MORE PRAISE FOR RICHARD LAYMON!

"Laymon is unique. A phenomenon. A genius of the grisly and the grotesque."

—Joe Citro, *The Blood Review*

"[Laymon has] an uncanny grasp of just what makes characters work. Readers turn the pages so fast they leave burn marks on the paper."

—*Horrorstruck*

"Laymon is incapable of writing a disappointing book."
—*New York Review of Science Fiction*

"One of the best, and most reliable, writers working today."
—*Cemetery Dance*

"I've read every book of Laymon's I could get my hands on. I'm absolutely a longtime fan."

—Jack Ketchum

"A brilliant writer."

—*Sunday Express*

"Laymon's writing's super-tight and characters well detailed and believable, which makes the savage termination of so many of them all the more shocking! The unbridled joy of a delightfully fertile and *wicked* imagination at work."

—*Terrorzone*

"Richard Laymon is a legend in dark fiction circles . . . a master of the macabre, a man on the cutting edge of the horror genre."

—*Scary Monsters Magazine*

THE TRAVELING VAMPIRE SHOW

Come and see—
the one and only known VAMPIRE in captivity!

—*VALERIA*—

Gorgeous!   Beguiling!   Lethal!

This stunning beauty, born in the wilds of Transylvania, sleeps by day in her coffin. By night she feeds on the blood of strangers.

See Valeria rise from the dead!

Watch as she stalks volunteers from the audience!

Tremble as she sinks her teeth into their necks!

Scream as she gulps their blood!

Where: *Janks Field, 2 mi. south of Grandville on Route 3*

When: *One Show Only—Friday, midnight*

How Much: *$10.*

(Nobody under age 18 allowed.)

THE TRAVELING VAMPIRE SHOW

RICHARD LAYMON

LEISURE BOOKS NEW YORK CITY

*This book is dedicated to Richard Chizmar,
owner, manager and coach of the CD Team.
You took us to the show.*

A LEISURE BOOK®

March 2001

Published by

Dorchester Publishing Co., Inc.
276 Fifth Avenue
New York, NY 10001

ISBN 0-8439-4850-7

The name "Leisure Books" and the stylized "L" with design are trademarks of Dorchester Publishing Co., Inc.

Printed in the United States of America.

Visit us on the web at www.dorchesterpub.com.

THE TRAVELING VAMPIRE SHOW

Chapter One

The summer I was sixteen, the Traveling Vampire Show came to town.

I heard about it first from my two best friends, Rusty and Slim.

Rusty's real name was Russell, which he pretty much hated.

Slim's real name was Frances. She had to put up with it from her parents and teachers, but not from other kids. She'd tell them, "Frances is a talking mule." Asked what she *wanted* to be called, her answer pretty much depended on what book she happened to be reading. She'd say, "Nancy" or "Holmes" or "Scout" or "Zock" or "Phoebe." All last summer, she wanted to be called Dagny. Now, it was Slim. A name like that, I figured maybe she'd started reading westerns. But I didn't ask.

My name is Dwight, by the way. Named after the Commander of the Allied Expeditionary Forces in Europe. He didn't get elected President until after I'd already been born and named.

Anyway, it was a hot August morning, school wouldn't be starting again for another month, and I was out in front of our house mowing the lawn with a push mower. We must've been the only family in Grandville that didn't have a power mower. Not that we couldn't afford one. Dad was the town's chief of police and Mom taught English at the high school. So we had the money for a power mower, or even a *riding* mower, but not the inclination.

Not Dad, anyway. Long before anyone ever heard of language like "noise pollution," Dad was doing everything in his power to prevent this or that "godawful racket."

Also, he was opposed to any sort of device that might make life easier on me or my two brothers. He wanted us to work hard, sweat and suffer. He'd lived through the Great Depression and World War Two, so he knew all about suffering. According to him, "kids these days've got it too easy." So he did what he could to make life tougher on us.

That's why I was out there pushing the mower, sweating my ass off, when along came Rusty and Slim.

It was one of those gray mornings when the sun is just a dim glow through the clouds and you know by the smell that rain's on the way and you wish it would hurry up and get here because the day is so damn hot and muggy.

My T-shirt was off. When I saw Rusty and Slim coming toward me, I suddenly felt a little embarrassed about being without it. Which was sort of strange, considering how much time we'd spent together in our swimming suits. I had an urge to run and snag it off the porch rail and put it on. But I stayed put, instead, and waited for them in just my jeans and sneakers.

"Hi, guys," I called.

"What's up?" Rusty greeted me. He meant it, of course, as a sexual innuendo. It was the sort of lame stuff he cherished.

"Not much," I said.

"Are you working hard, or hardly working?"

Slim and I both wrinkled our noses.

Then Slim looked at my sweaty bare torso and said, "It's too hot to be mowing your lawn."

"Tell that to my dad."

"Let me at him."

"He's at work."

"He's getting off lucky," Slim said.

We were all smiling, knowing she was kidding around. She liked my dad—liked both my parents a whole lot, though she wasn't crazy about my brothers.

"So how long'll it take you to finish the yard?" Rusty asked.

"I can quit for a while. I've just gotta have it done by the time Dad gets home from work."

"Come on with us," Slim said.

I gave a quick nod and ran across the grass. Nobody else was home: Dad at work, Mom away on her weekly shopping trip to the grocery store and my brothers (one single and one married) no longer living at our house.

As I charged up the porch stairs, I called over my shoulder, "Right back." I whipped my T-shirt off the railing, rushed into the house and raced upstairs to my bedroom.

With the T-shirt, I wiped the sweat off my face and chest. Then I stepped up to the mirror and grabbed my comb. Thanks to Dad, my hair was too short. *No son of mine's gonna go around looking like a girl.* I wasn't allowed to have much in the way of sideburns, either. *No son of mine's gonna traipse around looking like a hood.* Thanks to him, I hardly had enough hair to bother combing. But it was mussed and matted down with sweat, so I combed it anyway—making sure my "part" was straight as a razor, then giving the front a little curly flip.

After that, I grabbed my wallet off the dresser, shoved it into a back pocket of my jeans, hurried to the closet and pulled a short-sleeved shirt off its hanger. I put it on while I hurried downstairs.

Rusty and Slim were waiting on the porch.

I finished fastening my buttons, then opened the screen door.

"Where we going?" I asked.

"You'll see," Slim said.

I shut the door and followed my friends down the porch stairs.

Rusty was wearing an old shirt and blue jeans. That's pretty much what we *all* wore when we weren't dressed up for school or church. You hardly ever caught guys our age wearing shorts. Shorts were for little kids, old farts, and girls.

Slim *was* wearing shorts. They were cut-off blue jeans, so faded they were almost white, with frayed denim dangling and swaying like fringe around her thighs. She also wore a white T-shirt. It was big and loose and untucked, so it hung over her butt in the back. Her white swimsuit top showed through the thin fabric. It was a skimpy, bikini type thing that tied behind her back and at the nape of her neck. She was wearing it instead of a bra. It was probably more comfortable than a bra, and definitely more practical.

Mostly, in the summer, we all wore swimsuits instead of underwear. You never knew when you might end up at the municipal pool or at the river . . . or even when you might get caught in a downpour.

I had my trunks on under my jeans that morning. They were sort of soggy with sweat from the lawn mowing, and they clinged to my butt as I walked down the street with Rusty and Slim.

"So what's the plan?" I asked after a while.

Slim looked at me and hoisted an eyebrow. "Stage one's already been executed."

"Huh?" I asked.

"We freed you from the chains of oppression."

"Can't be mowing the *yard* on a day like this," Rusty explained.

"Well, thanks for liberating me.

"Think nothing of it," Rusty said.

"Our pleasure," Slim said, and patted me on the back.

It was just a buddy-pat, but it gave me a sickish excited lonely feeling. I'd been getting that way a lot, that summer, when I was around Slim. It didn't necessarily involve touching, either. Sometimes, I could just be *looking* at her and start to feel funny.

I kept it to myself, though.

"Stage two," Slim said, "we see what's going on at Janks Field."

I felt a little chill crawl up my back.

"Scared?" Rusty asked.

"Oh, yeah. Ooooo, I'm shaking."

I *was*, but not so much that it showed. I hoped.

"We don't *have* to go there," Slim said.

"*I'm* going," said Rusty. "If you guys are chicken, I'll go by myself."

"What's the big deal about Janks Field?" I asked.

"This," said Rusty.

The three of us had been walking abreast with Slim in the middle. Now, Rusty hustled around behind us and came over to my side. He pulled a paper out of the back pocket of his jeans. Unfolding it, he said, "These're all over town."

The way he held the paper open in front of me, I knew I wasn't supposed to touch it. It seemed to be a poster or flier, but it was bouncing around too much for me to read it. So I stopped walking. We all stopped. Slim came in close so she could look at the paper, too. It had four torn corners. Apparently, Rusty had ripped the poster off a wall or tree or something.

It looked like this:

The Traveling Vampire Show

Come and see—

the one and only known VAMPIRE in captivity!

—Valeria—

Gorgeous!   Beguiling!   Lethal!

This stunning beauty, born in the wilds of Transylvania sleeps
by day in her coffin. By night she feeds on the blood of strangers

See Valeria rise from the dead!

Watch as she stalks volunteers from the audience!

Tremble as she sinks her teeth into their necks!

Scream as she sups on their blood!!!

Where: *Janks Field. 2 mi south of Grandville on Route 3*

When: *One Show Only-Friday, midnight*

How much: *$10*

(Nobody under age 18 allowed)

Amazed and excited, I shook my head and murmured "Wow" a time or two while I read the poster.

But things changed when I got toward the bottom.

I felt a surge of alarm, followed by a mixture of relief and disappointment.

Mostly relief.

"Oh, man," I muttered, trying to sound dismayed. "What a bummer."

Chapter Two

A bummer?" Rusty asked. "You outa your mind, man? We've got us a traveling *vampire* show! A real live *female* vampire, right here in Grandville! And it says she's *gorgeous!* See that? Gorgeous! Beguiling! A stunning beauty! And she's a *vampire!* Look what it says! She stalks volunteers from the audience and bites their necks! She *sups* on their blood!"

"Bitchin'," Slim said.

"Might be bitchin' if we could *see* her," I said, trying to seem gloomy about the situation. "But there's no way we can get into a show like that."

Eyes narrow, Rusty shook his head. "That's how come we're going over there now."

"Oh," I said.

Sometimes, when Rusty came out with stuff like that, "Oh" was about the best I could do.

"You know?" he asked.

"I guess so." I had no idea.

"We'll look the place over," Slim said. "Just see what we can see."

"Maybe we'll get to see *her*," Rusty said. He seemed pretty excited.

"Don't get your hopes up," Slim told him.

"We *might*," he insisted. "I mean, she's gotta be around. *Somebody* put all those posters up, you know? And the show is *tonight*. They're probably over at Janks Field getting things ready right now."

"*That's* probably true," Slim said. "But don't count on feasting your eyes on the gorgeous and stunning Valeria."

He blinked at Slim, disappointment and vague confusion on his face. Then he turned his eyes to me, apparently seeking an ally.

I looked at Slim.

She raised both eyebrows and one corner of her mouth.

The goofy expression made me ache and laugh at the same time. Forcing my eyes away from her, I said to Rusty, "The gal's a vampire, moron."

"Huh?"

"Valeria. She's supposed to be a vampire."

"Yeah, so?" he asked, as if impatient for the punch line.

"So you think we're gonna maybe sneak up on Janks Field and catch her *sunbathing?*"

"Oh!"

He got it.

Slim and I laughed. Rusty stood there, red in the face but bobbing his head and chuckling. Then he said, "She's gotta be in her *casket*, right?"

"*Right!*" Slim and I said in unison.

Rusty laughed pretty hard about that. And we joined in. Then we resumed our journey toward Janks Field.

After a while, Rusty drew out in front by a stride or two, turned his head to look back at us, and said, "But seriously, maybe we *will* catch her sunbathing."

"Are you nuts?" Slim asked.

13

"In the *nude!*"

"Oh, you'd like that."

"You bet."

Scowling, I shook my head. "All you'd see is a little pile of ashes. And the first breeze that comes along . . ."

Slim started to sing like Peter, Paul and Mary, "The vam-mmmpire, my friend, is blowwwwing in the wind. . . ."

"And even if she *didn't* burn to a crisp at the first touch of sunlight," I said, "she'd sure as hell know better than to put on her vampire show with a *suntan*."

"Good point," Slim said. "She's gotta look pale."

"She could cover her tan with makeup," Rusty explained.

"That's a point," Slim agreed. "She probably uses a ton of makeup, anyway, to give her a convincing palor of undead-ness. So why *not* a tan underneath it?"

"An *all-over* tan," Rusty said, leering.

"We've gotta find you a girl," Slim said.

I suddenly wondered how *Slim* would look sunbathing in the nude, stretched out on her back with her hands folded under her head, her eyes shut, her skin slick and golden all the way down. It excited me to imagine her that way, but it made me feel guilty, too.

To push it out of my mind, I said, "How about Valeria?"

"There ya go," Slim said. "I hear she's stunning."

"I'll take her," Rusty said.

"You haven't even seen her yet," I pointed out.

"I don't care."

"Don't believe everything you read," Slim told him. "Valeria might turn out to be a pug-ugly, hideous hag."

"I bet she's incredible," Rusty said. "She *has* to be."

"Wishful thinking," I said.

Smiling as if he knew a secret, he asked, "Wanta put your money where your mouth is?"

"Five bucks says she's *not* gorgeous."

"I haven't got five bucks," Rusty said.

Which came as no surprise. His parents gave him an allow-ance of two bucks a week, which he was always quick to spend. I did better, myself, getting paid per chore and also doing some part-time yard work for a couple of neighbors.

"How much?" I asked.

"Don't bet, you guys," Slim said. "Somebody'll end up losing. . . ."

"Yeah," Rusty said. "*He* will. You wanta go in with me?"

"You've gotta be kidding," Slim said.

"Come on. You're always loaded."

"That's 'cause I don't squander my money foolishly."

"But this is a sure thing."

"How do you figure that?" Slim asked.

"Easy. This Traveling Vampire Show? Valeria's the main attraction, right?"

"Sounds like she's the *only* attraction," I threw in.

"And we all know it's bullshit, right? I mean, she's no more a vampire than *I* am. So she *has* to be gorgeous or you'd end up without any customers. I mean, you might be able to get away with having her be a fake *vampire*. Nobody's gonna expect a real one of those, anyway. But . . ."

"Some people might," I broke in.

"Nobody with half a brain," he said.

"I'm not so sure of that," Slim said.

We both stared at her.

"Maybe vampires *do* exist," she said, a sparkle of mischief in her eyes.

"Get real," Rusty said.

"Can you prove they don't?"

"Why would I *wanta* prove that? Everybody knows they don't exist."

"Not me," said Slim.

"Bullshit." He turned to me. "What about you, Dwight?"

"I'm with Slim."

"Big surprise."

"She's smarter than both of us put together," I said. Then I blushed because of the way she looked at me. "Well, you are."

"Nah. I just read a lot. And I like to keep my mind open." Smiling at Rusty, she added, "It's easy to have an open mind since I've only got half a brain."

"I didn't mean you," he said. "But I'm starting to wonder."

15

"To set *your* mind at ease, I doubt very much that Valeria *is* a vampire. I suppose there's a remote possibility, but it seems highly unlikely."

"Now you're talking."

"I also agree that, since she probably isn't a vampire, she'd *better* be beautiful."

Rusty beamed. "So, you want to back my bet?"

"Can't. You'll need someone to take a good, objective look at her and decide who wins. That'd better be me. I'll decide the winner."

"Fine with me," I said.

"I guess that'll be okay," said Rusty.

"Don't look so worried," Slim told him.

"Well, you always take Dwight's side about everything."

"Only when his side is the 'right' side. And I have a feeling that *you* might win this one."

"Thanks a lot," I told her.

"But I promise to be fair."

"I know," I said.

"So what're we gonna wager?" Rusty asked me.

"How much money do you want to lose?" I asked him.

I wasn't very confident about winning, anymore. He'd made a pretty good argument; if Valeria isn't a vampire, she *has* to be beautiful or there'd be no show. But I saw a hole in his case.

Valeria didn't have to be a real vampire for the show to work. She didn't need to be incredibly gorgeous, either. The Traveling Vampire Show might be successful anyway . . . if it was really and truly exciting or scary.

"Let's leave money out of the wager," Slim suggested. "Suppose the loser has to do something gross?"

Rusty grinned. "Like kiss the winner's ass?"

"Something along those lines."

I frowned at Rusty. "I'm not kissing your ass."

"It doesn't have to be that," Slim said.

"How about the loser kisses *hers?*" He nodded at Slim. *Her ass? The loser?*

Slim's face went red. "Nobody's kissing *my* ass. Or my anything else, for that matter."

"There goes my *next* idea," Rusty said, and laughed. He could be a pretty crude guy.

"Why don't we just forget the whole thing?" I suggested.

"Chicken," Rusty said. "You just know you're gonna lose."

"We might not even get to *see* her."

"If we can't see her," Slim said, "the wager's off."

"We don't even *have* a wager."

"I've got it!" Rusty said. "The winner gets to spit in the loser's mouth."

Slim's mouth fell open and she blinked at him. "Are you brain-damaged?" she asked.

"You got a better idea?"

"*Any* idea would be better than that."

"Like what?" he asked. "Let's hear *you* come up with something?"

"All right."

"Let's hear it."

Frowning as if deep in thought, Slim glanced from Rusty to me a few times. Then she said, "Okay. The loser gets his hair shaved off."

In that regard, Rusty had a lot more to lose than I did. He had a head of hair that would've put Elvis Presley to shame, and he was mighty proud of it.

Nose wrinkled, he muttered, "I don't know."

"You said it's a sure thing," I reminded him.

"Yeah, but . . . I don't know, man. My hair." He reached up and stroked it. "I don't wanta go around looking like a dork."

"It'll grow back," I said.

"Eventually," added Slim.

"Anyway, I'm not gonna let Dwight anywhere *near* me with a razor."

"I'll do the shaving," Slim said.

Hearing that, I suddenly didn't want to win this wager. I hoped Valeria would be the most amazingly beautiful woman in the world.

"How about it?" Slim asked.

"Count me in," I said.

I could tell by the look on Rusty's face that he wanted to back out. But honor was at stake, so he sighed and said, "All right. It's a bet."

Chapter Three

The dirt road leading through the forest to Janks Field was usually unmarked. Today, though, posters for The Traveling Vampire Show were nailed to trees on both sides of the turn-off. And a large sign—the side of a cardboard box nailed to a tree—pointed the way with a red-painted arrow. Above the arrow, somebody had painted VAMPIRE SHOW in big, drippy red letters. Below the arrow, in smaller drippy letters, was written, "MIDNITE."

"Nice, professional job," Slim commented.

"We probably aren't dealing with mental giants," I said.

"WHY ARE YOU TALKING SO QUIET?" Rusty boomed out, making us both jump.

We whirled around and watched him laugh.

"Good one," Slim said, looking peeved.

"A riot," I said.

"YOU TWO AREN'T NERVOUS, ARE YOU?"

Slim grimaced. "Would you pipe down?"

"WHAT'RE YOU SCARED OF?"

I wanted to bash him one in the face, but I held back. I don't think I've mentioned it yet, but Rusty wasn't exactly in the best of shape. Not a total lardass, but pudgy and soft and not exactly capable of fighting back.

Which might seem like an advantage if you want to slug a guy in the puss. But I knew it would make me feel lousy. And he was my best friend, after all—other than Slim.

Grinning, he boomed, "CAT GOT YOUR TONGUE?"

Slim pinched his side.

He gasped, "OW!" and twisted away. "That *hurt!*"

"Keep it down," Slim said.

"Jeez."

"We're gonna have to be sneaky going in," she explained, "or they'll toss our butts out and we'll never get a chance to see Valeria."

"Or don't you *want* to see her?" I asked Rusty.

"Jeez, guys, I was just screwing around."

"Let's hope nobody heard you," Slim said.

"Nobody heard me. We're *miles* from Janks Field."

"More like a few hundred yards," I told him.

"And sound really carries around here," Slim added.

"Okay, okay, I get the point."

The dirt road wasn't as wide as Route 3, so we didn't walk abreast. Slim took the lead. Rusty and I stayed pretty much beside each other.

There was no sunlight. Of course, there hadn't been any sunlight *before* we entered the woods—just a gray gloom. But now, with trees all around and above us, the gloom was deeper, darker. Things looked the way they do when you're out after supper on a summer night and you can see just fine, so far, but you've only got maybe half an hour before it'll be too dark for playing ball.

"If it gets much darker," I said, "Valeria won't *need* her casket."

Rusty put a finger to his lips and went, "Shhhhh."

I gave him the finger.

He smirked.

After that, I kept my mouth shut.

Our shoes were almost silent on the dirt road except for sometimes when one of us stepped on a twig. Rusty was breathing fairly hard. Every so often, he muttered stuff under his breath.

A very quiet tune seemed to be coming from Slim. "De dum, de doo, de do-doo. . . ." It blended in with the sounds all around us of buzzing flies and mosquitos and bees, bird tweets, and the endless flutters and rustling scurries of unseen creatures. "De-dum, de do, de doo."

Rusty made no attempt to shush her.

But suddenly he said, "Wait up."

Slim halted.

When we caught up to her, Rusty said in a hushed voice, "I gotta take a leak."

Slim nodded. "Pick a tree," she said.

He glanced from Slim to me. "Don't go anywhere, okay?"

"We'll stay right here," she told him.

I nodded.

"Okay," he said. "I'll be back in a minute." He stepped off the dirt road and made his way into the trees.

"Do you have to go?" Slim asked me.

"Nah."

"Me neither." She pursed her lips and blew softly through them. Then she said, "Sure is hot in here."

"Yeah," I muttered. I was broiled and drenched and itchy, my clothes sticking to me.

Slim's short blond hair was matted down in coils against her scalp and forehead. Sweat ran down her face. As I watched, a drip gathered at the tip of her nose and fell. Her white T-shirt was clinging to her skin and I could see through it.

"This vampire better be worth it," she said.

"Too bad we won't get to see her."

Slim gave me half a smile. "If she's in her casket, we'll have to bust her out of it. We're not gonna put ourselves through all this and not get a look at her."

"I don't know," I said.

"Don't know what?" she asked, and peeled her T-shirt off. In spite of her bikini top, she seemed to be mostly bare skin from the waist up. She wadded her T-shirt and mopped the sweat off her face.

I looked the other way.

"What don't you know?" she asked.

For a moment, I wasn't sure what we'd been talking about.

Then I remembered. I said, "She isn't gonna be by herself. I don't think so, anyway."

"You're probably right." Lowering the shirt away from her face, she smiled and said, "She needs casket-handlers."

"Right."

"Probably has a whole crew." She wiped her chest, her arms.

"And they might not be model citizens," I said.

Laughing softly, she lowered her head and began to wipe the sweat off her belly and sides. I sneaked a glance at her breasts. The thin pouches of her bikini top were stretched smooth with them. Around the edges of the fabric, I glimpsed pale slopes of skin.

"We'll have to be careful," I said.

"Yeah. If they look *really* scurvy, we'd better forget the whole thing."

Hearing footsteps, we both turned our heads and saw Rusty trudging toward us.

Slim continued to rub at herself with the balled shirt. I wanted her to put it back on, but I didn't say anything.

"All set," Rusty said. I saw him check her out. "What's going on?"

"Nothing much," Slim told him. "Just waiting for you."

"We're thinking we'll have to be really careful," I explained. "Valeria's gonna have . . ."

"Casket keepers," Slim threw in.

Rusty smiled and nodded.

"No telling how many people might be with the show," I said.

"And it's likely a scurrrrvy lot," added Slim with a bit of Long John Silver in her voice.

"They go around with a traveling vampire show," Rusty said, "they've gotta be at least a *little* strange."

"And maybe dangerous," I said.

Rusty suddenly frowned. "You guys aren't gonna chicken out, are you?" Before either of us had a chance to answer, he said, " 'Cause *I'm* going irregardless."

"Irregardless ain't a word, Einstein," Slim told him.

"Is too."

She wasn't one to argue. She just gave him a funny smile, then pulled her T-shirt on. "Let's go."

After that, none of us said anything. We weren't that far from Janks Field, so I think we were starting to get more nervous.

Janks Field was the sort of place that made you nervous no matter what.

First off, nothing grows there. It's a big patch of hard bare dirt surrounded by thick, green woods. But it's not bare on purpose. Nobody *clears* the field. As far as anyone knows, Janks Field has always been that way.

I've heard people say the dirt there is poison. I think they're wrong about that, though. Janks Field has more than its share of wildlife—the sort that lives in holes in the ground—ants, spiders, snakes, and so on.

Some people say aliens landed there, and that's why nothing will grow.

Sure thing.

Others say the field is cursed. I might go along with that. You might, too, after you know more about it.

The reason they call the place Janks Field isn't because it belongs to anyone named Janks. It doesn't, and never did. It's called that because of Tommy Janks and what he did there in 1954.

I was just a little kid at the time, so nobody told me much. But I do remember people acting funny the summer it all happened. Dad, being chief of police, wasn't home very often. Mom, usually cheerful, seemed oddly nervous. And sometimes I overheard scattered talk about missing girls. This went on for most of the summer. Then something big happened and everyone went crazy. All the grown-ups were pale and whispering and I caught bits and pieces like, "Some kind of monster . . ." and "Dear God . . ." and "their poor parents . . ." and "always knew there was something *off* about him."

As it turns out, some Boy Scouts had hiked into the field and found Tommy Janks sitting by a campfire. He was a deaf mute, so he never heard them coming. They caught him with a gob of meat on the end of a stick. He was roasting it over the fire. It turned out to be the heart of one of the missing girls.

Must've been awful, walking into a scene like that.

Those Boy Scouts became instant heroes. We envied them, hated them, and longed to be their friends. Not because they captured Tommy Janks (my dad did that), but because they got to *see* him cooking that heart over the fire. Those scouts were legends in their own time.

One of them, years later, ended up committing suicide and another . . .

That's another story. I'll stick to this one.

After my dad busted Tommy, he led a crew out to the field and they found the remains of twenty-three bodies buried there. Six belonged to the girls who'd disappeared that summer. The rest . . . they'd been there longer. Some, for maybe five years. Others, for more like twenty or thirty. I've heard that several of them might've been in the ground for a hundred years.

The field apparently hadn't been a cemetery, though; nobody found signs of any grave markers or caskets. There were just a bunch of bodies—a lot of them in pieces—tossed into holes.

Tommy Janks got himself fried in the electric chair.

The clearing got itself called Janks Field.

Chapter Four

There hadn't been a road to Janks Field, dirt or otherwise, at the time Tommy got caught cooking up the girl's heart. But Dad managed to drive in with his Jeep. He made the first tire tracks into that awful place. By the time the bodies and bones had been removed and all the investigations were over, the tracks were worn in. And people have been driving out to Janks Field ever since.

First, it was to gawk at where all those bodies had been found.

Before long, though, teens from Grandville and other nearby towns realized that the field was perfect for making out. At least if you and your girl had the guts to drive in there at night.

Not only did people go there to park, but some pretty wild parties went on sometimes. A lot of booze and fights and sex. That's what we heard, anyway.

We also heard rumors of witches and so on meeting at Janks Field to practice "black magic." They supposedly had naked orgies and performed sacrifices.

I sometimes thought it'd be pretty cool if they were sacrificing humans out there. I imagined bonfires, drums, nude and beautiful and sweaty girls leaping wildly around, chanting and waving knives. And a lovely, naked virgin tied to an altar, her body shiny with sweat, terror in her eyes as she waited to be sliced open in a blood sacrifice to the forces of darkness.

The whole notion really turned me on.

Turned on Rusty, too.

We used to talk about that sort of thing in hushed, excited voices. Not in front of Slim, though. I *couldn't* have said any of that stuff with Slim listening. But also we figured, being a girl herself, she might not want to hang out with us if she knew we had fantasies like that.

Whenever I imagined the Janks Field witch orgies, I always pictured Slim as the virgin tied to the altar. (I didn't mention that part to Rusty or anyone else.) Slim never got sacrificed because I came to her rescue in the nick of time and cut her free.

I don't know if any humans actually *were* sacrificed at Janks Field back in those days. It was fun to think about, though: sexy and romantic and exciting. Whereas the sacrifice of animals, which apparently *was* going on, just seemed plain disgusting to us.

The animal sacrifices disgusted and worried just about

everyone. For one thing, pets were disappearing. For another, people going to Janks Field for make-out sessions or wild parties didn't appreciate tripping over the dismembered remains of Rover or Kitty. Also, they must've been worried that *they* might be next.

Something had to be done about Janks Field. Since it was outside the city limits of Grandville, the county council chose to deal with it. They tried to solve the problem by installing a chain-link fence around the field.

The fence remained intact for about a week.

But then a concerned citizen named Fargus Durge entered the picture. He said, "You don't have orgies and pagan sacrifices going on in the town squares of Grandville or Bixton or Clarksburg, do you?" Everyone agreed on that. "Well, what's the difference between the town squares and Janks Field? The *squares're* in the middle of town, that's what. Whereas Janks Field, it's all by itself out there in the middle of nowhere. It's *isolated!* That's how come it's a magnet for every teenage hoodlum, weirdo, malcontent, deviate, sadist, satanist and sex-fiend in the county."

His solution?

Make Janks Field *less* isolated by improving access to it and making it a center of legitimate activity.

The council not only saw his point, but provided some funding and put Fargus in charge.

They threw enough money at the problem to bring in a bulldozer and lay a dirt road where there'd only been tire tracks before. They also provided funds for a modest "stadium" in the middle of Janks Field.

The stadium, Fargus's brainchild, consisted of high bleachers on both sides of an arena.

A very *small* arena.

The county ran electricity in and put up banks of lights for "night games."

On a mild June night a little over two years ago, Fargus's stadium went into operation.

It was open to the public unless otherwise booked for a special event. Anyone could use it day or night, because the

25

lights were on a timer. They came on at sundown and stayed on all night, every night, as a deterrent to shenanigans.

Fargus's "special events" took place every Friday and Saturday night that summer. Because the arena was so small, there couldn't be anything the size of basketball games, tennis matches, stage plays or band concerts.

The events had to be small enough to fit in.

So Fargus brought to the stadium a series of spectacular duds: a ping-pong tournament, a barbershop quartet, a juggling show, a piano solo, a poetry reading, an old fart doing card tricks.

Even though the events were free, almost nobody showed up for them.

Which was a good thing, in a way, because Fargus's big plan for the stadium hadn't included a parking lot. This was a major oversight, since most people drove to the events. They ended up parking their cars every which way on Janks Field. Not a *big* problem if only twenty or thirty people showed up.

But then one night toward the end of that summer, Fargus charged a five dollar admission and brought in a night of boxing and about two hundred people drove in for it.

Things were so tight in Janks Field that some of them had to climb over the tops of cars and pickup trucks in order to reach the arena. Not only did the field get jammed tight, but so did the dirt road leading in.

Regardless, just about everyone somehow made it into the stands in time to see most of the boxing matches.

They *loved* the boxing.

But when it came time to leave, all hell broke loose. From what I heard, and my dad was there trying to keep order (not on duty, but moonlighting), the logjam of cars was solid. Not only were there *way* too many cars in the first place, but some of them got flat tires from the broken bottles and such that always littered the field.

Feeling trapped, the drivers and passengers, in Dad's words, "went bughouse." It turned into a combination destruction derby/brawl/gang-bang.

By the time it was over, there were nineteen arrests,

countless minor injuries, twelve people who needed to be hospitalized, eight rapes (multiple, in most cases), and four fatalities. One guy died of a heart attack, two were killed in knife-fights, and a six-month old baby, dropped to the ground by its mother during the melee, got its head run over by a Volkswagen bug.

After that, no more boxing matches at Janks Field.

No more "special events" at all, duds or otherwise.

The stadium became known as Fargus's Folly.

Fargus vanished.

Though the "night games" were over, the huge, bright stadium lights continued to remain on from sunset till dawn to deter lovers, orgies and sacrifices.

And the grandstands and arena remained in place.

The Traveling Vampire Show would be the first official event to take place in Janks Field in almost two years—since the night of the parking disaster.

I suddenly wondered if it *was* official. Had somebody taken over Fargus's old job and actually booked such a bizarre event?

Didn't seem likely.

As far as I knew, the county had abandoned Janks Field. Except for paying the electric bills, they wanted nothing at all to do with the scene of all that mayhem.

I doubted that they would even *allow* a show to take place there—much less one featuring a "vampire."

Unless maybe some palms got greased.

That's how carnies got their permits, I'd heard. Just bribed the right people and nobody gave them trouble. A show like this would probably operate the same way.

Or maybe they hadn't bothered.

Maybe they'd just *shown up*.

I must've let out a moan or something.

"What is it?" Slim asked, her voice little more than a whisper.

"What's a show like this doing at Janks Field?" I asked.

Looking puzzled, Rusty said, "Why do you care?"

"I just think it's weird."

27

"It's a great place for a vampire show," Slim said.

"That's for sure," said Rusty.

"But how did they even know about it?"

Grinning, Rusty said, "Hey, maybe Valeria's been here before. Know what I mean?" He chuckled. "Maybe she's done some prime sucking in these parts. Might even be the one who put some of those old stiffs in Janks Field."

"And she likes to come back for old time's sake," Slim added.

"But don't you think it's odd?" I persisted. "Nobody just stumbles onto a place like Janks Field."

"Well, if you trip in a snake hole . . ."

Rusty laughed.

"I mean it," I said.

"Seriously?" Slim asked. "Somebody came out in advance to set things up. Don't you think so? And he probably asked around in town and found out about the place. That's all. No big mystery."

"I still think it's weird," I said.

"Weird is what you want," said Slim, "when you run a Traveling Vampire Show."

"I guess so."

"The only thing that really counts," Rusty said, "is that they're here."

But they weren't.

Or didn't seem to be.

We followed Slim out of the forest. The dirt road vanished and we found ourselves standing at the edge of Janks Field.

Way off to the right across the dry, gray plain stood the snack stand and bleachers. Overlooking them, gray against the gray sky, were the panels of stadium lights.

We saw no cars, no trucks, no vans.

We saw no people.

We saw no vampires.

Chapter Five

We started walking across the field.

"Guess we beat 'em here," Slim said, her voice hushed.

"Looks that way," said Rusty. He also spoke softly, the way you might talk late at night sneaking through a graveyard. He looked at his wristwatch. "It's only ten-thirty."

"Still," I said, "you'd think they'd be here by now. Don't they have to set up for the show?"

"Who knows?" Rusty said.

"How do we know someone *isn't* here?" Slim asked, a look on her face as if she might be kidding around.

"I don't *see* anyone," Rusty said.

"Let's just be ready to beat it," I said.

They glanced at me so I would know they got *both* meanings. Usually, such a remark would inspire some wisecracks. Not this time, though.

"If anything happens," Slim said, "we stay together."

Rusty and I nodded.

We walked slowly, expecting trouble. You *always* expected trouble at Janks Field, but you never knew what it might be or where it might come from.

The place was creepy enough just because it *looked* so desolate and because a lot of very bad stuff had happened there. Bad things *still* happened. Every time I went to Janks Field with Rusty and Slim, we ran into trouble. We'd been scared witless, had accidents, gotten ourselves banged up, bit, stung and chased by various forms of wildlife (human and otherwise).

Janks Field was just that way.

So we expected trouble. We wanted to see it coming, but we didn't know where to look.

29

We tried to look everywhere: at the grandstands ahead of us, at the mouth of the dirt road behind us, at the gloomy borders of the forest that surrounded the whole field, and at the gray, dusty ground.

We especially kept watch on the ground. Not because so many people had been found buried in it over the years, but because of its physical dangers. Though fairly flat and level, it was scattered with rocks and broken glass and holes.

The rocks were treacherous like icebergs. Just a small, sharp corner might be sticking up, but if your foot hits it, you find out that most of it is *buried*. The rock stays put and you go down.

You don't want to go down in Janks Field. (Forget the double-meaning.) If you go down, you'll come up in much worse shape.

Even if you're lucky enough to escape bites from spiders or snakes, you'll probably land on jutting rocks and broken glass.

The field was carpeted with the smashed remains of bottles from countless solo drinking bouts, trysts, wild parties, orgies, satanic festivities and what have you. The pieces were hard to see on gray days like this, but whenever the sun was out, the sparkle and glare of the broken bottles was almost blinding.

Of course, you never walked barefoot on Janks Field. And you dreaded a fall.

But falls were almost impossible to avoid. If you didn't trip on a jutting rock, you would probably stumble in a hole. There were snake holes, gopher holes, spider holes, shallow depressions from old graves, and even shovel holes. Though all the corpses had supposedly been removed back in 1954, fresh, open holes kept turning up. God knows why. But every time we explored Janks Field, we discovered a couple of new ones.

Those are some of the reasons we watched the ground ahead of our feet.

We also watched the more distant ground to make sure we weren't about to get jumped. That sort of thing had happened to us a few times before in Janks Field. If it was going to happen again, we wanted to see it coming and haul ass.

Our heads swung from side to side as we made our way toward the stadium. Each of us, every so often, walked sideways and backward.

It was rough on the nerves.

And it suddenly got rougher when Slim, nodding her head to the left, said, "Here comes a dog."

Rusty and I looked.

Rusty said, "Oh, shit."

This was no Lassie, no Rin Tin Tin, no Lady or the Tramp. This was a knee-high bony yellow cur skulking toward us with an awkward sideways gait, its head low and its tail drooping.

"I don't like the looks of this one," I said.

Rusty said, "Shit" again.

"No collar," I pointed out.

"Gosh," Rusty said, full of sarcasm. "You think it might be a stray?"

"Up yours," I told him.

"At least it isn't foaming at the mouth," said Slim, who always looked on the bright side.

"What'll we do?" I asked.

"Ignore it and keep walking," Slim said. "Maybe it's just out here to enjoy a lovely stroll."

"My ass," Rusty said.

"*That's* what it's here to enjoy," I pointed out.

"Shit."

"That, too."

"Ha ha," Rusty said, unamused.

We picked up our pace slightly, knowing better than to run. Though we tried not to watch the dog, each of us glanced at it fairly often. It kept lurching closer.

"Oh, God, this ain't good," Rusty said.

We weren't far from the stadium. In a race, we might beat the dog to it. But there was no fence, nothing to keep the dog out if we *did* get there first.

The bleachers wouldn't be much help; the dog could probably climb them as well as we could.

We might escape by shinnying up one of the light poles, but the nearest of those was at least fifty feet away.

31

A lot closer than that was the snack stand. It used to sell "BEER—SNACKS—SOUVENIRS" as announced by the long wooden sign above the front edge of its roof. But it hadn't been open, far as I knew, since the night of the parking disaster.

We couldn't get into it, that was for sure (we'd tried on other occasions), but its roof must've been about eight feet off the ground. Up there, we'd be safe from the dog.

"Feel like climbing?" Slim asked. She must've been thinking the same as me.

"The snack stand?" I asked.

"Yeah."

"How?" asked Rusty.

Slim and I glanced at each other. *We* could scurry up a wall of the shack and make it to the roof easily enough. We were fairly quick and agile and strong.

But not Rusty.

"Any ideas?" I asked Slim.

She shook her head and shrugged.

Suddenly, the dog lurched ahead of us, swung around and planted its feet. It lowered its head. Growling, it bared its upper teeth and drooled. It had a bulging, crazed left eye. And a black, gooey hole where its right eye should've been.

"Oh, shit," Rusty muttered. "We're screwed."

"Take it easy," Slim said. Her voice sounded calm. I didn't know whether she was talking to Rusty or the dog. Or maybe to both of them.

"We're dead," Rusty said.

Glancing at him, Slim asked, "Have you got anything to feed it?"

"Like what?"

"Food?"

He shook his head very slightly. A drop of sweat fell off the tip of his nose.

"Nothing?" Slim asked.

"You've *always* got food," I told him.

"Do not."

"Are you *sure?*" Slim asked.

"I ate it back in the woods."

"Ate what?" I asked.

"My Ding-Dong."

"You ate a *Ding-Dong* in the woods?"

"Yeah."

"How come we didn't see you?" I asked.

"I ate it when I was taking my piss."

"Great," Slim muttered.

"I didn't have enough to share with you guys, so . . ."

"Could've saved some for the Hound of the goddamn Baskervilles," Slim pointed out.

"Didn't know . . ."

The hound let out a fierce, rattling growl that sounded like it had a throat full of loose phlegm.

"*You* got anything, Dwight?" Slim asked.

"Huh-uh."

"Me neither."

"What're we gonna do?" Rusty asked, a whine in his voice. "Man, if he bites us we're gonna have to get rabies shots. They stick like a foot-long needle right into your stomach and . . ."

Slim eased herself down into a crouch and reached her open hands toward the dog. Its ears flattened against the sides of its skull. It snarled and drooled.

"You sure you wanta do that?" I asked her.

Ignoring me, she spoke to the dog in a soft, sing-song voice. "Hi there, boy. Hi, fella. You're a good boy, aren't you? You looking for some food? Huh? We'd give you some if we had any, wouldn't we?"

"It's gonna bite your hand off," Rusty warned.

"No, he won't. He's a good doggie. Aren't you a good doggie, boy? Huh?"

The dog, hunkered down, kept growling and showing its teeth.

On the ground around us, I saw small pieces of broken glass, little stones, some cigarette butts, leaves and twigs that must've blown over from the woods, a pack of Lucky Strikes that was filthy and mashed flat, a few beer cans smashed as flat as the cigarette pack, a headless snake acrawl with ants, someone's old sock . . . a lot of stuff, but nothing much good for a weapon.

Slim, still squatting with her hands out and speaking in the same quiet sing-song, said "You're a nice doggie, aren't you? Why don't you guys see if you can climb the nice snack stand, huh, doggie? Yeahhh. That's a good doggie. Maybe Dwight can give Rusty a nice little boost, and they can wait for me on top of the nice little snack stand? Is that a good idea? Huh, doggie? Yeah, I think so."

Rusty and I looked at each other.

We were probably both thinking the same things.

We can't run off and leave Slim with the dog. But she TOLD us to. When she says stuff, she means it. And she's smarter than both of us put together, so maybe she has some sort of fabulous plan for dealing with the thing.

I rebelled enough to ask Slim, "You sure?"

She sing-sang, "I'm so sure, aren't I, doggie? Are you sure, too? You're such a good doggie. It'd be so nice if you two lame-brain dingle-berries would do as I ask, wouldn't it, fella?"

With that, Rusty and I started easing ourselves backward and sideways.

The dog took its eye off Slim and swiveled its head to watch us. The threats in its growl told us to stay put, but we kept moving.

With only one eye, it couldn't watch both of us at once.

Ignoring Slim straight in front of it, the dog jerked its head from side to side like a frantic spectator at a tennis match. Its growl grew from threat to outrage, drowning out Slim's quiet voice.

She reached to her waist, grabbed her T-shirt and skinned it up over her head.

The dog fixed its eye on her.

"Go, guys!" she yelled.

Rusty and I dashed for the snack stand. I slammed my side into its front wall to stop myself fast. As I ducked and interlocked my fingers, I saw Slim in a tug-o-war with the dog.

She had her right knee on the ground. Her left leg was out in front of her, knee up, foot firm on the ground to brace herself against the dog's pull.

Rusty planted a foot in my hands, stepped into them and leaped. I gave him a hard boost. Up he went. I half expected him to drop back down, but he didn't. I didn't bother to look. Instead, I kept my eyes on Slim and the dog.

The dog, teeth clamped on its end of her T-shirt, growled like a maniac, whipping its head from side to side and back-pedaling with all four legs as if it wanted nothing more out of life than to rip the T-shirt out of Slim's hands.

On both feet now, she stood with her legs spread, her knees bent, her weight backward. The stance, her shiny wet skin and her skimpy white swimsuit top, almost made her look as if she were water-skiing. But if she fell here, she wouldn't be going into the nice cool river. And the dog would be on her in a flash, savaging her body instead of the T-shirt.

"Get up here," Rusty called down to me.

Slim's arms and shoulders jerked hard as the dog tugged.

She saw me watching. "Get on the roof!" she yelled.

And as she yelled, the dog let go.

Slim gasped and stumbled backward, swinging her arms, the shirt flapping. Then she went down.

The dog attacked her.

Shouting like a madman, I ran at them. Slim was on her back. The dog stood on top of her, digging its hind paws into her hips while it fought to rip her apart with its claws and teeth. Slim, gasping and grunting, held on to its front legs and tried to keep the thing away from her neck and face.

I grabbed its tail with both hands.

I think I only meant to pull the dog off Slim and give her time to run for the shack. But what happened, instead—I went slightly berserk.

As I jerked the dog away from her, I saw her scratches, her blood. That may be what did it.

Somehow I found myself *swinging* the dog by its tail. I was hanging on with both hands, spinning in circles. At first, the dog curled around and snapped at me. Its teeth couldn't quite reach me, though.

Pretty soon, it stopped trying and just howled as I twirled around and around and around.

While I swung the dog, Slim got to her feet.

I caught glimpses of her as I spun.

She was there, gone, there, gone . . .

Then she was on the move toward the snack stand. Closer. Closer. Around I went again and glimpsed her leaping. Around again and Rusty was pulling her up by one arm. Next time around, I glimpsed the faded seat of her cut-off jeans. Then I saw her standing on the roof beside Rusty.

Around and around I went. Glimpse after glimpse, I saw them shoulder to shoulder up there, staring down at me.

I saw them again. Again. They looked stunned and worried.

I was awfully dizzy by then and my arms were getting tired. I thought maybe I'd better end things soon—maybe by slamming the canine into a wall of the snack stand. So I started working my way in that direction.

Rusty yelled, "Don't bring it *here!*"

"Just let it go!" Slim called.

So I did.

Waiting until it was pointed *away* from the snack stand, I released its tail. The weight suddenly gone, I stumbled sideways, trying to stay on my feet.

I didn't see the dog at first, but its howl climbed an octave or two.

Then, still staggering, I spotted it. Ears laid back, legs kicking, it flew headfirst, rolling through the air as if being turned on an invisible spit.

Far out across Janks Field, it slammed the ground. Its howl ended with a cry of pain, and the dog vanished in a rising cloud of dust.

Slim's voice came from behind me. She said, "My God, Dwight."

And Rusty said, "Jesus H. Christ on a rubber crutch."

Then, growling like a pissed-off grizzly bear, the dog came racing out of the dust cloud.

Rusty yelled, "Shit!"

Slim yelled, "Run!"

I squealed a wordless outcry of disbelief and panic and sprinted for the shack.

Chapter Six

Leaping, I grabbed the edge of the roof. Rusty and Slim caught me by the wrists and hauled me up so fast I felt weightless. An instant later, the dog slammed against the wall.

I sprawled on the tarpaper, gasping for air, my heart whamming.

While I tried to recover, Slim sat cross-legged beside me and patted my chest and said things like, "Wow," and "You saved my life," and "You were a wildman" and so on, all of which made me feel pretty good.

While that went on, Rusty stood near the edge of the roof, leaning over the big wooden BEER—SNACKS—SOUVENIRS sign to keep an eye on the dog. He said, "It's still down there" and "I don't think it's even *damaged* from all that," and "How the shit are we gonna get outa here?" And so on.

After a couple of minutes, I sat up and looked at Slim. There were scratches on her face, shoulders, chest, arms and on the backs of her hands. She even had claw marks on the top of her right breast, running down to the edge of her bikini top. Those weren't bleeding, though. A lot of her scratches hadn't gone in deeply enough to draw blood—but some had.

"It really got you," I said.

"At least it didn't bite me. Thanks to you."

Looking over his shoulder, Rusty said, "You'll *still* have to get rabies shots." He sounded almost pleased by the idea.

"Screw that," Slim said.

"You *will*," Rusty insisted.

"You want to take a look at my back?" Slim asked me.

I crawled around behind her and winced. Her back, bare to the waist except for the tied strings of her bikini, was dirty and running with blood from her fall on the ground. In at least five places, bits of broken glass were still embedded in her skin.

"Oh, man," I muttered.

Rusty came around for a look and said, "Good going."

"I try my best," said Slim, smiling.

I started picking the pieces of glass out of her.

"You're gonna need a *tetanus* shot, too," Rusty told her.

"No way," Slim said.

"Besides," I said, "she had a tetanus shot last year after that moron stabbed her."

"That's right," Slim said.

"And one shot lasts like five or ten years," I added.

"Couldn't hurt to get another," Rusty said. "Just to be on the safe side. *And* the rabies shots."

After I pulled the pieces of glass out of Slim's back, she was still bleeding. "You'd better lie down," I told her.

She stretched out flat on the roof, turned her head sideways and folded her arms under her face.

Her back looked as if it had been painted bright red. Blood was leaking from ten or twelve slits and gashes. Nowhere, however, was it *gushing* out.

"Does it hurt much?" I asked.

"I've felt better. But I've felt a lot worse, too."

"I'll bet," I said. I'd seen Slim get injured plenty of times and heard about other stuff—like some of the things her father liked to do to her. Today's cuts and scratches seemed pretty minor compared to a lot of that.

"You're gonna need stitches," Rusty informed her. "A *lot* of stitches."

"He's probably right," I said.

"I'll be fine," she said.

"Long as the bleeding stops," I said, and started to unbutton my shirt.

"Unless infection sets in," said Rusty.

"You're sure the life of the goddamn party," Slim muttered.

"Just being realistic."

"Why don't you make yourself useful," I said, "and hop down and go get a doctor."

"Very funny."

I took off my shirt, folded it a couple of times to make a pad, and pressed it gently against several of Slim's cuts. The blood soaked through it, turning the checkered fabric red.

"Your mom's gonna kill you," Rusty said.

"It's an emergency." Where the blood on my shirt seemed worst, I pressed down firmly. Slim stiffened under my hands.

Rusty bent over us and watched for a while. Then he took off his own shirt, folded it, knelt on the other side of Slim and worked on her other cuts.

"Applying pressure should make the bleeding stop," I explained.

"I know that," Rusty said. "You weren't the only Boy Scout around here."

"The only one with a first aid merit badge."

"Screw you."

"Two Boy Scouts," Slim said, "and no first aid kit. Very prepared."

"We *used* to be Scouts," Rusty explained.

"*Used* to be prepared."

"Next time," I said, "we'll make sure and bring some bandages along."

"The hell with that," said Slim. "Bring guns."

Rusty and I laughed at that one.

After about five minutes, most of the bleeding seemed to be over. We kept pressing down on the cuts for a while, anyway.

Then Rusty looked at me and asked, "You were kidding when you said that about going for a doctor, right?"

"What do you think?" I said.

"Just wanted to make sure. I mean, I *figured* you must be kidding, you know? 'Cause I would've done it if I had to. I mean, if Slim really *had* to have a doctor. Like if it was life or death, I would've jumped on down and done it, dog or no dog."

It seemed like a strange thing for him to say.

Strange and sort of nice.

Slim said, "Thanks, Rusty."

"Yeah, well. It's just the truth, that's all. I mean, I'd do *anything* for you. For *either* of you."

"If you wanta do something for me," I said, "how about once in a while using underarm deodorant?"

Slim laughed and winced.

"Screw you, man! If anybody stinks around here, it's you."

"Nobody stinks," said Slim, the peacekeeper.

I checked underneath my bloody shirt again. Rusty looked under his, too. We both studied Slim's back for a while.

"Bleeding's stopped," I announced.

"Good deal," said Slim.

"But it'll probably start up again if you move around too much. You'd better just lay there for a while."

"Not like we're going anyplace anyhow," Rusty said.

I stood up, stepped to the front of the roof and leaned forward to see over the top of the sign. The dog, already staring up at me, bared its teeth and rumbled a growl. "Get outa here!" I shouted.

It leaped at me. I flinched and my heart lurched, but I held my position as the dog hit the wall about four feet up and tried to scramble higher. It worked its legs furiously, claws scratching at the old wood for a second or two. Then it fell, tumbled onto its side, flipped over and regained its feet and barked at me.

I muttered, "Up yours, bow-wow." Then I turned away.

Rusty, sitting cross-legged beside Slim, gave me a worried look. "What're we gonna do?" he asked.

"Stay right here," I told him. "At least for now. Give Slim's wounds a chance to dry up a little more. When we're ready to go, we'll figure out something about the dog."

"Maybe it'll be gone by then," Slim said.

"That's a good one," Rusty said.

"God, I'm being *nice* to it and the thing tries to rip my face off."

"Sometimes," I said, "being nice doesn't work."

"You can say that again."

"Sometimes, being nice . . ."

"Okay, okay," Rusty said.

I sat down beside Slim and turned my hands over. They were rust-colored and sticky. I wiped them on the legs of my jeans, but not much came off.

Rusty looked at his hands, too. They were as stained as mine. Frowning slightly, he brought his right hand close to his face. He stared at it for a few seconds, then raised his eyebrows and licked his palm.

"Oh, that's cute."

Lying on her stomach with her face toward me, Slim couldn't see Rusty. Rather than twisting around and maybe reopening some of her cuts, she asked me, "What's he doing?"

"Licking your blood off his hand," I explained.

He did it again. Smiling, he said, "Not bad."

"Grade-A blood, buddy," Slim informed him.

"I can tell." He sucked his red-stained forefinger. "Maybe those vampires've *got* something. Tasty stuff. Try some, Dwighty."

I shook my head. "No thanks."

"Scared?"

"I've got no problem with Slim's blood."

"As well you shouldn't," Slim pointed out.

"But I just got done swinging a filthy damn *cur* around by its tail."

"Weenie," Rusty said, grinning and lapping at his hand.

"Speaking of which," I said, "what've *you* been touching lately?"

Things dawned on him. He put his tongue back into his mouth and frowned at his hand. Looking a little sick, he shrugged his husky bare shoulders and said, "No big deal."

A smile on what I could see of her face, Slim said, "I'm *sure* Rusty must've washed his hands after going to the bathroom."

41

"I didn't piss on 'em, if that's what you mean." Then he managed to blurt out, "Not much, anyway," before he burst into laughter.

Slim and I broke up, too, but she stopped laughing almost at once—either it hurt or she was afraid the rough movements might start her bleeding again.

After a minute or two of silence, Rusty asked Slim, "Want me to lick your *back* clean?"

"*God* no!"

"Christ, Rusty," I said.

"What's the big deal?" he asked me. "I'm just offering to clean her up a little."

"With *spit*," Slim said. "No thanks."

"Get a grip," I told him.

Meeting my eyes, he said, "You can do it, too. You want to, don't you?"

"*No!*"

In fact, I did. Blood or no blood, the idea of sliding my tongue over the hot, smooth skin of Slim's back took my breath away and made my heart pound fast. Under the layers of my jeans and swimming trunks, I got hard.

But nobody knew it but me.

"You're out of your gourd," I said. "I'm not licking her and neither are you."

"What'll it hurt?" Rusty asked.

"Forget it," Slim told him.

"Okay, okay. Jeez. I was just trying to help."

"Sure," I said.

" 'Cause you know what? If we don't clean all that blood off Slim's back, it's gonna draw the vampire like a magnet."

"*What?*" I gasped, amazed.

"Points for originality," Slim said.

"You think it won't?" Rusty asked.

"I think there's no such things as vampires," I said.

"Me, too," said Rusty. "But what if we're wrong? What if this Valeria *is* one? All this blood's gonna bring her to us like chum brings sharks."

Though I didn't believe in vampires, I felt slightly nervous hearing him say those things. Because you never really know.

Do you?

Really?

Most of us *tell* ourselves we don't believe in that sort of stuff, but maybe that's because we're *afraid* to think they might exist. Vampires, werewolves, ghosts, aliens from outer space, black magic, the devil, hell . . . maybe even God.

If they do exist, they might *get* us.

So we say they don't.

"That's such bull," I said.

"Maybe it is and maybe it isn't," said Rusty.

"*Probably* it is," Slim threw in.

So I said, "If Valeria *is* a vampire, which she *isn't* . . . A, she's not even here yet. And B, even if she *gets* here, she can't do squat to us till after dark. And we'll be long gone by then."

"Think so?" Rusty asked.

"I know so."

Sure I did.

Chapter Seven

I eased myself down on my back. The tarpaper felt grainy against my bare skin, but at least it wasn't scorching hot the way it might've been on a sunny day.

"What're you doing?" Rusty asked.

"What does it look like?"

"We've gotta get out of here."

I shut my eyes, folded my hands across my belly, and said, "What's the big hurry?"

"You wanta get caught up here when *they* show up?"

Slim asked, "Why not? We came to see Valeria, didn't we?"

"To get a look at her—not to get *caught* at it."

"I'd rather get caught at that," Slim said, "than get my butt chewed by Old Yeller."

Rusty was silent for a while. Then he said with sort of a whine in his voice, "We can't just *stay* up here."

"It isn't just the dog," I told him. "The longer we wait, the less Slim'll bleed on the way home."

"But *they're* gonna show up."

"Maybe they'll have bandages," Slim said.

"Very funny."

"Let's give it an hour," I suggested.

"If we're real quiet," Slim said, "maybe the dog'll go away."

"Sure it will," Rusty muttered.

Then I heard some scuffing sounds. Turning my head, I opened my eyes. On the other side of Slim, Rusty was lying down. He let out a loud sigh.

The way we were all stretched out reminded me of the diving raft at Donner's Cove. Whenever we swam at the Cove, we always ended up flopping for a while on the old, white-painted platform. We'd be in our swimsuits, out of breath, dripping and cold from the river. Soon, the sun would warm us. But we wouldn't get up. You felt like you *never* wanted to get up, it was so nice out there. The raft was rocking softly. You could hear the quiet lapping of the water against it, and the buzz of distant motorboats and all the usual bird sounds. You could feel the soft heat of the sun on one side, the hard slick painted boards on the other. And you had your best friends lying down beside you. Especially Slim in one of her bikinis, her skin golden and dripping.

Too bad we *weren't* on the diving raft at the Cove. Too bad we were stranded, instead, on the scratchy tarpaper roof of the BEER—SNACKS—SOUVENIRS shack. Not surrounded by chilly water but by the wasteland of Janks Field. Not waves lapping peacefully at the platform, but the damn dog growling and barking and every so often hurling itself at the shack.

This just wasn't the same.

Not quite. The raft was paradise and this was the pits.

And even if the dog should magically vanish, I *knew* Slim

would start bleeding all over the place the minute we hit the ground.

She'd already lost a fair amount of blood.

She would lose a lot more on the way home.

What if she lost too much?

I turned my head. Blinking sweat out of my eyes, I looked at Slim. Her eyes were shut. Her face was cushioned on her crossed arms. It was speckled with tiny drops of sweat, and dribbles were running here and there. Her short hair, the color of bronze, was wet and coiled and clinging to her temple and forehead. She was marked from temple to jaw by three thin red stratches.

I found myself wanting to kiss those scratches.

And maybe also kiss the tiny soft curls of down above the left corner of her mouth.

While I was thinking about it, she opened her eyes. She blinked a few times, then raised her eyebrows. "Time to go?" she asked.

"Hasn't been an hour!" Rusty protested from the other side of Slim.

"I've been thinking," I said.

"Hurt yourself?" Rusty asked. Apparently, the rest period had improved his mood—if not his wit.

"I don't know about walking home from here," I said.

"You and me both," Rusty said. "We try, the dog'll have us for lunch."

"I'm not thinking about the dog."

"You oughta be."

"Dog or no dog, I don't like the idea of trying to walk home. Slim'll probably start bleeding again."

"Big deal," she said.

"It might be."

"It's not like I'll bleed *that* much," she said.

"What I was thinking, though, is that maybe one of us *better* go for help."

"Oh, joy," Rusty muttered.

"And what?" Slim asked. "Send out an ambulance for me? Forget it. I've got a couple of little cuts. . . ."

45

"More than a couple."

"Even still, it's no big crisis. I don't want to have a god-damn *ambulance* coming for me."

"What I thought was, I'll run to town and get somebody to drive me back here. Or I'll borrow a car and do it myself. Either way, we end up *driving* you home."

Slim's upper lip twitched slightly. "I don't know, Dwight."

"You wanta *leave* us up here?" Rusty asked.

"I'd be back in an hour."

"But shit, man, an *hour*. I don't want to be stuck up here for an hour."

"Take a nap."

"What if something *happens?*"

"I'll protect you, Rusty," Slim said, speaking loudly because her face was turned away from him.

He tossed a scowl at her. Then he said, "Anyway, what about the dog?"

"Long as you stay up here, it can't. . . ."

"I know *that*, man. What about *you?* You think it'll just let you leave?"

I shrugged. "I'll take care of it."

"Oh, yeah? Good luck."

He said it sarcastically, but I answered, "Thanks" and got to my feet. I stepped to the edge of the roof. Knees almost touching the back of the BEER—SNACKS—SOUVENIRS sign, I bent forward and looked down.

The dog, sitting, suddenly sprang at me and slammed against the shack.

"I think it's a moron," I announced.

"Do you have a plan or something?" Slim asked.

"Not exactly."

"I don't want you to get hurt."

I looked around at her, feeling a nice warmth. "Thanks," I told her.

Sitting up, Rusty said, "It's gonna have your ass, man."

The dog again threw itself at the shack, bounced off and fell to the dust.

I gave the sign a nudge with my knee. Though it felt sturdy, it was nailed to the roof on wooden braces made of two-by-fours. With a little effort, I could probably kick one of the braces apart and have myself a club—maybe with a few nails sticking out.

Only one problem.

When you're my dad's son, you don't go around destroying other people's property. Not even a crummy sign on a closed snack stand in Janks Field.

It's not only wrong, it's illegal.

If Dad ever found out that a son of his had kicked apart someone else's sign in order to make himself a club in order to beat the crap out of a stray dog . . .

"What're you doing?" Rusty asked.

"Nothing."

"Want help?" he asked.

A laugh flew out of Slim, but then she groaned.

"You okay?" I asked her.

"Been better." She grimaced slightly, then added, "Been worse, too."

"Do you have any fond feelings for the dog?" I asked.

"You kidding?"

I shrugged. "I mean, you're sort of an animal lover."

"That has its limits," she said.

"So . . . you won't be upset if something bad happens to this dog?"

"Like what?" she asked.

"Like something *really* bad?"

Looking me steadily in the eyes, she said, "I don't think so."

As I nodded, I saw Rusty giving me this very weird look. His eyebrows were rumpled in a frown, but his eyes looked frantic and his mouth seemed to be smiling.

"What?" I asked him.

"What're you gonna do?"

I shrugged, then walked over to where the sign ended. Down below, the dog watched me and followed. When I stopped, it stopped.

"Get outa here!" I shouted at it.

47

It barked and leaped, slammed the wall and tried to scurry up. Then it dropped. As it landed on its side in the dust in front of the shack, I jumped.

My plan was to land on the dog with both feet.

Cave it in.

On my way down, I heard it make a quick, alarmed whine as if it knew what was coming.

I braced myself for the feel of my sneakers smashing through its ribcage—and maybe for the sound of a wet *splot!* as its guts erupted.

But it had just enough time to scoot out of my way.

Almost.

Instead of busting through the dog, one of my feet pounded nothing but ground and the other stomped the end of its tail.

The dog howled.

I stumbled forward and almost fell, but managed to stay on my feet. As I regained my balance, I glanced back. The dog was racing off, howling and yelping, butt low, tail curled between its hind legs as if to hide from more harm.

Rusty, at the edge of the roof, called down, "Got a piece of him!"

The dog sat down, curled around and studied its tail.

"I'll be back as soon as I can!" I yelled.

My voice must've gotten the dog's attention. It forgot its tail and turned its head and stared at me with its only eye.

I muttered, "Uh-oh."

It came at me like a sprinter out of the blocks.

"Shit!" Rusty yelled. "Run! Go, man!"

I ran like hell.

Somewhere in the distance behind me, Rusty yelled, "Hey, you fuckin' mangy piece of shit! Over here!"

I looked back.

The dog, gaining on me, turned its head for a glance toward the voice.

Rusty let fly with a sneaker.

The dog barked at him . . . or at the airborn shoe.

The sneaker hit the ground a couple of yards behind it and

tumbled, throwing up dust. Not even a near miss. But the dog wheeled around and barked.

Rusty threw a second sneaker.

The dog glanced over its shoulder at me, snarled, then dodged the second sneaker (which would've missed it anyway by about five feet) and raced forward to renew its seige of the snack stand.

Chapter Eight

Afraid the dog might change its mind and come after me again, I ran for all I was worth until I reached the edge of the woods. Then I stopped and turned around.

The dog was sitting in front of the shack, barking and wagging its tail as if it had treed a pair of squirrels.

Up on the roof, Rusty waved at me, swinging his arm overhead like a big, dopey kid.

I waved back at him the same way.

Then Slim, apparently on her knees, raised herself up behind the sign. Holding onto it with one hand, she waved at me with the other.

My throat went thick and tight.

I waved back furiously and yelled, "See ya later!"

And a voice in my head whispered, *Oh, yeah?*

But who pays attention to those voices? We get them all the time. I do, don't you? When someone you love is leaving the house, doesn't it occur to you, now and then, that you may never see him or her again? Flying places, don't you sometimes think *What if this one goes down?* Driving, don't you sometimes imagine an oncoming truck zipping across center lines and wiping out everyone in your car? Such thoughts give you a nasty sick feeling inside, but only for a few seconds.

Then you tell yourself nothing's going to happen. And, turns out, nothing *does* happen.

Usually.

I lowered my arm, stared at my friends for a couple of seconds longer, then turned and hurried down the dirt road.

I ran, but not all-out. Not the way you run with a dog on your tail, but the way you do it when you've got a long distance to cover. A pretty good clip, but not a sprint.

Every so often, I had an urge to turn back.

But I told myself they'd be fine. Up on the roof, they were safe from the dog. And if strangers should come along—like some punks or a wino or The Traveling Vampire Show—Rusty and Slim could lie down flat and nobody would even know they were there.

Besides, if I returned, we'd all be on the roof again a couple of miles from home and no way to get there without Slim bleeding all over the place.

Going for a car was the only sensible thing to do.

That's what I told myself.

But the farther away from Janks Field I ran, the more I wished I'd stayed. A couple of times, I actually stopped, turned around and gazed up the dirt road to where it vanished in the woods.

And thought about running back.

Maybe I would've done it, too, except for the dog. I hated the idea of facing it again.

First, I felt sort of guilty about trying to kill it. Which made no sense. The damn thing had attacked Slim—it had *hurt* her and tried to rip her apart. For that, it deserved to die. Clearly. Without a doubt. But all that aside, I felt rotten about jumping off the roof to murder it. Part of me was glad it had scooted out of the way.

Second, the dog was sure to attack me if I returned to Janks Field on foot. It would try to maul me and I'd try to kill it again.

But I hope the dog wasn't the reason I decided to keep going. I hope it wasn't for anything selfish like that.

But you never know about these things.

The real whys.

And even if you could somehow sort out the whys and find the truth, maybe it's better if you don't.

Better to believe what you want to believe.

If you can.

Anyway, I didn't go back. I kept on running up the gloomy dirt road, huffing, sweating so hard that my jeans were sticking to my legs.

I met no one else. The road, all the way from Janks Field to Route 3, was empty except for me.

When I came to the highway, I stopped running. I needed to catch my breath and rest a little, but I also didn't want anyone driving by to get the wrong idea.

Or the right idea.

With Grandville only a couple of miles away, some of the people in cars going by were sure to recognize me. They might not pay much attention if I'm simply strolling along the road-side. But if they see me running, they'll figure something is wrong. They'll either stop to offer help or *tell* everyone what they saw.

Golly, Mavis, I was out on Route 3 this morning 'n who should I see but Frank and Lacy's boy, Dwight, all by himself over near the Janks Field turnoff, running like he had the Devil itself chasing after him. Seemed real strange.

Spose he was up to some sorta mischief?

Can't say, Mavis. He ain't never been in much trouble. Always a first time, though.

I wonder if you oughta tell his folks how you saw him out there.

I better. If he was my boy, I'd wanta know.

And so it would go. In Grandville, not only does everyone know everyone, but they figure your business is their business. Nowdays, you hear talk that "It takes a village to raise a child." You ask me, it takes a village to wreck a child for life.

In Grandville, you felt like you were living in a nest of spies. One wrong move and everyone would know about it. Including your parents.

After giving the matter some thought, I decided I didn't

51

want to be seen on Route 3 by *anyone*. So every time I heard a car coming, I hurried off and hid in the trees until it was out of sight.

I hid, but I kept my eyes on the road. If something that looked like a Traveling Vampire Show should go by, I wanted to know about it. I planned to call off my mission to town and run back to Janks Field.

When I wasn't busy dodging off to hide from cars, I wondered how best to get my hands on one.

My first thought had been to borrow Mom's car. But on second thought, she never let me take it without asking where I wanted to go. Janks Field was supposed to be off limits. She would be very angry (and disappointed in me) if I told her my true destination. Lying to her, however, would be even worse. "Once people lie to you," she'd told me, "you can never really believe them again about anything."

Very true. I knew it then and I know it now.

So I *couldn't* lie to her.

Which meant I couldn't borrow her car.

And forget about Dad's.

Both my brothers owned cars, but they loved to rat me out. No way could I go to either of them. . . .

And then I thought of Lee, my brother Danny's wife.

Perfect!

She would let me use her old red Chevy pickup truck, and she wouldn't yap.

I'd learned how to drive in Lee's pickup with her as my teacher. If she hadn't taught me, I might've *never* learned how to drive. Mom had been useless as an instructor, squealing *"Watch out!"* every two seconds. Dad had snapped orders at me like a drill instructor. My brother Stu was a tail-gating speed-demon; being taught how to drive by Stu would've been like taking gun safety lessons from Charlie Starkweather. Danny might've been all right, but Lee was in the kitchen when we started talking about it, and she volunteered.

That was the previous summer, when I'd been fifteen.

I spent plenty of time that summer hanging out with friends my own age: Rusty and Slim (calling herself Dagny) and a kid named Earl Grodin who had an outboard motorboat and wanted to take us fishing on the river every day. We *did* go fishing almost every day. Earl loved to fish. The strange thing was, he insisted on using worms for bait but he hated to touch them. So Rusty and Dagny and I took turns baiting his hook for him. And teasing him. You've never seen such a sissy about worms. Eventually, Dagny tossed a live one into her mouth. As she chewed it up, Earl gaped at her in horror. Then he gagged. Then he slapped her across the face as if to knock the worm out of her mouth so I slugged him in the nose and knocked him overboard. After that, he didn't take us out fishing any more. But the summer was almost over by then, anyhow, so we didn't mind very much.

We sure had fun on his boat while it lasted, but I had even better fun on the roads with Lee.

Being a school teacher, she had the summers off. She told me to drop by the house whenever I wanted driving lessons, so that's what I did.

The first time out, she told me to get behind the wheel of her big old pickup truck. She sat in the passenger seat, gave me a few instructions, and off we went. Their house was near the edge of town, so we didn't need to worry much about traffic. Good thing, too. Even though the driving part of the operation turned out to be easy, I did have trouble keeping my eyes on the road.

That's because Lee was a knockout.

You take a lot of beautiful women, they're shits. But not Lee. She was down-to-earth, friendly and funny. I'd say that she was just a normal person, but she wasn't. She was *better* than normal people. Way better. She didn't seem to know it, though.

When we went driving, she usually wore shorts. Not cut-off jeans, but real shorts. They might be red or white or blue or yellow or pink, but they were always very short and tight. She had great legs. They were tanned and smooth and very hard to keep my eyes away from.

On top, she might wear a T-shirt or a knit pullover or a short-sleeved blouse. Sometimes, when she wore a regular blouse or shirt, I could look between the buttons and catch glimpses of her bra. I tried not to do it often, though.

Mostly, I just stole glances at her legs.

I *would've* tried to sneak looks at her face, too—it was a terrific face—but I could look at that without being sneaky about it.

The first afternoon out with Lee, I learned how to drive. I didn't really need any more lessons after that. She knew it and I knew it, but we kept it to ourselves. Two or three times a week, for the rest of the summer, I went over to her house and we took off in the truck.

While I drove us through towns and over back roads, we talked about all sorts of stuff. We shared secrets, complained about my parents, discussed our worries and our favorite movies, laughed. We laughed *a lot*.

It was almost like being on a fabulous date with the most beautiful girl in town. Almost. What made it different from a date was that I held no hope of ever having any sexual contact with her. I mean, you can't exactly fool around with your brother's wife. Also, she was ten years older than me. Also, she was out of my league entirely.

All I could do was look.

Lee *knew* I was sneaking glances at her while I drove, but it didn't seem to bother her. Usually, if she noticed, she didn't mention it. Sometimes, though, she said stuff like, "Watch out, we're coming up on a curve," or "Don't forget about the road entirely." She was always cheerful when she said such things, but I always blushed like crazy. I'd mutter, "I'm sorry" and she would say, "Don't worry about it. Just don't crash."

Then one day I crashed.

For some reason, Lee wasn't wearing a bra that day. Maybe they were all in the wash. Maybe she was too hot. Who knows? Whatever the reason, I noticed it the moment she walked out of her house. Nothing showed through her bright red blouse, but her breasts seemed to be moving about more than usual. They were loose underneath the blouse, no doubt about it.

After noticing that, I tried to keep my eyes away from her chest as much as possible.

Maybe ten minutes later, I was driving along a narrow road through the woods, Lee in the passenger seat, when I finally just *had* to look.

I glanced over at her.

Between two buttons of her blouse, the fabric was pursed like vertical, parted lips. Looking in, I could see the side of her right breast. Her *bare* breast, smooth and pale in the shadows. Not very much of it actually showed—a crescent maybe half an inch wide, at most.

But much too much.

All of a sudden, I couldn't hear a word Lee was saying. I kept steering us along the road, smiling and nodding and turning my head to look at her—first at her face to make sure she wasn't watching me, then at the curve of her exposed breast.

I felt breathless and hard and guilty.

But I couldn't stop myself.

Suddenly, she yelled, *"Watch out!"* and flung her hands out to grab the dashboard.

My eyes jerked forward in time to see a deer straight ahead of us. I swerved and the deer bounded out of the way and I missed it just fine. But then I couldn't come out of the turn fast enough. I took out a speed limit sign.

We weren't hurt, though.

Next thing I knew, Lee and I were standing side by side in front of the truck, looking at its smashed headlight.

"I'm really sorry," I said.

"That's okay, honey," she said. "These things happen."

"Danny's gonna kill me."

She patted me on the back and said, "No, he won't. We'll just keep this between the two of us."

"But he'll see the damage."

"Let's you and I just forget you had a driving lesson today. Danny'll think I'm the one who crashed. That'll suit him just fine, anyway." She smiled at me. "You know how he loves to whine about 'women drivers.' "

"I can't let *you* take the blame," I protested.

"I insist."

"But . . ."

"If he finds out *you* did it, he'll tease you to death and he'll broadcast it to everyone he knows. You don't need that." Then, giving my shoulder a friendly squeeze, she added, "Besides, it's my truck. If I say I was driving it, I was."

Lee never told on me.

For the next week or so, Danny had a lot of fun at her expense. I was tempted to confess, but then everybody would've known Lee had lied. That would've made things worse all the way around.

Anyway, that's the kind of woman Lee was. I could count on her to help me retrieve Slim and Rusty, and she wouldn't blab about it.

I just hoped she'd be home.

Chapter Nine

I stayed fairly calm most of the way to Lee's house, but the sight of her pickup truck in the driveway turned me into a nervous wreck.

She's home!

I felt a lurch of panic.

Even under the best conditions, I sometimes chickened out about visiting Lee. That may seem strange, since we were such great friends. But you've got to understand how beautiful and special she was. As much as I liked being with her, I hated the idea of intruding on her. I wanted her *never* to think of me as a nuisance.

I didn't much want her to see me shirtless and sweaty and filthy, either.

All of a sudden, I changed my mind about asking for Lee's help. Instead of heading for her front door, I kept on walking.

Maybe I would just go home. If I told Mom the truth, she would take me out to Janks Field. Then she'd tell Dad all about it, and he . . .

"Dwight?"

My heart jumped. I turned my head and saw Lee in the doorway, holding the screen door open.

"Oh, hi," I called as if surprised to find her in this neck of the woods. "What're you walking away for?" she asked.

I stopped. "I'm not."

"How about a Coke?"

I shrugged. "Okay. Thanks." I hurried across her front lawn.

She stood there, holding the door and watching me, a look on her face as if she knew *everything* but considered it more fun to play ignorant.

Not dressed for company, she was wearing an old blue chambray shirt—probably one of Danny's. The sleeves were rolled halfway up her forearms and the top couple of buttons weren't fastened. Her shirt wasn't tucked into anything. (Maybe she wore nothing it *could* be tucked into.) Her legs were bare, and she didn't have on any shoes or socks.

As I trotted up the porch stairs, she asked, "Where you been hiding yourself?"

I shrugged and blushed. "Nowhere much," I said.

In the doorway, she gave me a hug. I didn't often get hugs from Lee; only if we hadn't seen each other for a long time. I put my arms around her. As she kissed my cheek and I kissed hers, she gave me a good solid squeeze, mashing me against the front of her body. Her shirt was soft against my skin. By the feel of her breasts, I knew she wasn't wearing any bra.

It was just about the best hug ever.

But we broke it up after a couple of seconds. Lee turned away, saying, "Come on, let's get those Cokes."

I followed her toward the kitchen, watching the back of her shirt. It draped her rear end, then stopped. The tail fluttered slightly as she walked.

"So what've you been doing with yourself?" she asked.

I suddenly remembered.

"Oh, yeah," I said.

That was all I needed to say.

About one stride into the kitchen, Lee stopped and turned around and raised her eyebrows.

"Maybe the Cokes better wait," I told her.

"What is it?"

"I was sort of wondering if you'd let me borrow your truck for about half an hour."

"Sure," she said, not even hesitating to think about it.

"Thanks."

I followed her through the kitchen. Her brown leather purse was on top of the table. She picked it up, reached inside, pulled out her keys and tossed them to me. I caught them.

"Thanks," I said again.

As I started to turn around, she said, "I've got nothing to do for a while. Want me to come along?"

I must've made a face.

"Guess not," she said and shrugged.

"It's not *that*. If you *want* to come along, it's fine with me. I just don't want to . . . you know, *impose* on you."

"When you're imposing, I'll let you know."

"Okay."

"And you're not." She gave me a quick smile. "Not yet, anyway." The smile gone, she added, "You *need* some help, don't you?"

"Well, I need a car. But it'd be great if you want to come along with me."

"You sure?" she asked.

"Sure."

"Where're we going?"

"Janks Field."

She let out a laugh, throwing back her head, then shaking it. When the laugh was over, she said, "That explains plenty."

"Still want to come?"

"You bet. But what's the problem?"

"Slim got attacked by a dog."

Lee grimaced. "Slim being Frances?" she asked.

"Right. Anyway, it didn't hurt her much, but she fell down and got some cuts. I was afraid she'd bleed all over the place if she tried to walk home, so I left her there with Rusty. They're on top of that snack stand."

"What about the dog?" Lee asked.

"It was still there when I left. But it can't get to them as long as they stay on the roof."

"So the idea is to drive out and rescue them?"

"That's it," I said.

"No problem. Just let me have a minute to get dressed. Go ahead and grab yourself a Coke. You look like you could use one."

"Okay. Thanks."

"If you want to wash up or something, feel free."

I nodded, and she left the kitchen. When she was out of sight, I sighed.

Cheer up, I told myself. She'll be back.

But "dressed."

Sighing again, I stepped over to the sink. I washed the dried blood off my hands, then splashed cold water onto my face. I used a wet paper towel to clean the sweat and grime off my arms and chest and belly. After that, I took a Coke bottle out of the refrigerator and pried its cap off.

I only managed a few swallows before Lee came in. She looked almost the same as before. Now, however, white shorts showed below the hanging front of her shirt. She wore white sneakers, but no socks.

"Ready to go?" she asked.

"All set."

"Want me to drive?"

"Sure." I tossed the keys to her. She caught them, then stepped past me and grabbed her purse off the table.

On our way to the front door, she said, "We'll come straight back here unless Slim turns out to need a doctor or something."

"Good idea."

Outside, Lee held the screen door.

I reached for the main door, meaning to shut it behind me, but she said, "Let's just leave it open. The more air gets in, the better."

So I left it open and stepped outside.

The screen door banged shut as I followed Lee down the stairs.

Walking ahead of me, she reached behind herself and hitched up the tail of her pale blue shirt. Both the seat pockets of her shorts were bulging. From one, she removed a white tin of bandages. From the other, she took a squeeze bottle of Bactine anticeptic. She dropped them into her purse as she walked.

Over at the driveway, she pulled open the driver's door of her pickup truck. I ran around to the other side. Still hanging on to my Coke, I opened the passenger door with one hand and climbed up.

Lee's purse was on the seat between us.

Leaning forward slightly, she punched a key into the ignition. She gave it a twist and the engine chugged to life. Then she sped backward out of the driveway, swung into the street and started working the forward gears, picking up speed. "We're off!" she proclaimed.

"Sure are."

She grinned at me. "How about a drink of that?" she asked.

"Sure." I handed the Coke to her. She didn't wipe the bottle's lip at all, just raised it to her mouth, tilted it high, and took a couple of swallows. Through the pale green of the glass, the Coke was a rich brownish red color.

There was still an inch of pop in the bottle when she handed it back to me. "Go ahead and finish it," she said.

I nearly always wiped off the lip of a bottle before drinking after anyone. But not this time. I put it into my mouth, knowing her mouth had just been there. She wasn't wearing any lipstick, but I almost thought I could taste her lips.

"So what were you three doing out at Janks Field?" she asked. "Looking for bones?"

"Looking for a vampire," I said.

She turned her head and hoisted her eyebrows.

"I know. Vampires don't exist. But there's supposed to be a vampire show at Janks Field tonight. One night only. The

Traveling Vampire Show. Rusty says they've got fliers for it all over town."

"This is the first I've heard about it," Lee said. "I haven't been into town yet today. Danny's off on one of his trips, so I slept in."

"Where'd he go?"

"Chicago. One of those sales conventions. So tell me more about The Traveling Vampire Show."

"There's supposed to be a real vampire. . . ."

"No kidding?" She looked at me and grinned. "I've never seen one of those, myself."

"Her name's Valeria. I guess she's supposed to go after volunteers from the audience."

"Cool," Lee said.

"Anyway, *we* can't go to the show. It doesn't even start till midnight and it's adults only and I'm never supposed to *go* to Janks Field at all."

"So of course you went there anyway."

"Yeah. You know, just for a look around. We thought we might get a chance to see Valeria."

"In daylight? You kids need to brush up on your vampire lore."

"Oh, we know all about *that*. We're not stupid."

She grinned at me.

"We just wanted to see what was going on. We figured maybe it'd be like a carnival and we could watch them setting up for the show, something like that. And maybe we'd get a look at Valeria."

Gorgeous! Beguiling!

I decided not to mention that Valeria was supposed to be a stunning beauty.

A blush suddenly spread over my skin.

Oh, God, don't let Lee find out about our wager!

"Thing is," I said, "we didn't seriously think she'd be spending all day in a *coffin*. You know? I mean, the whole thing's gotta be a fake-out. We figured we might actually see her wandering around in the daytime. Then we'd *know* she's a phony."

"So, did you see her?" Lee asked.

"I guess we got to Janks Field ahead of the show. Nobody was there except us. And that dog."

Chapter Ten

Lee drove down Route 3 at a safe speed just slightly over the limit but after the turn-off, in the seclusion of the dirt road, she poured it on. This didn't surprise me. I'd ridden with her many times before and knew all about her reckless streak.

I couldn't complain, though. *She'd* never crashed.

So I held my peace—along with the dashboard and door handle—while she ripped over the narrow, twisty road. The force of her turns sometimes bumped me against the door, sometimes threw me toward her.

I was tempted to let go and fall against Lee, not to punish her for the wild driving but to have the contact with her. It might've been embarrassing, though. And it might've made her crash into a tree or something. I didn't want to take the risk, so I held on tight.

We jerked from side to side, shook and bounced all the way to the far end of the road and burst out of the dense forest gloom into the open gray gloom of Janks Field and Lee almost sent me through the windshield the way she tromped on the brakes.

We skidded to a stop.

Parked near the shack where I'd left Slim and Rusty were three vehicles: a truck the size of a moving van, a large bus, and a hearse. All three were shiny black, and unmarked—no fancy signs announcing this was The Traveling Vampire Show, no paintings of bats or fangs or Valeria. Nothing at all like that. As if the show wanted to keep itself secret as it roamed the roads on its way from town to town.

Several people seemed to be unloading equipment from the truck.

"Looks like the show has arrived," Lee said.

"Guess so. If that's what it is."

"What else could it be?"

"I don't know," I said.

"I don't see your friends, though."

"Me neither."

"Think they're still up there?"

"They might be. Maybe they're lying down flat behind the sign."

"Let's find out," Lee said. She started driving forward.

My mouth jumped open, but I managed not to gasp. Instead, trying to sound calm, I said, "What're you doing?"

"We came to find Slim and Rusty. That's what we're going to do."

"But these *people!*"

"We've got every right to be here."

"Hope *they* see it that way."

"No sweat," she said, bravado in her smile but a flicker of worry in her eyes.

She drove slowly. Over the sound of the engine, I heard glass crunching under the tires.

"You sure about this?" I asked.

"Sure I'm sure."

"What if we get a flat tire?"

"I don't get flats." She gave me another one of those smiles. Then she added, "And if I do, we'll just have a couple of these strapping young chaps change it for us."

As she drove closer, a few of the workers stopped what they were doing and watched our approach. Others continued to go about their business. I counted twelve, in all. (There might've been more, unseen.)

Though I saw a variety of trousers on them—blue jeans, black jeans, black leather—they all seemed to be wearing shiny black shirts with long sleeves.

Studying their outfits, I noticed that all the workers weren't men. At least four seemed to be women.

I wondered if one of those might be Valeria herself.

Maybe they're *all* Valeria, I thought—and take turns playing the role. Or maybe the real Valeria is whiling away the afternoon in the bus.

Or in the hearse.

As Lee eased her pickup to a stop, I looked over at the hearse. I figured there might be a casket inside, but the rear windows were draped with red velvet. Lee shut off her engine.

A man was walking toward us.

Lee opened her door. It seemed like a bad idea.

"You getting out?" I asked.

"*You* don't have to," she said.

"What about the dog?"

She looked back at me. "Where is it?"

"I don't know, but it must be around here someplace."

"Maybe it decided not to stick around when it saw what was coming."

"Maybe that's what *we* oughta do," I said.

"We're fine," she told me, and climbed out.

I threw open my door, jumped to the ground and hurried around her truck. I came up behind Lee and halted by her side. The man stopped a few paces in front of us. He glanced at me, seemed to decide that I didn't matter, and turned his eyes to Lee.

He was so handsome he was creepy.

His long, flowing hair was black as ink, but he had pale blue eyes. The eyes might've looked wonderful on a woman; on him, they seemed unnatural and weird. So did his slim, curving lips. All his facial features were delicate, and he had smooth, softly tanned skin. Except for the slightest trace of beard stubble along his jaw and chin, he might've easily passed for a beautiful woman.

At least from the neck up. The rest of him was a different story. He had broad, heavy-looking shoulders and arm muscles that strained the sleeves of his shirt. The top few buttons of his shirt were unfastened as if to make room for his massive chest. He had a flat stomach and narrow hips, and wore black leather trousers with a sheath knife on the belt.

After sliding his eyes up and down Lee a couple of times, he smiled. I've never seen such white teeth. Even though the vampire was supposed to be Valeria, I couldn't help but check this guy's canines. They looked no longer or more pointy than anyone else's.

Sounding friendly enough, he said, "If you're here for tickets, I'm afraid we don't open the box office until an hour before show time."

"I can't buy any in advance?" Lee asked.

"Not until eleven o'clock tonight."

"But what if I come back tonight and you're sold out?"

"Oh, that won't happen. Not here. We sell out at some venues, but this arena isn't gonna fill up. Nice if it does, but it won't." He glanced at me, then said to Lee, "There is an age restriction, you know. The show's meant for adults, so no one under eighteen gets in. I think your brother's still a little on the young side."

"But he's the one who wants to see it," Lee protested.

The man flashed a grin at me. "I'll *bet* he does."

"A couple of his friends, too," Lee added.

"Well, if they're no older than he is. . . ."

"Maybe they're around here someplace. They came out ahead of us, so they should've been here by now. Teenagers? A husky boy and a slender blonde girl?"

The man frowned slightly and shook his head. "Haven't seen 'em. Nobody's here but our crew."

Turning her head in the general direction of the snack stand, Lee shouted, *"SLIM? RUSTY?"*

I watched the roof. Nobody popped a head up.

"If they do come along," Lee said to the man, "would you let them know we were already here?"

"I'd be glad to."

"Thanks. I *told* them that they were too young for a show like this. But they're *so* fascinated by the whole subject of vampires. . . ." She shook her head. "You know, teenagers."

"I know exactly," the man said. "I was one myself a few years ago. And fascinated by vampires."

"They just *had* to come out here and see what it was all about. I'm sure they were hoping I'd somehow be able to work magic and buy tickets for them. They seem to think I can do anything."

"I'd like to be able to help you. . . ."

"Lee," she said, and offered her hand.

"Lee," he said. He took it gently in his long fingers. "Pleased to meet you, Lee. I'm Julian."

"And this is my brother, Dwight."

Though I wished she hadn't used our real names, I smiled and held out my hand. Julian let go of Lee's hand and shook mine. His fingers felt warm and dry.

After releasing my hand, he faced Lee and asked, "Are you aware of what happens in our show?"

"Not really."

He performed a mock-embarrassed cringe and shrug. "Well, there's always a certain amount of blood-letting. Generally, quite a lot. In fact, it can get *very* gory. It looks worse than it is, but it can be shocking for people who aren't used to it."

"I see," Lee said, nodding slightly, a concerned look on her face.

"Also, clothing often gets torn in the heat of battle. It's not unusual for private parts to . . . become exposed."

Lee broke out a smile. "Sounds more interesting all the time."

Julian chuckled softly. "Well, I just want you to understand why we try to keep kids away from the show."

"I'm *almost* eighteen," I said, almost telling the truth.

"How old *are* you?" Julian asked me.

"Seventeen." I blushed as I said it. I hate lying.

"And your friends?"

"They're both seventeen, too," I said, and blushed even hotter because Slim, though sixteen like me and Rusty, looked more like fourteen.

I'm sure Julian knew I was lying. But he turned to Lee

anyway, and said, "I might be able to make an exception for them if they'll be accompanied by an adult."

"Oh, I'd be coming with them," she said.

"Then I suppose it'll be all right."

"Oh, that's wonderful. Thank you, Julian. Let me get my purse." She ducked into her truck and snatched her purse off the seat.

This has to be some kind of fake-out, I thought. She's not *really* going to buy tickets.

Standing beside me again, she asked Julian, "How much will that be for four tickets?"

"They're ten dollars each."

"So forty dollars," she said. She hung the purse from her shoulder, reached in and took out her wallet. Head down, she flipped through the bills.

I caught Julian staring at the front of her shirt.

He has the hots for her, I realized. That's why he's breaking the rules.

"Shoot," Lee muttered. "I don't seem to have forty in cash."

So that's it, I thought. She never *did* plan to buy any tickets.

I felt relieved, but also a little disappointed.

But then she said, "You wouldn't happen to take checks, would you?"

"From you," said Julian, "of course."

So she hauled out her checkbook and a ballpoint pen. With a smile at me, she nudged my arm. I realized what she wanted, so I turned around and bent over slightly. She braced the checkbook against my back and began to write.

Pausing, she asked, "Who should I make it out to?"

"Julian Stryker," he said. "That's Stryker with a y."

"Not to The Traveling Vampire Show?" she asked.

"To me. That's fine."

"You won't get in trouble?"

"I shouldn't think so. I'm the owner."

"Ah."

She stopped writing on my back. Straightening up, I watched her rip the check out of the book.

Her home address was printed on it, of course.

She handed it to Julian.

He held it open in front of him, studied it for a few moments, then slipped it into a pocket of his shiny black shirt. He patted it there and smiled at Lee. "If it bounces, of course, we'll require your blood."

She grinned. "Of course."

"Let me get your tickets," he said. He turned away and walked briskly toward the open front door of the bus. Like the hearse, the bus's windows were draped on the inside with red curtains.

I waited for Julian to vanish inside. Then I whispered to Lee, "That check has your *address* on it. Now he knows where you *live*."

"No big deal," she said. "While he's gone, why don't you take a look at the roof?"

I scowled toward the snack stand. It was only about twenty feet away, and none of the workers seemed to be watching us any longer. So I walked over to it, jumped, caught hold of an edge of the roof and pulled myself up.

Slim and Rusty were gone.

They'd left behind nothing, not even my shirt.

I dropped to the ground. No sign of Julian yet. I strolled back to Lee and reported, "They aren't there."

"Probably ran off when they saw what was coming."

"But what'd they do about the dog?"

Lee shook her head, shrugged, then smiled at Julian as he came out of the bus. In a quiet voice, she said to me, "They're probably on their way home."

"Sure hope so," I muttered.

"Four tickets for tonight's performance," Julian said, raising the tickets and smiling as he came toward us. With each stride, his black hair shook, his glossy shirt fluttered, and he *jingled*. The silvery, musical jingling sounded almost like Christmas bells, but not quite.

They sounded more like spurs.

I looked down at his boots. Sure enough, he wore a pair of spurs with big, silver rowels.

Had he been wearing them all along? Maybe, but I don't think so. Maybe he'd put them on while he was in the bus.

If so, why?

Why would he wear spurs at all?

I glanced around just to make sure there wasn't a horse nearby, and didn't see one. Of course, you could've fit half a dozen Clydesdales inside the truck and nobody'd be the wiser.

But I doubted there were any horses at all. More than likely, Julian wore the spurs as fashion accessories to his costume.

Maybe part of him longed to be Paladin.

The jingling went silent when he halted in front of Lee. He presented the tickets to her.

"Thank you so much, Julian," she said.

"My pleasure. We don't have reserved seating, so come early." His smile flashed. "And stay late. After the show, I'll introduce you to Valeria. You, your brother and his friends." He cast his smile in my direction.

"That might be nice," Lee said. "Thank you."

"Yeah, thanks," I threw in.

"The pleasure is mine," he said to Lee. "I'll look forward to seeing you tonight. All of you."

She blushed and said, "All four of us."

"Isn't that what I said?"

"Guess so." Nodding, she said, "Thanks again." Then she turned away and climbed into her truck. I hurried around to the other side and hopped into the passenger seat.

As she backed up, Julian walked away.

She swung the truck around and we started bouncing our way across Janks Field.

"You didn't have to buy *tickets*," I said.

"You want to see the show, don't you?"

"Well, yeah. I guess so. But Mom and Dad are never gonna *let* me."

"Maybe not." She tossed me a smile tinted with mischief. "If they know about it."

"Anyway, what about Slim and Rusty?"

"We've got *four* tickets and Danny's out of town. All four of us can go, just like I told Julian."

Holding back a groan, I muttered, "I don't know. I just hope they turn up. They were supposed to wait for me."

"I'm sure they're all right."

Chapter Eleven

As Lee steered us into the shadows of the dirt road, she said, "If I'd been up on that roof, I would've jumped down and run for the woods . . . probably before the Show even pulled into sight. A truck like that, it'd make a lot of noise coming through the woods."

"The bus, too," I added.

"They must've heard the engines in plenty of time to get away."

"But what about the dog?" I asked.

She shook her head. "Maybe it was gone by then."

"What if it wasn't?"

"Might've been distracted by the new arrivals."

"Yeah, maybe," I said, but I pictured Slim and Rusty racing over Janks Field, the yellow dog chasing them and gaining on them and finally leaping onto Slim's back and burying its teeth in the nape of her neck and taking her down. Rusty looking back over his shoulder . . .

Wrong, I thought. Rusty's slower than Slim. He would be dragging behind and first to get nailed by the dog.

Unless Slim held back to protect him.

Which she might do.

Probably *did* do.

So then, though she was the faster of the two, she would've been the one to get attacked.

In my mind, I once again pictured Rusty looking over his

shoulder. He watches Slim go down beneath the dog, then hesitates, knowing he should run back to help her.

But does he go back?

With Rusty, who knows?

I'm not saying he was a coward. He had guts, all right. I'd seen him do plenty of brave things—even *foolbardly* things, every so often. But he had a selfish streak that worried me.

Take for example how he snuck off, that morning, to eat his Ding-Dong.

Or what he did last Halloween.

Rusty, Dagny (later to be known as Slim) and I figured Janks Field would be the best of all possible places to visit on the spookiest night of the year. Maybe, as a bonus, we'd get to spy on a satanic orgy, or even (if we *really* lucked out) a human sacrifice.

But what had seemed like a great idea during the last week or two of October turned suddenly into a *bad* idea at just after sundown on Halloween. Confronted with walking out to Janks Field in the dark, I think we all realized that the dangers were more real than make-believe.

We'd gathered on the sidewalk in front of Rusty's house and we were all set to go. We wore dark clothes. We carried flashlights. We were armed with hidden knives—just in case. At supper, I'd told Mom and Dad that I would be going over to Rusty's to "goof around."

Which was not exactly a lie.

As we left Rusty's house behind and started walking in the general direction of Route 3, Dagny said, "I've been thinking."

"Hope you didn't strain nothing," Rusty said.

"Maybe we should do something *else* tonight."

"What do you mean?" he asked.

"*Not* go to Janks Field."

"You're kidding."

"No, I mean it."

"You wanta chicken out?"

"It's not chicken to be smart."

"Bwok-bwok-bwok-bwok-bwok."

"Hey, cut it out," I said.

Richard Laymon

"You gonna chicken out, too?" Rusty asked me.

"Nobody's chickening out," I said.

"Glad to hear it. I'd hate to think my two best friends are a couple of yellow-bellied cowards."

"Up yours," I said.

We kept on walking. Most of the houses in the neighborhood were well-lighted and had jack-o'-lanterns glowing on their porches. On both sides of the street, small groups of kids were making the rounds, walking or running from house to house with bags for their goodies. Most of them were dressed up: some in those flimsy plastic store-bought costumes (witches, Huckleberry Hound, Superman, the Devil, and so on); many in home-made outfits (pirates, gypsies, vampires, hobos, princesses, etc.); and a few (who probably lacked imagination, enthusiasm or funds) pretty much wearing their regular clothes along with a mask. Whatever their costumes, many of them laughed and yelled. I heard people knocking on doors, heard doorbells dinging, heard chants of "Trick or treat!"

We'd done that ourselves until that year. But when you get to be fifteen, trick or treating can seem like kid stuff.

And I guess it *is* kid stuff compared to a journey to Janks Field.

Walking along, seeing those kids on their quests for candy, I felt very adult and superior—but part of me wished I could be running from house to house the way I used to in my infamous Headless Phantom costume, a rubber-headed axe in one hand and a treat-heavy grocery sack swinging from the other.

Part of me wished we were hiking to anywhere *but* Janks Field.

Part of me couldn't wait to get there.

I have a feeling Dagny and Rusty might've felt the same way.

Regardless of how any of us felt, however, there was no more talk of quitting. Soon, we left town behind and walked along the dirt shoulder of Route 3. Though we had flashlights, we didn't use them. The full moon lit the road for us.

Every so often, a car came along and we had to squint and look away from its headlights. Otherwise, we had the old, two-lane highway all to ourselves.

Or so we thought.

When we finally came to the dirt road that would lead us through the woods to Janks Field, Dagny stopped and said, "Let's take five before we start in, okay?"

"Scared?" Rusty asked.

"Hungry."

That got his attention. "Huh?" he asked.

Dagny reached into a pocket of her jeans, saying, "Anybody want some of my Three Musketeers?"

"Big enough to share with a friend!" Rusty proclaimed.

"Sure," I said.

I took out my flashlight and shined it for Dagny as she bent over, pressed the candy bar against the thigh of her jeans, and used her pocket knife to cut it straight through the wrapper. Rusty took the first chunk, I took the next, the Dagny kept the third.

Before starting to eat, she slipped the knife blade into her mouth to lick and suck it clean.

Rusty and I started to eat our sections of the Three Musketeers.

In the moonlight, Dagny drew the blade slowly out of her tight lips like the wooden stick of an ice cream bar. Then she said, "Somebody's coming."

Those are words you don't want to hear, not on Halloween night at the side of a moonlit road, forest all around you, the town two miles away.

I suddenly lost all interest in the candy.

"Don't look," Dagny whispered. "Just stand still. Pretend everything's all right."

"You're kidding, right?" Rusty whispered.

"You wish."

Dagny stood motionless, gazing through the space between Rusty and me.

"Who is it?" I asked.

She shook her head.

73

"How many?"

"Just one. I think."

"What's he doing?" Rusty asked.

"Coming down the road. Walking."

"How big is he?" I asked.

"Big."

"Shit," Rusty muttered. Then he popped the last of his Three Musketeers bar into his mouth and chewed loudly, his mouth open, his teeth making wet sucky noises as they thrust into the thick, sticky candy and pulled out.

"What'll we do?" I asked Dagny.

"See who he is?" she suggested.

"Let's haul ass," Rusty said through his mouthful.

"I don't know," Dagny said. "Running off into the woods doesn't seem like a brilliant plan. If we stay here, at least some cars might come by. Anyway, maybe this guy's harmless."

"Three of us, one of him," I pointed out.

Dagny nodded. "And we've got knives."

Still chewing, Rusty glanced over his shoulder to see who was coming. Then he turned his head forward and said, "Double-shit. I don't know about you guys, but I'm outa here." He hustled for the darkness where the forest shrouded the dirt road. Looking back at us, he called, "Come on, guys!"

Dagny stayed put.

Therefore, so did I.

"Come on!"

We didn't, so Rusty said, "Your funerals." Then he vanished into the darkness enclosing the dirt road.

"Great," I muttered.

Dagny shrugged in the moonlight. *"Two* of us, one of him."

I stuffed the remains of my Three Musketeers into a pocket of my jacket, then turned around.

And understood why Rusty had run away.

What I suddenly didn't understand is how Dagny could've remained so calm.

Gliding up the middle of Route 3 was a ghost. A very tall ghost. Actually, a very tall person covered from head to ankles by a white bedsheet. With each stride, a bare foot swept out from under the sheet. But that's all I could see of the person except for his general shape. On top of his head was a black bowler hat. Around his neck hung a hangman's noose which served as a weight to hold the sheet in place.

There wasn't much wind, but the sheet flowed and trembled around the stranger as he walked.

So far, he remained in the middle of the road.

"Maybe he'll just walk by," I whispered.

"Who do you think it is?" Dagny asked.

"No idea."

"Who's that tall?"

"Can't think of anybody."

"Me neither." Dagny was silent for a moment, then said, "He doesn't seem to be looking at us."

True. To see us standing at the mouth of the dirt road—several feet beyond the edge of the highway—he would've needed to turn his head.

"Maybe he doesn't know we're here," I whispered.

We both went silent, side by side, as the sheeted figure glided closer and closer.

It stayed on the center line, face forward.

But I *knew* its head would turn.

And then it would come for us.

My heart pounded like crazy. My legs were shaking.

Dagny took hold of my hand.

As she squeezed my hand, we looked at each other. Her teeth were bared, but I couldn't tell whether she was giving me a smile or a grimace.

Turning our heads, we faced the stranger.

He kept walking. And then he was past us.

Dagny loosened her grip on my hand.

I took a deep breath.

The man in the sheet kept walking, kept walking.

We didn't dare say anything. Nor did we dare look away from him for fear he might turn around and come back toward us.

Soon, he disappeared around a bend.

"What was *that?*" Dagny asked, her voice hushed though

the sheeted man was far beyond hearing range.

"I don't know," I muttered.

"Jeezel peezel," she said.

"Yeah."

We both kept staring down the road.

"Is he gone?" Rusty called from somewhere among the trees.

"Yeah," I said. "You can come out now."

Rusty tromped out of the darkness. The moonlight flashed on the blade of the knife in his right hand. "What'd you wanta just *stand* here for?" he asked, sounding annoyed.

Dagny shrugged. "Why run?" she asked. "He didn't *do* anything."

"I was ready for him," Rusty said, raising his knife. "Lucky for him he kept going."

We all turned and stared at where the sheeted man had gone.

I really expected him to reappear, gliding toward us around the curve.

But the road was empty.

"Let's get out of here," Dagny said.

"Janks Field?" asked Rusty. When he saw how we looked at him, he said, "Just kidding."

So we headed north on Route 3, walking back toward town. We walked more quickly than usual. We often looked behind us.

When at last we reached the sanctuary of well-lighted streets, porches with glowing jack-o'-lanterns and houses with bright windows, we slowed to our usual pace. And we didn't look behind us quite so often.

"You know what?" said Rusty. "We should've gone after him."

"Sure," said Dagny.

"No, really. I mean it. Now we'll never find out who he was. And you know, he must not've been following us like we thought, so what *was* he doing? Where was he *going?* There isn't another town for twenty miles in that direction."

"Nothing but more forest," I added.

Shaking his head, Rusty said, "Shit. We should've followed him or something."

"Sure," said Dagny.

"Wouldn't you *love* to know what he was up to?"

"I don't think I *want* to know," Dagny said.

The thing about that night is that Rusty got scared and fled.

We could've gone with him, of course. It was our choice not to run off and hide. But after he knew that we were staying by the road, he didn't come back.

He didn't stick with us.

That's the point.

Rusty couldn't be completely trusted to watch out for Slim. In a bad situation, he might save his own hide and let Slim go down.

I never should've left them on the roof together.

Chapter Twelve

On our way back to Route 3, Lee drove the dirt road very slowly. We both scanned the woods in hopes of seeing Slim and Rusty.

Three times, Lee stopped her truck and tooted the horn. I climbed out and called their names. Then we waited. Nobody yelled back. Nobody showed up. So she drove on.

When we reached the two-lane highway, I said, "Maybe you'd better let me out."

She shook her head, but she didn't drive on. Most adults would've just stepped on the gas and whisked me off, but not Lee. "I don't think they're in the woods," she said. "By now, they're probably long gone." She put her hand on my leg. "Did you tell them where you'd be going?"

Blushing a little because of her hand, I said, "Not really. Just that I wanted to get a car and come back for them."

She patted my leg. "You know what? I bet they're looking for *you*. They probably headed straight for town. . . ."

"But we would've passed them."

"A lot of ways we could've missed them. Depends on when they left. And maybe they took short cuts."

"Maybe," I muttered. I supposed Lee was right about missing them one way or another. It was sure possible. "But I've got a feeling they're still out here," I told her. "I feel like something went wrong, you know? I mean, Slim already had all those cuts. What if she passed out? Or what if the dog attacked them? Or maybe Rusty broke his leg jumping off the shack. Or maybe they were captured by those people who run the vampire show. I thought they were a pretty creepy bunch. No telling *what* they might do if they caught someone like Slim."

Lee didn't smirk or laugh at me. She looked concerned. "You're right," she said. "Any of that stuff *might've* happened. Or something else, just as bad, that you haven't thought of." A smile crept in. "Though I think you've covered the bases fairly well."

I almost smiled, myself.

"The deal is," she continued, "they're probably somewhere in town by now—more than likely at *your* house, because they'd be needing to let you know what happened and your house would be about the best place to find you."

Nodding, I said, "I guess that's where they might go if they're okay."

"So let's look there first."

"Okay."

"If we don't find them at your place, we'll keep looking till we *do* find them. That sound good to you?"

"Sounds fine."

So then she pulled out onto Route 3, turned right, and headed for town. "We might even pass them along the way," she said.

We didn't.

The first thing I noticed as we approached my house was the empty driveway. It puzzled me for a moment. Mom

78

should've been back from the grocery store. Apparently, she'd had other errands to run.

A *lot* of errands, I hoped.

With a little luck, maybe she and Dad would never have to find out about any of this.

"Look who's here," Lee said.

Her words gave me a moment of pure joy, but it faded when I saw Rusty leaning back against an elm tree in the front yard, shirtless, his arms crossed.

No Slim.

Rusty looked carefree, though. He smiled and waved as we pulled up to the curb. On his feet were the sneakers that he'd thrown at the dog. I took that for a good sign.

But why wasn't Slim with him?

Feeling squirmy inside, I climbed out of the truck. Lee got out, too. As we walked toward Rusty, he asked me, "Where you been?"

"Out to Janks Field," I said. "Where's Slim?"

"She went home."

"Is she all right?"

"Fine. Except for, you know, the cuts." He smiled at Lee. "Hi, Mrs. Thompson."

"Hi, Rusty."

"So what happened?" I asked.

"Nothing much."

"You were supposed to wait for me."

"Yeah, well. We did. And then we thought we heard you coming . . . a car, you know? You were supposed to come back with a car, so we figured it must be you. Only what came out of the woods was a *hearse*. Man, I nearly. . . ." With a smile at Lee, he said, "It scared the heck out of us. I mean, a *hearse?* Give me a break. So we figured it wasn't Dwight coming to the rescue." Looking at me, he added, "Where would *you* get a hearse, right?" To Lee, he said, "Then a big black bus came out of the woods, and that's when we figured it must be the Vampire Show. So we beat it. We jumped down behind the shack and ran into the woods." He shrugged his meaty, freckled shoulders. "That's about it. When we got back

79

into town, we split up. Slim went to her place and I came here so I could tell you what'd happened."

"What about the dog?" I asked.

"Last I saw of that little . . . mutt . . . it was running toward the hearse like a madman, barking its tail off."

"So it didn't chase you guys?"

He shook his head. "Nope. We got off scot-free."

All my worries had been for nothing. That's usually how it is with worrying. More often than not, we get ourselves all in a sweat over something that *might* happen, then everything turns out just fine.

"What about Slim's cuts?" I asked. "Did they bleed much on the way home?"

"Nope. They were fine."

"They didn't reopen?"

"Huh-uh."

From what he said, I might just as well have stayed on the roof with them. It would've saved a lot of wear and tear on my nerves.

"Where did our shirts end up?" I asked.

"Slim has 'em. They're ruined anyway. She wore 'em home."

"Where'd her T-shirt end up?"

"Still on the ground, I guess. Did you see it when you were there?"

I shook my head. I hadn't seen Slim's T-shirt or any sign of the dog or the sneakers. . . .

"Wait," I said.

He suddenly looked worried.

"How'd you get your sneakers back?" I asked.

"Huh?"

"What'd you do, run halfway across Janks Field when the hearse and bus were already there and . . . ?"

"Heck no. We jumped off the *back* of the shack."

"Then how'd you get your shoes?"

"My shoes?" He looked down at his sneakered feet. "Oh!" He gave out a laugh and shook his head as if relieved. "You thought I threw *my* shoes at the dog!"

"I *saw* you throw them."

"Not *my* shoes. Those were Slim's."

"*Slim*'s shoes?"

"Sure."

"Jeez, man. Why didn't you throw your own?"

"It was her idea."

"Real nice."

"Don't blame me, she tossed me hers and told me to throw 'em, so I did."

"So then she had to go through the woods and all the way home barefoot?"

"No big deal. She was fine. Anyway, I offered her mine but she wouldn't take 'em."

"Not that they'd fit her anyway," I said, a little annoyed.

I had sure misjudged Rusty, giving him credit for what turned out to be mostly Slim's doing.

At least Rusty had done the throwing.

"Well," said Lee, "glad you both made it out of there all right. We had our doubts."

"We got out fine," Rusty said, smiling and bobbing his head. "In fact," he added, "Slim's coming over here as soon as she's gotten herself all bandaged and cleaned up."

"Good deal," said Lee. Then she turned to me. "I think I'll head on home, now. When Slim gets here, why don't the three of you talk things over and decide what to do about tonight?"

Rusty raised his eyebrows.

"Lee got us tickets for the show," I explained.

"No shit?" he blurted. Then he quickly added, "Excuse me, Mrs. Thompson."

"No problem, Rusty."

"Just slipped out."

"Tickets for all of us," I explained.

"Oh, man, this is *too* cool."

"I'll hang on to the tickets," Lee said, "and drive us out there tonight."

"Oh, wow. . . ."

"But you'll have to work things out, yourselves, with your parents. Handle them however you want. I won't tell on you, but I don't want to have a hand in any deceptions you decide to use."

"We'll figure something," I said.

"If we're going," Lee said, "we should probably leave from my place by about ten-thirty. We'll want to get there early enough to beat the crowd—if there *is* a crowd. And find ourselves a parking place."

"That'll be great," I said. "Your house by ten-thirty."

"And you're welcome to come over earlier. Always better not to wait till the last moment."

"We'll come over as early as we can make it," I told her.

Then she nodded, said, "See you later then," and headed for her truck.

Rusty and I watched her drive away.

"Your brother," he said, "is one lucky son of a bitch."

"You're telling me."

"Shit. What I wouldn't give . . ." He shook his head and sighed.

"Well, *we're* the ones going to the Vampire Show with her."

"Yeah! Fantastic! She got four *tickets?*"

"Bought 'em," I said. "They cost her forty bucks."

"She forked over *forty* bucks?"

"Well, not cash. She used a check."

"Do we have to pay her back?"

"She didn't say anything about it. I think she's treating us."

"Wow!"

"It didn't even matter that we're underage. The guy knew it, but he didn't care. Julian? He's the owner. He's the one we talked to when we went looking for you guys. He sort of warned Lee that it's an adults only show. . . ."

"What'd he say?"

"He said the show can be real gory. And *clothes* get ripped off."

"Holy shit!"

"Yeah. But Lee didn't seem to mind. She said she wanted the tickets anyway, so the guy went ahead and sold them to her. But only on the condition that she goes to the show *with* us. We can't, like, go without her."

"Ah. I bet he's got the hots for her."

"You know what else? If we stick around after the show, he'll introduce us to Valeria."

Rusty moaned almost as if in pain. "We get to meet her face to face?"

"If Julian keeps his word."

"Ohhhhh, man. This is gonna be *some night*, huh?"

"I'll say," I said. "If we can go."

"We're going. Man, we're going—I don't care *what*."

"Maybe I can finish mowing the lawn before Slim gets here."

Chapter Thirteen

Rusty sat on the porch stairs of my house and watched me finish mowing the front lawn. Then he stood around while I did the back yard and both sides. I was sweaty and out of breath by the time I'd finished. He came with me when I put the mower away in the garage.

Just as we were leaving the garage, Mom drove up. She parked in the driveway and climbed out of her car. She was dressed in her tennis whites—a good clue as to where she'd been.

"I was afraid you'd given up on the yard," she said.

"No. I just took a little break."

"Hello, Russell."

"Hi, Mrs. Thompson."

"How's everything?" she asked him.

"Just fine, thank you."

After a quick glance around, she asked us, "Where's d'Artagnan?"

She could only mean Slim.

"On her way over," I said, though I was starting to wonder why she hadn't shown up yet.

"She had to stop by her house," Rusty explained.

To deflect a possible interrogation, I asked Mom, "How was the tennis?"

She beamed. "I *trounced* Lucy."

"Good going," Rusty said.

"Shouldn't you have let her win?" I asked.

I asked that because Lucy Armstrong was the principal of Grandville High—where Mom taught English and where Rusty, Slim and I were students.

"She wins often enough with no help from me. It's high time I got the upper hand. I beat her in three straight sets and she had to pay for our lunch. Just wasn't her day, I guess." Mom looked us over for a moment, then said, "Have you fellows had lunch yet?"

"Not yet," I said.

"Well, why don't you come inside the house and I'll make you some sandwiches?"

She trotted up the porch stairs ahead of us, her tiny white skirt flouncing. I guess she was in pretty good shape for a person her age, but personally I wished her skirt could've been a little longer—like maybe long enough to cover her underwear?

Not that Rusty seemed to mind the view.

Inside the house, I said, "If you'd rather do something else, I can go ahead and make our sandwiches. No problem."

"Sounds good. Any time I can get out of making a meal. . . ." She smiled. "I'll just go ahead and take my bath."

Did she *have* to say that in front of Rusty? He was probably already imagining her in the tub. That's the kind of guy he was. I know, because that's also the kind of guy *I* was. Except not about my own mother. Not about Rusty's mother, either; you wouldn't *want* to imagine her naked. But Slim's mom was another matter. She looked a lot like Slim, only taller and curvier. Whenever she was around, I had a hard time taking my eyes off her. Slim noticed, too, and seemed to think it was funny.

Rusty watched my mother climb the stairs. If she'd been Slim's mom in a tiny skirt like that, I would've been doing the same thing, so I tried not to let it annoy me.

"We might take a walk into town or something after we eat," I called up the stairs.

She stopped climbing, turned with one foot on the next stair, and looked down at me. I bet Rusty liked *that* view.

"So if we're not here . . ." I said, and shrugged.

"Just be back in time for supper."

"What're we having?" I asked.

"Hamburgers on the grill." Smiling, she added, "There'll be enough for your friends if they'd like to join us."

"That might be neat," I said.

Rusty, looking embarrassed, shrugged and said, "Thank you. I'll have to check with my folks, though."

"We can go over to your place and ask," I threw in.

"Good idea," Rusty said.

"I'll just go ahead and count on the three of you for burgers," Mom said. "If somebody doesn't show up, more for the rest of us."

"Great," I said.

"Thank you, Mrs. Thompson," Rusty said.

Around adults, he was always excessively polite. Not unlike Eddie Haskell on *Leave it to Beaver*, even though he looked more like a teenaged, overweight version of the Beave.

"Come on," I told him, and led the way into our kitchen. I walked straight to the refrigerator. "Lemonade or Pepsi?" I asked.

"You kidding me? Pepsi."

I opened the door, pulled out a can and handed it to him.

"Aren't you having one?" he asked.

"I had a Coke over at Lee's house."

He snapped off the ring tab and dropped it into his Pepsi the way he always did. I figured someday he would swallow one of those ring-tabs and choke on it, but I didn't say anything. I'd already warned him about it often enough so that I suspected he kept on dropping the rings into his cans just to annoy me.

Acting as if I hadn't even seen him do it, I stepped over to the wall phone.

"What're you doing?"

"Gonna call Slim, see why she isn't here yet."

"Good idea."

I dialed her house.

As I listened to the ringing, Rusty took a drink of his Pepsi, then went over to the kitchen table and sat on a chair. He looked at me. He raised his eyebrows.

I shook my head.

So far, the phone had jangled seven or eight times. I let it continue to ring in case she was at the other end of her house, or something. I knew the ringing wouldn't disturb anyone, because nobody lived there except Slim and her mother. And the mother was probably away at work.

After about fifteen rings, I hung up.

"Not home," I said.

"She's probably already on her way over. . . ."

Just then came a thump of plumbing, followed by the *shhhhh* sound of water rushing through the pipes of the house. Mom had started to run her bath water.

Rusty lifted his gaze toward the ceiling—as if hoping to see her.

"Hey," I said.

He grinned at me. "Maybe Slim's taking a bath. Has the water running. Can't hear the phone."

"Maybe."

After gulping down some more Pepsi, he suggested, "How about we give her five minutes, then try again?"

"If she's running bath water, she'll be in the tub five minutes from now."

"But she'll hear the phone," he explained.

"Not if she's taking a shower."

"Girls don't take showers."

"Sure they do."

Leering, Rusty said, "Nah. They just love to lounge in a tub full of sudsy hot water. They do it for *hours*. By candle light. Sliding a bar of perfumed soap over their bodies."

86

"Right," I said.

"Hey! Just thought of something! How would you like to be *Slim's* bar of soap?"

"Get outa here," I said.

"No, really. Think about it."

"Shut up."

"Or would you rather be *Lee's* soap? Sliding all over her. Just think of all the places. . . ."

"Knock it off, okay?"

"You're blushing!"

I turned away from him, picked up the phone and dialed Slim's number again. This time, I only let it ring twelve times before hanging up.

"Let's go," I said.

"Where to?"

"Slim's house."

"Want to catch her in the tub?"

"I want to make sure she's all right."

"She's fine."

"She should've been here by now. She's not taking any bath, not with all those cuts on her back. Maybe a quick shower, but she would've been done with that a long time ago and it only takes five minutes to walk here. So where is she?"

"What about our sandwiches?"

"I'm not hungry," I said. "And you ate a Ding-Dong in the woods."

"That was *hours* ago."

"We'll get something later. Come on."

"Shit," Rusty muttered. He polished off his Pepsi, then scooted back his chair and stood up.

On our way to the front door, I said, "Slim *did* make it home, didn't she? You stuck with her the whole way?"

"Almost. We split up at the corner."

"At the *corner?*"

"The corner of *her* block."

"Great," I muttered, throwing open the screen door.

Rusty followed me onto the porch and down the stairs.

"So you don't *really* know she made it home?"

"Her house was right there."

"You should've walked her to the door."

"Oh, sure."

"And even if she made it *into* her house," I said, "nobody was there to take care of her. Maybe she got inside and passed out, or something."

"What was I supposed to do, go in with her? Then you'd be riding my ass for being alone in the *house* with her."

I guess he was right about that.

"You could've at least made sure she was all right," I muttered. "That's all."

Speaking slowly, in a clipped voice that sounded as if he might be running short of patience, Rusty said, "She told me she'd be fine. She said she didn't *want* any help. She told me to go over to your place and she'd be along as soon as she got done bandaging herself up."

"How was she supposed to put bandages on?" I asked. "The cuts are on her *back*."

"Don't ask me. I'm just telling you what she said."

I said, "Damn it." My throat felt tight and achy.

"Don't worry, Dwight." He sounded a little concerned, himself. "I'm sure she's fine."

Chapter Fourteen

Even though Slim didn't have a father and her mother worked as a waitress at Steerman's Steak House, she lived in a better neighborhood than mine and in a better house.

That's because they inherited the house and some money from Slim's grandparents.

Slim's mother, Louise, had grown up in the house and continued to live there even after she got married. This was because she and her husband, a low-life shit named Jimmy

Drake, couldn't afford to move out. At the time of the wedding, she was already pregnant with Frances (Slim), and Jimmy had a lousy job working as a clerk in a shoe store. After Slim was born, Jimmy wouldn't allow Louise to have a job.

Actually, this wasn't unusual. Back in those days, most men preferred for their wives to stay home and take care of the family instead of run off to work every day. A lot of women seemed to like it that way, too.

In this case, though, Louise *wanted* to work. She hated living in her parents' house. Not because she had problems with *them*, but because of Jimmy's behavior. He drank too much. He had a violent nature and a horny nature and he enjoyed having people watch.

Slim never told me *all* the stuff that went on, but she said enough to give me the general picture.

To make it fairly brief, when she was three years old (so *she'd* been told), her grandfather fell down the stairs (or was shoved by Jimmy) in the middle of the night, broke his neck and died. That left Jimmy with the three gals.

God only knows what he did to them.

I know some of it. I know he tormented and beat all of them. I know he had sex with all of them. Though Slim never exactly came out and said it, she hinted that he'd forced them into all sorts of acts—including multi-generational orgies.

At the time it came to an end, Slim was thirteen and calling herself Zock.

She seemed strangely cheerful one morning. Walking to school with her, I asked, "What's going on?"

"What do you mean?" she asked.

"You're so *happy*."

"Happy? I'm *ecstatic!*"

"How come?"

"Jimmy (she never called him Dad or Pop or Father) went away last night."

"Hey, great!" I was ecstatic, myself. I knew Slim hated him, but not exactly why. Not until later. "Where'd he go?" I asked.

"He took a trip down south," she said.

"Like to Florida or something?"

"Further south," she said. "*Deep* south. I don't exactly know the name of the place, but he's never coming back."

"Are you sure?" I asked, hoping she was right.

"Pretty sure. Nobody *ever* comes back from there."

"From where?"

"Where he went."

"Where'd he go?"

"The Deep South," she said, and laughed.

"If you say so," I told her.

"And I do," said she.

By then, we were almost within earshot of the crossing guard, so we stopped talking.

Though the subject of Jimmy's trip came up quite a lot after that, I never learned any more about where he'd gone. "Deep South," was about it.

I had my suspicions, but I kept them to myself.

Anyway, the grandmother died last year. She passed suddenly. Very suddenly, while in a checkout line at the Super M grocery market. As the story goes, she was bending over the push-bar of her shopping cart and reaching down to take out a can of tomato sauce when all of a sudden she sort of twitched and tooted and dived headfirst into her cart—and the cart took off with her draped over it, butt in the air. In front of her were a couple of little tykes waiting while their mother wrote a check. The runaway cart crashed through both kids, took down the mother, knocked their empty shopping cart out of the way, kept going and nailed an old lady who happened to be heading for the exit behind her *own* shopping cart. Finally, Slim's grandma crashed into a display of Kingsford charcoal briquettes and did a somersault into her cart.

Nobody else perished in the incident, though one of the kids got a concussion and the old lady broke her hip.

That's the true story of how the grandmother died (with the help of a brain aneurism) and that's how Slim and her mother ended up living by themselves in such a nice house.

Side by side, Rusty and I climbed the porch stairs. I jabbed the doorbell button with my forefinger. From inside the house came the quiet *ding-dong* of the chimes.

But nothing else. No footsteps, no voice.

I rang the doorbell again. We waited a while longer.

"Guess she's not here," I said.

"Let's find out." Rusty pulled open the screen door.

"Hey, we can't go in," I told him.

Stepping in front of me, he tried the handle of the main door. "What do you know? Isn't locked."

"Of course not," I said. In Grandville, back in those days, almost nobody locked their house doors.

Rusty swung it open. Leaning in, he called, "Hello! Anybody home?"

No answer.

"Come on," he said, and entered.

"I don't know. If nobody's home . . ."

"How're we gonna know nobody's home if we don't look around? Like you said, maybe Slim passed out or something."

He was right.

So I followed him inside and gently shut the door. The house was silent. I heard a ticking clock, a couple of creaking sounds, but not much else. No voices, no music, no footsteps, no running water.

But it was a large house. Slim might be somewhere in it, beyond our hearing range, maybe even unable to move or call out.

"You check around down here," Rusty whispered. "I'll look upstairs."

"I'll come with you," I whispered.

We were whispering like a couple of thieves. Supposedly, we'd entered the house to find Slim and make sure she was okay. So why the whispers? Maybe it's only natural when you're inside someone else's house without permission.

But it wasn't only that. I think we both had more on our minds than checking up on Slim.

I was a nervous wreck, breathing hard, my heart pounding, dribbles of sweat running down my bare sides, my hands trembling, my legs weak and shaky as I climbed the stairs behind Rusty.

Over the years, we had spent lots of time in Slim's house but we'd never been allowed inside it when her mother wasn't home.

And we'd never been upstairs at all. Upstairs was off limits; that's where the bedrooms were.

Not that Slim's mother was unusually strict or weird. In those days, at least in Grandville, hardly any decent parents allowed their kids to have friends inside the house unless an adult was home. Also, whether or not a parent was in the house, friends of the opposite sex were *never* allowed into a bedroom. These were standard rules in almost every household.

Rusty and I, sneaking upstairs, were venturing into taboo territory.

Not only that, but this was the stairway where Slim's grandfather had met his death. And at the top would be the bedrooms where Jimmy had done many horrible things to Slim, her mother and her grandmother.

There was also a slight chance that we might find Slim taking a bath.

And neither of us was wearing a shirt. That's fine if you're roaming around outside, but it makes you feel funny when you're sneaking through someone else's house.

No wonder I was a wreck.

At the top of the stairs, I said, "Maybe we oughta call out again."

Rusty shook his head. He was flushed and sweaty like me, and had a frantic look in his eyes as if he couldn't make up his mind whether to cry out with glee or run like hell.

In silence, we walked to the nearest doorway. The door was open and we found ourselves in a very spacious bathroom.

Nobody there.

The tub was empty.

Good thing, I thought. But I felt disappointed.

What was nice about the bathroom, it had a fresh, flowery aroma that reminded me of Slim. I saw a pink oval of soap on the sink. Was that the source of the wonderful scent? I wanted to give it a sniff, but not with Rusty watching.

We went on down the hall, walking silently, Rusty in the lead. A couple of times, he opened doors and found closets. Near the end of the hall, we came to the doorway of a very large, corner bedroom.

Slim's bedroom. It had to be, because of the book shelves. There were *lots* of bookshelves, and nearly all of them were loaded: rows of hardbounds, some neatly lined up, while others were tipped at angles as if bravely trying to hold up neighboring volumes; books of various sizes resting on top of the upright books; neat rows of paperbacks; crooked stacks of paperbacks and hardbounds; neat stacks of magazines; and scattered non-book items such as Barbie dolls, fifteen or twenty stuffed animals, an archery trophy she'd won at the YWCA tournament, a couple of little snow globes, a piggy bank wearing Slim's brand new Chicago Cubs baseball cap and her special major league baseball—autographed by Ernie Banks.

In one corner of the room stood a nice wooden desk with a Royal portable typewriter ready for action. Papers were piled all around the typewriter. On the wall, at Slim's eye level if she were sitting at the desk, was a framed photo of Ayn Rand that looked is if it had been torn from a LIFE or LOOK magazine.

Slim's bed was neatly made. Its wooden headboard had a shelf for holding a radio, books, and so on. She had a radio on it, along with about a dozen paperbacks. I stepped over for a closer look at the books. There were beat-up copies of *The Temple of Gold, The Catcher in the Rye, Dracula, To Kill a Mockingbird, Gone With the Wind, The Complete Tales and Poems of Edgar Allan Poe, Jane Eyre, The Sign of the Four, The October Country, Atlas Shrugged* and *The Fountainhead.* I hadn't actually read any of these books myself (except *The Catcher in the Rye*, which was so funny I split a gut laughing and so sad that I cried a few times), but Slim had told me about most of them. Of all the books in her room, these were probably her favorites, which is why she kept them on her headboard.

When I finished looking at them, I turned around. Rusty was gone.

I felt a surge of alarm.

Instead of calling out for him, I went looking.

I found him in the bedroom across the hall. The mother's bedroom. Standing over an open drawer of the dresser, his back toward me, his head down. He must've heard me come in, because he turned around and grinned. In his hands, he held a flimsy black bra by its shoulder straps. "Check out the merchandise," he whispered.

"Put that away. Are you nuts?"

"It's her mom's."

"My God, Rusty."

"Look." He raised it in front of his face. "You can see through it."

"Put it away."

"Dig it, man. It's had her tits in it." He put one of the cups against his face like a surgical mask, and breathed in. The soft pouch collapsed against his nose and mouth. As he sighed, it puffed outward. "I can smell her."

"Yeah, sure."

"I swear to God. She hasn't washed this thing since the last time she wore it."

"Gimme a break."

"C'mon and smell it."

"No way."

"Chicken."

"Put it back, Rusty. We've gotta get out of here before somebody catches us."

"Nobody's gonna catch us."

He breathed in slowly and deeply, once again sucking the fabric against his nose and mouth.

"For God's sake."

"Okay, okay." He lowered it, folded it in half and stuffed it into the drawer.

"Is that the way you found it?" I asked.

"What do you think, I'm a moron?" He slid the drawer shut. "Let's go."

"Hang on." He pulled open another drawer. "Undies!"

He started to reach in, so I rushed over and shoved the drawer shut. He jerked his hands clear in the nick of time.

But I'd shut the drawer too hard.

The dresser shook.

On top of the dresser was a tall, slim vase of clear green glass with three or four yellow roses in it.

The vase toppled forward.

Gasping, I tried to catch it.

I wasn't quick enough.

It crashed down onto a perfume bottle and they both shattered. Glass, water and perfume exploded, filling the air. Roses flew off the front of the dresser. As they bumped their bright heads against the front of Rusty's jeans, a cascade of scented water spilled over the edge of the dresser, ran down and poured onto the carpet.

Chapter Fifteen

We gazed at the mess, stunned and silent.

The air of the bedroom carried an odor of perfume so sweet and heavy that it almost made me gag.

After a while, Rusty muttered, "Shit. You really did it this time."

"*Me?*"

"Huh? You think *I* slammed the drawer?"

"Oh, *you* had nothing to do with it. All you did was open it in the first place so you could paw through her stuff. If you weren't such a degenerate . . ."

"If *you* weren't such a prude . . ."

Then we both fell silent and resumed gazing at our catastrophe: the puddle on the dresser top bristling with chunks and slivers and specks of glass; the wet patch on the carpet that looked as if a dog had taken a leak there; the bits of colored glass sprinkled on and around the wet patch; the yellow roses at Rusty's feet, some of their petals fallen off.

"What're we gonna do?" Rusty asked.

I shook my head. I couldn't believe we'd found ourselves in such a predicament.

"Clean it up?" Rusty asked.

"I don't think we *can*. That perfume . . . we'll never get the smell out of the carpet. The minute someone comes upstairs, they're gonna know something's wrong."

"Not to mention," said Rusty, "we can't exactly *un*break the glass."

"Whatever we do, we'd better do it fast and get out of here."

"Wanta just leave?" Rusty asked.

"I want to make it all go away!"

"Rotsa ruck."

"Okay," I muttered, sort of thinking out loud. "We can't make it go away. And it'd probably take us fifteen minutes just to clean up all the glass. Then the place'll *still* smell like a perfume factory. And in the meantime, we might get caught up here."

Rusty nodded, then said, "If we just go away—leave everything exactly the way it is right now—they might not even realize anyone was here. I mean, if shutting a drawer too hard'll knock that vase over, *anything* will. They'll think it was just an accident."

"I don't know," I said.

"C'mon, man. A *lot* of stuff could've knocked the thing over. Like even the front door slamming."

"Maybe so."

"So let's haul ass."

We walked backward away from our mess, watching it as if to make sure it wouldn't pursue us. On the other side of the doorway, we whirled around and ran for the stairs. When we were a block away from Slim's house, we looked at each other, shook our heads and sighed.

"I feel like such a rat," I said.

"Accidents happen," Rusty said. "Thing is, we got away with it. Long as nobody blabs. . . ."

"I don't know."

"You don't *know?*"

"Lying to Slim . . ."

"You'd rather have her find out we went sneaking through her house? That'd go over big."

"If we explain why . . ."

"And what were we doing in her *mother's bedroom?*"

"*I* just went in to look for *you.*"

"Oh, so you wanta tell Slim what *I* was doing in her mom's room?"

I shook my head. I sure couldn't tell Slim the truth about *that.*

"You'd *better* not."

"Why'd you have to *do* that?"

"Felt like it," he muttered. "Anyway, *you* would've done the same thing if you had the guts."

"Would not."

"Only *you* would've gone through *Slim's* drawers." Grinning, he raised his eyebrows. "What *were* you doing by yourself in Slim's room, huh?"

"Looking at her books."

"Oh, sure."

"I didn't even know you were gone."

"Uh-huh. Sure."

"Go to hell."

Laughing, he patted me on the back.

"Hands off," I said.

He took his hand away. His smile sliding sideways, he said, "Seriously, you're not gonna tell Slim about any of this, right?"

"I guess not," I said.

"You *guess* not? C'mon, man! I've never told on *you.*"

"I know," I said, and went a little sick inside at the reminder of all the things Rusty knew about me. "I won't tell. I promise."

"Okay. Good deal. It's just between you and me."

"Right."

"Shake on it."

I looked around. There were houses on both sides of the street and a few people nearby, but nobody seemed to be watching us. So I shook hands with Rusty. His hand was bigger than mine, and very sweaty. He didn't pull any funny stuff, so I guess he was being sincere.

"If anything comes up," he said, "we didn't even go in Slim's house today."

"What if somebody saw us?"

"We'll claim it wasn't us."

"Sure thing."

"We just stick to our story, no matter what."

"But if somebody *saw* us . . . somebody who *knows* us . . ."

"Simple. We just say he's confused about which day it was. You know? We'll say we *did* go into Slim's house yesterday, but not today. Get it?"

"I guess so."

"But don't worry. It'll never come up. It's not like anybody got murdered in there."

"That's true," I admitted.

But I got a sick feeling again, because the truth was a lot worse than a broken vase and perfume bottle. Sure, it wasn't murder. If it ever got out what really happened in Slim's house, however, people would be giving me and Rusty (*especially* Rusty) funny looks from now till Doomsday.

"Never happened?" Rusty asked.

"Never happened."

"Great." He smiled as if vastly relieved. "That's that."

"All we've gotta do now," I said, "is find Slim."

"She'll turn up."

"I wonder if we should check with her mom."

"At Steerman's?" Rusty asked. "Oh, great idea! And tell her what? 'Gosh, Mrs. Drake, have you happened to see your daughter lately? She seems to be missing. We've already checked at your house, but she isn't there.' "

"We don't have to tell her that."

"We go anywhere near her, she's gonna *know* it was us in her bedroom."

I supposed he was right about that.

"Anyway," he said, "you think they'll let us into that restaurant without our shirts on?"

"We could pick up a couple of shirts at your house," I suggested.

"We can't go to Steerman's."

"But we've gotta find Slim! I mean, where the hell *is* she? How can she just disappear? Maybe somebody jumped her or something. You never saw her make it into her house and she isn't *in* her house and she didn't show up at *my* house and we haven't spotted her on the streets—so where *is* she?"

"She might've gone to the hospital."

At this point, we were only two blocks away from the police station. "I think I wanta talk to Dad about it."

"Your *father?* Are you nuts?"

"Maybe he knows something."

"He's a *cop!*"

"That's the point. If somebody grabbed Slim, the quicker we get the police on it, the better."

"What'll we tell him about going to Slim's house?"

"Never happened."

Leading the way, I turned the corner toward the police station.

Rusty reached out, clapped a hand on my shoulder and stopped me. "Hang on a minute."

"What for?"

"You'll get us all in trouble."

I turned around and faced him. "If that's what it takes to find Slim. . . ."

He bared his teeth as if in pain, then said, "I know where she is."

"What?"

"I know where Slim is."

"That's what I thought you said. What're you talking about?"

"I didn't exactly tell you everything before."

"Like what?"

"We didn't exactly walk home together."

"Right. You split up at her corner."

"Well, that's not exactly the way it happened."

"Exactly how *did* it happen?"

"We actually split up . . . back at Janks Field."

"What?"

He shrugged his bare, freckled shoulders and held out his hands, palms upward as if feeling for raindrops. But there was no rain. "Thing is, Slim wouldn't leave."

"What?"

"Well, we were up on the roof of the snack stand, you know."

"Where you were supposed to *stay*," I reminded him.

"Well, that's the thing. Slim *did* stay. But I didn't. When we heard these engine noises, we looked over the top of the sign and pretty soon here comes this hearse outa the woods. I go something like, 'Oh, shit, it's *them*.' But Slim goes, 'Hey, all right!' like she's excited about it. The dog goes running over to bark at the hearse, so I tell Slim we'd better head for the hills while the gettin's good. Only she won't do it. She says there's no reason to run away, and besides, *you'll* get all bent outa shape if you come back looking for us and we aren't there."

"So you ran away *without* her?"

"She *refused* to leave. What was I supposed to do?"

"Stay with her!"

"Hey, man, it was her choice to stay."

"It was *your* choice to run."

"She *told* me to go on without her. 'Don't let me stop you,' That's what she said. She also said, 'Maybe I can get a look at Valeria and see who wins the bet.' So I jumped down and that's the last I saw of her."

"Jesus," I muttered.

"She planned to wait for you, man. I figured that's exactly what she *did* do. When you came driving up to your place with Lee, I figured Slim was gonna be with you."

"She wasn't *on* the roof."

"Yeah, I know, I know."

"So why'd you lie?"

"I don't know." His voice was whiny. "I figured . . . if you found out I'd left her there, you'd give me all sorts of shit about it. . . ."

I almost slugged him in the face, but the sight of my raised fist put such fear in his eyes that I couldn't go through with it. I lowered my arm. I shook my head. I muttered, "You *left* her there."

"*You* left both of us."

"That was to get help, you idiot. Don't you know the difference?"

"Nobody *made* her stay behind."

"So where the hell *is* she?" I blurted.

"How should I know?"

"Damn it!"

"I thought she'd be at her house by the time we got there."

"Well, she wasn't," I snapped. I gave Rusty a scowl, then started walking away. He stuck with me, walking by my side, his head down.

After a while, he said, "Look, she's gotta be somewhere. She wasn't on the roof of the shack when you and Lee got there, so she must've jumped down sometime after I did. She probably ran into the woods. . . ."

"Then why isn't she home yet?"

"Maybe she hung around to keep an eye on things. And to wait for you to show up."

"But I *did* show up."

"Maybe she'd quit by then and started for home."

"Then where *is* she?"

"On her way?" he suggested.

"It's not that far. Lee and I left Janks Field—must've been a couple of hours ago."

"Hour and a half?"

"Whatever, Slim had *more* than enough time to get home."

"Maybe we just haven't looked in the right place yet."

"She'd be looking for *us!* And she would've *found* us a

long time ago if she'd made it back to town. Which means she didn't."

"So what do you think happened?" Rusty asked.

Shaking my head, I told him, "Somehow, she's out of commission."

"Huh?"

"Too weak to travel. Passed out. Trapped somehow. Maybe even a prisoner. Or worse."

"Worse like what?"

"Do I have to spell it out?"

"You mean like raped and murdered?"

Hearing him speak the words, I cringed. "Yeah. Like that."

We walked in silence for a while. Then Rusty said, "I bet it'll turn out that she's fine."

"She'd *better* be."

Chapter Sixteen

We're going to the cops," I said, and turned a corner toward the police station.

"Do we *have* to?" Rusty asked.

"Yeah."

"Your dad'll find out we went to Janks Field."

"I don't care," I said. I did care, but getting in trouble with my parents didn't seem like much of a big deal just then.

"He'll ground you," Rusty warned.

"Maybe."

"What about the show?"

"I'm not gonna be *allowed* to go to that no matter what. And at this point, I don't give a hot crap about that stupid Vampire Show. I just want to find Slim. The best way to do that is to tell Dad everything that happened."

Rusty looked shocked. "Not about *Slim's* house."

"We can say we rang the doorbell, but didn't go in."

"No! That'll be admitting we were there!"

"We *were* there."

It went on like that for a couple more minutes, but we both shut up as we approached the front doors of the police station.

I went in first. Right away, I regretted it.

With everything else going on, I hadn't given any thought to Dolly.

The Grandville Police Department was comprised of six cops, my dad included. Two cops per shift, all of whom could be brought into action in case of an emergency.

Since there were no actual police to spare for desk duty, civilians had been hired to act as receptionist/clerk/dispatchers. Dolly worked the day watch.

She was a skinny, bloodless prude. Pushing forty, she lived with her older sister. She disapproved of men in general, and me in particular. The only times she ever seemed happy were when she got to gloat over someone else's misery.

When I walked through the door, she looked at me from behind the front desk. The corners of her lips curled upward. "Dwight," she said.

"Hello, Dolly."

One of her thin, black eyebrows climbed her forehead to show how much she didn't appreciate any hint of a reference to the Broadway musical.

"Russell," she said and gave him a curt nod.

"Good afternoon, Miss Desmond."

She eyed both of us as we approached her. Mostly, she eyed our bare chests. Even though the office was air-conditioned, heat was suddenly rushing to my skin. "Let me guess," she said. "You've come to report the theft of your shirts."

Rusty laughed politely. It sounded very fake. On purpose, I'm sure.

"We've been mowing lawns," I explained. Not quite a lie. I *had* been mowing the lawn, Rusty participating as an observer. "Is Dad here?"

"I'm afraid not," she said, obviously pleased by her announcement. "What seems to be the trouble?"

"I just need to talk with Dad about something."

"Would it be police business?"

"Sort of," I said.

She tipped her head to one side and fluttered her eyelashes at me in some sort of mockery of flirtation. "Perhaps you would like to share it with me?"

"It's sort of personal," I said.

"In trouble again, are we?" She glanced from me to Rusty, then back to me. "What is it this time?"

"Nothing," I said. "We didn't do anything. I just need to talk to Dad for a minute."

"No can do," she said, oh so chipper.

"Do you know where he is?"

"Out on a call." Grinning, she batted her eyelashes some more. "I'm not at liberty to divulge his exact whereabouts. Police business. You understand."

Rusty nudged my arm and whispered, "Let's just go."

"You can radio him, can't you?" I said.

"No can do."

"Come on, Dolly. Please. This is important."

Her eyes narrowed. "This *does* have to do with your shirts, doesn't it." She spoke it as a fact, not a question.

"No," I said. Though, in a way, our shirts *were* involved.

She leaned forward, folded her arms on the desktop and slid her tongue across her lips. "Tell me."

"No can do," I said.

Off to my side, Rusty snorted.

Dolly stiffened and her eyes flared. "Are you smart-mouthing me, young man?"

"No," I said.

"I don't *like* a smart-mouth."

"I'm sorry. I didn't mean to. . . ."

"Your father will hear about this."

I blushed. Again.

She noticed and seemed pleased. "He'll hear alllll about how you and your pal Russell came barging in here half-naked and got *smart* with me."

"Let's get out of here," Rusty said.

"Speaking of *pals*," Dolly said, "where's Frances? Why isn't *she* here? She's *always* with you two." Dolly leaned further over the desk top and stretched her long neck forward like a curious turtle. "Has something happened to her?"

Mouth hanging open, I shook my head.

"She hasn't lost *her* shirt, has she?"

"No."

"Why isn't she with you?"

While I tried to think of a good lie, Rusty kept silent.

"What've you two *done* to her?" Dolly demanded.

"Nothing! She's fine. Are you out of your mind?"

"Out of my mind?" she screeched.

Oh shit, I thought. Now I've done it.

"Frances is fine!" I blurted.

"OUT OF MY MIND???"

"I didn't mean it!"

"He didn't mean it!" Rusty echoed.

"WHERE'S MY GUN???"

I yelled, *"FUCK!!!"*

Dolly cried out, *"WHAT DID YOU SAY?"*

By then, we were racing for the door, Rusty in the lead.

"WHAT DID YOU SAY, DWIGHT THOMPSON? WAS THAT THE F WORD YOU SAID? YOUR FATHER IS GOING TO . . ."

The door shut behind me, cutting off the rest of her words.

We ran around the corner before we slowed down. Rusty was out of breath and laughing at the same time.

"It's not funny," I said.

"The hell . . ."

"If she tells Dad what I said . . ."

"You're fucked."

"It's not funny," I repeated, and looked around to make sure nobody was within earshot. We were walking along Central, the main street through Grandville's business district. Though a few cars were going by and I could see a couple of people in the distance, the area was pretty much dead. Just by the deadness, I knew without looking at a clock that the time must be about two o'clock. That's how the town *is* between two

105

and three o'clock on just about every weekday afternoon.

It was a strange time of day. You could go into the hardware store, the restuarants, the Woolworths, the barber shop, the pharmacy, or just about any other business establishment in the downtown area and you'd be lucky to find another living soul—except for those who worked there.

Since nobody was around, we didn't need to worry about being overheard.

I didn't care much for the quiet, though. It gave me an uneasy feeling. If you're in a forest and nobody's around, all the better. A forest is supposed to be quiet and peaceful. Not a town, though. A town is meant to be bustling with people. When it's almost deserted, it feels wrong. At least to me.

It made matters worse, the day being so gray and hot.

It especially made matters worse that Slim was missing.

Just in case I might happen to forget for one minute to worry about her, I couldn't turn my eyes anywhere without seeing posters for the Traveling Vampire Show. They were tacked to utility poles, taped to store windows and doors, and several littered the sidewalk and street. I even saw one in a curbside trash basket.

"Somebody was sure busy putting up posters," I muttered.

"You should've been here this morning. They were everywhere."

"They're almost everywhere now."

Rusty shook his head. "Half of 'em aren't even here anymore." He patted his seat pocket. "I got mine. And we've got *tickets!* I can't believe it."

I gave him a look.

"Cheer up, buddy."

"I'll cheer up when we find Slim. If my dad hasn't killed me by then for saying fuck to Dolly."

"You know what?" Rusty said. "I bet Dolly won't even tell on you. She *can't*. She threatened us with a gun."

"She didn't really. . . ."

"She went, 'Where's my gun?' After that's when you yelled fuck."

We were walking past the recessed entryway of a toy store

just then. The doors stood wide open, but I glanced in and didn't see anyone.

"Stop saying that, okay?"

"What, fuck?"

"Come on, Rusty, quit it. We're in enough trouble already."

"Dolly won't tell."

"*Every*body tells in this town."

Not everybody, I reminded myself. There's Lee. She was probably the only adult I knew who didn't take delight in snitching on people.

"Know why I keep saying fuck?" Rusty asked.

"Cut it out."

"Because I'm so fucking hungry."

I was awfully hungry, myself. Here it was, somewhere past two o'clock in the afternoon, and I'd eaten nothing all day except for a bowl of Raisin Bran at about nine.

"Okay," I said. "You stop talking dirty and we'll get something to eat."

"Deal."

"Central Cafe?"

"Great," Rusty said. "How much money you got?"

"Seven or eight bucks."

"Can I borrow some off you? Just enough for a cheeseburger and fries. And a chocolate shake."

"Sure."

"I'll pay you back."

He almost never paid me back for anything, but I said, "Fine."

As we walked along, Rusty moaned softly. He said, "I *love* Flora's cheeseburgers."

"They're pretty decent," I admitted.

"Decent? They're fabulous. How about the way she butters up those buns and *grills* 'em so they crunch?"

I was on the verge of drooling when we arrived at the Central Cafe. Looking through the windows, I saw nobody at any of the booths or tables, though one guy was sitting at the counter. Behind the counter stood Flora.

Taped to one of the windows was a poster for the Traveling Vampire Show.

"Oh, shit," Rusty said.

He pointed to a sign on the restaurant's door.

NO SHIRT. NO SHOES. NO SERVICE.

"Oh, well," I said.

He said, "Fuck!"

I said, "Shhh."

"When did they put *this* up?"

"It's probably always been here."

"I don't think so. Why don't we give it a try, anyway?"

"Not me. Let's just go someplace else."

"Chicken."

Not in the mood to argue, I walked away from the door and Rusty. He hurried after me.

"I *really* wanted one of those cheeseburgers," he said.

"Me, too. But we lost our shirts in a good cause."

"If I'd known we were gonna end up starving . . ."

"You'll live," I said.

He groaned. "We should've had those sandwiches back at your house when we had the chance."

"Well, we didn't."

"We can go back."

"Your place is closer," I said.

He contorted his face to let me know what a lousy idea it was.

I decided not to let him off the hook.

"Why don't we go there and get something to eat? You can ask your mom about having supper at my place tonight, and maybe I can borrow one of your shirts."

He sighed. Then he said, "Yeah, okay."

"A clean one, preferably."

A smile broke out. "Up yours," he said.

Chapter Seventeen

When Rusty's house came into sight, so did a crowd of parked cars.

"Oh," Rusty said.

"What?"

He looked at me and bared his teeth. "Mom's day to host her bridge club."

"Oh."

"Forgot all about it." Looking pained, he said, "There'll be like a dozen ladies in the living room."

I nodded.

My mother also belonged to a bridge club, though not the same one as Rusty's mom. I'd been in our house when she hosted her group. The air was so thick with cigarette smoke you wondered how they could see their cards . . . or breathe. And the noise! I had no problem with the clinking of glasses and coffee cups that sounded as if you were in a crowded restaurant. The constant chatter wasn't so bad, either. What I couldn't stand were the outcries of surprise and delight that kept blasting through the house: ear-splitting whoops and squeals and cackles and shrieks.

"We can't go in," Rusty said.

"What about the back door? We could sneak into the kitchen."

Rusty scowled. "I don't know," he muttered. "Mom'll be running in and out . . . and no telling who else." He shook his head. "We'd get caught. Then Mom would have to *introduce* us to everyone."

I grimaced.

Our mothers *always* introduced us to company. It's a horrible, embarrassing experience even when you're fully dressed.

I sure didn't want to be paraded shirtless in front of all Mrs. Baxter's lady friends.

It would be even more humiliating for Rusty, since his physique was nothing to brag about.

"But I've *gotta* get some food in me," he said.

He frowned down at the sidewalk as if pondering his options. Then he said, "We might as well try and sneak into the kitchen. We can grab something to eat and then haul ass."

"What about shirts?"

"Forget it. How'm I supposed to get to my room?"

I gave him a look.

"It's not *my* fault," he said.

"I know."

"But at least we can grab some food."

In case we were being watched from the living room, we kept our eyes away from Rusty's house until we were past it. On the other side of the driveway, we ducked behind the parked station wagon and made our way to the garage. Then we went around the garage to the back yard and crept up the stairs to the kitchen door.

Rusty bent forward. Hands cupped to the screen, he peered in. Then he eased open the door.

I followed him into the kitchen. Nobody was there except for us. Both doors to the rest of the house were shut—probably to keep the bridge club ladies from noticing the kitchen's clutter.

The doors kept out most of the smoke, but not the noise. Mrs. Baxter's group sounded exactly like my mother's—like a gang of merry female lunatics.

The kitchen counters were littered with dirty glasses, cups, plates and silverware. By the look of things, Mrs. Baxter had served cherry pie a la mode to her friends. On the table in front of us were two pie tins, empty except for crumbs of crust and spilled red filling.

Rusty ran a fingertip across the bottom of a pie tin, came up with a gob of filling and stuck it in his mouth.

I didn't bother.

Hunched over, head swiveling as he glanced from door to

door, Rusty tiptoed around the table and made his way to the refrigerator. He pulled it open. I stepped up beside him. The chilly breath of the refrigerator drifted against my skin. It felt great.

With both of us standing close to the open refrigerator, Rusty found a pack of Oscar Meyer wieners. He pulled out a hot dog, stuck it into his mouth like a somewhat droopy orange cigar, then offered the package to me. I slipped out a wiener and poked it into my mouth.

Rusty, Slim and I often ate cold hot dogs—but only when no adults were around. Put a mother into the picture, and a wiener *has* to be heated and slipped onto a bun. Like it's the law. Only problem is, the bun is usually dry. To make the bunned hot dog edible, you need to slather it with mustard or ketchup (and Rusty always needed *pickle relish*, a disgusting concoction), which killed the taste of the wiener.

I chowed down my cold dog and accepted Rusty's offer to have another.

While we held them in our mouths, Rusty put the package away and pulled out a big brick of Velveeta cheese.

"Mmm?" he asked.

Nodding, I affirmed, "Mmm."

We turned away from the refrigerator, I eased its door shut, and we headed across the kitchen. Rusty took a cheese slicer out of a drawer. At a clear place on the counter, he set down the Velveeta and peeled back its shiny silver wrapper. With the taut wire of the slicer, he cut off an inch-thick slab.

He handed it to me. As I sank my teeth into it, he started to cut off another slab.

One of the doors behind us *swooshed* open.

We both jumped.

Through the swinging door stepped Bitsy.

The actual name of Rusty's fourteen-year-old sister was Elizabeth. Her nickname used to be Betsy. Like everyone else in Rusty's family, however, she was on the husky side. So Rusty started calling her Bitsy. She *liked* it, but her parents didn't. They seemed to think it drew attention to her size, and not in a flattering way.

When the door swung open, I figured we'd had it.

Rusty gasped and whirled around like a burglar caught in the act.

Seeing that the intruder was only Bitsy, though, he rolled his eyes upward. I smiled at her, my tight lips hiding my mouthful of yellow cheese goo and my right hand holding a wiener.

"Hi, guys," she said. She looked glad to see us.

Especially glad to see me. She was always glad to see me. She was smitten with me, and had been for years. Maybe because I was such a handsome fellow. Or maybe because I always treated her like a regular person and never teased her and often stuck up for her when Rusty started giving her crap.

As the door swung shut behind her, Bitsy blushed and smiled into my eyes, then checked out my bare torso, then met my eyes again and said, "Hi, Dwight."

I nodded, swallowed some Velveeta and said, "Hi, Bitsy. How you doing?"

"Oh, fine, thank you." As if suddenly worried about her own appearance, she patted her hair and glanced down at herself. Her hair, as usual, resembled a shaggy brown football helmet but without the face guard or chin strap. She was wearing an old T-shirt and cut-off blue jeans—the same sort of outfit Slim normally wore, except Bitsy was barefoot. Plus, her T-shirt was more ragged than Slim's and she wasn't wearing a bikini top underneath it. She could've used one. Or a bra. Especially since her T-shirt was so thin you could pretty much see through it.

"Hey, Bits," Rusty said. "Wanta do us a favor?"

"Like what?"

"Get us some shirts."

She frowned slightly at him. "What for?"

"To *wear*, stupid."

I gave him a look. One thing that always puzzles me; people smarting off when they're asking for someone's help. It seems not only rude but incredibly dumb.

Trying to sound extra-nice to make up for Rusty, I said, "Our shirts got ruined over at Janks Field."

Bitsy's eyes widened. "You were at *Janks Field?*" She glanced at Rusty. "You're not supposed to go there."

"Thanks, Dwight. Now she's gonna tell on me."

To Bitsy, I said, "You won't tell on him, will you?"

"If you don't want me to."

"Thanks."

"You're welcome."

"Anyway, our shirts got ruined when we were there." Seeing the concern in her eyes, I explained, "A dog attacked us."

"Oh, no!"

"We're all right, but our shirts got wrecked. We've been running around without them all day and we're getting pretty sunburned."

"You've got a good tan," she told me, blushing.

"Thanks. But anyway, we just want to borrow a couple of shirts so we don't get burnt any more than we already are when we go back out."

"What *sort* of shirts do you want?" she asked.

"Anything," I said.

"Just go in my closet and grab us a couple, okay?"

"In your *closet?*"

"Want me to draw you a map?"

With a sort of pleased, now-the-tables-are-turned look on her face, she said to Rusty, "But I'm not supposed to *go* in your closet."

Rusty's eyes narrowed. "You have my permission. This once."

"Well well well," she said.

"Just do it, okay?"

"Why can't you do it yourself? They're *your* shirts. It's *your* closet."

Before Rusty could answer and probably make matters worse, I told her, "We don't really want to meet the bridge club, you know?" Shrugging, I glanced down at myself. "No shirts? It'd be kind of embarrassing."

Nodding and blushing, she stared at my bare torso.

"C'mon, Bits. We haven't got all day."

113

I scowled at Rusty. "Leave her alone. She doesn't have to get the shirts if she doesn't want to."

"I'll get them," she said, speaking to me.

"Thanks."

"You're welcome. How many do you need?"

"Twenty-eight, you moron," Rusty said.

"Just two will be fine," I told her.

"What about Slim?" she asked.

The sudden reminder made me go sick inside. Trying not to let it show, I said, "What about her?"

"Does she need one, too?"

"Let's *ask*," Rusty said, and looked over his shoulder.

"Slim isn't with us," I explained.

"Why not?"

Rusty and I spent a little too long thinking about that one. Bitsy suddenly looked worried. "Is she all right?"

"She's fine," Rusty said.

"No she's not," Bitsy said. Her eyes turned to me. "Something happened to her, didn't it?"

Considering Bitsy's crush on me, you might've expected her to be jealous of Slim. But it didn't work that way. Instead of hating Slim, she idolized her. I'm pretty sure she wished she could *be* Slim: cute and slender and athletic and smart and funny, and hanging out with me almost every day.

"Where *is* she?" Bitsy asked.

I shrugged.

"She had to stay home and do the laundry," Rusty said.

Bitsy's eyes stayed on me. Clearly, she didn't believe Rusty's explanation. She wanted to hear it from me.

"Why don't you go ahead and get us the shirts?" I said, a gentleness in my voice that surprised me. "Just two shirts. We'll wait in the backyard, okay? And I'll tell you about Slim."

"Okay."

When Bitsy shoved open the door, the noise of the bridge ladies swelled. The door swung shut, coming half-open again on our side and fanning in a few gray rags of smoke.

Rusty muttered, "Shit."

Then he cut off another thick slab of Velveeta cheese, folded the end of the wrapper, and returned the cheese to the refrigerator. While he still held the door open, he asked, "Another dog?"

I shook my head.

He shut the door. Both of us holding what was left of our wieners and cheese, we hurried outside and down the stairs to the backyard. Over near a corner of the house, we stopped to wait for Bitsy and finish eating.

"Jush wha' we nee'," Rusty muttered, his words mushy from a mouthful of partly-chewed lunch.

"Don't worry about it," I said.

He swallowed and said, "Why'd you have to go and tell her about *Janks Field?*"

I shrugged. "I have a hard time lying sometimes."

"Tell me about it."

"Sorry. But look, she'll be all right."

"Easy for you to say, she isn't *your* sister."

The screen door swung open. Bitsy rushed out and bounded down the stairs. Her hands were empty. I figured something must've gone wrong. As she hurried toward us, though, I saw that the front of her T-shirt bulged more than usual.

"Got 'em," she said. Stopping in front of us, Bitsy patted her bulge. Her T-shirt was so thin I could see the wrinkled bunch of fabric underneath it.

Rusty put out his hand and snapped his fingers. "Give," he said.

Fixing her eyes on me, Bitsy asked, "Where's Slim, really? Something's wrong, isn't it?"

"You have to promise not to tell," I said.

Rusty groaned.

"I promise."

"She'll tell."

"No, I won't." She raised her right hand. "I swear."

"First time something doesn't go her way. . . ."

She threw a glare at him. "I will not."

I said, "We're going to look for Slim right now. She was

115

still at Janks Field last time we saw her. So that's where we're going."

"How come you went off without her?"

I gave Rusty a look, then faced Bitsy and said, "She wanted to stay behind."

"How come?"

"To look at some stuff," I said. "Anyway, we have to get back and find her."

Bobbing her head slightly as if she now understood, Bitsy reached with both hands under the bottom of her T-shirt and dragged out a couple of shirts. They were both wrinkled, but looked clean.

"This one's for you," she said, and handed me a checkered, short-sleeved shirt.

"Thanks," I said.

"You're welcome."

"And this one's for you."

The shirt she held out toward Rusty had nothing wrong with it that I could see, but he snatched it from her grip and muttered, "Thanks a lot."

Turning again to me, she said, "Are you sure Slim doesn't need a shirt, too?"

"Nah," I said. "She has ours."

"What happened to *hers?*"

"The dog got it," I said.

"I thought you said it wrecked *your* shirts."

"Indirectly," I said.

"Huh?" Bitsy asked.

"Shit on a stick," Rusty said, "why not just blab *everything?*"

Holding the stub of my wiener in my mouth, I put on the shirt.

"I'm coming with," said Bitsy.

Chapter Eighteen

"The hell you are!" Rusty blurted.

"She's my friend, too."

"You're not coming."

Glaring at her brother, Bitsy said, "If you don't let me come, I'm gonna tell."

Rusty's eyes flashed at me. *"See?"* Then he shoved the rest of his wiener into his mouth.

Bitsy turned to me. "You don't mind me coming, do you?"

Here was my big chance to redeem myself with Rusty and ruin Bitsy's day . . . or week, or month. I didn't want to do it. But I wasn't crazy about having her tag along with us, either. "It's fine with me," I said.

She gave Rusty a glance of triumph.

"The only thing is," I said, "it might be dangerous."

"That's okay."

"I wouldn't want you to get hurt."

"I don't mind."

"Do you mind if you get *us* hurt?" Rusty asked her.

"I'm not gonna do that."

"Oh, yeah? What if we get chased and you're too slow and we have to run back to *rescue* your fat ass and like Dwight gets *killed* all because of *you?*"

"Quit it, Rusty," I said.

A stubborn look in her eyes, Bitsy told him, "You just don't want me to come. But it's okay with Dwight. He said so."

She looked at me for confirmation.

"Sure," I said. "If you really want to, you can. But we *are* going to Janks Field. No telling what might happen. There's the dog, and . . ."

"I'm not scared."

"You oughta be, you little twat."

"Rusty!"

She turned on him. "I'm gonna *tell!*"

"Go ahead. See if I care." To me, he said, "Damn it, Dwight, we can't take her to Janks Field. She's my *sister*. What if something *does* happen to her?"

"We'll make sure she's all right," I told him. To Bitsy, I said, "Are you really *sure* you want to come? It's not just dangerous, it's a long walk. Five or six miles," I added, exaggerating slightly.

"Is not," she said.

"Round trip."

"I can walk that far."

"Sure you can," Rusty muttered.

"I'm coming," Bitsy said. "Right, Dwight?"

"If you really want to," I told her.

"I do."

"One thing, though. You can't come with us barefoot. It's a long walk and Janks Field has all sorts of broken glass and stuff. . . ."

"Spiders and snakes," Rusty added.

"You have to put some shoes on," I told her.

An eager look in her eyes, she said, "Wait right here." Then she swung around and trotted to the back stairs. She hustled up them, pulled open the screen door and entered the kitchen. The door banged shut.

Rusty and I looked at each other.

I nodded.

We split.

Ran like hell around the corner of the garage, cut across the neighbor's yard, made it to the sidewalk and didn't stop running till we reached Route 3. Panting and drenched with sweat, we stopped by the side of the pavement. I walked in slow circles while Rusty bent over and held his knees.

When he had his breath back, he straightened up and grinned at me and shook his head. "Good man," he said.

"Yeah, well."

He patted me on the back, and we walked up Route 3. On

both sides of us, the woods were tall and thick. Though the sunless afternoon made the road ahead of us look gloomy, in there among the trees there was hardly any light at all.

After a while, Rusty said, "Bet she never thought *you'd* ditch her."

"I know."

"That's why it worked."

"Yeah."

He patted me on the back some more. "I can't believe you did that to her."

I glowered at him.

"Just kidding, man. It was brilliant."

"I didn't want to hurt her feelings."

"Blew that one."

"If she'd just listened to reason . . ."

"Ha!"

"I *tried* to talk her out of coming."

"You did your best. Anyway, she had no business butting in like that. Not to mention threatening to *tell* on us. Serves her right." Rusty chuckled softly.

"What?" I asked.

"Just thinking about the look she must've had on her face when she came back out and we were gone."

"It's not funny."

The humor left his face. "Just hope she doesn't decide to come after us. I wouldn't put it past her." Scowling, he looked over his shoulder.

I looked back, too. The road behind us was deserted, at least to where it curved out of sight about thirty feet away. "Maybe we'd better hurry," I said.

We picked up our pace.

Every so often, we glanced back.

I felt lousy about ditching Bitsy.

I told myself that she had no business going with us in the first place. She wasn't really one of us and we *might* be running into trouble. If things went bad, she could hardly be counted on to take care of herself. Saving her would be *our* job and we didn't need that sort of responsibility.

Still, I'd tricked her. I'd betrayed her. I'd probably broken her heart.

I almost wished she would show up just so I could stop feeling so guilty.

Because of the twists in Route 3, we couldn't see very far behind us. Bitsy might've been back there, closing in. At any moment, she might come hustling around a bend, jiggling and waving.

I half expected it to happen.

Every so often, cars went by. We stayed along the edge of the road, walking single file, and ignored them. Though most of the people in the cars probably recognized us, nobody called out or stopped. With any luck, we might not even get talked about; it wasn't as if we were doing anything interesting, just walking.

By the time we were about halfway to the Janks Field turn-off, Bitsy still hadn't appeared. Maybe because we were walking too fast. So I slowed down.

Rusty gave me a grateful look. Our fast pace had been rough on him.

We kept glancing back every so often. Rusty, I'm sure, hoped he wouldn't spot Bitsy on the road behind us. I didn't want her with us, either, but I might've been relieved to find her coming along.

When we finally reached the dirt road leading to Janks Field, I stopped and looked back toward town. There was a fairly long stretch before the first bend. Staring at the empty lanes, I realized this was where the sheeted man had come gliding toward us last Halloween night. The memory gave me a little shiver up my back.

What was he doing out here that night? I wondered.

Who was he?

Where is he now?

I almost expected to see the sheeted figure in its silly bowler hat and not-so-silly hangman's noose come drifting up the road toward us.

Would it be as scary on a summer afternoon?

Maybe even scarier.

What if he's just on the other side of the bend?

To stop myself from thinking about it, I said to Rusty, "Maybe we'd better wait here for a few minutes and see if Bitsy turns up."

"Are you nuts?"

"What if she *is* coming after us?"

"All the more reason to get going."

I shook my head. "And leave her alone out here? We're two miles from town."

He gave me a disgusted look. "She knows the way home."

"But she might keep on looking for us. If she thinks we're somewhere just ahead of her, no telling *where* she might go."

Rusty sighed. "She probably never came after us at all. She probably went straight to her bedroom, crying."

"Maybe," I admitted. "But let's at least give her five minutes or something to catch up. In case she . . ."

"Hi guys."

Rusty flinched and gasped, "Shit!"

Even though I recognized the voice, I jumped. A moment later, warmth and relief spread through me. I turned and searched the deep shadows of the woods alongside the dirt road.

"What's up?" Slim asked, stepping out from behind a tree.

"Hey *hey!*" Rusty blurted. "I *knew* you were okay."

I'd known no such thing, myself. As she came toward us, my throat tightened and tears filled my eyes.

She looked fine.

She looked *great*. Her short blond hair was wet and clinging to her scalp. Her skin was shiny and dripping, scratched here and there from her encounter with the dog. On top, she wore nothing except her white bikini. Her cut-off jeans hung low around her hips. Her feet were wrapped in shirts, mine on her right foot, Rusty's on her left.

Seeing the look on my face, she said, "Hey, Dwight, it's okay."

I hurried to her and spread out my arms, aching to hug her. But then I remembered all the cuts on her back, so I didn't do it. She looked into my eyes. She had tears in her eyes, too.

Her lips and chin quivered a little. Suddenly, she threw herself against me and wrapped her arms around me and hugged me hard.

Not wanting to hurt her, I put my hands on her shoulders.

Her hot, wet face nuzzled the side of my neck. She was breathing hard, her chest and breasts pushing against me. I could feel the pounding of her heart. Each time she took a breath, her flat belly touched mine.

"You guys gonna do it?" Rusty asked.

"Shut up," Slim said.

"Do I get some of that?"

Neither of us bothered to answer him.

After a while, Slim loosened her hold on me and tipped her head back. "I sure am glad to see you," she whispered.

"Same here," I said.

She looked at Rusty. "You too, I guess."

"How's the back?" I asked.

"Not bad."

I turned her around by the shoulders. The cuts looked raw and gooey. None seemed to be bleeding at the moment, but her skin was ruddy with a mixture of sweat and old blood. The bikini ties in the middle of her back were still white in a few places. Mostly, though, they were red.

"Has it been bleeding?" I asked.

"Not much." She turned around to face me. "Just for a little while right after I jumped down off the shack," she said, and glanced at Rusty.

"What'd *I* do?" he complained.

Instead of answering, she looked over her shoulder. "Let's get off the road before someone comes along." As we followed her into the trees, she said, "I've been staying out of sight."

"Good idea," I told her.

"Waiting for you. I knew you'd be coming back for me sooner or later."

"We've been looking all over for you," I said.

"I've been right here." She stopped and turned toward us. "A long time," she added.

"How long?" I asked.

She shrugged. "More than an hour, I bet."

"Why?" Rusty asked.

She gave him a peeved look. "We were *supposed* to wait for Dwight."

"I know, I know."

"Some of us do what we *say* we'll do."

"You didn't exactly stay put either," he told her.

"No, I didn't. But I came here so I could *meet* him." To me, she said, "I figured if you came back with a car, you'd have to slow down for the turn and I'd have a chance to run out and stop you."

"I *did* come back in a car," I said.

Her head jumped forward, eyes going wide, mouth dropping open—a look of total, dumb surprise. "Huh?"

"In Lee's pickup."

"When?"

"I don't know. Around noon, I guess. Twelve, twelve-thirty, something like that."

With a few minor changes in her face and posture, she looked intelligent again, but perplexed. "That must've been right after I took off," she said.

"Should've stayed," Rusty told her.

"You've got to be kidding. I couldn't get out of there fast enough after what I saw."

"What?" I asked.

"The way they killed the dog."

"They killed the dog?"

Chapter Nineteen

Good for them," Rusty said.

Slim frowned at him. "Why don't *you* shut up?"

"What crawled up *your* ass and . . ."

"Rusty!" I snapped.

"What'd I do?"

Eyes on Rusty, Slim said, "I didn't really appreciate getting *left* up there."

"You should've come with me."

"We were supposed to wait for Dwight."

"Yeah, but . . ."

"Yeah, but," she mimicked him. "Yeah-but, yeah-but you turned yellow and ran away and *left* me up there." To me, she said, "You should've seen him freak out. Nothing was even *there* yet. We just heard cars coming through the woods, and he goes ape like it's the end of the goddamn world. And then this *hearse* drives onto the field. That did it, the hearse. He goes, *'Oh, shit! It's a hearse! We gotta get outa here!'* I told him to calm down. I mean, big deal. A hearse. It's just part of the vampire show. It's part of what we went there to *see*, you know? It was probably *Valeria's* hearse. I thought he *wanted* to see Valeria. But huh-uh, all he wants is to *vamoos*."

"You were scared, too," Rusty said.

"Yeah, a little. But I didn't run away."

"Duh. Yes you did."

"Later."

"You should've left when I did. Don't go calling *me* a chicken. I just had the foresight to haul my ass out of there sooner than you."

"I planned to stick it out." To me again, she said, "I told Rusty we should just relax and lie down flat so they wouldn't see us."

"They *would've* seen us. The minute someone climbed the bleachers. By then, we might not've been *able* to get away."

"So he said, 'You wanta stay, stay. I'm gonna get while the gettin's good.' "

I could *hear* Rusty say it.

"Of course, my shoes and shirt were down on the ground. My shirt was no big deal, but I didn't want to leave my shoes behind."

"But you did," Rusty pointed out.

"Yeah, that's for sure. After they did that to the dog, I stopped worrying about my feet. I grabbed both your shirts and jumped off the back of the shack and ran like hell for the woods."

"What *did* they do to the dog?" I asked.

"Right off, it went running toward the hearse, barking like a maniac."

"I saw that," Rusty said.

"Yeah, and then you took off." Turning her eyes to me, she said, "I got down flat on my stomach and looked around the end of the sign. The hearse was coming straight toward me. It had a bus coming along behind it. Like a school bus, only black."

"I've seen it," I said.

"When you drove out with Lee?" Slim asked.

"Yeah."

"So what all did you see?"

"The hearse, the bus, that big truck that looked like a moving van, a bunch of people unloading stuff."

"Wait'll you hear," Rusty said.

"Hear what?"

"He's got . . ."

"Hey!" I blasted him. "I'll tell her. But I'd like to hear about the dog first, okay?"

"Okay, okay." To Slim, he said, "What'd they do, run it over?"

"Let *her* tell it."

"So sorry." He smirked at Slim, "Proceed."

"Okay, so the dog ran straight for the hearse, barking its butt off. I thought it'd jump out of the way at the last second, but it didn't. What it did, it stopped in front of the hearse and planted its feet in the dirt and sort of hunched down and *barked* like a madman. So then the hearse stops. I'm thinking these are decent people who don't want to run over a dog. Boy, was I wrong. What happens next, the bus drives up behind the hearse and stops and its door opens. And these *people* come pouring out. Like maybe fifteen of them, and they're all dressed in black and carrying spears."

"Spears?" I blurted.

"Spears. Big long ones. Like maybe six feet long, with steel tips."

"You're shitting us," Rusty muttered.

"Yeah, I wish."

"What did these people look like?" I asked.

"Jungle bunnies?" Rusty asked.

I winced. Ever since Slim had read *To Kill a Mockingbird*, she'd gone on the warpath if anyone used that sort of language.

She glared at Rusty.

"You know." He smiled. "The spears."

"Don't be an asshole," she told him.

"Just asking."

"Well, don't. You want to be a bigoted shit-for-brains, don't do it in front of me."

I looked at Rusty and shook my head. "Nice going."

"Big deal."

Still looking angry, Slim said, "Matter of fact, all of them were white."

"Glad to hear it," Rusty said.

Ignoring him, I asked, "What did they look like?"

"Just normal, I guess." She glanced at Rusty, but he made no comment so she turned her attention to me and continued. "Mostly men, I think. And a few women. They all wore these shiny black shirts that looked like satin or silk or something. Anyway, they split into two groups. One bunch went around one side of the hearse, one around the other. Before the dog noticed anything was wrong, they closed in on it. They surrounded it, then started poking at it with their spears. They could've killed it with one good thrust, but nobody did that. They just kept poking at it, giving it little jabs."

Slim went silent. She had a hurt look in her eyes as if she could feel the dog's agonies. After taking a few deep breaths, she said, "I couldn't see the dog at all . . . just those people around it, going at it with their spears. I could sure hear it, though. It was yelping and squealing and whimpering. You could tell. . . . It was like they just wanted to *torture* it."

"Good God," I muttered.

"Sick," Rusty said.

"Finally, they stepped back to let someone through. The dog was down on its side. Its tongue was hanging out and it was panting for air, and it was just *covered* with blood. It was sort of trying to get up." Slim's voice broke. She shook her head and looked away from us.

Rusty looked as if he might throw up.

With both hands, Slim wiped sweat away from her eyes. Some tears, too, I think. Then she took another deep breath and said, "The guy they let through, he got down on one knee and shoved his spear. . . ." Breathing hard, she shook her head. Then as if in a race to get her story done, she blurted, *"He picked it up off the ground with his spear and ran with it to the back of the hearse and somebody'd already opened the door back there and he shoved the dog in like food on the end of a stick and . . ."* She paused to take a few quick breaths, then went on. *"He pulled the spear back a second later, and the dog wasn't on it anymore. It was like somebody in the hearse . . . I don't know."*

Rusty and I both stared at her.

Head down, she kept wiping her face with both hands. It took her a long time to calm down. Then she said, "After that, that's when I figured it was time to go."

We were silent for a while longer. Then I said, "God almighty."

After more silence, Rusty said, "So you think somebody in the hearse *ate* the dog?"

She shrugged her shiny, tanned shoulder. "I don't know," she muttered.

"Or drank its blood," I suggested.

"Valeria *is* supposed to be a vampire," Rusty reminded us.

"I don't know who was in the hearse," Slim said.

"Maybe nobody," I said. "Maybe they just put the dog in there to get it out of sight."

"I don't know," Slim muttered. "Anyway, that's what happened. And I thought if they got their hands on me . . . I might get it like the dog. So I turned around and belly-crawled to the back of the roof and jumped down and ran like hell."

"Did they see you?" I asked.

"I don't know. Maybe not. I didn't hear any shouts. No one came after me. I don't think so, anyway. When I got into the woods, I kept changing directions to throw them off. Just in case someone *was* after me. Then I hid for a while."

"Where'd you hide?" Rusty asked.

She shrugged again. "Under some old tree. It had fallen over and there was a space between it and the ground. I just barely fit in."

"How long do you think you stayed in there?" I asked.

"Seemed like ages." She shrugged again. "Maybe half an hour, I don't know."

"I bet that's where you were when Lee and I were at Janks Field."

"Maybe. I don't know."

"Did you hear anyone calling your name?"

She shook her head.

"I called out for you and Rusty."

"When was that?"

I shrugged. "I don't know. Maybe around twelve-thirty, I guess. Twelve-fifteen, twelve-thirty, something like that."

Slim frowned as if thinking about it, and shook her head again. "I must've been *some*where in the woods."

"You weren't on the roof."

Surprise on her face, she said, "You looked?"

"Yeah. I went over and jumped up and . . ."

"Went over to the *shack?*"

"Yeah."

"What about all those *people?*"

"They weren't paying much attention to us. Julian had gone into the bus . . ."

"Who's that?"

"Julian Stryker. He's the owner of the show."

Looking surprised but not at all pleased, Slim said, "You met the *owner?*"

I nodded.

"What'd he look like?"

"I can see *this* coming," Rusty said.

I glanced at him, then looked back at Slim. "He wore a black shirt. . . ."

"They *all* wore black shirts, numbnuts," Rusty reminded me.

Ignoring the remark, I said to Slim, "He had long, black hair. He was . . . I guess women would probably think he was really handsome."

"Gorgeous?" Slim asked.

"I didn't think so, but . . ."

"Was he carrying a spear?" Rusty asked.

I glared at him.

"Did he wear silver spurs?" Slim asked.

"Yeah."

"That's him," she said.

"Knew it," said Rusty.

Me, too. But I asked, "The guy who . . . picked up the dog and took it to the hearse?"

Slim nodded.

"Oh, man," I muttered.

"What?"

"We asked him about you and Rusty."

"What'd he say?"

"That he hadn't seen you."

"Wait'll you hear the *good* part," Rusty said, a strange smile on his face.

"Lee bought tickets from him," I explained. "Four tickets for tonight's performance of the Traveling Vampire Show. One for each of us."

Chapter Twenty

Slim stared at me. She looked a little stunned. "You're kidding," she said.

"They cost her forty bucks," I said.

"But nobody under eighteen's allowed."

"Julian made an exception for us."

"He's got the hots for Lee," Rusty explained.

Slim's upper lip lifted slightly. Eyes turning toward Rusty, she said, "Maybe that's why. Or maybe he *did* see us. Me, anyway. If he saw me running away—if *any* of them did— he might figure I watched them kill the dog. Maybe he wants to *get* me."

A touch of scorn in his voice, Rusty said, "Why would he want to *get* you?"

"To stop me from telling what I saw."

I could think of other reasons he might want Slim. They made me feel cold and tight inside. I decided not to mention them.

A grin on his face, Rusty said, "Maybe he wants to stick a spear up your ass."

"Real funny," Slim muttered.

I punched him. My fist smacked his soft upper arm through the sleeve of his shirt.

Face going red, he gasped, *"Ah!"* and grabbed his arm and gazed at me with shocked, accusing eyes. As I watched, his eyes filled with tears. "Real nice," he said.

I turned to Slim. She looked as if she wished I hadn't hit him, but she didn't seem *angry* at me. More as if she thought the punch had probably not been the most terrific idea.

Though tears shimmered in Rusty's eyes, he wasn't exactly

crying. They weren't streaming down his face or anything. Frowning at me, he rubbed his arm.

"I didn't hit you that hard," I said.

"Hard enough. It *hurt*, man."

"You shouldn't have said what you did."

"I was just being funny."

"You *weren't* being funny," Slim assured him. "And you wouldn't be making cracks like that if you'd watched them with the dog."

"Sorry," he muttered, still rubbing his arm.

"And as a matter of fact," Slim said, "that guy really *might* want to stick a spear up my ass. Or up yours. Anyone who'll do a thing like that to a dog . . . he wouldn't think twice about doing it to a person."

"Maybe we'd better forget about going to the show tonight," I said.

Rusty's mouth fell open. He looked as if I'd punched him again. "Shit," he said. "We can't not *go!*"

"I'm not going," Slim said. "No way."

He turned to me. "I wanta see the show, man! Don't you? I mean, *Valerie!* If we don't go tonight, we'll *never* see her. *You* wanta see her, don't you?"

"It might not be such a good idea," I said.

"It'd be a *lousy* idea," Slim said. "*I'm* sure not going anywhere near those people again, and I don't think you guys should, either. They're a bunch of sickos."

"Just because they killed that stupid *dog?* Hey, *Dwight* tried to *jump* on the damn thing. Is he a sicko, too?"

"It's different."

"Dog would've been just as dead. Except he missed. He sure as hell *planned* to land on it."

She glanced at me, shook her head, and said to Rusty, "You know good and well it was different. Stop being a creep, okay?"

"I just don't wanta get rooked outa the show," he said. "I don't care *what* they did to that stupid dog. Look how it messed *you* up. It deserved what it got."

"Didn't deserve *that*." Slim looked from Rusty to me and

said, "Anyway, let's get out of here. I want to go home and get cleaned up."

Home.

I remembered what we'd done there.

It all rushed in: sneaking into her bedroom, looking at her things, Rusty fooling with her mother's bra, and the awful accident with the vase and how we'd left the mess behind. A nasty flood of heat flashed through my body.

Rusty cast me a warning glance.

And suddenly an idea popped into my head. Trying to keep my relief from showing, I frowned and said, "Maybe we'd better go over to Lee's house first and tell her about what happened. See what she thinks."

Rusty looked pained. "She hears what they did, man, she isn't gonna *take* us."

I gaped at him, astonished that he didn't realize a trip to Lee's house would save us from going to Slim's. The mess in her mother's room was sure to be discovered sooner or later, but I preferred later. The longer we could put it off, the better.

"She *shouldn't* take us," Slim said. "None of us should go to that show."

"Anyway," I said, "we *have* to tell Lee what happened."

"No, we don't."

"Yes, we do. Otherwise, she'll be waiting for us." To Slim, I explained, "We're supposed to be at her house at 10:30 tonight." To Rusty, I said, "We can't just not show up when she's expecting us."

"So we *do* show up. I've got no problem with that."

"I think we'd better tell her now," I said.

Slim nodded in agreement.

"Besides," I said, "her house is closer than Slim's. We can stop there first and borrow some bandages."

Rusty opened his mouth as if all set to argue. Before any words came out, however, a light of understanding filled his eyes.

He got it.

He got *something* anyway.

"Good point," he said. "Bandages. Lee *must* have bandages.

Everyone has bandages. Okay. Let's go there first."

"Okay by me," Slim said.

Not saying a word, I raised one foot off the ground and pulled off my sneaker.

"What're you doing?" Slim asked.

"Giving you my shoes."

"You don't have to do that."

I smiled at her and shrugged and pulled off my other sneaker. Holding them both toward her, I said, "I insist."

"Hey, no. C'mon. I can't wear your shoes."

"Sure you can."

"If she doesn't want to wear 'em . . ."

I gave Rusty a look that shut his mouth.

"Put them on," I told Slim. "Please."

"I don't know."

"If it hadn't been for *your* shoes, I would've gotten chomped by the dog."

"Glad to help."

"*I'm* the one who threw 'em," Rusty reminded us.

"You did a good job," I told him.

"Saved your butt."

"I know. You both did."

"Yeah, well, remember that when you wanta rook me outa Valeria."

"Sure." To Slim, I said, "I *want* you to wear them. Please."

"But what about *you?*"

"I'll be fine."

With a look of embarrassed but grateful surrender, she nodded and said, "All right." Then she took the sneakers from my hands, turned away and walked over to the remains of an old, fallen-down tree. She sat on its trunk, facing us, and set both sneakers beside her. While Rusty and I stood there and watched, she brought up one foot, crossed it over her knee, and removed the shirt that she'd been using to protect it. The bottom of her bare foot looked filthy. I glimpsed some blood on it before she put my sneaker on.

"Are your feet okay?" I asked.

"A few little nicks. No big deal." She let the shirt fall to the ground, then brought up her other foot.

When she had both my shoes on, she stood up. "Feels much better," she said. Then she crouched and plucked our shirts off the ground. Holding them out in front of her, she shook her head. "These are really wrecked, guys. I'm sorry."

They were not only covered with dirt and blood, but torn in a few places.

"Want them?" she asked.

Rusty shook his head.

"We can throw them away when we get to town," I said, holding out my hand. "I'll carry 'em."

She was about to give them to me when Rusty asked her, "Don't you want to wear one?"

"Thanks anyway. They're filthy. You want me to get infected?"

"You can't walk back to town looking like that. Everybody's gonna wonder how you got all wrecked up."

I nodded. "You'd better wear a shirt."

She frowned at the shirts in her hands. "I'd rather let people see me. . . ."

"You can borrow mine," Rusty said. He started to unfasten the buttons of the shirt he was wearing.

Shaking her head, Slim said, "It'll get blood on it. I've wrecked enough shirts for one day."

"I insist," Rusty said.

"No, really. . . ."

"You can wear Dwight's shoes. . . ."

"Okay."

He pulled his shirt off.

"Thanks," Slim said. She handed the two ruined shirts to me, then stepped closer to Rusty. "You'd better put it on me, though." She turned her back to him.

He gave me a strange smile—somehow smug and embarrassed at the same time—then slipped the shirt up Slim's arms and eased it onto her shoulders. "There you go," he told her.

Turning to face us, she fastened a couple of the middle buttons. "Thanks, guys," she said.

The shirt was way too large for her. It drooped over her shoulders. The sleeves reached down to her elbows. The single pocket hung below the rise of her left breast. The tails were so long that they completely hid her cut-off jeans.

She looked so cute it hurt to look at her.

I wished I could put my arms around her and hold her and never let go.

Instead of giving it a try, I just stood there, staring at her and feeling like I almost wanted to cry.

I don't know what it was about Slim.

I'd seen Lee a few hours earlier wearing my brother's big old work shirt. Even though it fit Lee pretty much the same way as Rusty's shirt fit Slim, even though Lee was probably the most beautiful woman I'd ever seen, the sight of her hadn't made me feel like my heart might break.

Maybe because Lee wasn't *cute*.

Slim was cute; Lee was spectacular.

I loved both of them. They both had ways of making me ache for them. But different ways. And different sorts of aches. In different places.

"What's wrong?" Slim asked me.

"Nothing."

"Ready to go?"

"Yeah."

"Let's go," Rusty said. He led the way, Slim walking behind him.

I followed, staying a few paces behind Slim, watching her.

With only my socks between my feet and the forest floor, I felt pokes and jabs with every step. I didn't mind, though. I was glad that my own feet, not Slim's, were the ones being hurt.

When we reached the pavement of Route 3, I said, "Wait up."

They stopped walking. I checked the bottoms of my socks.

135

They had picked up some dirt and debris, but they weren't really damaged yet.

"Want your shoes back?" Slim asked.

"Nope. I'm fine." I pulled off my socks, stuffed them into the pockets of my jeans and then we all resumed our hike back to town.

Chapter Twenty-one

As we entered the outskirts of town, I remembered about Bitsy. She hadn't followed us, after all, probably so hurt by my betrayal that she'd gone back to her bedroom and cried. I once again felt rotten about ditching her . . . on top of everything else I felt rotten about.

God, it's hard not to feel rotten.

I should've felt wonderful because we'd found Slim alive and well.

But I didn't. And I felt cheated because I had to feel lousy about Bitsy and about what we'd done in Slim's house and about slugging Rusty and about the poor damn dog getting speared and about God-only-knows what else.

On top of all that, it looked as if we wouldn't even get to see the Traveling Vampire Show.

Things could've been worse, though; at least we weren't on our way to Slim's house.

When we came to Lee's block, I saw her pickup truck in the driveway.

"She's home," I said.

"How about if we *don't* tell her about the dog?" Rusty suggested, looking over his shoulder at us with a pained expression on his face. "Please? She doesn't have to know *everything*, does she?"

"She has to know about that," Slim said.

"We're not going, anyway," I pointed out. "So why *not* tell her?"

Rusty stopped walking, turned around and raised his open hands to halt us. "Hold it up," he said.

We stopped.

"What if we change our minds?" he asked. "It's a long time between now and midnight. Maybe we'll wanta go after all, but we won't be able to if we've already spilled the beans to Lee."

Looking mildly amused, Slim said, "Oh, you think sometime between now and midnight it'll turn out that they *didn't* gang-stab the dog."

Gang-stab? Slim sometimes got creative with her language.

"I just mean, you know, maybe we'll decide to go *anyway*. Do we really wanta miss the Vampire Show on account of a stupid dog?"

"It isn't because of the dog," Slim said. "It's because what they did to it was heinous. These are heinous people."

Rusty looked annoyed.

"Abominable," I explained. "Shockingly evil."

He glanced at me. "I know what it means. I'm not stupid, you know."

"I know."

"Anyway, it's not like they'll do anything horrible *tonight*. They wouldn't dare." Eyes on Slim, he said, "I bet they wouldn't even've done that to the dog if they'd known you were watching. They *sure* aren't gonna pull stuff like that in front of an audience."

"Wouldn't think so," I said.

"They'd have the cops all over 'em."

Slim shook her head. "I don't plan to find out." Not waiting for any more arguments from Rusty, she stepped past him. He turned to follow her, and I took up the rear.

"Just because *you* don't want to see the show," he said to Slim's back, "have you gotta ruin it for the rest of us?"

"Leave her alone," I said.

We cut across Lee's front lawn. After two miles of walking mostly on pavement, the soft, dry grass felt good under my bare feet. When we reached the porch, I took over the lead and trotted up the wooden stairs. The screen door was shut, but I could see through it. The main door was open. Instead of ringing the doorbell or knocking, I called out. "Lee? It's Dwight. Are you here?"

"Come on in." Her voice sounded as if it came from somewhere deep in the house.

I opened the screen door and we all stepped into the foyer. The stone floor felt cool but hard.

The living room was just to our left. Lee's voice hadn't come from over there, but I looked for her anyway. She didn't seem to be there. At least I couldn't see her.

Though all the curtains were open, the afternoon was so gloomy that not much light made it through the windows. The room looked the way it might look at dusk if nobody'd turned on any lamps.

"I'll be right in," Lee called.

"Okay." I realized she might assume I was alone. Just to play it safe, I let her know, "Slim and Rusty are here, too."

"Good deal."

"Hi, Mrs. Thompson!" Slim called.

"Hi, Slim."

"Hello again," Rusty called.

"Hello, Rusty." After a small pause, Lee added, "Sit down and make yourselves comfortable. I'll be in in a minute."

Rusty suddenly announced, "If this isn't a good time for you, we can leave."

"No, it's fine. Don't go away. I'm almost done."

"Nice try," Slim whispered.

Rusty grinned, then walked into the living room and plopped down on the sofa.

Slim glanced at the bottoms of her shoes—my shoes—then entered the living room.

"Take a load off," Rusty told her.

She looked around at the furniture, then shook her head. "Think I'll stand. I'm a mess."

I checked the bottoms of my feet. They felt sore from the hike. They were dirty and even had a couple of dark smudges that made me suspect I'd stepped in a couple of oil drips. I didn't see any blood or cuts, though, so I took the socks out of my pocket and put them on. Then I walked into the living room. The carpet felt good and soft.

I wanted to sit down, but it didn't seem right to leave Slim standing by herself.

After a couple of minutes, Lee came in. "Sorry about that," she said. "I was mopping the kitchen floor."

She *looked* as if she'd been mopping a floor: some hair drooped across her forehead, her skin gleamed with sweat, the sleeves of her big blue shirt were rolled halfway up her forearms and her feet were bare. The front of the shirt was tied together just below her breasts. She wore small, white shorts. Like her shirt, the shorts looked like what she'd had on when she drove me to Janks Field.

To Slim, she said, "I understand you had some dog trouble this morning."

"Just a bit. Thanks for going out to rescue me."

"Yeah, thanks," Rusty added.

"Sorry we missed you," Lee said. Concern coming into her eyes, she said to Slim, "I thought you went home afterward."

Slim looked puzzled.

"You aren't cleaned up and it looks like you're wearing someone else's shirt and sneakers."

"I haven't been home," Slim said.

Lee gave Rusty a glance.

He seemed to blush, cringe and shrug all at the same time.

"It turns out Slim stayed behind," I explained. "At Janks Field. Rusty left, but she stayed for a while. Rusty told us a little fib when he said they'd left together. We went back and found her."

"Where *were* you?" Lee asked her.

"I ran off and hid in the woods," Slim said. "I guess that's how I missed you."

"That was a *long* time ago."

Slim shrugged. "I just stayed hidden. I didn't want to walk all the way home because I'd lost my shirt and shoes. Besides,

139

Dwight was supposed to show up." She smiled at me. "And he did."

"We *both* did," Rusty pointed out.

To Lee, I said, "We figured maybe we could borrow some bandages from you."

She turned to Slim. "All right if I take a look?"

"Sure." Slim unbuttoned her shirt, took it off, then turned around.

At the sight of her back, Lee pursed her lips.

"Most of that's from broken glass," I explained.

"You'd better come with me, Slim. We'll get you cleaned up and bandaged."

Looking a little embarrassed, Slim nodded.

"You guys wait here," Lee told us. "We won't be long."

We watched Slim and Lee leave the room. A couple of minutes later, water came on and rushed through the pipes.

Rusty met my eyes. "Sounds like somebody's taking a bath," he whispered.

"Or a shower."

"Who do you think it is?"

"Who do you think?"

A smile spreading across his cherubic face, Rusty said, "Wanta find out?" He started to rise from the sofa.

"Stay put," I said.

He stood up. "I know we can't *look*. As if they'd leave the *door* open. But maybe we can hear something."

"Forget it."

"Come on, man."

"Don't you think we've screwed up enough for one day?"

Looking disappointed in me, he said, "You're such a chicken."

"If you say so."

"Come on. It'll be cool."

"No."

"I tell you what. You wait here where it's nice and safe and *I'll* go listen."

"No you won't."

He lifted his eyebrows. In a quiet, taunting voice, he said, "Slim's probably *nude* in there, you know."

"Knock it off."

"Maybe Lee, too. Maybe she got in the shower with Slim to help wash her back."

I saw it in my mind. Rusty was obviously seeing it in his mind, too, and I didn't like that. I stepped up close to him— so close that our stomach's touched—and looked him in the eyes.

"Okay, okay," he muttered. "Forget it. Never mind." He backed away and sank onto the sofa.

After a while, I calmed down. I walked to the other side of the room and sat in an armchair.

We both sat in silence.

Rusty was careful not to look at me.

The water kept rushing through the pipes.

Chapter Twenty-two

When the water shut off, Rusty lifted his head and looked at me.

"What?" I asked.

"Nothing."

"What?"

"Nothing. You're not so pure, that's all. You're no purer than me, you're just scared of getting caught."

"Up yours."

"It's the truth."

"Shut up, okay? They might be able to hear us."

He closed his mouth and gave me a smug, knowing smile. He knew he was right, and I knew he wasn't far from wrong.

We didn't say anything else. After a while, we heard a door unlatch. Then came quiet footsteps and voices.

Lee saying, "I'll have to give him a try."

Slim saying, "I've got an extra copy of *The Temple of Gold* I can let you read."

"Great."

"I'll bring it over sometime."

Then they walked into the living room. Lee, dressed the same as before, was carrying my sneakers, Rusty's shirt, and a brown paper grocery bag with its top crumpled shut.

Slim, with nothing in her hands, had the clean, fresh look of someone who'd just taken a bath or shower. She wore clothes that must've belonged to Lee: a loose white T-shirt, red shorts, white crew socks and white sneakers. The T-shirt completely covered her shorts, but I could see through it enough to tell their color. I could also tell where bandages had been applied, and that she no longer wore her bikini top.

Her bikini and cut-off jeans were probably in the grocery bag Lee was carrying.

Evidently, Lee didn't own a bra in Slim's size.

When I realized I was staring at Slim's chest, I quickly turned my eyes to Lee. "How'd it go?" I asked.

"I think she'll live. But since she refuses to see a doctor, I guess she'll have to go stitchless."

"My cuts aren't that bad," Slim said.

"They aren't that *good*, either." Lee dropped the sneakers in front of my feet, stepped toward the sofa and tossed the shirt to Rusty.

While I put on my shoes and Rusty put on his shirt, Lee set the grocery sack on the coffee table. Then she sank onto the sofa beside Rusty, settled back against the cushion, swung her legs onto the coffee table and crossed her ankles. She sighed as if relieved to be off her feet.

Still fastening his buttons, Rusty turned his head and stared down at her.

Life was suddenly good again for him.

Lee glanced at him, smiled, then said to all of us, "The kitchen floor's gotta be dry by now. If anyone wants a Coke or something, feel free. I'm not moving, though. You'll have to help yourselves."

None of us spoke up.

Slim walked past me. She smelled like a strange, wonderful combination of lemons and marshmallows. Through the back of her T-shirt, I saw eight or ten bandages. She went to a wicker chair near the lamp table and sat down. Perched near the front of the seat, she folded her hands on her lap and kept her back straight.

Glancing from Slim to me, Lee asked, "So, all set for tonight?"

Slim hadn't told her about the dog?

"Not sure yet," I said.

"We're still working on it," said Rusty. He gave Slim a perplexed look.

Slim's shoulders moved slightly.

Rusty returned his gaze to Lee's slumped, lounging body. "Any ideas?" he asked her.

"Nothing spectacular. Anyway, I think you should work it out for yourselves."

Looking at me, Rusty said, "I can get permission to sleep over at your house. Your mom and dad still go to bed at ten?"

"Around then."

"So we wait till they hit the sack, then we sneak out."

"I don't know about sneaking out," I said.

"It'll work. It's always worked before."

I could've killed him for saying that in front of Lee.

She looked at me and lifted her eyebrows. She seemed amused and curious.

"We didn't do anything much," I told her.

"Hey, don't worry about it. I won't tell."

"I know."

"But I'd like to hear about it sometime."

"Sure."

"And I'll tell you about the times *I* used to sneak out at night."

"*I'd* like to hear that," Rusty said.

She lifted a hand off her belly, reached over and patted him on the leg.

His face went crimson.

143

Mine probably did, too.

"We'll see," she told him.

"If we have to sneak out of someone's house," I said to Rusty, "why not *yours?* Why does it always have to be *my* house?"

"I'm already invited for supper," he pointed out.

"What's that got to do with it?"

"I'll already *be* there."

"Right. So then I explain how you've asked me to spend the night at *your* place. And then we go over *there* after . . ."

"Just can't wait to see Bitsy again, huh?"

I grunted as if I'd been slugged in the stomach. "Oh yeah," I muttered.

"I'm sure she'd *love* to see you. . . ."

"Never mind."

"Here's how to work it," Slim suddenly said.

I gaped at her.

Rusty actually went, "Huh?"

"Dwight, you tell your parents you've been asked to spend the night at Rusty's house. Rusty, you tell yours that you're invited to stay at Dwight's. Then you both come over to *my* house."

Stunned again, I mumbled, "Your house?"

"It'll be perfect," she said.

I pictured the mess in her mother's bedroom.

"I don't get it," Rusty asked. "Why do we wanta go to your house?"

"We won't have to worry about sneaking out when it's time to leave."

"We won't?" I asked.

"We'll have the whole house to ourselves."

"Really?"

Smiling and nodding as if very pleased with herself, she said, "That's right."

"What about your mom?" I asked.

"She'll be gone. She's got a date tonight."

"What do you mean?" Rusty asked. He had a dumbfounded

look on his face as if he'd just woken up from a nap and couldn't figure out what was going on.

"A *date*, you know? With a *guy*."

"Tonight?" I asked. I was feeling slightly dumbfounded myself.

"Who's the lucky guy?" Lee asked.

Slim shrugged, this time using only one shoulder. "I don't know. She met him at Steerman's last night."

"You don't know his name?"

"Charlie something. From across the river. He lives over in Falcon Bay. Anyway, he's taking Mom out tonight in his cabin cruiser."

"He's got a *cabin cruiser?*" I asked.

"A thirty-foot Chris-craft."

"Holy shit!" Rusty blurted. Then he said, "Sorry, Mrs. Thompson."

Lee reached over and patted his thigh again. I wished she would stop doing that.

"Mom won't even be coming home at the end of her shift," Slim explained. "Charlie's meeting her at the restaurant. Then he's taking her out for a night on the river."

"How do *I* meet this guy?" Lee asked.

"Hey," I said.

She laughed.

Eyes on Slim, Rusty asked, "So when's your mom getting home?"

"I'm supposed to expect her when I see her." Slim tried to smile, but it didn't come off very well. "When she says that, I usually don't see her till the next day."

I tried not to look upset. "She leaves you alone all night?"

"Sometimes."

Why was this the first I'd heard about it?

"It's no big deal," she said. "I *am* sixteen."

"So am I, but . . . *I* wouldn't like it."

Slim met my eyes. "It's okay. Really."

"It's not *that* okay," Lee said. "If you ever feel like coming over here . . ."

"Thanks."

"Let me know the next time your mom's planning to pull an all-nighter, okay? You shouldn't have to stay alone like that."

"Anyway," Slim said, "it'll work out great for tonight. After supper, we can all hang out at my house till it's time to go. There won't be anyone around to stop us."

"Sounds great," Rusty said.

"Yeah," I said.

"Why don't you come over, too?" she asked Lee.

"Thanks, but I'll pass. I'll probably take a nice long nap after supper. Wouldn't want to fall asleep in the middle of the vampire show."

"If you change your mind . . ."

She shook her head. "Not me. But let's not have any hanky-panky over there. You really shouldn't be having boys in the house when your mom's not home."

"Yeah, but we won't do anything."

Looking at each of us, Lee said, "I want everyone to be on their best behavior, okay?"

"We will be," Slim said. She glanced from Rusty to me. "Won't we, guys?"

"Sure thing," said Rusty.

I nodded in agreement.

"Okay," Lee said. "So then just come on over here around ten, ten-thirty."

"We'll be here," Slim said.

Chapter Twenty-three

When we left Lee's house a couple of minutes later, Slim led the way. We hurried after her, but she managed to keep ahead of us until we reached the corner.

There, she turned around, faced us, and set her grocery bag

down on the sidewalk. "Can one of you give me a shirt?"

We must've looked perplexed.

"Come on, come on." She snapped her fingers. "Dwight, let me have yours."

"It's actually Rusty's."

"She can have it," Rusty said.

I took it off and handed it to her.

"Thanks."

"You're welcome," Rusty said.

As she slipped into the shirt, she said, "I don't mind much if you guys see me like that, but . . ." She shook her head. "Not everyone else in town." She started fastening the buttons. "Lee wouldn't let me put my own stuff back on after I showered. I wanted to at least put my swimsuit back on, but she said it's too dirty. Which it is. I'm probably better off not wearing it." Slim finished with the buttons. "All set."

"Almost," I said. "What happened to telling Lee about the dog?"

"Oh, that."

"Yeah."

She shrugged. "I don't know. I just didn't want to screw things up for you guys."

"All *right!*" Rusty blurted.

"I mean, it's pretty clear you've both got the hots to see Valeria in action."

"You betcha."

"I'm not so sure I do," I told her.

"Well, it's up to you. I just didn't want to be the one to ruin it. *I'm* still not going. But let's hang out at my place anyway, okay? Then when it's time to go you can just head over to Lee's without me. If you feel like it."

"She'll wonder why you didn't come," I said.

"Tell her I got a headache or something."

"The trots," Rusty suggested.

She scowled at him. "Not the trots, a headache."

"You got your period!"

Slim and I both blushed furiously.

"No," she said.

"Why not say it's your period?"

"Forget it."

"Can't go to vampire shows when you've got your period, you know. All that blood? Drive's 'em crazy and they come after you."

"Jeez," I muttered.

"It's the *truth*, man. It'd be like going into bear country or swimming in shark-infested waters."

Glaring at him, Slim said, "Get bent."

Rusty started to laugh.

Slim reached toward his face. Very quickly, she tucked down her middle finger, hooked it in place with the pad of her thumb, built up some force in her finger and let it go. It flicked upward, nail thumping Rusty's nose.

His eyes bulged. His face went red. His laughter stopped. Staggering backward, he cupped a hand over his nose.

"No more talk like that," she told him.

"Shit," he gasped.

"You never know when to quit," she said.

He blinked at her, his eyes red and watery.

I didn't feel sorry for him. And I was glad Slim had hurt him. Now, *both* of us had brought tears to Rusty's eyes.

He sniffled a few times. Then he muttered, "Now you've done it," and lowered his hand.

Bright red blood was running out of his nostrils and spilling over his upper lip.

"Oh, great," Slim muttered.

Rusty sniffed and licked the blood. "Happy?" He tipped back his head.

"You'd better lie down," I told him.

He stepped off the sidewalk and stretched out flat on some-one's front yard.

"You'll be all right in a minute," I said.

Slim squatted down beside him. Patting him on the chest, she said, "Too bad, sport. You can't go to a vampire show with a bloody nose. Drives 'em crazy. They'll come right after you and suck you dry."

"Screw you," he said.

Calmly, Slim reached toward his face, tucked down her middle finger and gave his nose another hard flick.

"OW! DAMN IT!"

"Be nice, Rusty, and these things won't befall you."

"Go to hell," he muttered.

Chuckling, Slim stood up. She said to me, "Poor Rusty, everybody's beating up on him."

"He likes it," I said. "He must."

"I do not," he said from the ground.

"Anyway," Slim said, "where're we going now?"

"My place?" I suggested. "We can hang out there till supper time. You're going to eat with us, aren't you? Dad's grilling burgers."

"Sure. But why don't I meet you there? I want to run home and change clothes."

She saw the look on my face.

"What?" she asked.

"Do you *have* to?"

She stared down at herself, holding her arms away from her sides, bending her knees, grimacing as if she'd just gotten up from a face-first fall into a mud puddle.

"You look fine," I said. She looked *great*, but I didn't want to push it.

"Yeah, well, I like to wear my own stuff. Anyway, it'll only take a few minutes." She started to turn away.

"No, wait," I said.

She faced me.

"Why don't you not go?"

She raised her eyebrows, put her head forward and spoke slowly as if talking to a goon. "I want my *own* clothes?" She lifted her voice at the end so it sounded like a question. "I want clothes that *fit?* And shorts that aren't *red?* And *something* to wear under them?"

"Okay," I said.

But I must've looked pained, because her mocking attitude changed to concern. "What is it?"

I shrugged.

Someone was sure to discover the mess in her mother's

bedroom, anyway, sooner or later. This might be a good time for Slim to find it. She would have no reason to suspect Rusty and me, especially if she went by herself so she couldn't see the looks on our faces or hear us say something stupid.

I should've told her, "Nothing's wrong. Go on ahead."

But I didn't want her to leave.

Before I could think of what to say, Rusty spoke up. "He's scared you'll get lost."

Slim met my eyes.

My eyes must've looked astonished, because I could hardly believe that Rusty had come up with an explanation that was so close to the truth.

Especially since I hadn't realized it, myself, until the words came out of him.

"I just think we oughta stick together," I said. "It's been a weird day, you know? We didn't know *where* you were, and . . . I don't want you to get lost again."

"I was never lost."

"But *we* didn't know where you were. We were afraid maybe *they'd* gotten their hands on you. . . ."

"And shoved a spear up your ass."

Just when I was starting to appreciate Rusty again, he had to say that.

Slim smirked down at him. "You didn't *know* about the spears then, moron."

"We assumed them."

Slim and I laughed. But then we looked at each other and I said, "Anyway, I've spent most of the day *worrying* about you, and we finally found you and now you want to go off by yourself."

"Just for a few minutes. . . ."

"What if they *are* after you?" I asked. "Somebody might've seen you run away. . . ."

"Even if they did, they don't know where I live."

"They might."

"They have *ways*," Rusty said from the ground.

"Bull."

"*Magic* ways."

"Yeah, right."

Rusty sniffed a couple of times, then took his hand away from his face. All around his mouth, he was smeared with blood. He looked as if he'd been eating someone raw. Smiling, he said, "Maybe they put the *dog* on your scent."

"It's dead."

"They put its *ghost* on you."

Slim looked uneasy for a moment. Then she smiled and said, "Good one."

"Maybe *you* should be the writer," I told him.

"Slim can write 'em. I'll be the idea man."

"Anyway," Slim said, "they can't possibly know where I live."

"What if they're watching us right now," I asked, "and they follow you home?"

She almost smirked, but not quite. Instead, she turned her head and looked over her shoulder.

"Maybe they're already *at* your house," Rusty added, kidding around.

"Yeah, right."

"Anything's possible," he said.

"Anything is *not* possible."

"What if they're *waiting* for you?"

I looked down at Rusty, impressed and a little annoyed. He'd just given a whole new meaning to the mess Slim would find in her mother's room. Now, instead of wondering about the mystery of it, she might figure the gang from Janks Field had paid a visit to her house.

"I'll take my chances," she told Rusty. "See you guys later." Again, she turned away.

Again, I said, "No, wait." Then I looked down at Rusty. "Get up. If she's going, we're going with her." To Slim, I said, "Is that okay?"

"Okay by me."

"How's the nose?" I asked Rusty.

"Hurts."

"Is it still bleeding?"

He sniffed a couple of times. "I donno. Maybe not."

"Come on. We're going with Slim."

151

Chapter Twenty-four

As we climbed the porch stairs, my stomach started to feel funny. Not indigestion funny, scared funny. I was nervous about Slim finding the spilled perfume and broken glass in her mother's room, but it wasn't just that. Dumb as it may seem, I half believed that Julian or some of his gang *might* be hiding in the house.

Because of Rusty's remarks.

Sometimes people say stuff that doesn't make any sense, but it gets to you anyway. This was one of those times.

I *knew* Slim's house was empty, but the fear wouldn't go away.

It didn't help matters, watching her open the screen door and front door without unlocking either of them.

Anybody might be in her house.

When I started to follow Slim through the doors, Rusty grabbed my arm. I frowned back at him.

"Maybe we should wait out here," he said.

"Huh?"

"Her *mother's* not home."

In the foyer, Slim turned around. "You're coming over tonight, aren't you? So what's the difference?"

"I thought tonight we'd sneak in the back way," Rusty explained. "We don't want your neighbors seeing us, do we?"

She made a face to show us what she thought of nosy neighbors. "If they don't like it, they can lump it."

"You're only gonna be a minute, right?" Rusty asked. "Why don't we just wait out here for you?"

"Don't you want to come in and wash up?" she asked him.

"Nah, I'm fine."

"You're a bloody mess," she said.

"That's okay."

"I think we should go in with her," I said, still worried for no good reason that she might have intruders.

Slim nodded. "Yeah, come on."

Leering at her, Rusty said, "If we come in, can we go upstairs?" Before she could answer, he added, "We've never seen your bedroom."

Her eyebrows lifted.

Rusty nudged me. "*You'd* like to see her bedroom, wouldn't you?"

Scowling, I shook my head.

"How about it?" he asked Slim. "Do we get to see your bedroom?"

"In your dreams." She whirled around and hurried toward the stairway. As she trotted up, she looked over her shoulder. "In or out, I don't care. But stay downstairs."

When she was gone, Rusty grinned at me.

"You jerk," I whispered. "What're you trying to pull?"

"Just playing it safe, you know? We don't wanta be around when she finds the surprise in her mom's room, do we?"

"I guess not."

"Outa sight, outa mind."

"Sure."

"No matter what, we act dumb."

"Right."

I hated the whole idea of being dishonest with Slim, but we'd already deceived her. If we tried to tell the truth now, we'd look like jerks.

Expecting Slim to shout at any moment, I gazed at the top of the stairs. So did Rusty. We stood side by side, watching and listening. Quiet sounds came from the second floor: footsteps, the creaking of a board, soft skids and bumps that might've been drawers opening and shutting.

Rusty leaned toward me. "She hasn't noticed it yet."

"Guess not."

"Maybe she won't."

Nodding, I whispered, "The smell might've dissipated."

He turned his head and frowned at me.

"Spread out and faded away," I explained.

"I know that. I'm not stupid."

"Hey, guys," Slim called. "You want to come up here a minute?" She sounded a little worried.

We glanced at each other. Rusty looked like a school kid ordered to the principal's office.

"Oh, man," he murmured.

I ran to the stairs and raced up them two at a time, Rusty pounding along behind me. At the top of the stairs, I *knew* I would see Slim down the hallway, standing in front of her mother's bedroom.

She wasn't there.

The hallway was empty.

"Slim?"

"Over here." Her voice had come from the left—the direction of both the bedrooms.

Heart thumping hard and fast, I hurried down the hallway, certain to find Slim inside her mother's bedroom.

The two doors were on opposite sides of the hallway.

As I neared them, I smelled the sweetness of the spilled perfume. Maybe the scent had dissipated, but it certainly hadn't vanished.

I turned toward the mother's door.

"Dwight?"

I spun around. Slim was in her own room. I hurried to her door and got there just before Rusty. We both stopped and gazed in.

Slim was standing beside her bed, a nervous look on her face. She was barefoot. She still wore Lee's red shorts, but she'd taken off the shirts and put on her own bikini top. The powder-blue one, a favorite of mine. The matching bottoms looked as if they been tossed onto her bed along with the two shirts she'd taken off.

"What's wrong?" I asked.

In a small voice as if she feared being overheard, she said, "Somebody's been in my room."

I shriveled inside. Before I could say anything, Rusty asked, "What do you mean?"

She turned sideways, raised a long, tanned arm and pointed a finger at her pillow.

On top of it lay a paperback book, wet and chewed and torn. Though the book looked as if it had been mauled by a vicious dog, its cover was intact enough for me to read the title.

Dracula.

My breath knocked out, I looked at Rusty. He looked at me. Then we both shook our heads.

Slim still had her eyes on the wreckage of *Dracula*, so I took a fast look at the paperbacks on her headboard. They were lined up neatly, just the same as when I'd seen them earlier. Then, however, *Dracula* had been among them.

"How the hell did *that* happen?" Rusty asked.

I almost blurted out, "*I* didn't do it," but I caught myself in time.

I'd looked at the books, but I hadn't touched them and certainly hadn't chewed on any of them.

Neither had Rusty. The books had been fine when I went looking for him and found him in the mother's room. After that, neither of us had been alone in the house.

Slim kept staring at the book.

"Did *you* do it?" Rusty asked.

"No!" I blurted.

"Not you. Slim."

"Huh? Me?" She looked at him. "Are you nuts?"

He shrugged. "I don't know. Did you?"

"No!"

"You had *time* to do it."

"I was changing my clothes."

"Didn't you *see* it?"

Slowly, she shook her head. "Not right away. It must've been like that, but . . . I got undressed over there." She nodded toward her dresser. "Then I came over here and tossed the stuff on the bed and that's when I noticed."

"That's when you yelled?" I asked.

She shook her head some more. "I put my top on first."

An image filled my mind of Slim standing there in just the

red shorts, breathing hard as she stared down at the decimated book, her breasts rising and falling.

"This is crazy," Rusty muttered. He looked worried.

Apparently, he didn't suspect me. Maybe he'd glanced into the room on our way out and seen that nothing was out of place.

To Slim, he said, "Are you sure you didn't do this, like to freak us out or something?"

One glance gave him all the answer he needed—and more.

"Slim wouldn't do that to a book," I said. "For *any* reason."

"That's right," she said.

"So if she didn't, who did?" Half grimacing, half smiling, he added, "Or *what?*"

Slim bent over slightly, reached down and picked up the book. "It's still wet." She lifted it close to her face and sniffed. "Smells like saliva."

"Human or dog?" I asked.

"Or vampire?" asked Rusty.

Slim scowled at him. "It's broad daylight."

"We'd better look around," I said. "Whoever did this might still be in the house."

"Or *whatever*," Rusty threw in.

Slim looked around as if confused about what to do with the book. Then she carried it across her room and dropped it into a wastebasket next to her desk. It hit the bottom with a ringing thump.

She pulled open a desk drawer and took out two knives. One was a hunting knife in a leather sheath. The other was a Boy Scout pocket knife. Not speaking a word, she brought the knives to us. She handed the hunting knife to me, the pocket knife to Rusty. Then she went to her closet, silently opened its door and stepped inside.

In the closet, most of Slim was out of sight.

She stepped backward with her straight, fiberglass bow in one hand and a quiver of arrows in the other.

Turning toward us, she slung the quiver over her back so the feathered ends of a dozen or more arrows jutted up behind her right shoulder. The strap angled downward from her shoulder to her left hip, passing between her breasts.

With both hands free, she planted a tip of her fiberglass bow against the floor. She pulled down at the top, used her leg for some extra leverage, bent the bow and slipped its string upward until its loop was secure in the nock.

Left hand on the grip, she raised the bow. Then she reached up over her shoulder with her right hand and slipped an arrow out of the quiver. She brought it down silently in front of her and fit its plastic nock onto the string.

At the end of the long, pale shaft was a steel head that looked as if it were made of razor blades.

"Watch my back," she whispered.

I drew the hunting knife out of its sheath. Rusty opened the blade of the pocket knife. We followed Slim out of the room.

Much of her back was hidden behind the quiver of arrows. The quiver was brown leather and nicely tooled. She'd won it by taking first place in a YWCA Fourth of July archery contest a couple of summers earlier. Most people hadn't expected a fourteen-year-old girl to win it, but I'd known she would.

Chapter Twenty-five

Just a week before the archery contest, we had hiked out to Janks Field for a secret practice session. It was the end of June, a hot and sunny afternoon. The desolate expanse of Janks Field, scattered with a million bits of broken glass, sparkled and glittered in the sunlight as if someone had sprinkled gems over its bare gray earth. Even with our sunglasses on, we had to squint as we walked onto the field. There wasn't so much as a hint of a breeze. The air felt heavy and dead. It smelled dead, too. Or something did.

"What's that *smell?*" I asked.

"Your butt," Rusty said.

"Something's dead," said Slim.

"Dwight's butt," Rusty explained.

"Huh-uh." Slim shook her head. She was thirteen that summer and calling herself Phoebe. "It's bodies."

"Dwight's . . ."

"I bet they never found 'em all," she said. "You know, the stiffs. The corpses. And you know what? It *always* smells like this."

"Does not," Rusty said. He would argue with a rock.

"Yeah, it does," Phoebe said. "I smell it every time we're here. It's just worse sometimes, like on really hot days."

"Bunk," Rusty said.

"I think she's right," I said.

"Oh, yeah, she's *always* right."

"Pretty much," I said.

Grinning, Phoebe said, "Right as rain."

"Where do you want to shoot?" I asked her.

"Here's fine."

I'd carried the target all the way from home. We'd constructed it that morning in my garage: a cardboard box stuffed with tightly wadded newspapers, an old *Life* magazine photo of Adolf Eichmann taped to one side.

I set the box down on a mound of dirt so that Eichmann's face was on the front and tilted upward at a slight angle.

Phoebe paced off fifty feet.

Rusty and I stood slightly behind her.

With her first arrow, she put out one of Eichmann's eyes and knocked the box askew.

That's when I knew she would win next week's archery contest.

She held fire while I straightened the box and came back.

Her second arrow poked through Eichmann's other eye. He looked as if his big, black-rimmed spectacles had come equipped with feathered shafts.

Though the impact had twisted the box, she managed to put her next arrow into Eichmann's nose.

Then someone called out, "Well, if it ain't Robin Hood and his merry fags."

Even before turning around, we recognized the voice.

Scotty Douglas.

When we did turn around, we saw that he wasn't alone. Scotty had his sidekicks with him: Tim Hancock and Andy "Smack" Malone.

Smack got the nickname because it was what he enjoyed doing to kids like us. But he was no worse than Scotty and Jim.

Sneering and smirking, the three guys swaggered toward us like desperados on their way to a gunfight.

Nobody had any guns, thank God.

Their empty hands dangled in front of them, thumbs hooked under their belts.

Slim had the bow.

Rusty and I appeared to be unarmed, but we both had knives in our pockets. So did Scotty's gang, probably. Except their knives were sure to be bigger than ours, and switchblades.

In big greasy hair, sideburns down to their jaws, black leather jackets, white T-shirts, blue jeans, wide leather belts and black motorcycle boots with buckles on the sides, they were a trio of Marlon Brandos from *The Wild One*, half-baked but scary.

Scotty and Tim were older than us by a couple of years, and Smack was at least a year older than them. Bigger, too. In spite of his hood costume, Smack looked like an eight year old balloon boy somebody'd pumped up till he was ready to burst. Hairy, though. His belly, bulging out between the bottom of his T-shirt and the belt of his low-hanging jeans, was extremely white and overgrown with curly black hair that got thicker near his belt.

Smack was in the same grade as his buddies because he'd gotten held back once or twice. He wasn't exactly a sharp tool. Neither were Scotty or Tim, for that matter.

Scotty raised his hands. "Don't shoot," he told Phoebe.

Though she lowered her bow, she kept an arrow nocked and her hand on it. "We were here first," she said.

"So what?" Scotty asked.

"So maybe you can go somewhere else till we're done."

"Maybe we don't wanta."

"Maybe we *like* it here," said Tim.

Grinning like a dope, Smack glanced at his two pals and said, "Anyways, she didn't use the magic word."

They laughed. Smack was such a card.

"Please," Phoebe said, even though she knew the magic word would work no magic on these three losers. We all knew that. We knew they wouldn't simply go away. Not until they'd had their "fun" with us, whatever that might be.

Scotty, Tim and Smack came to a halt about four or five paces away from us. They smiled as if they owned us.

Flanked by his buddies, Scotty asked, "Please what?"

"Please go away and leave us alone." Though she must've been shaking inside, she seemed very calm.

"What'll you give us if we do?" Scotty asked.

"What do you want?" Phoebe asked.

Pursing his lips, Scotty stroked his chin with his thumb and forefinger and frowned as if giving deep thought to the matter. "Wellllll," he said, "let me seeeee."

"You guys better leave us alone," Rusty said, a whine in his voice. "Dwight's dad's the police chief."

As if they didn't already know that.

"As if we give a shit," said Scotty. Fixing his eyes on me, he asked, "You gonna tell on us?"

"No," I said.

"That's what I thought."

Rusty glanced at his wristwatch. Then he looked surprised. "Oh, gosh, I have to get home."

"To your *mommy?"* Smack asked. He gave his pals a hopeful glance, and looked disappointed when they didn't laugh or even crack smiles over his wit.

"Go home if you want," Scotty said.

"Really? You mean it?"

"Sure. Go."

Trying again, Smack said, "You don't wanta keep your *mommy* waiting."

Rusty acted as if he hadn't heard that. To Scotty, he said, "You really gonna let us go?"

160

"Gonna let *you* go, fatso."

"Me?"

"You."

"What about *them?*"

"What about 'em?"

"You gonna let them go, too?"

"What's it to you?"

Lips twisting all crooked, Rusty said, "I don't know."

"You going or aren't you?" Scotty asked.

"I don't know."

"He don't know much," Smack said, and chuckled.

"I'll give you till three," Scotty said. "You're still here, you get what they get. One."

Rusty's mouth fell open. Appalled, he glanced at me, at Phoebe.

"Two."

He raised a hand and blurted, "Wait! Wait! What're you gonna do to *them?*"

"Whatever we want," said Tim.

"Three."

"WAIT!" Rusty cried out, tears coming to his eyes.

"Missed your chance, lard-ass."

"Did not! It was a *time-out!*"

"That's what you think."

Tim spoke again. "Missed your chance, porky."

Scared as I was—and I was straining not to mess my pants—it occurred to me as peculiar that these two skinny snakes were making cracks about Rusty's weight when their own pal, Smack, was about a ton heavier than Rusty. Showed how much they cared about their buddy.

Suddenly in tears, Rusty pleaded, "Gimme another chance. C'mon. Please? It ain't fair."

The three creeps thought *that* was funny. They laughed and glanced at each other and shook their heads.

I didn't find it very amusing.

"Let him go," I said.

Scotty smirked at me. "Gonna tell your *daddy* on us?"

"Just let him go, that's all."

To Rusty, he said, "You wanta leave?"

Sniffling and sobbing, Rusty nodded.

"Okay, you can leave."

"Th . . . thanks."

"But first you gotta suck my dick."

For half a second, I thought he was kidding. But then he unzipped his jeans. Walking toward Rusty, he reached into his fly and my stomach sort of dropped because this was getting worse than I'd ever thought and if they did perverted sex stuff to Rusty they'd do it to me and Phoebe, too, and then maybe they would have to kill us so we wouldn't tell on them.

About two steps away from Rusty, Scotty whipped out his tool and said, "Get on your knees and open wide," and Phoebe shot an arrow into his leg.

It punched through Scotty's jeans and thunked deep into the side of his right thigh. He squealed, jerked up his leg and grabbed near where the arrow had entered. On one foot, he twisted away and hopped a couple of times. Then he fell sideways. He landed hard on the ground and squealed some more as the pieces of broken bottles jabbed into him.

Instead of attacking us, Tim and Smack just stood there. They looked at Scotty, then at Phoebe, shock on their faces. They couldn't believe Mr. Tough Guy had gotten himself shot down. Especially they couldn't believe the shooting had been done by a skinny little tomboy with a bow and arrow.

Squirming on the ground and whimpering, Scotty cried out, "*Get her, guys! Get 'em all!*"

By then, Phoebe had another arrow on the string of her bow.

When Tim and Smack turned to her, she drew back the string to her chin and aimed at Tim's face.

Flinging his hands up in front of his face, he yelled, "No! Don't! I give!"

As she swept her weapon in Smack's direction, he gasped something like, *"Eeek!"* and threw both hands toward the sky.

"Get down," she told him.

"Huh?"

"Get down on the ground."

He looked as if he wanted to say something else. Then he shut his mouth and sank to his knees.

"All the way down," Phoebe said. "Lie down."

He eyed the ground in front of him. It glittered with bits and chunks of shattered bottles. Also, there were a couple of snake holes in the dirt. If he followed Phoebe's orders, he would have to lie down on them.

His sweaty face flushed a deeper shade of red than before. "Hey," he said. "C'mon. I didn't do nothing."

"Down," Phoebe said.

I don't know whether it was the razor sharp arrowhead a few inches in front of his nose or the look in Phoebe's eyes, but something convinced him to obey orders. Hands on the ground, he eased his trembling body down onto the dirt and broken glass and snake holes.

"Stay put," Phoebe told him. Then she turned toward Tim.

He cringed away from her.

"I want my arrow back," she said.

Tim looked down at Scotty curled on his side, the arrow jutting up from his leg. Scotty was quietly weeping, and not moving at all except to gasp for breath. Probably he didn't want to get cut up any worse by the glass he was lying on.

Wrinkling his nose, Tim faced Phoebe. "Your arrow?"

"That one right there."

"How'm I suppose to . . ."

"Jerk it out."

"But . . ."

Scotty spoke up. In a tight voice that seemed to vibrate with pain or rage, he said, "Touch the fuckin' arrow and I'll eat your heart."

"But . . ."

"I'll kill your mom and fuck your sister. I'll . . ."

Giving him a dirty look, Tim bent down and jerked out the arrow. Scotty screamed, clutched his wound and lay there twitching.

Phoebe uncocked her bow and slipped the arrow into her old, raggedy quiver.

Tim handed the other arrow to her. "Thanks," she said. She

waved it toward me and Rusty. The steel head looked as if it had been dipped in red paint. A couple of drops fell to the ground. "My lucky arrow," she said.

Not bothering to clean Scotty's blood off its tip, she swept the arrow over her shoulder and dropped it into her quiver.

"You lie down, too," she told Tim.

Without protest or hesitation, he stretched out on the ground.

To Rusty and me, Phoebe said, "I guess that's enough target practice for one day. Let's go home."

We went to the target first. I plucked the arrows out of Eichmann's eyes and nose and gave them to Phoebe. Then I picked up the cardboard box.

Scotty, Smack and Tim stayed on the ground.

We started walking away, Phoebe in the middle.

They stayed down.

When we were pretty far away but still within earshot, Phoebe stopped and turned around. She shouted, "*We won't tell if you don't!*"

They never did.

We never did.

In the woods after we got away from them, we laughed nervously, shook our heads, slapped each other on the back, and told Phoebe "Good going" and "Way to go" about a million times.

Then I saw she had tears in her eyes.

When I saw that, my own eyes went hot and wet.

I'm not really sure why either of us got weepy like that, but I suspect there were plenty of reasons. They had to do with fear and loyalty and bravery and cowardice and humiliation and pride. They also had to do, I think, with the joy of survival.

Pretty sure we didn't spill any tears over damages inflicted on Scotty or his pals.

After that time in Janks Field, by the way, they were no longer pals. They stayed away from each other, and *really* stayed away from me, Rusty and Phoebe.

They were so scared of Phoebe that they never even dared

to give us dirty looks. Many times, in the first few months after the incident, I saw each of them cross streets or start walking in the opposite direction just to avoid us—Scotty with a pretty good limp.

One week after her target practice in Janks Field, Phoebe won the Fourth of July archery contest (junior division) with a final, amazing shot that would've done Robin Hood proud.

She made the shot, of course, with her lucky arrow.

And won the hand-tooled leather quiver.

Chapter Twenty-six

On both sides of the quiver, I could see the powder blue strings of Slim's bikini top, her bandages and bare, tanned skin down to the waistband of Lee's red shorts.

I was half lost in how Slim looked from behind, half dwelling on the summer she won the quiver and pretty much paying no attention at all to anything else as I followed her to the door of her bedroom.

One step into the hallway, she stopped.

"What?" Rusty asked.

As if he didn't know.

Slim went, "Shhhh." Then she walked straight across the hallway and into her mother's bedroom. We went in after her, spread out, and stared at the mess we'd left behind. A puddle, prickly with broken glass, remained on top of the dresser. The carpet below the dresser now looked dry, but dangerous with shards from the demolished vase and perfume bottle. A few bright yellow rose petals lay among the remains as if they'd been blown there from somewhere else.

The flowers were gone.

For a moment, I thought that Rusty or I must've thrown them away.

Then I remembered that we hadn't touched them.

A chill crawled up the back of my neck.

Rusty and I glanced at each other.

He, too, had noticed the roses were gone.

"We better get outa here," he whispered.

Ignoring him, Slim stepped around the mess on the carpet and walked slowly through the room. We stayed with her. Since both her hands were busy with the bow and arrow, she stood by, ready to shoot, while I looked under the bed and Rusty opened the closet door. When she entered the master bathroom, I crept in behind her.

The bathroom held flowery scents.

No trace of the yellow roses, though.

And no trace of any intruders.

Turning around, Slim pointed her arrow away from me. Her eyes met mine. She gave me a quick, nervous smile. Then she came toward me and I backed out of the bathroom.

Rusty looked glad to see us.

For the next ten or fifteen minutes—or hour—we searched the house.

It was hard on the nerves.

In some ways, I felt major relief. Because of the *real* intruder, Slim would never have to know about our invasion of her home.

But the relief came with a large price.

Someone *else* had come into her house, roamed its silent rooms, stood beside Slim's bed while neatly slipping the paperback copy of *Dracula* out of her headboard and *chewing* the book. Someone had stolen into her mother's bedroom and made the yellow roses disappear.

Chewing the book seemed like the act of a madman.

Taking the roses seemed like something a woman might do. *Or the Frankenstein monster*, I suddenly thought, remembering Karloff's smile when the little girl gave him a flower.

As we crept through the house, upstairs and down, entering every room, opening every door, glancing under and behind furniture, checking everywhere large enough to conceal a person, I prayed that we would find no one.

I was a nervous wreck.

Not a moment went by that I didn't expect someone to jump out at us.

Julian Stryker, maybe. Or Valeria (though I'd never seen her). Or some of their black-shirted crew.

Maybe armed with spears.

I tried to convince myself that this was impossible, that they had no way of knowing where Slim lived, but it certainly *wasn't* impossible. There were many ways to learn such things.

By following us, for instance.

I gripped the knife tightly. My mouth was dry. My heart thudded. Sweat dripped down my face, fell off my ears and nose and chin, and glued the clothes to my skin. I felt as if a cry of terror was ready to explode from my chest.

But we found no one.

"I want to finish changing," Slim said when our search was done.

"We'll go with you," I told her.

If Rusty had said that, she would've answered with a crack. "In your dreams," maybe. But I'd said it, so she knew I wasn't being a wiseguy.

"Okay."

We followed her upstairs. In her bedroom, she dropped her bow and arrow onto her bed. Facing us, she said, "You guys can wait in the hall." Then she took off her quiver. Not paying much attention to what she was doing, she dragged the leather strap up against her left breast. It snagged the underside of her bikini and lifted the fabric. As the rising strap pushed at her breast, she realized what was happening, saw us watching, and quickly turned her back.

"In the hall," she reminded us. "Okay?"

"We're going, we're going," Rusty said.

I said, "I'll leave the door open a crack."

"Fine."

We hurried out of her room and I pulled the door almost shut.

Rusty quietly mouthed, "Did you see that?"

I gave him a dirty look.

He mouthed, "Oh, like you didn't look."

Speaking in a normal voice, I said, "Why don't you go to the bathroom and wash your blood off? I'll start cleaning up the glass."

He shook his head. "I'll help."

"You'll get blood on stuff."

He inspected his hands. They looked as if they'd been smeared with rust-colored paint. Palms up, he closed and opened his fingers. The stickiness made crackling sounds. "Maybe I better," he admitted. "But you've gotta come, too."

"You're not scared, are you?"

"Up yours," he said. He gave me the finger, then turned his back on me, marched to the bathroom at the end of the hall, and vanished through its doorway. A moment later, the door bumped shut. I heard a soft, ringing thump as Rusty locked it. Soon, water began running through the pipes.

I stood alone in the hallway.

And didn't like it.

Even though we had searched the house, we weren't necessarily safe. Separated like this, we could be picked off one at a time.

"Slim?" I asked.

"Yeah?" she said from inside her room.

"You okay?"

"Fine."

"You almost . . . ?"

She swung the door open so quickly it startled me. She grinned.

She now wore a clean white T-shirt and cut-off jeans and a pair of old tennis shoes that must've been white on a distant summer when she'd been Dagny or Phoebe or Zock. Through the thin cotton T-shirt, I could see her bikini top.

Stepping out of her room, she looked down the hall. "Rusty in the john?" she asked.

The water still ran.

"Yeah. He's washing up."

She nodded. "Thought so." Then she looked me in the eyes

and said, "I'm sure glad you guys are here. This stuff would've scared me silly if I'd been by myself."

"Are you kidding? Nothing scares you."

"*Everything* scares me."

"Yeah, sure. You're the bravest person I know."

A smile broke across her face. "That's what *you* think." She glanced toward the bathroom.

The door remained shut. The water still ran.

Tilting her head back slightly, she stared into my eyes.

Slim's eyes, pale blue in sunlight, were dark blue in the dimness of the hallway—the color of the summer sky at dusk. Intense, hopeful and nervous, they seemed to be searching for something in my eyes.

She had never stared at me quite that way before. I wondered what it meant.

What if she wants me to kiss her?

Could that be it? I wondered.

Do it and find out.

But maybe that *wasn't* what she wanted.

We kept gazing into each other's eyes. Soon, I was sure that she *did* want me to kiss her. She didn't just want it, she was *waiting* for it. Waiting for me to catch on and take her into my arms and put my lips on hers.

I wanted to do it, too. I *ached* to do it. I'd been longing to kiss her for so long, and now she was almost *begging* for my lips.

I couldn't force myself to move.

Do it! Come on! She wants me to!

I stood there like a lump—except that lumps don't sweat and tremble.

I felt more frightened than when we'd been searching the house, but this fear was mixed with desire for Slim and disgust with myself for being such a coward.

Just do it!

Making an excuse for myself, I thought, *If I try to kiss her now, Rusty might catch us.*

The water still ran.

What's taking him so long, anyway?

169

Then I thought, *Who cares if he sees us kiss? Just go ahead and do it. Do it now before she changes her mind. . . .*

A toilet flushed.

The sound of it came like a signal for Slim to shut down the power of her gaze. Whatever'd been going on, it was over. A mild smile lifted the corners of her mouth. With her eyes and smile, she seemed to be saying, "Oh, well. Missed our chance. Maybe next time."

At least that's what I think they were telling me. They might've been saying, "You dumb jerk, you missed your chance." But I don't think so.

Then she reached up and flicked my nose the same as she'd done to Rusty, but not as hard. Not nearly as hard.

Gently.

Then she said, "Want to help me pick up the glass?"

"Sure."

We turned and entered her mother's room.

Chapter Twenty-seven

We no sooner started picking up the pieces of broken glass than Slim said, "I'll get my wastebasket." She hurried off and came back quickly.

When she set it down, I dumped in a handful of glass and saw her ruined copy of *Dracula* at the bottom.

"Mom won't be too happy about this," Slim said.

"She doesn't get home till tomorrow?"

"Probably not." Frowning slightly, Slim started to gather shards from the dresser top.

"What if we clean all this up," I said, "and get rid of the smell and replace the broken stuff? She'll never have to find out anything happened."

"Is that what *you'd* do?" Slim asked.

170

I looked up at her.

"If it was *your* mom's stuff?"

"Maybe."

"You wouldn't, either." A grin spread across her face. "You're *way* too much of a Boy Scout for that."

"Think so, do you?"

"I know so."

I suddenly felt ashamed of myself for not living up to her ideas about me.

And I felt very glad she didn't know everything.

"Anyway," she said, "I don't think we'd get away with it. We'd have to find a matching vase and perfume bottle. . . ." She shook her head. "Even if we could lay our hands on exact matches, Mom would figure it out somehow. Then I'd be in trouble for trying to trick her." She dumped a handful of glass into the wastebasket. "Only thing is, it'll really scare her if she finds out somebody came in the house and did this stuff. It'd be nice if she *didn't* have to find out."

I dropped more glass into the wastebasket.

Slim continued to clean off the dresser top for a while. Then she blurted, "I've got it!" She grinned down at me. "How about this? First, forget about *Dracula*. She hasn't got a clue about what I read. All we have to do is get rid of the evidence. As for this mess . . . I was just being helpful. I came in to water her roses, seeing as how she was having an overnighter with her boyfriend, and had a little accident. Knocked the vase over. It hit the perfume bottle, broke the perfume bottle and *presto!*"

Somebody applauded.

I looked over my shoulder and found Rusty standing in the doorway, clapping his hands. "Bravo!" he said. "Good plan."

Slim obviously thought so, too. Beaming, she said, "Not bad, huh?"

"It's perfect," I said.

"You oughta be a writer," Rusty told her.

"Thank you, thank you, thank you." She might've performed a full bow if her hands hadn't been full of broken glass. All she did was duck her head.

171

I dumped more glass into the wastebasket, then said to Rusty, "Wanta give us a hand here?"

He started clapping again.

"Ha ha."

"Did I miss anything?" he asked.

I remembered the way Slim had stared into my eyes. Feeling myself blush, I said, "Not much."

"You almost missed your chance to help us clean this up," Slim told him.

"I tried."

"What'd you do in there," I asked, "take a bath?"

His face flushed scarlet. "I had to *go*, okay? Thanks for bringing it up."

Slim chuckled.

"Very funny," Rusty muttered.

"You like it so much in there," she said, "how about going back and getting us some paper towels? There should be a roll under the sink where the TP is. Maybe you can bring the whole thing."

"Sure." He hurried away.

Slim waited until his footsteps faded, then whispered, "Do you think Rusty had anything to do with this?"

I felt a blush coming on. Quickly, I asked, "What do you mean?"

"He's acting sort of funny."

"He is?" I hoped *I* wasn't.

"Like he feels guilty about something."

I shook my head. "I don't know. He seems okay to me."

"Do you think he might've done this stuff?"

"Why would he chew up your *book?*"

She shrugged. "It's *Dracula* and he's all excited about the Traveling Vampire Show? Maybe he thought it'd be a cool trick to play . . . freak us out."

"I don't know," I muttered. "I don't think so. Anyway, he was with me."

"Maybe he came in and did this on his way back from Janks Field. Before he went over to your place."

As I shrugged, I heard footsteps coming down the hallway.

172

We went silent, but we both looked at Rusty when he walked in.

"What?" he asked, handing the roll of paper towels to Slim.

"Thanks," she said.

"What's going on?"

"We were just trying to figure out how all this happened," Slim explained. She turned away, tore off some paper towels, wadded them up and started to mop the top of the dresser.

Rusty gave me an alarmed look.

I almost shook me head, but realized that Slim was facing the mirror and might see me.

"If none of us did this stuff," she said, "who did?"

"How about ghosts?" Rusty suggested. The playful tone of his voice sounded forced. "I mean, you've *gotta* have ghosts in this place, everything that's happened here."

She stopped cleaning and turned around. Frowning, she asked, "Like what?"

"You know."

"No I don't. What do you mean, 'everything that's happened here'?"

Rusty seemed shocked by her tone. It shocked me, too.

"Like with your dad and grandfather."

"You've gotta be dead to be a ghost," Slim said, her voice sharp.

"I know, but . . ."

"And Jimmy Drake isn't."

"I didn't say he is."

"You said his ghost . . ."

"He *might* be dead, right? I mean, he left town and you've never heard from him again. So he *could* be dead, couldn't he?"

Seeming calmer, Slim looked at Rusty with narrow eyes and said, "I guess so."

"Anyway," Rusty said, "it was just a thought."

"A lame thought," I told him, wishing he hadn't brought up the subject of Slim's father. "You don't even believe in ghosts."

"This just seems like the sort of thing a guy like Jimmy

173

Drake might do," Rusty explained. Then his eyes widened. In a hushed voice, he said, "Maybe he *was* here. Maybe he came back . . . you know, from wherever he went . . . and did this stuff."

Slim stared at him.

"In the flesh," Rusty said. "Not a ghost or anything, but *him*. What if he's *back?*"

"He's not," Slim said.

"How do you know?"

"If he came back, he wouldn't piddle around chomping on books and breaking a couple of things. It's not his style. They're just *things*. They're not people. They don't . . ." She turned away and resumed wiping the dresser top.

"I think it has something to do with the vampire show," I said—partly because that's what I really thought, partly to get the subject off Slim's father because I knew she didn't like being reminded of what he'd done to her and the others. "Maybe it's a warning."

Nodding, Rusty added, "To keep our mouths shut."

"I don't know," Slim muttered.

"What I think we should do," I said, "is finish cleaning this stuff up and then go over to my house. We can have supper there like we planned, but maybe we shouldn't come back here afterwards."

"*They* might be waiting for us," Rusty pointed out, smiling as if he thought it were a joke.

"Where *will* we go?" Slim asked.

"I don't know yet. We oughta think of a place where nobody'll be able to find us. But the main thing is, we should stay together from now on."

Slim turned around. Finally smiling, she raised her eyebrows. "From now on?"

"Cool," Rusty said.

"At least till the vampire show leaves town," I explained.

"What about tonight?" she asked. "I'm *not* going to the show. I'm not stepping foot in Janks Field till those creeps are long gone."

"Well *I'm* going," Rusty said. Eyes on Slim, he shook his

head. "I'm not gonna miss it just because *you're* a chicken."

"Hey," I said.

"Well, I'm not. We don't even know it was *them*. It might've been anyone."

"It isn't about this," Slim said. "It's about torturing and killing that poor dog."

"That poor dog went after you like a hunk of raw meat."

"Let's not start this again," I said. "Let's just finish and get outa here before something else happens."

It took about half an hour longer to complete the clean-up: vacuuming the carpet, wiping it with a damp sponge to take away some of the perfume, dumping the wastebasket in Slim's garbage can in the alley behind her house and throwing in some old newspapers to hide the book and bits of glass, then finally putting everything away.

Back upstairs after returning the wastebasket to her bedroom, Slim brushed her hands against the front of her cut-off jeans. "I guess that does it."

"Guess so," I agreed. "Anything you want to take with you?"

"Depends on what we'll be doing."

"Going to the vampire show," Rusty said.

"Maybe *you* are." To me, she said, "Anyway, I guess I'll just leave everything here for now. We can always come back and get stuff, depending on what we decide to do."

"Go the vampire show," Rusty repeated. This time, he grinned.

"Yeah, sure," Slim said.

Downstairs, we hid all the weapons on the floor behind the living room sofa where we could get to them quickly if we needed them.

"I'll be right back," she said. Leaving us there, she hurried toward the back of her house. She returned a couple of minutes later with an inch-long strip of Scotch tape sticking to her fingertip.

"What're you gonna do with that?" Rusty asked.

"Old Indian trick," she said, and ushered us out of the house.

Standing in the entryway, she pulled the front door shut. Then she squatted down and I realized what she was doing. Not exactly an "old Indian trick." More like a James Bond trick. She was sticking one end of the tape to the door's edge, the other end to the frame.

When she stepped away, I glanced down but couldn't quite see the transparent tape.

Neither would an intruder, more than likely.

Opening the door would either break the tape or pull it loose at one end or the other. Then we'd know that someone had entered Slim's house.

"Did the same to the kitchen door," she announced.

"Good idea," I said.

Smirking, Rusty said, "Why not balance buckets of water on top of the doors and *really* nail 'em."

She looked at him and raised her eyebrows.

I said, "Make it *holy* water."

"*There's* an idea," Slim said.

Rusty frowned. He didn't get it. So we both tried to explain to him about vampires and holy water while we crossed to the sidewalk and turned toward my house.

When we finished, he said, "I knew that."

Chapter Twenty-eight

Mom's car was gone from the driveway. The house seemed empty when we entered it, but I called out anyway and got no answer.

"She must've gone somewhere," I muttered. It seemed odd that Mom would leave the house this late in the afternoon.

"Maybe she went to the store," Slim suggested.

"Maybe." That didn't seem likely, since she'd done her grocery shopping that very morning. But maybe she'd forgotten to pick up buns or something, and decided to make a last-minute run.

On the kitchen table, I found a note in Mom's handwriting.

Honey,

Your father just called from the hospital. He has been hurt, but he tells me it is nothing to worry about. I am going to be with him. Don't know when I'll be back. Go ahead and eat without us. Burgers are in the fridge. I'll call when I can.

Try not to worry, your dad's fine.

Love,

Mom

Slim and Rusty watched in silence while I read the message a couple of times. It gave me a cold lump in my stomach. When I finished with it, I said, "My dad's in the hospital."

Slim winced. "What's wrong with him?"

Shaking my head, I handed the note to her. Rusty stepped up close beside her and they read it together.

"He can't be very bad," Slim said. "He was in good enough shape to phone your mom."

"But he can't be that good," Rusty said, "or he wouldn't be at the hospital."

Scowling, I shook my head.

Slim put down the note. "What do you want to do?"

"I don't know," I muttered.

"Want us to go away?" Rusty asked.

"No. Huh-uh." I pulled out a chair and sank onto it. "Why couldn't Mom tell me what's wrong with him?"

"She said he's fine," Slim pointed out.

"He can't be *fine*."

She picked up the note and stared at it for a while. "Your dad got hurt," she said, "but he's fine. That's what it says."

"Doesn't make any sense," I muttered.

" 'Got hurt,' " Slim said. "Your mom wouldn't have worded it that way if he'd had something like a heart attack. Sounds like maybe he had an accident."

"Or got shot," Rusty suggested.

Slim gave him a dirty look. "Whatever happened," she said, "it's nothing really serious but he does need some sort of treatment."

"Why couldn't she just *tell* me?" I blurted. "He must've told *her*."

"I don't know," Slim muttered.

"Maybe she thought it'd scare you," Rusty said.

"But it's not supposed to scare me *not* being told?"

Slim put her hand on my back. It made me feel better, but not a whole lot. "We don't have to wait for your mom to call. Why don't we phone police headquarters? I bet somebody there can tell us what happened."

I checked the kitchen clock.

"Dolly'll still be on duty," I said.

"So?" Slim asked.

I shook my head. Much as I hated the idea of talking to Dolly, I stood up and headed for the wall phone.

Rusty met my eyes. He looked as if he were in pain, himself. "Or you could call the hospital," he said.

"How do we know which one?" Slim asked.

While the town of Grandville had a hospital of its own, the county hospital over in Clarksburg was better equipped for major emergencies. In nearby Bixton was a Catholic hospital staffed mostly by nuns. People from our area could end up in any one of them, depending on one thing or another.

"Start with the nearest," Rusty suggested.

"Easier to ask Dolly," Slim said.

We hadn't gotten around to telling her about our run-in with the vicious little dispatcher. Under the circumstances, however, I figured Dolly would be sympathetic. Even if she couldn't stand me, she liked my dad. For good reason; anyone else would've fired her a long time ago.

"Guess I'll call her," I said.

Just as I reached for the phone, it rang. I jumped and jerked my hand back, my heart pounding like mad.

Before the second ring, I snatched the phone off its hook. Hardly able to breathe, I said, "Hello?"

"Dwight?"

It was a mother, but not mine. And she didn't sound happy.

"Is Russell there?"

"Yeah. Yes. He's right here."

"Please send him home right away."

"Would you like to talk to him?"

Teeth bared, Rusty put up his hands and shook his head.

"I'll talk to him when he gets here. As for you, young man, I must say I'm terribly disappointed in you."

I felt my own lips peel back. My stomach suddenly felt even worse than before.

"I'm sorry," I said.

"You ought to be. Elizabeth has always been very fond of you."

"I'm fond of her, too."

"You have a strange way of showing it."

"I'm sorry," I muttered.

"Send Russell home immediately, please." With that, she hung up.

Rusty and I stared at each other.

"You're supposed to go home right away," I said.

"Shit."

"Bitsy must've told on us."

"Told you she would, man. Shit. The little bitch."

"Hey," Slim said.

"Well, she is. I knew she'd spill her guts."

"What'd you guys do to her?"

"We sort of ditched her," I said. "She wanted to go with us to look for you. We tried to talk her out of it, but she wouldn't take no for an answer."

"Always has to have her own way, or she goes crying to mommy, the little twat."

Slim scowled at him. "Quit it."

"Anyway," I said, "I finally said she could come with us but she had to put shoes on. So when she went into the house for her shoes, we took off."

"That wasn't very nice," Slim said.

"I know. But she was being a pest. And anyway, it was for

her own good. I mean, we were heading for Janks Field. Do *you* think we should've taken Bitsy to Janks Field?"

"You've got a point."

"So now we're neck-deep in shit," Rusty said.

"You'd better get going," I told him.

"What about you guys?" he asked.

I shook my head.

"We'll stay here," Slim said, "and try to find out what's going on with the chief."

"What about tonight?"

"You worried about the goddamn vampire show?" Slim blasted him. "Dwight's *dad's* in the hospital, you cretin! Get outa here!"

She hurried ahead of him and opened the kitchen door.

Watching me over his shoulder as he walked toward the door, Rusty said, "We'll still try'n make it, though, right? I mean, if your dad's okay and everything?"

I just shrugged and shook my head.

"I'll call you," he said.

Then Slim shut the door behind him and we were alone. Our eyes met.

We'd both had it drilled into our minds that, unless an adult was present, we should never be in a house with a member of the opposite sex.

It had been different when Rusty was with us. Now he was gone. We were suddenly free to do *anything*, and I'm sure we both knew it.

Knew it, and felt embarrassed by the knowledge.

Slim shrugged and said, "Do you want to call Dolly?"

"I guess I could." I stepped over to the phone. And stared at it. And kept staring.

I didn't want to make the call.

Not because of Dolly, but because of what she might say about my father.

In a soft voice, Slim asked from behind me, "Are you okay?"

"Yeah, but I don't know. Maybe I'd better wait for Mom's call."

"She might not call for an hour or two."

"I know, but . . . maybe I'd better wait."

"Want *me* to call Dolly and see what's going on?"

"No, that's okay."

"Are you sure? I'll do it if . . ."

The phone rang. Its sudden jangle made me flinch. My insides cringed.

I grabbed the handset. "Hello?"

"Honey, it's me."

Mom.

I shriveled.

"Did you see my note?"

"Yeah."

Tell me!

"I would've called sooner, but people were using the phones. And then I *did* call, but our line was busy."

"How's Dad?"

"Oh, he's fine. He said to say hello."

"Well, what happened?"

"He had a little accident in his patrol car, honey. A dog ran out in front of him. You know how your father is about animals. He swerved to miss it, and everything would've been fine except his front tire picked that moment to blow out. So then he lost control of the car and smacked into a tree."

"Hard?" I asked.

"Hard enough," Mom said. "You know how your father feels about seat belts."

According to Dad, only sissies wore them. It seemed like a strange attitude for a chief of police, but he'd grown up in the Great Depression, fought in World War Two. . . .

"How *is* he?" I asked.

"Well, he broke his left arm and cracked a few ribs. He also hit his head on the windshield hard enough to break it. The windshield, not his head." She laughed, but it sounded a little tense. "You know how hard your father's head is. Anyway, he apparently *was* knocked unconscious for a while. But then he came to and drove himself over to County General."

"Why County General?" I asked.

"Well, he feels it's better equipped, and he was almost as close to it as . . ."

"Where was he?"

"Out on Route 3."

On Route 3 and a dog ran out in front of his car?

A chill scurried up my back and the skin on the nape of my neck stiffened with goosebumps.

"Anyway," Mom said, "he's fine, but they're going to keep him overnight."

"What for?"

"Just as a precaution. Because of the head injury, mostly. They want to keep an eye on him till morning."

"Oh. Okay."

"Anywhoooo, I thought I'd like to stay here at the hospital with him."

"All night?" I asked.

"I don't *have* to stay. . . ."

"No, it's fine."

"If you'd rather not stay by yourself, I could come home."

"No, you don't have to do that."

"Or I'm sure you could spend the night with Rusty or one of your brothers."

"Danny's out of town."

"Well, Lee's home. Or go over to Stu's."

"I'll be okay here," I said.

"That's fine. You're certainly old enough to stay by yourself. There's ground beef in the fridge. You can make yourself a hamburger if you want. We were going to grill them on the barbecue tonight. . . ." Her voice trembled and stopped and I knew she was weeping. After a while, she sniffed and said, "If you'd rather get take-out, there's money in the drawer. . . ."

"I'll be fine," I said. "Don't worry about me. Tell Dad hi for me, okay?"

"I will, darling. Oh, he said I should let you know that he missed the dog."

"He should've hit the dog and missed the tree," I said.

I heard Mom laugh softly. "I'll tell him that. And I'll give him your love."

"Thanks."

"Anything else before we hang up?"

"Not that I can think of."

"Okay then, honey. You can call us here if anything comes up." She gave me the hospital's phone number and Dad's room number. Then she said, "I guess that's about it for now."

"Guess so."

"Okay, we'll see you in the morning."

"See you then," I said.

"Be good."'

"I will."

"Bye."

"Bye," I said, and hang up.

Chapter Twenty-nine

So he's pretty much all right?" Slim asked when I turned around. Nodding, I realized she'd heard only my side of the conversation. I wasn't sure what she knew and what she didn't. So I explained, "They're keeping him overnight because he hit his head, but . . . other than that, he broke his arm and cracked some ribs."

"But his head'll be all right?"

"They think so."

"He missed a dog and hit a tree?"

I smiled. It must've looked strange, because it brought a frown to Slim's face. "He was out on Route 3," I explained, "and a dog ran out in front of his car."

Slim made a face as if she were smelling something horrible but amusing. "A *one-eyed* dog?" she asked.

"I didn't ask."

"Woo."

"Yeah."

"When did this happen?"

"I don't think it was *that* long ago."

"*Our* dog's been dead since about noon."

"Yeah." I shook my head. "Had to be a different dog."

"Maybe the one that chewed up my *Dracula*."

"The very same," I said.

She grimaced.

I grimaced.

"Maybe we've got *ghost* dogs," she said.

"Or someone wants us to *think* so," I said, which got her laughing. "Anyway," I continued, "it wasn't a ghost *or* a dog that chewed up your *Dracula*."

"Are you *sure?*"

"Pretty sure. For one thing, there's no such thing as ghosts."

"Are you *sure?*"

She was seeming very playful.

"Pretty sure."

"Don't be."

"Anyway, if there *are* ghosts, they can't *bite* stuff. They don't have any . . ."

"Teeth?" she asked.

Grinning, I shook my head. "That's not what . . . I mean, they're just . . . like *spirits*. They don't have *substance*."

"A matter of opinion."

"Anyway, ghost or not, a dog would've had to paw the *Dracula* off your bookshelf. Or bite it out. Either way, it would've messed up your other books. But they were all in a neat row. That could only be done by a human."

"Or a vampire," she added, "speaking on behalf of our absent Russell."

I laughed. "Daylight," I reminded her.

Her smile evaporated. "Which leaves us with humans. I'm glad we're out of my house."

"My mom isn't coming home till tomorrow morning, so I guess there's no reason you can't stay here."

"No reason you can't go to the vampire show tonight, either."

"I don't know."

"You don't want to miss that."

"I might."

"Oh? You'd rather stay home and watch television?"

"Maybe. If you'll be here."

"I'll be here unless you throw me out, I guess."

"I wouldn't throw you out."

"What about Rusty?" she asked.

"What about him?"

"He *really* wants to see that show."

"He's probably grounded."

"He'll find a way to get out."

"Maybe."

"He will. And then he'll show up here, all rarin' to go."

"I almost hope he doesn't," I said.

We suddenly ran out of words, so we stared at each other. Again, we both seemed awfully aware of being together in an empty house. Nobody to see us. Nobody to tell on us. Nobody to stop us.

We were only a few feet apart. A couple of steps forward and I'd be close enough to put my arms around her, pull her up against me, kiss her . . .

I couldn't move.

She wasn't moving either, just gazing into my eyes. She looked solemn and hopeful.

I ached to take those steps and hug her, feel her body against mine, feel her lips. . . .

A smile broke across her face and she said, "Maybe we'd better eat."

Saved! But disappointed.

"Good idea," I said. "Cheeseburgers sound okay?"

"Cheeseburgers sound great."

"We can do 'em outside on the grill."

"Why don't you get the fire started and I'll make the patties?"

"Great."

I hurried to the refrigerator, found the package of ground chuck, and gave it to Slim.

"How many you want?" she asked.

185

"I don't know, how many do *you* want?"

"I haven't thought about it."

"Do you make 'em thick or thin?" I asked.

"Thin's better. I don't like them raw in the middle."

"Me either. So if you're making them thin, I'll have two."

"Okie-doke. Maybe I'll have two, too."

We both smiled like idiots.

Slim set the package of meat down on the counter, then stepped over to the sink and started to wash her hands. I watched her standing there, bent over slightly, the bottom of her T-shirt hanging crooked across the rear of her cut-off jeans. Her rump filled the seat of her jeans. A fringe of threads brushed against the backs of her thighs. Her legs were smooth and tanned all the way down to her ankles.

She looked over her shoulder. "What?" she asked.

"Nothing."

She smiled. "Nothing, huh?"

"Just looking," I said, and blushed.

We had another of those staring contests where I wanted to go to Slim, but was afraid to, and she looked as if maybe she hoped I would come over and kiss her.

This time, it didn't go on very long before she said, "Maybe you'd better go out and start the fire."

"Yeah, guess so. Back in a while." I hurried outside.

Nowadays, most people have grills that run on propane. It's easy to use and doesn't pollute the environment (God perserve us from the fumes of backyard barbecues!) When I was growing up, however, we never had a propane grill. We never had charcoal lighting fluid, either. Dad claimed the fuel odor gave food a bad taste, but I'm pretty sure he was just trying to protect my brothers and I from the scourge of doing something "the easy way." So while every other family in Grandville started their barbecue fires by squirting fuel on the briquettes, we had to build ours the "natural way," like Boy Scouts on a campout, by crumpling paper, piling on the kindling, then adding the briquettes on top.

At least he allowed us to use matches. Could've been worse.

Usually, I resented that we weren't allowed to use fuel. Tonight, though, I welcomed the distraction of building a fire the hard way.

For one thing, it kept my mind occupied so it wouldn't dwell too much on Dad's accident . . . or on the murdered dog . . . or on the chewed book or the missing yellow roses . . . or on my betrayal of Bitsy . . . or on the Traveling Vampire Show. . . .

Also, it kept me out of the kitchen.

I was glad to be outside in the murky afternoon, watching flames lick at my sticks and briquettes, with Slim safely out of sight.

Alone with my fire, I missed her and longed to be with her—but I felt a wonderful sense of relief. At least for a while, there was no need to worry about how to act with Slim in a house without adults.

It remained in my mind, along with all my other concerns, but didn't overwhelm me because my main thoughts were focused on adding sticks and briquettes to the fire.

I jumped a little when the screen door banged shut.

Slim came trotting down the back steps with a bottle in each hand.

They weren't bottles of soda pop.

"You think your parents'll mind if we drink up some of their beer?"

If she'd been Rusty, I would've blown my stack.

But she was Slim, and she looked so good, and she had that smile.

"They'll just kill us is all," I said, smiling.

"Never fear. My mom drinks the same brand. We can replace these with some of hers."

"Then *she'll* have missing bottles."

"She's keeps a zillion of them around. She'll never know the difference."

"We will," I said. I must've said it funny.

Slim laughed and said, "Gad-zooks, I hope so."

187

Chapter Thirty

We sat on the stairs outside the back door and sipped our beers. We were side by side, so we didn't have to worry about staring at each other. We could look straight forward at the lawn or grill, or down at the beer bottles we were holding, or somewhere else.

When we first sat down, there were a couple of inches between us. As we talked and sipped, they disappeared somehow, through no fault of mine. I didn't move, so Slim must've. Before you know it, her upper right arm was touching my upper left arm.

I tried not to think too much about it, but I couldn't quit thinking about it.

Even though Slim and I had been best friends for all those years and done so much together, it was almost as if we were on a first date. Everything about her seemed new and wonderful and scary.

When our bottles were about half-empty, Slim said, "Think the charcoal's ready?"

I considered jumping up to check, but that would've broken the contact between our arms. We might not be able to get our positions just the same when I came back.

"I'd give it another ten minutes or so," I said.

She nodded, sighed, took another sip of beer, then said, "I'm not in any hurry."

"Me neither."

"It's kind of nice, just sitting here."

"Yeah."

"Just the two of us," she added.

My heart started pounding like mad. Afraid to look at her, I stared toward the barbecue grill and nodded.

"Not that I've got anything against Rusty," she said.

I managed to laugh. "You don't?"

"He's okay."

"For a pain in the butt."

This time, she laughed. Then she said, "What really bugs me is that he's always around. I know he's your best friend and all, but . . ."

I was tempted to turn my head toward her, but I stopped myself. "But what?" I asked.

"Sometimes I just wish he'd take a long walk off a short pier, that's all."

"Same here."

In a low voice, she said, "Thing is, it'd be nice if just the *two* of us could do stuff sometimes."

Now I *had* to turn my head. Looking her in the eyes, I asked, "Really?"

"Yeah. Not that I want to hurt his feelings or anything."

Our faces were so close together that her eyes made tiny jerking movements from left to right as if she couldn't make up her mind about which of my eyes to look at. I could smell a sweet warm scent of beer on her breath.

"Just that I sort of like being alone with you," she said. "Like now."

"Same here," I whispered.

Then Slim reached down between her legs and set the beer bottle on the next lower step. Turning herself sideways, she put her arm around my back. I set down my bottle. When I turned, my knee pushed against her knee. We both leaned toward each other and put our arms around each other and kissed.

Her lips were cool from the beer, and soft, and *hers*. I'd kissed girls before. A few times, anyway. In fact, I'd kissed Slim before, at least on the cheek a couple of times when she was going away on trips with her mom. But there'd never been another kiss like this one.

The way Slim kissed me, I figured she must be in love with me just the same as I was in love with her. She hugged me so hard it hurt. I took it easy on her, though, because I could feel the bandages under her shirt.

The kiss went on and on. I felt as if I were sinking into Slim. I was in her and she was in me. I had her breath in my mouth and in my throat and in my lungs. I had the tips of her breasts touching me softly through our clothes. I wanted it to go on forever.

Way too soon, she loosened her hold on me. Her lips moved away from mine. Her breasts stopped touching me. But she remained so close that our noses almost touched, and she stared into my eyes.

I stared back into hers.

This time, the staring didn't make me nervous. This time, it just felt good.

After a while, she tilted her head sideways and kissed me again. This time, her lips barely touched mine before she took them away. "You're all spitty," she whispered. She eased away from me, but not very far. She was wet around the mouth herself, and a little bit red. Smiling softly, she leaned toward me again. She stretched out the neck of her T-shirt and rubbed it across my mouth. Then she moved back and wiped her own mouth in the same place. "Kissing can be messy, huh?" she asked.

I opened my mouth. For a moment, I thought I might've forgotten how to talk. But I managed to say, "Guess so."

"Think the fire's ready yet?"

"Maybe. I'll be right back."

Leaving my beer on the step, I stood up and started toward the grill. As I walked, I could feel a slippery wetness in the lining of the swimming trunks that I wore under my jeans. It dismayed me. I mean, we'd just been kissing. It had been the most wonderful kiss of my life. It had been overwhelming, but sweet and pure, not sexual. At least that's what I'd thought while it was happening. I hadn't had a hard-on—at least I didn't think so—and I certainly hadn't ejaculated.

I'd sure leaked, though.

A hot, sick feeling flooded through me.

While I still had my back to Slim, I glanced down. The

front of my jeans was safely hidden by the hanging front of my shirt. Rusty's shirt, actually.

Vastly relieved, I looked down at the fire. The paper and kindling had burnt away, but the charcoal briquettes were just about right: the gray had almost reached their black centers.

"Looks ready," I called to Slim.

"I'll get the burgers." She took another swig of beer, then reached down again and set her bottle on the step. Standing up, she plucked at the legs of her cut-offs. Then she turned around and rushed up the stairs. At the top, she swung open the screen door. She vanished into the kitchen.

I waited for the door to bang shut. My back to the house, I looked down and pulled aside the front of my shirttail.

No wet spot on my jeans.

One less thing to worry about.

Pretty soon, the kitchen door swung open and Slim came out with a platter of burgers in her hands. Though her hair wasn't much longer than mine, a wispy flap of it draping her forehead and the fringe around her ears bounced as she trotted down the back stairs. So did her bikini top. I could see it jouncing up and down ever so slightly through the front of her T-shirt. The crew neck of her T-shirt drooped a little to the right from when she'd pulled at it to wipe off our mouths.

"I put salt and pepper on them," Slim said as she came toward me. "Also, I found the buns."

"Good deal," I said.

While she held the platter, I removed the patties one at a time. They felt cold and greasy in my fingers, and sizzled when they hit the grill.

I looked at my hands. "Guess I'd better wash."

"You could've used this." Slim reached behind her back. Her hand returned holding a spatula, which must've come from a back pocket.

"*Now* you tell me."

She grinned. "Go ahead and wash up. I'll watch the burgers."

"Right back," I said. Taking the platter with me, I ran to the house. I set it on the counter next to the buns. The buns were already on another plate, open and slathered on both sides with mayonnaise.

Slim knew what we liked.

I hurried over to the sink. When I tried to wash my hands, I found that cold water wouldn't take off the grease. I had to use hot water and soap.

Through the window in front of my face, I could see Slim standing by the barbecue. Pale smoke was rising in front of her and drifting away on the breeze. She was frowning slightly. I couldn't tell whether she was worried about something or just thinking hard. Maybe she was concentrating on the burger patties, trying to judge when to turn them over. She had the spatula ready in her right hand, but wasn't using it yet. Her left arm hung by her side. She stood with her left leg stiff, all her weight on it, that side of her rump sort of pushing out against the seat of her cut-offs.

I might've kept staring at her forever, but the water burnt my hands. I gasped and jerked them out from under the faucet. They were stinging, so I let cold water run on them for a while. Then I dried them on the dish towel.

Slim was a big fan of cheeseburgers. So was I, for that matter. So I hurried to the fridge and took out our Velveeta. Carrying it to the counter and unwrapping it, I found myself remembering the Velveeta at Rusty's house. And his mother's bridge club. And Bitsy catching us. And how we'd run away from her.

Life had seemed wonderful for the past few minutes, but now I started feeling a little rotten again.

In my mind, I saw the eagerness on Bitsy's face when she thought we'd be taking her with us.

Then I heard Rusty's mother. *Elizabeth has always been very fond of you.*

I found our cheese slicer in a drawer.

I must say I'm terribly disappointed in you.

I pushed the tight wire of the slicer down through the block of Velveeta. When I had four slabs, each about half an inch thick, I put them on the plate with the buns. Then I picked up the plate and hurried outside.

Slim watched me trot down the stairs. She still had that frown on her face. As I neared her, she smiled. "Velveeta," she said.

"Yep."

"Just a sec."

Fire was leaping around the patties, fueled by their dripping grease. Slim had already flipped them over. Their upturned sides were brown and glistening, striped with black indentations from the grill. They sizzled and crackled and smelled delicious. As I watched, Slim pressed down on each of them with the spatula, squeezing them flatter, making juices spill out their sides. Each time she mashed one, the fire underneath it went crazy.

After pressing all four of them, she switched the spatula to her left hand. With her right, she picked up the slabs of Velveeta. She laid them out, one on top of each patty.

Until she came to the fourth slab of Velveeta.

She gave me a quick grin. "This'll be mine," she said, and took a bite. A blissful look on her face, she started to put the remaining three-quarters of the slice on the fourth patty. Instead of letting it go, however, she brought it quickly back to her mouth and snapped off another quarter of it. "Gotta even up the sides," she said through her mouthful. Then, reaching through the smoke and flames, she neatly set the remaining strip in the center of the patty.

By then, the cheese on the other burgers was starting to melt. "These are going to be great," Slim said.

"Yeah."

"But you know what?"

"What?" I asked.

"I've been thinking about Rusty."

"Uh."

"He really wants to see the Vampire Show."

"Yeah, I know."

"I've been thinking, it might not be so easy for him to get out of his house tonight. They probably won't *let* him out, and he won't be able to *sneak* out in time if they're keeping an eye on him."

193

"Maybe it's just as well," I said. "It might be better if we *all* miss it."

"He really has his heart set on it, though."

"Yeah, I know."

"He'd be so disappointed," Slim said, and looked at the grill. Melted Velveeta was starting to spill down the sides of the patties and drip into the flames. "Uh-oh." Quickly, she stabbed the spatula underneath one of the burgers, lifted it off the grill and slid it onto a bun.

"Should we go to Rusty's rescue?" I asked.

"I think we'd better." Slim scooped off another burger.

"I thought you liked it better without him around," I said.

"I do," she said. She flashed me a sly smile, then transferred another burger from the grill to a bun. "But he's still our friend."

"Yeah."

"More appreciated in his absence than in his presence. . . ."

I laughed.

She took off the last burger, the one with half as much Velveeta. "This one's yours," she said.

"Okay."

"I'm kidding," she said. "It's . . ."

"No, really, I'll take it. I'd *rather* have that one."

She laughed softly and shook her head. "If you want it that much, you can have it." She set the top of the bun in place and pressed it down with her open hand. "She's all yours."

Chapter Thirty-one

The sun normally would've been blazing in our eyes at this time of the evening, but it couldn't get through the heavy clouds. Though the air felt muggy, a breeze came along every so often. A warm breeze. It felt pretty good, anyway.

We sat at the picnic table near the back of the lawn. It was painted green and had benches along both the long sides. Slim and I sat across from each other.

The cheeseburgers tasted great but they were very messy to eat. Juices and Velveeta dripped off their sides, ran down our chins, dribbled down our hands and fell onto the table. After just a few bites, I ran into the house to get napkins.

We'd finished our beers and needed something to drink with our burgers. So I went to the fridge. I half intended to grab a couple more beer bottles, but couldn't bring myself to do it. I took out a couple of Pepsis instead.

Then I hurried outside.

Watching me, Slim said, "Ah, Pepsi."

"If you'd rather have more beer . . ."

She shook her head. "This is just what I wanted."

I put the cans on the table, gave Slim a couple of napkins, then sat down.

"Anyway," she said, "we don't want Rusty's parents to smell beer on our breath."

"Why are they *gonna* smell beer on our breath?"

She gave me a whimsical, tilted smile. "We drank beer."

"I know that, but . . ."

"And we're going over to Rusty's house when we get done eating."

"We are?"

"We want to rescue him, don't we?"

"I guess so."

"Well, we can't exactly go in and kick butts, you know? I mean, this is Rusty's family."

"Right."

Her smile spread. "What we've got to do is *kiss* butts."

When she said that, I suddenly remembered the wager about Valeria. Rusty had suggested that the loser would have to kiss Slim's butt. And I'd imagined myself doing it. I imagined it now, too, and my face went red.

"That's a figure of speech," Slim pointed out.

"I know."

"Anyway," she said, "if we were *literally* going to kiss their butts, we wouldn't need to worry about beer on our breath."

"We'd have *bigger* worries."

We both had a pretty good laugh, and then we went on eating. When we were done, we carried everything into the house and cleaned up. Slim washed the spatula, knife and platter. I dried them and put them away. Soon, every trace of our supper was gone except for the two empty beer bottles.

"What'll we do with those?" I asked.

"Find a sack. We'll take them over to my place. We'll put them with my mom's empties, then grab a couple of fresh ones and bring them back here."

I grinned. "Good plan."

"Elementary, my dear Thompson."

My dear.

She only said it to make a play on Sherlock Holmes, but the words gave me a warm feeling, anyway.

"We'd better take care of that, first," she said. "Get it out of the way before we try to liberate Rusty."

I found a grocery sack. The brown paper kind. (This was before anyone came up with the notion of "saving the trees" by providing plastic grocery bags—which now *decorate* the trees and fences and streets and rivers and never go away.) Mom used the grocery bags to line our wastebaskets and sometimes to wrap packages for mailing. So she had a good collection of them.

I got one and held it open for Slim. With the empty bottles in her hands, she bent down in front of me, the top of her head almost touching my belly. The bottles clinked together as she set them on the bottom of the sack.

Then she straightened up. We looked each other in the eyes. Smiling softly, she said, "Let me smell your breath."

I set the sack down beside me. Slim moved in close, very close. She put her nose in front of my mouth and sniffed. I expected a smart remark, but didn't get one. Instead of commenting on my breath, she put her mouth against mine and kissed me. Her arms went around me. She pressed her body against mine.

I thought about hugging her, but was afraid of her cuts. She didn't have any cuts on her rear end, though. I could put my hands down there. I *wanted* to. But I didn't dare. After all, that was below the belt.

While I was still struggling to work up the nerve, Slim took her mouth away and stepped back. "Your breath's fine," she whispered.

"Yours, too."

"Smells like beer and cheeseburgers."

"I thought you said it's fine."

"It *is*," she said. "Only thing is, Mr. & Mrs. Simmons are going to know you've been drinking."

"You, too."

She smiled. "Maybe if we don't let them kiss us . . ."

"They'd better not try."

"Why don't you go and brush your teeth?"

"I don't think that'll take care of it."

"Can't hurt. I'll brush mine when we get to my place."

"Well . . ."

"Go ahead, I'll wait here."

I ran up the stairs two at a time and hurried into the bathroom. After brushing my teeth, I used the toilet. This was the tough part about wearing swim trunks instead of underwear; they had no fly. Usually, I tried to maneuver myself out through the leghole of the trunks and the zipper of my jeans. But I didn't feel like struggling, so I just dragged everything down around my ankles. My skin was hot and damp from being trapped inside all those clothes. In front, I was slippery as if I'd been dipped in liquid soap. I could hardly hold on to take aim. But the air felt great on all those hot, wet places.

Before flushing, I used a lot of toilet paper to dry myself. Then I pulled up my trunks and groaned at the way their hot, clammy lining clung to me. Quickly, I tugged them down again. I took off my shoes, jeans and trunks, then put my jeans back on. The dirty clothes hamper was next to the toilet. I dropped my trunks in, put my shoes on, then washed my hands and left the bathroom. Without anything on under my jeans, I felt dry and loose and free.

I could *stay* like this, I thought. Nobody'll ever know.

But I knew I didn't dare.

In my bedroom, I shut the door and turned on the light. I unbuttoned Rusty's shirt, took it off, turned toward my bed and gave his shirt a toss.

On the pillow of my bed was a yellow rose.

My stomach dropped.

I leaped to my open closet, pulled a clean shirt off a hanger, then snatched Rusty's shirt off the bed and ran to the door. I jerked it open.

"Slim!" I shouted.

"Yeah?" Her voice sounded far away. "What is it?"

I slapped the light switch. As darkness collapsed all around me, I raced down the hallway to the top of the stairs and then I ran down the stairs.

Slim was standing in the gloom of the kitchen, the grocery sack in her hand. "What's wrong?" she asked.

"Somebody's been here." Holding the two shirts in my left hand, I grabbed Slim's arm with my right. I hurried to the back door, pulling her.

I felt a little better the moment we were outside, but I didn't actually feel safe until we'd reached the sidewalk out front. When we came to the end of the block, we stopped. I tried to put on my shirt, but it wasn't easy with Rusty's shirt in one hand.

"I'll hold it," Slim said.

I gave Rusty's shirt to her, and put on my own.

"So what happened?" she asked.

"I went to my bedroom to change shirts," I explained. "When I looked at my bed, there was a rose on the pillow. A *yellow* rose."

The left side of Slim's upper lip lifted, baring some teeth. "Like one of my *mom's* yellow roses?"

"Yeah."

"Ooo."

"It was just lying there on my pillow."

"Everything else was okay?"

"Far as I could tell. But I didn't exactly hang around to find out."

Or put on underwear, I thought. But Slim didn't need to know that.

"I was afraid they might still be in the house. And I thought about you being alone in the kitchen." I finished buttoning my shirt. Then I took Rusty's shirt from Slim. "Figured I'd take this back to him."

She nodded.

We stepped off the curb and crossed the street.

"Are we still going to your place?" I asked.

"We have to," she said. "Then we've got to go to *your* house again. If we don't take care of the beer, you'll get the shaft from your parents."

"Guess we never should've drunk it in the first place."

She smiled at me. "Can't say I regret it."

"This is a lot of trouble to go through."

"The cover-up's the price you pay for doing the crime."

I laughed. "Did you just think that up?"

"I think so."

"Good one."

She slipped her hand into mine. We walked side by side through the quiet evening.

Chapter Thirty-two

When we came to Slim's house, she set the grocery sack down on the stoop and crouched in front of the door.

"The tape looks okay," she said. "Stay here. I'll check the back door before we go in."

I waited. A couple of minutes later, Slim opened the front door from inside.

"*Entre,*" she said.

The sack in one hand, Rusty's shirt in the other, I stepped over the threshold.

Slim shut the door and locked it. "If anyone came in while we were gone," she said, "they didn't use the doors."

"I guess that's good news," I said.

She seemed amused. "Vampires, of course, can turn into bats or wolves . . . or even a mist. You go turning into *mist*, you can get in just about anywhere."

"It's not dark yet," I pointed out.

She smiled. "Not *technically*. Of course, if we want to get picky about it, vampires can't enter *anyplace* without an invitation."

"That *is* good news."

"But *people* can."

"Not so good."

"I want to brush my teeth. Why don't you put that stuff down and come upstairs with me? You can stand guard. Just in case."

"Okay."

We went upstairs together. She turned on the bathroom light, then said, "I'll be out in a minute," and shut the door.

She didn't lock it, or I would've heard the ping.

It was good to know that she trusted me.

Standing outside the door, I heard water start to run.

Night hadn't yet fallen, but the hallway was almost dark. I thought about taking a walk to the other end for a quick look into the bedrooms. But I wanted to stay close to Slim. And I really didn't *want* to see the bedrooms: what if they weren't the same as when we'd left?

What if someone was *hiding* in one of them? Hiding in silence, waiting for us. . . .

It didn't seem likely. If I'd had to put money on it, I would've wagered that nobody was in either of the rooms, nobody was in the entire house except me and Slim.

Still, I felt chills crawling up my back as I stared into the gloom at the end of the hallway.

I wished Slim would hurry up.

Finally, she shut the water off. I expected the door to open, but it didn't.

Then I heard a steady splashing sound.

200

Oh.

Not wanting Slim to come out and wonder if I'd been listening to her, I walked away from the door. The sound diminished. Though I could still hear her, I stopped a few strides down the hall.

And stared toward the two bedrooms.

Nobody's here, I told myself. They were here before, but then they left and went to my house.

And to Rusty's? I wondered. He'd been at Janks Field the same as us.

I heard the toilet flush.

Soon after that, the bathroom door opened, light spilling into the hallway.

"Dwight?"

"I'm here." I hurried to the door.

Slim looked a little worried. "Where'd you go?"

"Nowhere. Just over there." I nodded to the side.

Stepping out of the bathroom, she looked down the hallway. "Did you hear something?"

I shook my head. "Not really. I was just . . . waiting for you."

"Let's go to my room," she said.

"Okay."

My heart suddenly pounding, I stayed by Slim's side and we left the lighted doorway behind.

Hurrying at the last moment, she entered her bedroom ahead of me and flicked the light switch. We stood motionless. Only our heads turned.

"Looks fine," Slim whispered.

"Yeah."

She turned toward me.

Nobody's home and we're in her bedroom. . . .

"I've made a decision," she said.

Oh, God.

I was almost too nervous to ask, but I managed to say, "What?"

"I'm going after all," she said.

"Huh?"

"To the Traveling Vampire Show. If you guys are going to it, so am I."

"But I thought . . ."

"Yeah, well . . . things have changed. If I *don't* go with you, where am I supposed to stay that's safe? They've been *here*—somebody has been, anyway."

I almost confessed, but stopped myself. Rusty and I had been in her house, all right, and we'd broken the vase and perfume bottle in her mother's room. But we hadn't chewed her book or taken the yellow roses.

"And they've been to *your* place," Slim continued. "*Your* parents are at the hospital. My mom's away for the night. I'm sure as heck not going to stay here by myself. Or at your place. I *wouldn't* stay at Rusty's, since I happen to not be able to stand his parents." She shrugged. "Maybe at Lee's, but . . ."

"Not there," I said. "Julian has her address on the check she gave him."

"As if he needs addresses," Slim said.

"But why are they doing this?" I asked. "If it *is* them? I just don't get it."

"To scare us, I guess. So we won't talk."

"About the dog?"

"I don't know. They might be afraid the cops'll come if I tell. Maybe they've got a *lot* to hide. I mean, you know?"

"If they're so afraid we'll tell on them, why don't they . . ." Not wanting to say it, I shrugged.

"Take us prisoners?" Slim suggested. "Or kill us?"

"Something like that," I admitted.

"I don't know," Slim said. "But that'd be awfully drastic. If they're trying not to draw attention to themselves, killing some kids doesn't seem like a brilliant way to go about it."

I almost smiled. "You're right about that."

"On the other hand," she said, "if they're trying to scare us, why did they give us tickets for tonight's show?"

"They didn't *give* them to us. They *sold* them."

"And got their hands on Lee's address," Slim said. "But why do they need her address? They didn't need *ours*. They just followed us, or something."

I shrugged. "Maybe in case they *hadn't* been able to follow us? That sort of thing doesn't always work. They might've lost us. But if they *did*, they'd still know where to find Lee." When I said that, I got a slightly sick feeling inside.

"I wonder if *she's* had any visitors," Slim said.

"Maybe we'd better call her."

"Yeah. In a minute. I want to change first."

"Huh?"

"Like you."

I blushed and raised my eyebrows as if I didn't know what she was talking about. Which was pretty much true.

"The dark shirt," she said.

"Oh."

"It's a good idea."

"Thanks." I hadn't worn a dark shirt on purpose. After seeing the rose on my pillow, I'd just grabbed it. But I saw no harm in allowing Slim to think I'd chosen a dark shirt for purposes of camouflage.

She walked to her closet, turned on its light and began to search through the clothes hangers.

"I'd better wait in the hall," I said.

"You don't have to." The words were hardly out of her mouth before she pulled off her T-shirt. Her back was toward me and she had her bikini top on, along with about a dozen bandages. Then she reached behind her. "Don't get worried," she said, and untied the back string. As she untied the neck string, she said, "It's just too hot."

She let her bikini top fall to the closet floor.

I stood there gaping at her naked back, stunned and thrilled and scared, hardly able to believe that she had actually taken off her top in front of me.

This had never happened before.

Maybe because we'd never been alone together.

She spread some hangers apart. As she reached out for a blouse with her right arm, she turned her body slightly. Just in front of her armpit, and a little lower, was a pale, smooth slope—the side of her right breast.

She probably didn't know I could see it. And I only did see

it for a moment before she pulled the blouse off the hanger and turned away again.

Turned away so that both her breasts were facing the closet. I couldn't see them, but I sure knew they were there.

They'd be in plain sight if only I were standing in the closet. *Or if she turns around.*

Please turn around, I thought. Please.

I suddenly hoped something would happen to *make* her turn around. Maybe a sudden noise. Like the telephone ringing?Or a shout?

I could shout.

But I didn't. As much as I ached for Slim to turn around, I didn't want to do anything that might make her think less of me.

She turned around.

Her blouse was already on, however, and most of the buttons were fastened.

I hoped I wasn't blushing too badly when she looked up at me. "How's this?" she asked.

Her long-sleeved blouse was black and made of a shiny fabric. Somewhat too large for her, it hung down so low it almost hid the front of her cut-off jeans.

"That oughta keep you from being seen," I said.

"Does it look weird?" she asked.

"Looks great."

"I mean, with my shorts. A long-sleeved blouse . . ."

"Do you have a black skirt?"

She made a face at me. "I have one, but I'm not about to wear it."

"Long jeans?" I suggested.

"It *does* look weird."

"It's fine."

"How about if I do this?" She rolled the sleeves halfway up her forearms. Then she turned her back to me, unfastened her cut-offs and tucked in the tails of her blouse. Zipped and buttoned, she faced me again. "Better?"

Pulled tight and smooth, the blouse showed every contour.

The smooth mounds of her breasts were tipped with stiff nipples.

"You look fine," I said.

She frowned. "What?"

Before I could say anything, she turned around and looked at herself in the mirror. Her frown deepened. Her hands came up and she touched her nipples. "Can't go around like this," she said.

In the mirror's reflection, our eyes met.

I shrugged.

Her hands slid down below her breasts, clutched her blouse and pulled it upward, dragging its tails out of her cut-offs. When she stopped, it was still tucked in but now had plenty of slack in it. No longer taut against her breasts, it draped them but didn't reveal every detail.

Her eyes again met mine in the mirror. "Better?" she asked.

I nodded.

She turned around and came to me, a smile spreading over her face. "Are you all right?" she asked.

"Fine."

"Are you sure?"

"Sure."

"You seem awfully nervous."

"I do?"

"Yeah."

"I'm okay."

"Do *I* make you nervous?"

"Maybe a little."

Reaching down, she took hold of my wrists. "These?" she asked, and lifted my hands and placed them on her breasts. Through the thin fabric of her blouse, I felt their heat and smoothness. I felt how springy they were. I felt the push of her nipples.

Chapter Thirty-three

In Slim's bathroom, I tried to clean myself up.

"Are you okay?" she asked through the door.

"Fine," I said. I tried to make my voice sound calm even though I was so embarrassed I wanted to cry.

"Can I do something to help?" she asked.

"No. Thanks. Everything's okay."

"Oh, sure." She didn't sound very chipper, herself.

"Just . . . I'll be out in a minute."

"I'm sorry, Dwight."

"Isn't your fault."

"Of course not."

I blushed furiously.

What did she think had happened to me?

She hadn't asked.

Does she know?

My hands leaping away from her breasts, I'd blurted, "Gotta go," then run from her bedroom and down the hall to the bathroom.

Maybe she thinks I got hit by the trots.

From the other side of the door, Slim said, "It's fine if you want to take a shower or something."

A shower might be the best solution, but I said, "No, that's okay."

"Come on, Dwight. You take a shower, and I'll throw your stuff in the wash. It won't take that long. We'll get everything nice and clean."

"I don't know," I muttered. The wads of toilet paper had taken care of the worst of it, but I was still very sticky and my jeans . . .

"Why don't you just hand your pants out through the door?" Slim said.

"Nah."

"Come on, Dwight."

Slim opened the door, but only a few inches. Her arm reached in. "Just hand them to me."

"They're a mess."

"It's all right. Come on." The fingers of her upturned hand waved back and forth, gesturing for me to approach.

"Can't you just leave me alone for a while?"

"Give me your pants, Dwight." This time, she sounded serious.

"They're gross."

"They *are* not."

"That's what you think."

"I know what happened," she said, her voice suddenly going soft. "And I know why it happened. I know all about that sort of stuff. Thanks to Jimmy."

"Oh, God," I muttered, and hoped she hadn't heard me.

"*He* was gross," Slim said. "Everything *about* him was gross. But nothing about you is gross, Dwight. Nothing. There's nothing for you to be ashamed of or embarrassed about. Okay? So just let me have your pants and I'll wash them for you. Please."

"Okay."

Blushing like crazy, I climbed out of my jeans. On the back of the bathroom door was a full-length mirror. I saw myself walking toward it, my hair mussed, my face scarlet, my shirt not quite long enough to cover my equipment, my jeans swaying by my side, my legs bare all the way down to the tops of my white socks.

"Here," I said, and put my jeans into Slim's hand.

"Thanks," she said. Her arm retreated. A moment later, she said, "What about your trunks?"

Expecting the question didn't save me from the embarrassment of it.

"I got rid of them back at my house," I confessed. "They were too hot."

"Ah," she said. "Okay. No problem. I'll go downstairs and throw these in the washer. Why don't you go ahead and take a shower?"

"Be careful, okay?"

"I will be. You, too." The bathroom door eased shut.

I thought about things for a minute or two, then took off my shirt and socks and stepped over to the bathtub. I started the water running. When it felt about right, I climbed into the tub, slid the frosted door shut, and started the shower. The spray came out cold. A few seconds later, however, it was good and hot.

I tried to get myself clean with just my hands and the water. After some rubbing, though, my skin still felt slick and tacky in the places where I'd made the mess.

Bending over, I removed a bar of soap from the tray.

The fresh scent of the soap reminded me of Slim.

Of course, I thought. It's her soap.

Suddenly, the realization struck me that I was taking a shower in the very same tub where Slim took her showers or baths. She had been naked in this very place. She had slid this very bar of soap over her bare skin. It had touched her face, glided over her breasts, slicked the skin of her buttocks, even rubbed her *down there*.

Never mind, I told myself.

But as I stood in the spray, I couldn't stop myself from thinking about it. I got pretty excited all over again. I imagined Slim coming back upstairs after throwing my jeans in the washer . . . easing open the bathroom door and sneaking inside . . . taking off all her clothes, then sliding open the shower door.

Mind if I join you in there?

Don't mind at all.

It'll never happen, I thought. Not in a million years.

It might.

What had already happened was too fantastic to believe.

She put my hands on her breasts!

If she'll do that, I thought, what *else* will she do?

She knows all about sex, thanks to that bastard Jimmy

208

Drake. She's *experienced*. We're alone in the house. We've got all night—if we skip the vampire show. Taking a shower together could be just the beginning!

I was done washing myself, but I decided to keep on showering.

No hurry, I thought.

She'd already had plenty of time to take my jeans out to the garage behind her house, throw them into the washing machine, start the machine, and return to the house. By now, she might be just outside the bathroom door.

On the rim of the tub was a plastic bottle of shampoo. I picked it up, opened it, and poured some of the yellow goo into the palm of my hand.

I'll be sudsing my hair when she comes in.

I'll act very surprised.

I won't have to *act*, I realized. I really *will* be surprised. I'll be shocked.

It would take a miracle to have Slim get in the shower with me.

But she put my hands on her breasts.

Right. And I had an *accident* like some kind of sex-starved kid.

I *am* a sex-starved kid.

I rubbed the foamy shampoo into my hair and scalp. The shampoo didn't smell the same as the soap. Like the soap, however, its aroma reminded me of Slim.

I lathered my hair for a long time, giving Slim plenty of time to show up.

She isn't *going* to show up, I finally had to admit.

She's probably waiting outside the bathroom door—and wondering what's taking me so long. Maybe she even decided to wait by the washing machine and not come back until my jeans are finished.

I put my head under the hot spray. I spent a fairly long time rinsing away the suds, still hoping for Slim to come in. Finally, I bent down and turned off the water. I rolled the door open. Hanging on to its edge, I leaned out slightly and looked around. The bathroom was aswirl with white steam.

No Slim.

I climbed out of the tub. Dripping, I took a few steps and pulled a pale blue towel off its bar. Slim's towel. It had to be hers; her mother's tub was in the master bathroom. The towel was the same powder blue color as Slim's bikini. The one she was wearing tonight. The one with the top she'd removed in her closet.

Drying myself, I wondered if the towel had been in the wash since the last time she'd used it. I didn't think so. It seemed clean and fresh, but didn't smell or feel the way towels do before they've been used.

This one had been against Slim, all over.

When I was done drying myself, I wrapped it around my waist and tucked a corner down to hold it in place. It jutted out quite a lot in front, so I didn't go to the door or call out for Slim.

To pass a little time, I stepped over to the counter. The mirror above it was all fogged up. Even though I couldn't see myself in the mirror, I combed my hair with a pink comb I found on the counter. Then I sprayed my armpits with Slim's deodorant. It was Right Guard, and it's odor reminded me of her.

It seemed that Slim's special scent was made of many different aromas—her soap, her shampoo, her deodorant. Now those scents were on me. I liked having the same smell as Slim—or almost the same.

She had other aromas, too, at different times. Perfumes. Suntan oil. Foods she'd eaten. Sometimes, she carried outdoor scents: she smelled like wind or rain or grass or sunlight.

The towel was no longer sticking out, so I went to the door. I expected Slim to be on the other side of it.

She wasn't.

I stepped out and looked down the hall. Light from her open bedroom door spilled onto the carpet like a yellow fluid.

"Slim?" I called.

No answer came.

Not from her bedroom. Not from downstairs. Not from anywhere.

What if *they* got her?

The thought made me feel squirmy.

Maybe they were hanging around the house all along, hiding, waiting to get Slim alone. . . .

She's probably still in the garage, I told myself. Safe and sound. Waiting to take my jeans out of the washer.

I might as well wait in her bedroom, I thought.

As I walked toward the glow from her room, the towel started to come loose. I grabbed it, held it up, and kept on walking—suddenly very aware of being naked except for the towel.

Stepping into the light, turning toward her doorway, I suddenly imagined Slim was waiting for me in her bed. Maybe with a sheet pulled up almost to her shoulders.

Her shoulders bare.

Her face smiling.

That's why she hadn't answered when I called out; she didn't want to ruin the surprise.

Chapter Thirty-four

Wrong.

Slim's bed was empty. She didn't seem to be in her room at all.

"Slim?" I asked, just to make sure.

A fluttery feeling in my stomach, I left her room and walked to the head of the stairway.

"Slim!" I called out.

She didn't answer.

So I trotted down the stairs. Straight ahead of me was the front door. I suddenly imagined it swinging open, Slim's mother coming into the house and gaping up at me in shock, blurting out, *What're YOU doing here, young man? Where are your clothes?*

Something had gone wrong with her overnight plans, and here she was.

It could happen.

Of course, it didn't.

It's been my experience that worst case scenarios are very rare indeed. Rare to the extent that you can almost count on them not happening.

But sometimes they do.

The moment I turned away from the front door, my terror of being caught by Slim's mother vanished and my fears for Slim resumed.

The kitchen light was on. The back door stood open and the screen door was shut.

Earlier, Slim had entered the house this way to open the front door for me. She had also, probably, gone out this way to take my jeans to the garage.

I walked across the linoleum floor. It felt clean and slick under my bare feet.

At the screen door, I stopped and looked out.

The two-car garage stood at the far right corner of the lawn. Though its doors were shut, the windows of the laundry room were bright.

Slim has to be in there, I told myself.

But what if she's not?

She *is!* She knows I've got no pants until she comes back with my jeans. She's just staying with them till they're done.

Probably.

I couldn't stand the idea of waiting for her—not knowing for sure if she was there—so I opened the screen door and hurried down the back porch stairs.

Night had come. It was warm. Soft breezes blew against me, and they smelled of rain—rain that had been holding off all day but was sure to fall sooner or later.

Almost naked, I was glad to have the darkness. The trees and fences gave me some protection, but not enough, from the eyes of neighbors who might be looking out their windows.

If I should be seen in Slim's back yard wearing nothing but a towel . . .

I suddenly realized that *Slim* would be seeing me in nothing but a towel. I couldn't turn back, though. I had to make sure she was safe.

It'll be embarrassing, I thought, but it can't be any worse than what's already happened.

After retucking the towel to secure it around my waist, I opened the laundry room door.

I stepped in.

Slim wasn't there. Neither machine was running, but the air felt hot and smelled faintly of detergent. I stepped up to the washer and opened its top. Bending down and peering into the shadows, I felt moist heat rise against my face. The machine had been used recently, but it was empty now.

I stepped over to the drier. It was a front-loader. When I bent over to open it, my towel started to come loose. I grabbed the towel at its tuck by my hip. Holding it in place, I bent lower and peered into the drum.

At the bottom was a tangle of damp fabrics.

Feeling a little confused, I squatted down directly in front of the drier, reached in with my right arm, and plucked at the clothes. I separated them enough to find my own jeans, Slim's cut-off jeans and the pants of her powder blue bikini. Nothing else.

"You got me."

Though I recognized Slim's voice, it came from behind and startled me. My arm hopped up and banged against the top of the drier's door hole. *"OW!"* I yelped. I jerked my arm clear. Grabbing where it hurt, I shot to my feet and twisted around.

The laundry room had its own door into the rest of the garage. Though the garage housed the big old Pontiac that used to belong to Slim's grandmother (who'd checked out in the Super M checkout line the previous year), it was mostly used for storage. They kept a freezer chest there. And an extra refrigrator.

The door had been shut when I came into the laundry room. Now it was open and Slim stood in the doorway, a look of

213

concern on her face, a beer bottle in each hand. Her shiny black blouse was large enough so that it reached below her groin. Cut higher at the sides, it let me see bare skin to her hips. Her legs were bare all the way down to the sneakers on her feet.

I noticed all that in about half a second.

During the same half second, while my arm rang with pain, I realized that I'd lost my towel.

The hand of my wrecked arm was almost where I needed it to be. Fast as I could, I cupped myself.

Slim smiled as she watched me squat and snatch up the towel.

When I had it around me again, her smile vanished. "Sorry I startled you," she said.

"It's okay."

"You really whacked your arm."

"It'll be okay."

"I keep messing you up." She looked serious when she said it. But then she must've found some humor in her wording, because a smile crept across her face. "Rusty would've liked that one," she said.

"Yeah."

"Anyway, I'm sorry." She stepped out of the doorway and came toward me, the bottles swinging by her bare hips, her breasts moving softly under her blouse. She set the bottles on top of the washer. "Let me see your arm," she said.

Holding the towel together with my left hand, I raised my right arm. The front of my forearm was crossed by a red mark. Slim frowned at it. Then she gently took hold of my wrist and elbow, lifted my arm toward her face, and kissed the red place. I still felt as if someone had whacked my arm with a crowbar, but now I could feel Slim's lips. They felt cool and soft.

Looking up into my eyes, she asked, "Does that make it better?"

"Makes it fine," I told her.

She lowered my arm and let go of it. "I didn't mean to surprise you," she said. "I thought you were in the house."

"I got worried about you."

"I was just out here."

I shrugged. "Guess so. It's just . . . you were gone so long."

"I couldn't come in till the wash was done." She lowered her head to look at herself. Her open hands, down by her sides, gestured toward her bare thighs. As if to point out that she was naked below her hanging shirttails.

As if I hadn't noticed.

"Since I was doing a wash anyway," she said, "I figured I might as well throw in some of my own stuff." She blushed slightly, looked as if she might add something, then turned away. "Only trouble is, I can't get the drier to work."

I found myself smiling.

"Looking forward to wet jeans?" Slim asked.

I shook my head. "It's just . . . I thought you'd vanished again."

Her eyebrows soared. "What do you mean, vanished *again*? I've never vanished."

"I *thought* you had."

"Ah, but I *hadn't*. I always knew where I was."

"I guess so."

"I know so." She laughed a couple of times. Then she said, "So what'll we do about the drier?"

After shrugging, I asked, "What's wrong with it?"

"It doesn't go. Watch." She went to the drier. As she bent over to shut its door, the tail of her blouse slid upward a couple of inches. I tried to look away. Before I could succeed, however, she straightened up.

Before I could feel either relief or disappointment about that, however, she leaned over the top of the drier and reached for the control knobs and her blouse tail *really* slid up.

"See?" she asked.

I saw, all right.

"It *should* be going. But it's not."

I said, "Hmm."

She straightened up and turned around. I must've been as red as ketchup, but she acted as if she didn't notice. She also pretended not to notice the front of my towel sticking out. "Why doesn't it want to work?" she asked.

"I'm sure it *wants* to."

She smirked, but I could see she was a little amused, too. "You know what I mean," she said.

"You sure you're turning it on right?" I asked.

"I *know* how to turn on a drier."

"I'm sure you do."

"And what's *that* supposed to mean?" she asked.

I tried not to grin. "Oh, nothing."

She reached up with her right hand, flicked her middle finger and thumped the tip of my nose. Not very hard, but hard enough to make me blink and take a step backward. Also, my eyes watered.

"Oh, no," Slim said, suddenly looking appalled. "I'm sorry. God, why do I keep *doing* this stuff?" She put her hands on both sides of my face, drew my head toward her and kissed me on the nose. Then she kissed me on the mouth.

I almost reached for her breasts. I remembered last time, and how they'd felt. But I also remembered the result.

Taking her by the wrists, instead, I moved her hands away from my face. Her mouth went away, too.

"I'd better take a look at the drier," I said.

Looking me in the eyes, she nodded slightly. "Good idea," she said, her voice low and shaky.

She stepped aside. I went to the drier. "Nothing at all happens when you turn it on, right?"

"The drier?"

"Right, the drier."

"Right. Nothing at all happens."

"Sounds like it might be a problem with the power."

"Sure," Slim said.

"Was it working before?"

"Yeah. Mom did the wash a couple of days ago. It was working fine."

Holding on to my towel, I stepped around the side of the machine and looked behind it with high hopes of finding the power cord unplugged. But it looked secure in its socket.

"It *is* plugged in," Slim told me. "I already checked that."

"You did?"

"I'm not an idiot."

I looked at her and grinned. "I know."

"So what do you think it is?"

"It might be a dead outlet. Have you got an extension cord?"

"Sure. Right back." She whirled around. Her blouse fluttered and rippled behind her as she ran toward the doorway. The air flapped its tail.

She leaped through the doorway and vanished into the other side of the garage.

While she was gone, I squatted beside the machine, scooted it away from the wall, reached behind it and pulled the plug out of the wall socket.

Slim came back with the coil of an extension cord dangling from one hand. "Here you go," she said.

"Thanks."

I took it from her and pushed the dryer's plug into the extension. Holding my towel with one hand, I stood up and followed Slim to an outlet near the door.

"Try this one," she said.

I pushed the prongs of the extension cord into the holes of the outlet.

Slim said, "Ahhh" as the drier came to life.

Chapter Thirty-five

Leaving our clothes in the drier, we went back to Slim's house. I led the way, using my left hand to hold my towel secure. Slim carried the beer bottles.

In the kitchen, she set the bottles on the table. "Maybe you'd better give Lee a call."

"Oh, yeah," I said.

Slim swept her hand toward the wall phone.

"Now?" I asked.

"Don't you think you should?"

"I guess so," I admitted. I frowned at the phone, reluctant to make the call.

"What's wrong?"

I shrugged. "I don't know."

"We'd better make sure she's all right."

"Yeah."

"And find out if *she's* had any weird stuff happen."

"How about if we wait and call later?"

"What's wrong with now?"

"I don't know." I happened, just then, to glance at Slim's legs.

She grinned. "It's a *phone* call, Dwight. She won't be able to see us."

"I know, but . . ." I shrugged.

"Want me to leave the room?"

"No!" The word burst from my mouth.

Slim flinched.

"Don't leave," I said, trying to make my voice calm. "You'll probably vanish again."

"I told you, I *haven't* vanished."

"That's your opinion."

A glint of mischief in her eyes, she said, "I oughta know."

"Don't go anywhere," I told her.

I stepped over to the phone, made sure my towel was secure, then lifted the receiver off its hook. I knew Lee's number by heart. While I dialed it, Slim pulled a chair away from the kitchen table and sat down.

Lee's phone started to ring.

With the table in the way, I didn't need to worry about seeing anything lower than Slim's belly.

I listened to the quiet ringing and we gazed into each other's eyes.

It started out as that intense, curious, hopeful stare that we'd been giving each other so much lately. Our *love* stare, I guess. But then Slim's gaze faltered, and so did mine. Soon, we were frowning at each other.

"How many times has it rung?" she asked.

"I don't know, seven or eight."

"Give it a few more."

"She usually gets it in two or three if she's home."

"Maybe she's in the bathroom or something."

Maybe she's busy, I thought, and doesn't want to be bothered by a phone call right now and she's wondering what sort of jerk is keeping at it this long.

As I let it continue to ring, I began to hope Lee *wouldn't* answer. She was one of my favorite people, not only beautiful but one of my best friends, so I hated to make a nuisance of myself.

Finally, I hung up.

"Well," Slim said.

"Yeah."

"I wonder what *that* means."

"Maybe she went somewhere," I said.

"Or she's taking a bath," Slim said. "If she's running the water, she might not even hear the phone. Or maybe she heard it, but didn't want to get out of the tub."

I pictured Lee lounging in her bathtub, wet and shiny.

"*I* sure don't get out to answer the phone," Slim said, and I pictured *her* in her bathtub.

Starting to get excited, I sat down at the kitchen table across from Slim.

"Or she might've been on the toilet," Slim added. "There's no telling. Why don't you call her back?"

I didn't relish the idea of standing up just then. "Why don't we give her a while?"

"Yeah. How about five or ten minutes? Maybe she'll get done with whatever she's doing."

"Good," I said.

"I'm sure she's fine."

"I hope so."

"I mean, *we* had some weird stuff happen, but nobody *did* anything to us. We might've gotten a little scared, but we didn't get hurt."

I nodded in agreement.

"While we're waiting . . ." She went silent and let a smile spread over her face.

It was a type of smile I'd seen on Slim before, but not very often. It had a slyness to it. It always meant trouble.

"Uh-oh," I said.

Slim scooted back her chair. I tried to keep my gaze high as she stood up and turned around. Mostly, I succeeded.

"Where're you going?" I asked.

Striding away, she looked over her shoulder. "Back in a minute. Don't worry, I won't vanish."

"Please don't," I muttered.

I watched the black tail of her blouse drift against her rear end as she left the kitchen. When she was beyond the reach of the kitchen light, all I could see was a pair of walking legs. Soon, they were eaten by the darkness.

I was tempted to stand up and go after her, but I still had a towel problem.

"You okay?" I called.

"Fine."

"What're you doing?"

"You'll see."

On her way back, I saw her legs first. Then I noticed the pale shapes of her face and forearms. By her side, she was carrying something more pale than her skin.

It turned out to be a newspaper.

I looked away and tried to seem interested in the clock while Slim sat down and scooted her chair closer to the table.

Then I faced her and asked, "What's the paper for?"

"Time to put my big plan into action."

"What big plan is that?"

"Operation Rescue Rusty."

I groaned.

Slim chuckled.

By the time she finished explaining, I no longer needed to worry about embarrassing protrusions of my towel. I sighed, pushed myself away from the table, and went to the phone. I was trembling slightly and my heart was pounding.

I dialed, then turned toward Slim.

She looked very pleased with herself.

I showed her my teeth and she laughed.

Over at Rusty's house, someone picked up a phone.

"Hello?"

I cringed. "Hello, Mrs. Simmons."

"Hello, young man."

"Is Rusty there?"

"I'm afraid he's incommunicado at the moment."

"Oh. Yeah. I sort of thought so. I feel awful about what we did. You know, ditching Elizabeth."

"You have no idea how much you hurt her feelings, Dwight. Frankly, I didn't except such behavior from you."

"I'm awfully sorry. Really. I just wasn't thinking straight. I was so worried about Slim. . . ."

"Well, yes. I can understand your concern, but it was no excuse. Elizabeth fully expected you to wait for her."

"I know. I feel rotten about it. Anyway, I was thinking about doing something to cheer her up."

Mrs. Simmons was silent.

"I thought maybe Slim and I might come over and take her with us to the movies."

Mrs. Simmons remained silent.

"There's a double-feature at the drive-in. *What Ever Happened to Baby Jane*'s playing with *The House on Haunted Hill*."

"Haven't you *seen* those movies?" she asked.

"The House on Haunted Hill."

"I thought so."

"But that was a couple of years ago, and we missed our chance to see *What Ever Happened to Baby Jane* when it played at the Crown. Anyway, I'm pretty sure Elizabeth hasn't seen either one of them, and Slim and I don't mind seeing *The House on Haunted Hill* again. It was really good."

"I'm not sure I want Elizabeth to see that sort of movie. They're both supposed to be dreadful. I don't want her coming home with nightmares."

"Bette Davis and Joan Crawford are in *Baby Jane*," I pointed out.

"I'm well aware of that."

"They were really big stars in your generation."

That got a laugh out of Mrs. Simmons. "*My* generation, huh?"

I wasn't quite sure what to make of that, so I changed the subject slightly. "Anyway, I bet Elizabeth would get a kick out of going to the drive-in with us. We'll pay for her ticket and buy her snacks and stuff."

"And who, exactly, will be driving?"

"Slim. We'll be going in her car."

"I see."

She trusted Slim. I figured we had it made.

Then she said, "I don't know, Dwight."

"I think Elizabeth might especially like spending some time with me after . . . you know, feeling so *abandoned* this afternoon."

"I suppose you'll want *Rusty* to accompany you likewise?"

"Doesn't matter to us. It's fine either way."

"He's grounded, you know."

"He doesn't have to come. The thing is, this is really for Elizabeth."

"I'll have to ask her."

I heard some clatter that meant she was setting down the phone. Pressing the mouthpiece of Slim's phone against my belly, I said quietly, "I think we're in business."

Slim looked tickled. She also looked as if she'd known all along that her plan would succeed. Largely because her plans *always* succeeded.

Almost always.

After a while, Mrs. Simmons returned to the phone. "Dwight?" she asked.

"I'm here."

"My husband and I have talked it over. We've also discussed the matter with Elizabeth, and she's willing to forgive and forget."

"Oh. Good."

"So we'll allow her to go with you."

"Great."

"Rusty, too. He's still grounded, mind you. This will be the exception to the rule."

"Fine." I grinned at Slim.

"But I want you to promise you won't do anything to make us regret our decision."

"I promise, Mrs. Simmons."

"When will you be picking them up?"

"Maybe in about half an hour?"

Slim nodded her approval.

"Very good. We'll see you then."

"Great."

"And Dwight?"

"Yes?"

"This is a very thoughtful thing you're doing. It goes a long way toward putting you back in our good graces."

"Thank you, Mrs. Simmons."

"See you soon," she said.

"Real good. Bye."

"Bye."

I hung up.

Grinning, Slim began to applaud. "Bravo," she said. "*A fine* performance."

"Thank you, thank you . . ."

"While you're on a roll, how about giving Lee another try?"

I dialed Lee's number. It rang and rang and rang.

Chapter Thirty-six

Slim picked up the two fresh bottles of beer and we went into the living room. On the foyer floor was Rusty's shirt and the bag containing my dad's two empty beer bottles—just where I'd left them before hurrying upstairs to stand guard on Slim while she brushed her teeth.

At the time, I'd figured we would be out of the house in about five minutes.

Funny how one thing leads to another.

Or not so funny.

Watching Slim squat by the bag to take out the empty bottles and put in the full ones, I could hardly believe what had happened after I'd followed her upstairs. There was a dreamlike quality to it. As if several of my fantasies—and dreads—had come to life. But I knew I hadn't dreamed any of it; there squatted Slim in nothing but her blouse and here stood I in nothing but a towel. Our clothes were in the drier. All of it had actually happened.

And we were still dealing with the consequences.

Not to mention the consequences of drinking my dad's beer.

Drinking those two bottles of beer (and trying to conceal the deed) had led us back to Slim's house . . . where she'd gone upstairs to brush her teeth and change into a dark blouse . . . and all the rest had happened.

Consequences within consequences.

But *good* consequences. Mostly.

Standing up, Slim said, "You be in charge of the beer." Then she walked over to the sofa. Her back was toward me, so I watched the tail of her blouse slide up as she bent over and pulled the sofa away from the wall.

She crouched and took out the weapons: her bow, her quiver of arrows, and the two knives Rusty and I had carried while helping her search the house for prowlers.

"What'll we do with those?" I asked.

"Take 'em with us." She raised her arm to lift the strap of the quiver over her head. When she did that, her blouse glided up a couple of inches. I kept my eyes on her face until the quiver was on her back and her blouse was down where it belonged.

"Let's go see if the clothes are dry," she said.

I picked up the bag, the two empty bottles, and the shirt I'd borrowed from Rusty.

"Aren't you forgetting something?" Slim asked.

I must've looked puzzled.

A smile spread across Slim's face. "I only washed your *jeans*."

"Oh!"

She laughed.

I set everything down again, said, "Right back," and headed for the stairway feeling a little stupid.

I was about halfway up when Slim said, "Dwight?"

I stopped and looked around. "You'd better leave my towel up there," she said. "Put it back where you got it, okay?"

Leave her *towel?*

"Okay," I said.

"And check around the bathroom. We don't want to leave any *evidence* behind."

"Okay."

"And could you check my bedroom, too? I think I left the light on."

"I'll check," I said and continued up the stairs. At the top, I looked back down at her and said, "Stay put, okay?"

"I will."

"And yell if anything happens."

"I will."

On my way down the hall to her bedroom, the towel started to slip. I held it by the tuck . . . and wondered why I bothered. After all, she wanted me to leave the towel in the bathroom. What would I do then?

Stepping into her bedroom, I was about to flick the wall switch when I saw that the closet light was also on. I walked toward it, striding over the place where Slim and I had been standing when she'd put my hands on her breasts. Then I was in the closet, standing where she'd stood when she took off her T-shirt. I looked down. The powder blue top of her bikini lay on the floor, just where she'd dropped it.

Maybe she didn't want it left on the floor.

As I thought about picking it up, however, I remembered Rusty fooling with Slim's mother's bra. What if I picked up the bikini top and got an urge to bury my face in it . . . and Slim suddenly showed up and caught me?

So I let it stay on the floor.

I yanked the string to shut the light off, then rushed back across Slim's room, hit the switch on my way out, and hurried through the hallway toward the glow from the bathroom.

At the top of the stairs, I paused and saw Slim looking up at me.

"Everything okay?" she asked.

"No problem. Your closet light was on."

"You get it?"

"Yeah."

"Thanks."

"I'll be right down," I said, and entered the bathroom. I started to shut the door, then changed my mind and left it open a few inches so I would be able to hear her . . . in case.

The first thing I did was take off the towel. Naked, I went to the bar where I'd found it. I folded it neatly and hung it up.

Then I crouched over the bathtub. I turned on the water and rinsed the tub, then used toilet paper to wipe some hairs that had collected over the drain. I tossed the paper into the toilet and flushed.

The counter and sink looked fine.

So I put on my shirt, then my socks and shoes.

And stood there, staring down at myself. The tails of my shirt hung down pretty much the same distance on me as Slim's blouse did on her. But there was a difference. Slim had nothing down there capable of sticking out.

I did, and it was.

Slim had already caught a look at it in the laundry room when I lost my towel. Still, I wasn't about to go downstairs this way.

She *said* to leave the towel up here, I reminded myself.

If she can go around in just her blouse, I can go around in this.

What if her mom comes home?

Never mind her mom coming home; in my condition I wouldn't be able to stand in front of Slim for ten seconds without having another accident.

To solve the problem, I took off my shirt. Obviously, I

couldn't tie it around my waist by its short sleeves. When I turned my shirt upside-down, however, the corners of the front tails were able to reach around my waist. I tied them together with a half knot over my left hip. The arrangement looked ridiculous and didn't cover any of my left leg, but it concealed what needed to be hidden. I looked at myself in the mirror and shook my head.

Then I swung open the bathroom door, flicked its light off, and stepped into the hallway.

From the foot of the stairs, Slim grinned up at me. "Good grief," she said.

"I had to put your towel back."

As I trotted down the stairs, she stared at me and kept grinning. "You could've just *worn* the shirt, you know."

"I *am*."

"Up where it belongs."

"No, I couldn't."

"I am," she said.

"I know, but. . . ." I shrugged. "It's different."

"Chicken." Though the grin remained on her face, I caught a hint of disappointment in her eyes.

My God, I thought.

Turning away, Slim said, "We'd better get a move on. I put the knives in the bag with the beers, by the way."

"Good idea." I picked up the bag, the two empty beer bottles and Rusty's shirt. Then I followed Slim into the kitchen. She grabbed her purse off the counter and swung its strap over her other shoulder. Then we went outside.

The wind was stronger than before, but warm. It felt good blowing against me. I watched how it flapped and lifted Slim's blouse.

Was she angry with me?

Did she feel cheated because I'd worn the shirt around my waist? Had she hoped to catch glimpses of *me* underneath its tails?

Even as I wondered about it, the rear of her blouse was flipped up by the wind and I saw her pale buttocks.

Then she opened a door and entered the laundry room. I

stepped in behind her, pulled the door shut, and followed her through the other door to the main area of the garage.

She stopped at the rear of the Pontiac. With one hand, she reached into her purse. Her hand come out holding a key case. She fumbled with it, found the key she wanted, then bent over and slid it into the key hole of the trunk.

When the trunk was open, she set her bow inside. She took the quiver off her back and put it into the trunk, too. Then she took the bag from me, set it down near her quiver and bow, and shut the lid.

Next, she opened the driver's door and tossed her purse onto the seat. After closing the door, she said, "Over here."

I followed her to a corner of the garage. We stopped at a collection of cardboard cartons containing empty beer and soda bottles. Slim took our two empties from me, knelt down, studied the situation for a while, then found a carton with four vacant openings. She slipped Dad's bottles into two of them.

Grinning up at me, she said, "That's half the trick."

I felt half-relieved.

We went into the laundry room. The drier was still going, but it stopped when Slim opened its door. Squatting, she reached inside the machine and pulled out my jeans. She felt them here and there. "I think they're dry. It's hard to tell when they're hot like this. They might still be a little damp."

"It's okay."

She handed the jeans up to me. While she reached into the machine to take out her cut-offs and bikini bottoms, I draped my jeans over the top of the washer.

I tugged the half-knot at my hip.

My shirt pulled free.

Slim turned her head and stared up at me.

Even as I felt myself growing and rising, I swung the shirt behind my back, put my arms into its sleeves, pulled it up, drew it together in front and began to fasten its buttons.

A gentle smile spread over Slim's face.

My heart pounded like crazy.

I've lost my mind, I thought.

"Oh, dear," Slim said. "Look at you."

"Sorry." I snatched my jeans off the washer.

"No. Don't put them on yet."

"But . . ."

"Just wait."

While I waited, Slim stood up. She put her bikini pants and cut-off jeans on top of the drier. Then she leaned over the machine and twisted a knob—to shut it off, I guess.

Coming toward me, she said, "I know a way to get rid of that."

"Get rid of what?"

"That." Her eyes went to it.

"You do?"

There was mischief in her smile. "I know many things."

"Jeez."

She squatted in front of me.

Oh, my God! She's gonna blow me!

My heart hammered.

"I don't know, Slim."

She tilted back her head and smiled up at me. "It'll be all right. We don't want you messing up your clean jeans, do we?"

"No, but . . ."

She raised her hand toward me.

Okay. Not the same as her mouth, but still . . .

Her middle finger curled down. She caught it under her thumb and let fly, thumping the tip of my erection.

"OW!!!" I cried out.

Chapter Thirty-seven

Sitting in the passenger seat of the Pontiac on the way to my house, I gave Slim a dirty look. She grinned at me. In the darkness, she couldn't have seen much of the look I'd given her, or known what I was thinking. But she said, "It worked, didn't it?"

She *did* know what I was thinking. "Yeah, but jeez!"

"You're fine."

"Easy for you to say, you're not the one who got thumped."

"I've had a few thumps."

Remembering Jimmy Drake, I decided not to pursue the subject.

"The car's working good," I said.

"She's a peach," Slim said, and patted the steering wheel.

That's what her grandmother used to say about the car, *She's a peach.*

Up to the moment of her grandma's demise, it had been the old woman's car and nobody else had been allowed to drive it. Slim's mother used the hot little M.G. that had belonged to Jimmy. (Apparently, he'd gone on his mysterious trip without it.)

Slim, however, hated everything about Jimmy, including his car. *Especially* his car. Before going away, he often forced her to take rides with him. He drove her to secluded places and did terrible things to her.

After Jimmy's departure, Slim refused to go anywhere in the M.G. Her grandmother drove her in the Pontiac when she *had* to have a ride. Otherwise, she did her traveling by foot. This was fine with Slim. I think, if she'd gotten herself stranded in the middle of Death Valley and her mother came to the rescue in Jimmy's old M.G., Slim would've shaken her head and told her, "Thanks anyway, I'd rather walk."

When her grandmother died, Slim lost her transportation. Her mother continued to use the M.G., while the Pontiac sat unused in the garage. It seems that Slim's mother wanted nothing to do with *that* car. Who knows why? Maybe she simply enjoyed the nice little M.G., even if it *had* belonged to a bastard like Jimmy. Or maybe awful things had happened to her in the Pontiac—or *nice* things that were too painful for her to think about, now that her mother was dead.

Like I say, who knows?

Whatever the reason, the Pontiac got itself abandoned in the garage. It sat there for almost a year.

A few months before the Traveling Vampire Show came to town, Rusty and I went over to Slim's house on a hot, sunny morning, figuring the three of us might head over to the river. The M.G. wasn't in the driveway, so Slim's mom was probably away. Slim might've been gone, too, but we knew she hadn't taken off with her mother. Not in the M.G.

We knocked on the front door, but nobody answered. So then we went around back. The garage door was open. We found Slim in the driver's seat of her grandmother's big green Pontiac, gazing through the windshield. When she heard us coming, she turned her head and smiled. "Hey, guys," she said out the open window.

"Hi," I said.

"What's up?" Rusty asked.

"Not much. Hop in."

While Rusty nodded and eyed the back door, I hurried around to the other side and climbed into the front seat. Leaving the door open for Rusty, I scooted to the middle.

Slim was in a T-shirt and cut-off jeans. Her legs looked tan and smooth. Her feet were bare. The way she looked made me feel great. So did the smell of her. I sighed and smiled. "What're you doing?" I asked.

She shrugged. "Just thinking," she said.

Rusty scooted in beside me. "Gonna take her for a spin?"

When he said that, I noticed the key in the ignition.

"Not today."

"Come on, Dagny, let's see what she'll do."

Leaning toward the wheel, she looked at Rusty. "It's Slim," she said. "Slim, not Dagny."

This was the first we'd heard of it.

"*Slim?*" Rusty asked. "All of a sudden you're Slim? What happened to Dagny?"

She shrugged, smiled, and said, "Now I'm Slim, that's all."

"If you say so," Rusty said.

I said, "Fine with me. Any name you want's fine with me."

Rusty went, "Oooooo."

Ignoring him, I said, "Anyway, Slim, want to come with us to the river? Maybe we can take a canoe out, or . . ."

"Forget it, man," Rusty interrupted. "Let's go for a spin!"

"Can't," Slim said.

"Sure we can."

"A," she said, "I don't know how to drive. B, I don't have a driver's license. C, two of the tires are flat. D . . . ," she twisted the ignition key. It triggered a few dismal clicking sounds, then nothing.

Rusty muttered, "Crap."

"Dead battery?" I said.

Slim nodded. "That's what I think, too." Frowning, she stared out the windshield. One of her hands idly stroked the steering wheel, which was sheathed in leopard skin.

You don't see leopard skin steering wheel covers too much anymore. In fact, the last one I remember seeing was on Slim's grandmother's Pontiac. Back in those days, steering wheel covers weren't at all uncommon. Old people seemed especially fond of them. When you saw a leopard skin cover on a steering wheel, you could pretty much bet that the car was owned by an old woman.

Anyway, Slim lightly stroked the leopard skin along the top curve of the wheel while she concentrated on her thoughts. After a while, she said, "I don't know much about cars."

Rusty let out a laugh.

She leaned forward, looked past me and frowned at him.

"Thought you knew *everything*," he said.

"I know more than you, numbnuts."

"Hah!"

"But not about this."

"Whatcha mean, J. D. Salinger don't teach you how to fix a car?"

Ignoring Rusty's crack, she gave the key another twist. Silence.

"How about Ayn Rand!" Rusty called out. "Why don't you look up 'dead batteries' in *Alice Shrugged*."

I gave him a shot with my elbow.

"Ow!" He grabbed his arm. "Damn it!"

"It's *Atlas*," Slim said. "Not Alice. Anyway, are you guys interested in helping me fix the car? My mom wants nothing to do with it. She'll just let it sit here forever. But if we can get it running, it's as good as mine. I can get my driver's license and then we can drive *all over* the place."

"I'll teach you how to drive," I said, really eager.

"Great."

I pictured the two of us roaming the back roads together, just as Lee and I had done the previous summer when I was learning to drive in her pickup truck.

"What about me?" Rusty asked.

"You don't have a license," I pointed out.

"Who cares? I'm a great driver. We can *both* teach her."

I'd seen samples of Rusty's driving prowess a few times after he had "borrowed" his family car in the middle of the night. We'd been lucky to live. For various reasons, we'd never told Slim about the excursions, so she had no idea what a lousy, dangerous driver Rusty was.

Shaking my head, I muttered, "I don't know."

Slim patted my thigh and said, "If we get this baby going, you can *both* be my teachers. We'll drive all over the place! It'll be great!"

So we didn't go to the river that day. We worked on the Pontiac, instead.

Apparently, Slim's grandmother had kept it in fine shape while she was alive. Its troubles were mostly the result of the car not being used for almost a year.

Rusty really came through. He figured out all the problems

as we went along. Slim and I provided money to buy whatever he suggested: some new belts and hoses, mostly, but also a new battery. He installed them. He also patched the flat tires.

Within a week, we had the Pontiac running.

On back roads outside the town limits, Slim drove. Rusty and I took turns sitting beside her, giving instructions, once in a while grabbing the wheel to keep us on course. We had a few close shaves, but no accidents.

After about two weeks, Slim was driving as well as anyone I'd ever known . . . and a zillion times better than Rusty. Her mom took her over to the DMV in Clarksburg. A couple of hours later, she came back with her temporary driver's license.

There was no stopping us, then. Slim behind the wheel (and sometimes me or Rusty), hardly a day went by when we didn't go for a drive someplace. We had already explored most of the nearby back roads, so we hit every town within fifty miles of Grandville. We followed the roads that ran alongside the river, stopping whenever we felt like wandering around on foot or taking a swim. At night, sometimes we cruised downtown Grandville. Once a week, we took the Pontiac to the drive-in movie show. We were having ourselves a fine time until about the middle of July.

That's when the Moonlight Drive-in had its very first "ALL-NIGHT SHOCKFEST." From sunset till dawn, the drive-in out on Mason Road would be showing one horror movie after another.

We wanted to go and stay for the entire event.

Not a chance.

Even though Slim would be driving and everyone trusted her, we were ordered to be home by midnight. By "we," I mean me and Slim. Both my parents were pretty strict about that sort of thing, and so was Slim's mother. Rusty's parents thought of themselves as strict, too, but they were easy to fool. Rusty could've tricked them and stayed out all night, no problem. He had no reason to do it, though, since Slim and I both had to be back by twelve.

Our parents thought they were being generous, giving us till midnight.

We didn't see it that way. They *always* let us stay out till midnight when we went to the drive-in. But this wasn't just the usual double-feature—this was the first ALL-NIGHT SHOCK-FEST. *Six* different horror movies would be shown and we wanted to see them all.

Thanks to our midnight deadline, we would only have time to watch two of them.

Didn't seem fair.

We pushed for one o'clock, figuring we might get in three of the movies. That would at least be *half* of them. Getting to see half sounded pretty good.

But my parents wouldn't go along with it. Therefore, neither would Slim's mother.

Midnight. Take it or leave it.

Midnight, it seems, is the magic hour for parents. Somewhere along the line, maybe someone was too impressed by *Cinderella*. Or maybe midnight was when the gates of the city got locked, back in the old days when cities *had* gates. More than likely, the fixation on being home by midnight had primitive, superstitious origins. Midnight, the witching hour, "when churchyards yawn" and all that. Who knows?

I do know this. The need to be home by midnight was what got us into trouble . . . the fact that we left the drive-in exactly when we did.

Chapter Thirty-eight

We arrived at the Moonlight Drive-in early enough to find a parking place fairly close to the screen. Though the sun had already gone down, it wasn't quite dark enough yet for the movies to start. "Big Girls Don't Cry" was coming from the speaker box on the post beside our car. Kids were still playing on the swings and slide and teeter-totters below the giant screen.

We had plenty of time for a trip to the snack bar, where we bought Cokes and hot dogs and buttered popcorn. Back at the car, I took the driver's seat. Slim sat beside me, and Rusty sat by her other side. "Walk Like A Man" was playing on the speaker. I leaned out the window, grabbed the metal box off its post and brought it inside. I cranked the window up a few inches and hung the speaker over its edge. And we were all set.

About ten minutes later, the Shockfest began.

The first movie turned out to be *Bucket of Blood*. It's about this goony beatnik who wants to be an artist, but he's no good at it. Then he accidentally kills a cat, which was pretty funny in an awful way. To conceal the cat's body, he covers it with clay. Presto! He has himself a perfectly good sculpture. Everybody's amazed by how detailed and lifelike it is. Knowing a good thing when he sees it, he starts murdering gals and covering *their* bodies with clay.

We loved it. We kept laughing and going, *"Oh, no!"* But it scared us, too. A couple of times, Slim grabbed my leg and squeezed it.

After *Bucket of Blood* was over, we went to the restrooms. We also paid another visit to the snack bar, where we picked up boxes of Juicy Fruits, Good 'n Plenty and Milk Duds.

The second show was *The Killer Shrews* and even scarier than *Bucket of Blood*. Shrews are supposedly the fiercest creatures in the world, but they're so small they don't go after people. *These* shrews, though, were the size of dogs. (Looking back on it, I'm pretty sure they *were* dogs.) They kept trying to get at a group of people stranded on this island. Wanted to rip them up and eat them. The people took refuge inside a house and boarded up the place to keep the shrews out. But the damn things kept getting in, anyway. It was pretty horrible. Several of the people got themselves eaten.

When I saw *The Night of the Living Dead* a few years later, it reminded me of *The Killer Shrews* . . . and of what happened after we left the drive-in. I found myself reminded of that night about a zillion times because the main actor in *The Killer Shrews* turned out to be Festus in *Gunsmoke*. After Chester got replaced by Festus, I could hardly ever watch *Gunsmoke* without thinking about *The Killer Shrews* and what happened on the way home.

At about eleven-thirty, the movie ended. An intermission started, and the area around the snack stand lit up. Here and there, headlights came on and engines started. Apparently, we weren't the only people who needed to get home.

Since I was already behind the wheel, I asked Slim, "Want *me* to take us back?"

She was *supposed* to do all the driving that night. In fact, she always drove us to and from the drive-in movies. But I figured it would be easier if we just stayed in our seats and I took the wheel.

Slim didn't answer for a few seconds. Then she said, "We told everyone *I'd* be driving."

"Yeah, true. Maybe you'd better."

"I suppose so."

Leaning out the window, I reached over and hooked the speaker box onto its pole. Then I brought myself back into the car and opened the door.

And realized my mistake. If I went around to the other side of the car so Slim could scoot over behind the wheel, I would end up sitting next to Rusty on the way home.

I wanted to sit next to Slim, not Rusty.

"What's wrong?" she asked.

I couldn't tell her. We were pals, buddies, best friends. If she found out I *needed* to sit next to her, she might realize how I really felt. It might scare her.

"Nothing," I said. "I'm fine."

"Are you sure? If you really *want* to drive . . ."

"Nah, that's okay." I climbed out and shut the door. Starting to feel lousy, I walked around to the other side. By the time I reached the passenger door, Slim and Rusty had both scooted over.

I sat beside Rusty and swung the door shut.

Leaving the headlights off, Slim drove slowly forward down

the slope of the hump from which we'd viewed the movies. At the bottom, she made a sharp turn onto the cross-lane.

She put on the parking lights. A couple of times, she stopped to let people walk by. At the end of the lane, she waited for a car to pass us before she pulled out.

She didn't cut anyone off. She didn't do anything wrong or even rude. Neither did Rusty or I.

In fact, we're pretty sure that what happened a few minutes later had nothing to do with any of the cars from the drive-in. Those exiting ahead of us had all turned the other way at Mason Road. And none came out after us. None that we noticed, anyway.

For a while, Slim's Pontiac seemed to be the only car on the road. We were about ten miles north of town, midway between Grandville and Clarksburg.

We had forest on the right.

On the left was the old graveyard. If it had a name, we didn't know it. Nobody'd been buried there since about 1920. We'd explored it a few times, though never at night. It had a lot of very cool tombstones and statues and stuff.

Driving by, the three of us snuck glances at it the way we usually did. I think we wanted to make sure nobody was digging up bodies . . . or crawling out of any graves.

No one was.

But a car sat between the old stone posts of its entry gate. A car without any lights on.

"Uh-oh," Slim said. I felt our speed decrease slightly. "Was that a cop car?"

"Didn't look like one," Rusty said.

"It wasn't," I confirmed. Being the son of Grandville's police chief, I knew what every cop car looked like: not just ours, but those of all the nearby towns, plus the county cars and state cars.

"Thought it might be a speed trap," Slim said.

"Nope," I told her.

"Cool place to make out," Rusty said.

Slim and I both laughed.

"Don't you think?"

"No," Slim said. "For one thing, it's right by the road where everyone can see you. Not to mention the *bone* orchard. You wouldn't catch *me* making out there."

"Wouldn't catch *you* making any . . ." Rusty tipped his head back and stared at the rearview mirror.

"What?" Slim asked.

"I think it's coming," he said.

"Huh?" Slim glanced at the rearview mirror. "I don't . . . oh."

I was already looking over my shoulder and knew why she'd said, "Oh." A car was coming, all right, but without headlights on. It looked like a clump of shadow hurling toward us from the rear.

"That the car from the graveyard?" Slim asked.

"Think so," Rusty said.

Slim groaned.

Rusty and I both looked over our shoulders.

Rusty muttered, "Shit."

By the velocity of the car's approach, I expected it to swerve and zip around us. But it didn't. It stayed behind us. Just when I expected it to slam into our tail, Slim hit the gas. We shot forward, the sudden acceleration pushing me into the seat.

The other car shrank into the distance, then started to grow. It looked like a big old black Cadillac.

"Here it comes," I said.

"What's the *matter* with that bastard!" Slim blurted.

"You'd better get moving," Rusty told her.

"I *am* moving."

"Faster."

We picked up more speed. The Cadillac quit growing. It didn't shrink away, either. It matched our speed and stayed about twenty feet behind us.

Moonlight glinted on its hood and windshield. I couldn't see inside it.

Slim said, "I don't like this."

She rounded a bend in the road too fast. The tires sighed. As the forces pulled at me, I grabbed the door handle to keep myself from leaning into Rusty. He let himself tilt against Slim. She muttered, "Get off me," and shoved at him with her elbow.

I looked back. The Cadillac was still on our tail.

"I'm slowing down," Slim said and took her foot off the gas.

"Here it comes," I warned.

I braced for the impact. There wasn't one. When I looked back again, the car was no more than two feet from our rear. But the space seemed to be growing.

"Looks like they don't want to hit us," I said.

"What *do* they want?" Slim asked.

I shook my head.

Rusty said, "Maybe they're just trying to scare us."

"If that's all," Slim said, "they've succeeded. They can go home now."

"Could be anything," I said.

"*Is* it the car from the graveyard?" Slim asked.

"You got me," I said.

"I think so," said Rusty.

"It looked like it might've just been sitting there *waiting* for us."

"Or for *some*one," I said. "Maybe just waiting for *any*one to go by."

Her voice low and steady, Slim said, "Either way, we're it."

"Long as all they do is follow us . . . ," Rusty muttered.

"We'll get to town pretty soon," I said.

"We're not *that* close," Slim pointed out.

"Five minutes?"

"More like ten," Rusty said.

"Who do you think they are?" Slim asked.

"God knows," I muttered.

"How about Scotty or one of those guys?" Rusty asked.

"They wouldn't dare," Slim said.

"They'd *love* to nail us," I said.

"Yeah, but they know what'll happen if they try."

"You wouldn't happen to have your bow handy, would you?" Rusty asked.

"No. But they don't know that."

"I almost hope it *is* Scotty," I said.

"As opposed to whom?" Slim asked.

"I don't know. Some creep like Starkweather or . . ."

"Hey," Rusty said. "Maybe it's an *artist* and he wants to make us into statues. Slap some clay on us. . . ."

"Crap!" Slim cried out.

Startled, I leaned past Rusty and looked at Slim. Her head was turned away, her short hair blowing. Just as I noticed the engine noises growing louder, the dark shape of the Cadillac filled her side window. It was no more than three feet away, in the lane for oncoming traffic.

So far, there *was* no oncoming traffic.

The big car stayed beside us. Its windows were rolled up. I tried to see through them, but couldn't.

Slowly, the front passenger window began to lower.

"Watch out!" I yelled.

Slim hit the brakes. We were thrown forward in our seats and the Cadillac burst ahead. It zoomed up the road for a few seconds, then cut back into our lane.

Its brake lights came on, bright red in the darkness.

"Oh, shit," Rusty muttered.

"Shit is right," Slim said.

We stopped dead in our lane.

The Cadillac, about fifty yards ahead of us, also seemed to be stopped.

Its red brake lights went out.

Slim shut off our headlights and darkness slammed down on us.

At the rear of the Cadillac, white lights came on.

"Back-up lights," I muttered.

They began moving slowly toward us.

"Here it comes," Slim whispered.

"I don't feel so good," Rusty said.

"What'll we do?" I asked.

Nobody said anything.

The car continued to back up. About ten feet in front of us, it stopped. All its lights went dark. It sat there.

And sat there.

"If anyone else comes along . . . ," I said.

"We'll see their headlights," Slim said. "I'll get us out of the way."

"Speaking of which," said Rusty, "where *is* everyone?"

"Still at the movies," Slim explained.

"That's where *we* oughta be," I said. "We wouldn't be in this fix if we'd stayed for the whole thing."

"Parents," Rusty muttered as if it were a curse word.

Slim chuckled softly, then added, "I guess we'll have the last laugh if we end up getting killed."

"We'll be all right," I said. "They obviously aren't gonna ram us, or they would've done it by now. The thing is . . ." I wasn't sure how to say it.

"What?" Slim asked.

"If someone gets out of the car . . ."

She leaned forward and looked at me. "Someone gets out and tries to come for us on foot, he'll have to deal with Chief Pontiac."

"Gonna run him over?" Rusty asked.

"If he needs it."

We waited.

The Cadillac sat in front of us, dark, its doors shut.

Slim looked at her wristwatch. "I know his game," she said. "He's trying to make us late."

"What time is it?" I asked.

"Quarter till twelve."

"We can still make it."

"Not if we keep sitting here."

"If we're late," I said, "my Dad's gonna kill me."

That got a pretty good laugh from Slim and Rusty.

Then Slim said softly as if speaking to herself, "Let's just see what happens," and stepped on the gas. As we bolted from a standstill, she cut into the other lane.

The Cadillac sprang forward and swung to the left, blocking us.

Slim hit her brakes and swerved to the right.

The Cadillac swerved and blocked us again.

We stopped. It stopped.

We sat there in the dark, ten feet apart.

"Screw this," Slim said. She threw her door open.

"What're you *doing*?" I yelled.

"Stay here." She started to climb out.

"Grab her!"

Rusty didn't even try. Either he knew better than to interfere with Slim or he was eager for her to handle the situation.

Slim dodged her open door and headed for the Cadillac, taking long, quick strides. I jumped out. "Wait!" I called.

She stopped and waved me away. "Get back in the car," she said.

"Slim!"

She whirled away and walked straight to the driver's door of the Cadillac.

I felt my stomach drop as she bent over and knocked on the window.

"Get away from there!" I called.

She knocked again. "Hey!" she yelled.

I hurried between the two cars. Glancing toward ours, I saw that Rusty had scooted over. He now sat in the driver's seat.

Slim was still leaning toward the window of the Cadillac. As I stepped around its rear, she said, "What's going on, mister?" From her tone of voice, I figured the window must be open. "Why're you . . ."

She suddenly tried to leap backward, but a hand shot out and grabbed the front of her T-shirt. It jerked hard. With a gasp, she stumbled forward and her head plunged into the open window.

"*NO!*" she squealed.

I ran toward her.

Watching.

Not wanting to believe my eyes.

Slim was inside the window to her shoulders, squirming and kicking, shoving at the window frame with her left hand to keep herself from being dragged in.

Her right arm was already inside the car.

I hit her hard in the midsection.

Tore her out of the window.

Tackled her.

Landed on top of her, smashing her against the pavement, where we almost got run over by the Pontiac. "Get in!" Rusty yelled. The passenger door flew open. "Get in! Quick!"

I scurried up, pulling at Slim. I hurled her into the front seat. Already in motion, the car started to take off without me. I chased it, running in the V of its open door.

"Hey!" I yelled.

Rusty slowed down and I dived in.

Next thing I knew, we were speeding toward town.

I leaned out and pulled the door shut. Panting for air, I sat up straight.

Rusty was stoked. "Holy jumpin' Jesus!" he said. "Wow! Jeez! Did you see that? They *grabbed* her. Holy shit! Couldn't believe it! Shit!" He slapped Slim on the thigh. "They almost got you."

Slim quit gasping for breath long enough to say, "Tell me about it."

"You all right?" I asked her.

"I'm here. That's what counts. Thanks, guys."

"No sweat," said Rusty.

Twisting my head, I looked out the rear window. The road behind us looked empty.

"I don't see 'em," I said.

"Me, either," said Rusty.

"When they come, don't stop. Don't stop for anything."

"You betcha!"

"They won't," Slim said. "They won't be coming." She lifted her right hand and jangled a bunch of keys.

"Holy shit!" Rusty said.

"You got their *car* keys."

"It was easy."

As Rusty raced into town that night, Slim told us that there'd been two men in the car: one behind the wheel and another in the passenger seat. They were strangers to her.

She described them to us—and ten minutes later to my father—as being about thirty years old, white, slender, with crew cuts. They were dressed in blue jeans and white T-shirts. Though she'd only seen them in the darkness for a few seconds, she was fairly certain that the two men were identical twins.

Dad drove off to look for them.

By the time he got out to Mason Road, however, the Cadillac was gone, along with the twins who'd tried to take Slim.

They weren't found during the weeks that followed, either.

Maybe they'd just been "passing through" and were long gone.

But we were afraid they might be out there, somewhere.

We didn't talk about it much. Hardly ever. Probably because all three of us had a pretty good idea about what they would've done to Slim if they'd taken her away in their Cadillac. We didn't want to think about it.

Especially since they might make another try for her.

We knew their car.

And they knew ours.

After that night, I kept a sharp eye out for dark Cadillacs. I'm pretty sure we all did, though we didn't talk about it.

And our car—Slim's—remained in the garage for almost a month after our close call on the way home from the Horrorfest. It didn't come out again until the night of the Traveling Vampire Show.

Chapter Thirty-nine

Slim waited in the driveway while I ran into my house and placed the two full bottles of beer in the refrigerator. I was almost weak with relief as I hurried back to her car.

I climbed into the passenger seat. "That's it," I said.

"Beautiful," she said. "Pulled that off without a hitch."

We looked at each other and grinned.

Then she backed out of the driveway and steered for Rusty's house. "When we get there," she said, "maybe you'd better go in without me."

"You sure?" I was hoping to have her there for moral support.

"I can do without Rusty's mom and dad. Besides, they'll start asking me a lot of questions if I go in. I'm sure they must've heard about my 'disappearance.'"

"Probably." The real reason she wouldn't go into the house with me, I figured, was because she didn't want Rusty's parents to see how she was dressed. They were used to seeing her in T-shirts, not fancy blouses. Plus, her shiny, long-sleeved blouse didn't exactly go with her ragged cut-off jeans. Rusty's mom and dad were sure to wonder why she'd dressed so strangely.

"Just say we're in a hurry and I'm waiting in the car."

I nodded. With Slim waiting in the car, I might be able to get out of the house faster.

Too soon, we reached Rusty's house. Slim pulled up to the curb and stopped. "I'll even leave the engine running," she said.

"*Sure* you don't want to come in?" I asked.

"You'll be fine."

"Okay. See ya."

I climbed out of the car. Somebody must've been watching for us, though, because the front door opened before I could get there. Bitsy came out. Rusty, still in the doorway, called "We're going now!" to his parents.

An answer came from somewhere inside the house, but I couldn't make it out.

Rusty shut the door.

All *right!* I wouldn't have to face the parents, after all.

As Rusty followed his sister down the porch stairs, I said, "Hi, Bitsy."

Smiling and looking shy, she said, "Hi, Dwight. Thank you for inviting me to the movies."

"Oh, you're welcome. Glad to have you."

She had dressed up for the occasion. Instead of her usual

T-shirt and cut-off jeans, she was wearing a sleeveless sun-dress. Instead of being barefoot, she wore sandals. Hanging from one shoulder was a white, patent leather purse.

"You look very nice tonight," I said. What was I *supposed* to say?

"Thank you, Dwight."

"You're a life-saver," Rusty told me.

"No sweat."

He hurried ahead. I'd left the passenger door open. He climbed in.

Smiling at me, he said, "Maybe you two lovebirds should sit together in the back."

"That was the plan," I said.

Sure it was.

I opened the back door and held it for Bitsy. Then I got in and shut the door.

"Hey, Slim," Rusty said.

"Hey, Rusty." Looking over her shoulder, she said, "How you doing, Bitsy?"

"Oh, just fine, thank you. Thank you for asking me to come with."

"Our pleasure," Slim told her. Facing forward again, she took off.

Bitsy smiled at me from her side of the back seat, but didn't try to come any closer. "I'm sorry to hear about your father's accident," she said.

Thanks for reminding me, I thought.

"Thanks," I said.

"Is he going to be all right?"

"I guess so. They're just keeping him overnight in the hos-pital to be on the safe side."

"I'm sure that's a good idea."

"Hey, Bitsy?" Slim said.

"Yes?"

"We're stopping by Lee Thompson's house before we head over to the drive-in."

"Really? What for?"

"Don't be such a nosy pain in the ass," Rusty said.

I said, "Leave her alone" at about the same moment Slim said, "Cut it out, Rusty."

Even though there wasn't much light in the back seat, enough came in through the windows for me to see Bitsy turn her head toward Rusty and cast a self-satisfied smile in his direction. I saw the smile, but he didn't. He was looking straight ahead.

To Bitsy, I explained, "My brother's out of town for the weekend. We just want to drop in on Lee and make sure she's okay."

"Is something wrong?"

"A lot of weird stuff's been going on today," Slim said.

"Like what?"

"Come *on*, guys," Rusty said, a pleading whine in his voice. "She *tells*. I don't want my mom and dad knowing *all* my business."

"I won't tell," Bitsy said.

"Bullshit," Rusty said.

Slim stopped the car. Looking out the window, I saw that we were at the curb in front of Lee's house. Her pickup truck was parked in the driveway.

The windows of her house were dark.

"Doesn't look like she's home," Rusty said.

"I'll go see." I opened my door.

"I'm coming with you," Rusty said, opening his.

"Me too," said Bitsy.

Slim shrugged, shut off the engine and killed the headlights. Moments later, all four of us were walking toward the front door of Lee's house.

"Did Lee *go* somewhere?" Rusty asked in a hushed voice.

"We don't know," Slim said.

"It's funny the lights are off," I muttered.

"Maybe she's taking a nap," Rusty said.

"We tried to call a couple of times," I told him. "I don't think she slept through the ringing."

"Might've," Slim said. "But not likely."

On the front stoop, I reached for the doorbell but Rusty

grabbed my wrist. "Don't," he whispered. "What if somebody's *in* there?"

"Like who?"

"You know. Like *them*."

"You mean Julian?" I asked.

"Yeah. Or some of his gang."

"Who's Julian?" Bitsy asked.

Slim went, "Shhhh."

When I lowered my arm, Rusty released my wrist. I stepped up to the screen door, put my nose against it, then cupped my hands on both sides of my eyes to block out the faint glow of light from the street.

I could just barely see in.

The main door was wide open. Beyond it, I saw only blackness and shades of gray.

"LEE!" I shouted, startling everyone.

Rusty gasped. Bitsy sucked in a quick breath, making a high-pitched *"Uh!"* Slim grabbed my arm but didn't make any noise.

Only silence came from inside the house.

Though I hated to raise my voice again, I yelled, *"LEE! YOU HOME? IT'S DWIGHT!"*

After my shout, a long silence.

Rusty broke it, whispering, "Maybe she went over to a neighbor's."

"Maybe."

"Who's Julian?" Bitsy asked again.

"From the Vampire Show," Slim said.

Bitsy did that *"Uh!"* again.

"Tell her *everything*, why don't you!" Rusty burst out in an angry whisper.

"I'm going in," I said.

Slim, still gripping my arm, gave it a squeeze. "Wait here. I'll be right back." Then she let go, whirled around and ran back to her Pontiac. Bending over behind it, she opened its trunk.

"What's she doing?" Bitsy asked.

Slim reached into the trunk, then took a step away from it

and swung her quiver of arrows behind her back.

Rusty groaned.

"What?" Bitsy demanded.

"Nothing."

Slim bent over the trunk again. This time, she came up with her bow in one hand. I couldn't exactly see what she had in her other hand, but knew it must be the two knives.

She came running toward us, leaped up the stairs and lurched to a halt. "Here, you guys." She held out the knives. Rusty took the sheath knife and I took the pocket knife.

"What's going on?" Bitsy asked.

"Why don't you go and wait in the car?" Rusty said.

"Fat chance."

"Go on. It might be dangerous."

"So?" Turning to me, she said, "I don't have to wait in the car, do I?"

"Might be a good idea," I said.

Slim gave a quick shake of her head. "We don't really want her in the car by herself."

"No," said Bitsy. "We don't."

"If you stay," Rusty told her, "you've got to do everything we tell you to."

"I'm not taking orders from *you*."

"Just stick with us," Slim told her, then whipped an arrow out of her quiver, fit it onto her bowstring and drew the string back a few inches.

"Who's *in* there?" Bitsy asked.

"We don't know," I said. "Maybe nobody."

Rusty put his face close to Bitsy's. "Maybe a *vampire!*"

She straightened her back. "No such thing."

"Keep telling yourself that, squirt."

"There *isn't*."

"Let's go," Slim said. "Me first. Dwight, you wanta get the door?"

First, I opened the pocket knife. Holding it in my right hand, I used my left to pull open the screen door.

Slim walked in. Rusty followed, staying close to her back.

Bitsy went into the house behind him. I took up the rear and eased the screen door silently shut.

In the foyer, we stopped moving. We listened.

There were a few quiet sounds of the sort that houses always make: creaks, clicks, humms and buzzes from some sort of appliances. I heard breathing sounds and hoped they came only from us.

Slim's black shirt moved like a shadow in the darkness. She seemed to be swiveling slowly, scanning the living room, ready to shoot.

All of a sudden, my left arm got grabbed. I flinched and gasped, then realized it was only Bitsy.

Only.

She clung to my arm with both hands and pressed her body against it as if she'd mistaken my arm for a pole she hoped to climb. My upper arm was clasped against one of her breasts so tightly that the small, soft mound seemed to be mashed flat. My forearm was pressed to her belly. I could feel her heartbeat and breathing. She wore a flowery perfume so sweet I almost gagged.

It wasn't exactly the same as if she'd been Slim.

I resisted the urge to push her away.

"Somebody get a light," Slim whispered.

"Let go," I told Bitsy.

She held on. I made my way toward a wall switch, anyway, with Bitsy clinging to me. When I got within reach of where a switch should be, I said, "Let go. Come on, I need my arm."

At last, she released me.

Without her body mashed against it, my arm felt strangely cool. I raised it and flicked a light switch. Two lamps came on in the living room, one at each end of the sofa.

No Lee.

No strangers.

No one at all.

Everything looked just the same as usual.

"Okay," Slim whispered, "let's check the rest of the house."

Again, she led the way, walking slowly, her bow partly drawn back, ready to let an arrow fly if we should come under attack.

Chapter Forty

We made our way through the entire house, turning on lights in every room, looking in closets, glancing behind furniture and drapes. In the bedroom, I dropped and peered into the space between the bed and the floor while Rusty checked the adjoining bathroom.

Lee was nowhere to be found.

Nobody seemed to be in the house except the four of us.

Done with our search, we returned to the living room. Slim swung her arrow over her shoulder and dropped it into her quiver. Rusty sank onto the sofa. I folded my knife shut and stuffed it into a front pocket of my jeans.

"Can we go to the movies now?" Bitsy asked.

We all looked at her.

She frowned. "What?"

"We're worried about Lee," Slim exlained.

"Don't you think she just *went* someplace? I mean, people *go* places. We don't want to miss the movies, do we?"

"Screw the movies," Rusty said. "We were never gonna go to the movies anyway."

"Were, too." She gave me a betrayed look. "We were, weren't we? You *said* so."

I nodded to Bitsy, but spoke to Rusty. "We figured to head on out to the Moonlight and take in the first one, anyway."

"Why not both?" Bitsy asked.

"We're supposed to be back here by ten-thirty. . . ."

"*Dwight!*" Rusty blurted.

"We might as well tell her the truth."

"She'll *tell* on us."

"Will not," she protested.

"Like hell."

252

Slim said to Bitsy, "This has to be a secret, okay? We've let you come along tonight, but if you ever want to do anything with us again . . ."

"Ever in your whole life," Rusty added.

". . . you'll have to keep quiet about what goes on. We can't have you going home and telling your parents about everything we do."

"About *anything* we do," Rusty said.

Bitsy raised her right hand as if taking an oath. "I promise."

Looking disgusted, Rusty shook his head and muttered, "She'll tell."

"Will not."

I gave Slim the nod.

She nodded in return, then said to Bitsy, "We think somebody's after us. Maybe someone from the Traveling Vampire Show."

"What for?"

"To shut us up," Rusty said.

"We don't really know what they're up to," Slim explained. "I saw them . . . do something horrible to a dog today. Maybe they want to scare us into keeping quiet about it. The thing is, weird stuff has been happening ever since. Someone was in my house this afternoon. They chewed up a book in my bedroom. . . ."

"Like a dog," Rusty added.

"The book was *Dracula*," Slim pointed out. "Which is about vampires."

"Not that we think a vampire did it," I said.

"But maybe someone from the show. Also, there was this flower vase in my mother's room. It had yellow roses in it. Somebody broke the vase and took the roses. Then one of the roses turned up in Dwight's room."

"At *your* house?" Bitsy asked me, looking shocked.

I nodded. "They put it on my pillow."

"Now we've got this with Lee missing," Slim continued. "She and Dwight drove over to Janks Field this morning looking for me and Rusty, and they talked to the main guy of the Vampire Show."

"Julian Stryker," I said.

"Lee bought tickets for tonight's performance, but she paid with a check. The check had her name and address on it. So Julian and his bunch had an easy way to find out where she lives."

"You think they *took* her?" Bitsy asked.

The question made me go cold inside.

"We don't know," Slim said.

"She ain't *here*," Rusty added.

"But there're no signs of foul play." I wanted to talk myself and the others out of believing that Lee had been taken away.

"Not unless you count the open door," Slim said.

"She might've left it like that for the breeze," I said. "Anyway, she isn't expecting us for a couple more hours, so maybe she *did* go somewhere."

"Without her truck?" Slim asked.

"She might've walked over to . . ."

"Without her purse?"

"Purse?" I asked.

"It's on a counter in the kitchen."

"I saw it," Bitsy threw in.

Slim said, "I think Lee would've taken it with her if she'd gone off on her own."

"*You* hardly ever take a purse with you," I pointed out.

"Yeah, well . . . I'm a little different. Most women take their purses *every*where."

"Maybe she took a different one," I said. "She has more than one."

"Let's have a look," Slim said.

All of us followed her into the kitchen. Nodding at Lee's brown leather purse, she said to me, "Why don't you do the honors? You're family."

"Sure." I moved Lee's purse from the counter to the kitchen table, where the light was better. Then I frowned at Slim. "Do you really think we oughta do this? It's sort of invading her privacy."

"*I'll* look," Rusty volunteered.

"No you won't," I said. "We don't need *you* going through her stuff."

"Oh, yeah? What's . . . ?" He shut up, no doubt suddenly afraid I might tell what he'd done that afternoon in Slim's mother's bedroom.

Slim said, "We just need to see how full it is . . . if maybe she went off with some other purse."

"It feels pretty heavy," I said.

"Would you rather have me look?" Slim asked.

"Yeah, maybe so."

I stepped aside. Slim handed the bow to me, then opened Lee's purse. As we all watched, she lifted out the billfold. Holding it out of the way, she bent over the purse and peered in. "Checkbook, lipstick, keys. . . ." Then her lips moved, but she said nothing. She reached down into the purse.

Her hand came up holding four stiff red papers the size of postcards cut in half lengthwise.

The first time I'd seen them, they had been in the hand of Julian Stryker when he came out of the bus at Janks Field.

Then I'd seen Lee tuck them into her purse.

Slim studied one of them. Meeting my eyes, she said, "Tickets for tonight's performance of the Traveling Vampire Show."

"All *right!*" Rusty blurted.

Slim and I looked at him. He seemed delighted.

"The *tickets*, guys. We can still *go*."

"Not without Lee," I said.

"Go where?" Bitsy asked.

Rusty scowled at her. "To the Traveling Vampire Show."

"What about the *drive-in?*"

"Screw the drive-in."

Bitsy glanced hopefully from me to Slim and back to me again. This time, neither of us came to her defense. Her face turned sullen, lower lip bulging out.

Slim set the tickets on the kitchen table. "Guess Lee didn't switch purses. This one has all the main stuff in it." She put the billfold back inside. Leaving the tickets on the table, she closed the purse. Then she turned toward me. She looked worried.

"You really think they took her?" I asked.

"It's a possibility. But maybe Lee just went off without her purse, no big deal. She might've gone for a walk, gone on a ride with a friend, whatever, and she'll turn up before long. I mean, you guys had *me* kidnapped or God-knows-what this afternoon just because you couldn't find me for a couple of hours. Lee could be *anywhere*, perfectly safe, planning to get back here in plenty of time to take us to the show."

"We're gonna *miss* the show if we don't get going," Bitsy complained.

"Not *that* show, you wad. The *vampire* show."

Slim pretty much ignored them. "If she'd just gone off, though, she probably would've taken her purse and shut the front door. So maybe something happened that made her leave in a big hurry."

"An emergency," I said.

Slim nodded. "Maybe she ran out of the house to help someone. Or to get *away* from someone."

"Maybe she *did* get away," I said.

In my mind, I saw Lee fleeing out the back door of her house, Stryker and his gang in hot pursuit . . . chasing her with spears as she ran through her yard and down the long embankment toward the river.

What if she didn't make it?

"Another possibility," Slim said, "is that someone came into the house and took her away."

"Stryker?" Rusty asked.

"He's a likely suspect," Slim said. "But maybe he isn't involved at all. Look at what's happened to *us*. Like how that car came after us on the way home from the drive-in a few weeks ago. And that weird guy in the sheet on Halloween last year. And all the troubles we've had over at Janks Field *before* today. They had nothing to do with the Vampire Show."

"Maybe," Rusty said. "Maybe not."

"Get real," I told him.

"Who really knows?" he said, wiggling his eyebrows and trying to sound like Karloff. "Maybe it's the ghost of Tommy Janks. He's doing it all . . . pulling all the strings."

"Get bent," Slim said.

"I want to take a look out back," I said and handed the bow back to Slim. "If someone *did* come after Lee, maybe she ran off."

"Out the *back* door?" Rusty asked, using his normal voice.

"Yeah." I walked toward it.

"The front door's the open one," he reminded me.

"If someone comes in the front door," I explained, "what you do is run out the back and shut it behind you to slow 'em down. . . ."

"Or maybe so they don't realize you went out," Slim added.

"Right," I said. I stepped up to the back door and opened it. A warm wind blew in against me. I pushed on the screen door.

It stayed shut.

Because its inside hook was fastened.

"Guess she *didn't* run out the back," I admitted.

"So much for that theory," said Slim.

"She still could've gotten away."

"Maybe she didn't *need* to," Rusty said.

"That's right," I said.

"So what do you want to do?" Slim asked me.

I shrugged. I had to do something, but didn't know what. I felt miserable: confused, helpless, scared.

Even as we stood in the kitchen chatting about theories, Lee might be running for her life with Stryker or someone hot on her tail. Or maybe she'd already been captured. Someone might be taking her farther and farther away. Or torturing her. Or raping her. Or killing her. Or she might be perfectly fine. Maybe she'd walked over to a friend's house for supper or gone for a stroll to enjoy the wild, windy night.

"I don't know," I muttered.

Bitsy raised her hand as if she were in a classroom.

"We know, we know," Rusty said. "In your brilliant opinion, we should forget about Lee and go to the drive-in."

"Shows how much you know," Bitsy said.

"What is it?" Slim asked.

Bitsy frowned and opened her mouth, but no words came out.

"Spit it out," Rusty said.

"Shut up," I told him. Then I looked at Bitsy. "Is there something you want to say?"

She glanced around at all of us, then said, "Just that you shouldn't be so worried about Lee. She just *went* somewhere, that's all."

Rusty smirked. "Thanks for the news flash."

Bitsy scowled at him, then looked at me and said, "Nobody's *after* anybody. I mean, you've got it all wrong."

"About what?"

"Everything. That guy you keep talking about . . . Stryker? From the Vampire Show? He didn't do any of that stuff. You know, sneak into your houses and chew on the book and do things with the roses." Blushing fiercely and looking ready to burst into tears, Bitsy said, "I did it."

Chapter Forty-one

I think my mouth fell open. I know Slim's did.

Rusty blasted, *"You!"*

"I'm *sorrrrry*," she brayed, and then started to bawl. Face red and twisted, tears rolling down her cheeks, she sobbed out, "I didn't *mean* to! I'm *sorrrrry!!!*"

"You little shit!"

"Knock it off," I told Rusty.

Standing there, Bitsy lowered her face into her open hands. Her shoulders jumped up and down. She gasped and snorted.

Slim started making faces at me and nodding toward Bitsy.

I got the message. Stepping up to Bitsy, I murmured, "It's all right," and put my arms around her.

Her arms whipped around me like a springing trap.

258

I stroked her head with one hand and patted her back with the other while she shuddered and twitched. Her face was shoved against my chest. I felt her hot breath through my shirt. Soon, I felt wetness, too. From her tears. And, I'm afraid, from her slobber.

I kept saying, "It's all right" and "Everything's fine" and "It doesn't matter," and so on for quite a while until Bitsy finally calmed down.

Then Slim said softly, "Let's go sit down." She led the way. Bitsy and I followed her, Bitsy sniffing and clinging to my arm.

In the living room, Slim pointed to the sofa. So I sat down on it, Bitsy still hugging my arm.

Slim sank onto the front edge of a chair. She propped the bow on the floor between her feet and held it upright in front of her. She couldn't lean back because of her quiver.

Rusty sat in another chair, looking disgusted and shaking his head.

"We're not mad at you, Bitsy," Slim said.

"You're not?"

"No. Are we, Dwight?"

"No," I said. "It's no big deal, Bitsy."

"No big deal," Rusty echoed, glaring at her. "Fuckin' psycho."

Bitsy gasped. From the look on her face, she was about to blurt, *"I'm gonna tell!"* But no words came out. Our warnings must've gotten through to her.

Slim frowned at Rusty. "You're not helping matters."

He rolled his eyes upward.

To Bitsy, Slim said in a gentle voice, "What happened, anyway? What made you do it?"

She gave Slim a pouty look, then whined, "I don't knowwww. They ditched me."

"Rusty and Dwight."

"Yeah. I got sent in for my shoes, only when I came back out they were already gone. It was all just a trick to get rid of me."

"A pretty mean trick," Slim muttered.

Which made me feel crummy again.

"Yeah," Bitsy said. "It was really mean. I went after 'em. I could've caught up, too, 'cause I knew they were going to Janks Field to look for you. Only they didn't *want* me with 'em, or they would've waited." Bitsy looked into Slim's eyes. "See, the thing is, you've always gotta have it just the three of you. Nobody wants me butting in. They've gotta have you all to themselves, and I guess you *wanta* be the only girl." She pushed out her lower lip again. "Maybe you're not the *only* girl around that wants to have fun sometimes."

I saw Slim's eyes go shiny. She swallowed, licked her lips, then asked in a soft voice, "You blamed *me* for the guys ditching you?"

"Sorta," Bitsy muttered.

"And that's why you went over to my house?"

"I guess." She lowered her head and continued. "It wasn't locked or anything."

"It hardly ever is."

"I knew nobody was gonna be there, 'cause of how your mom works over at the restaurant and you don't have a dad or anything . . . and the guys said you were over at Janks Field. So I just went in."

"Freak," Rusty muttered.

"Stop it," I told him.

"Well, she is."

"Leave her alone," Slim said. Then she said to Bitsy, "Did you go in on purpose to wreck things?"

"No," she said. It was almost a whimper.

"Why *did* you go in?"

She shrugged with one shoulder. "I don't know."

"But you went up to my bedroom and chewed on my *Dracula*?"

"I guess so."

Rusty sneered. "You don't *know?*"

"I guess I chewed on some book."

"Why that one?" Slim asked.

"Just . . . I don't know . . . I knew you liked it a lot."

"That's why you chewed on it? To hurt me?"

"I guess so."

"Why none of the others?"

Another shrug. "I don't know. I guess maybe I didn't feel like it." She raised her head to meet Slim's eyes. "It made me feel *awful*, wrecking your book." Her lower lip bulged, her chin shook and she started crying all over again. "I'm *sorrrrry!*" she blubbered.

I started patting her back.

Slim said, "It's all right, Bitsy. Don't worry about it."

"I'll . . . buy you . . . a new one."

"Doesn't matter," Slim said. "But I don't get it. If you suddenly felt so bad about wrecking *Dracula*, how come you went into my mom's room and started breaking things?"

Here we go.

"I *didn't*," she blurted.

Meeting my eyes, Rusty shook his head slightly.

"You didn't break the vase?" Slim asked. "Or the perfume bottle?"

"They was . . . already busted. I just . . . I took the *flowers*, that's all . . . They looked so . . . they was on the floor like . . . like nobody wanted 'em and they got thrown down . . . and they looked so *sad*."

Looking perplexed, Slim said, "But you didn't break any glass?"

Bitsy shook her head.

Then Slim laid off the questions for a while and I patted Bitsy until she calmed down. When she was done crying, Slim asked, "So what happened after you picked up the roses?"

"Nothing."

"Nothing else at my house?"

"Huh-uh."

"So you left my house, and then what?"

Lowering her head, she muttered, "I guess I went and gave a rose to Dwight."

"You went over to his house and sneaked in?"

She nodded slightly.

"What time was that?" I asked.

She shrugged. "I don't know."

"Wasn't my *mom* home?"

Again, the small nodding motion. Then the soft voice murmured, "I guess so."

"You snuck around in my house while my *mother* was there?"

"I'm sorry."

"Jeez."

Rusty looked pleased with himself. "*Told* you she's a psycho."

"I didn't hurt nothing," Bitsy said.

"What *did* you do in Dwight's house?" Slim asked.

"Nothing. Just gave him the flower, that's all."

"You put it on my *bed*," I said.

"I'm sorry."

"Good God," I muttered.

"What else did you do?" Slim asked.

The way Bitsy's face suddenly flushed crimson, I wished Slim had kept the question to herself.

"Nothing," Bitsy said.

"Oooo, boy," Rusty muttered.

"What did you do?" Slim asked again.

Once too many times.

Bitsy's head jerked up and she snapped at Slim, "Nothing! I didn't do *nothing*! You can go to hell! You can *all* go to hell!" Then she leaped up and ran for the foyer.

For a moment, the three of us were too stunned to move or speak. Then Rusty yelped, "Shit!"

Slim called, "Bitsy, wait."

From where I was sitting on the sofa, I could see the girl hustle toward the front door. "Bitsy!" I yelled.

Then Rusty pounded by

"Good God," Slim said. She sprang up, dropping her bow to the carpet and struggling to pull off her quiver.

I leaped up and went after Rusty.

"Stop or I'm gonna cream you!" he shouted.

His sister flung open the screen door and ran outside. The door, starting to swing shut, bounced off Rusty as he charged through.

"Rusty!" I yelled. Hot on his heels, I swept the closing door out of my way, rushed across the stoop and leaped down the stairs.

Bitsy was chugging across Lee's front yard, short hair bouncing, skirt flapping behind her, Rusty closing in. Though he was large and clumsy and slow, his little sister was slower.

"Rusty!" I shouted. "Let her go!"

He reached out and grabbed a shoulder of her sleeveless sundress. "Gotcha!"

They matched strides, linked by his arm.

"Let go!" I yelled at him.

"Stop!" he yelled at her.

He didn't let go. She didn't stop.

I reached out and grabbed the back of Rusty's shirt collar. I was about to give it a sharp tug when Bitsy suddenly let out a squeal.

Rusty's body blocked my view of her. When I saw her again, she was careening sideways out of control. Rusty must've jerked her shoulder.

I heard Slim yell, *"Jesus!"*

Letting go of Rusty and trying to slow down, I twisted my head around and caught a glimpse of Bitsy spinning like a frenzied figure skater. Her arms were flung out. Her skirt was twirling high.

I lost track of her for a moment as Rusty and I nearly collided.

By the time I saw her again, she must've just crashed to the ground. She tumbled wildly, flipping over a couple of times, and came to rest on her back.

We hurried toward her.

She was gasping for air. Her arms and legs were spread out as if she hoped to make snow angels in August. The top of her sundress, buttons ripped open down to her belly, was hanging off one shoulder and showing her bare right breast. Her skirt had gotten shoved up so it covered nothing below her waist. I thought at first that she was wearing some sort of tight, skin-colored underwear. Just as I realized my mistake, Slim crouched beside her, blocking my view. She shut Bitsy's dress top and lowered the skirt just before Rusty and I got there.

Rusty scowled down at her. "Y'okay?" he asked.

She just kept gasping.

"It's your own stupid fault," he said. "I *told* you to stop."

In a gentle voice, Slim said to Bitsy, "There was no reason to run away."

"Yeah," Rusty said. "We weren't gonna hurt you."

I glared at him. "Why'd you have to throw her down?"

"All I wanted to do was make her stop running away. She wasn't supposed to get hurt."

"Fucker."

It wasn't a very nice thing for Bitsy to call her brother, but I was glad to hear it. For one thing, I felt the same way. For another, I didn't think she'd be making cracks like that if she had sustained any really serious damage.

Rusty scowled down at her for a while, then said, "Look, you weren't supposed to get hurt. Okay? I'm sorry. It was an accident."

"Like fun," Bitsy muttered.

"Why don't we get you off the ground?" Slim said to her. "We can go back inside and see if you need to be patched up. I happen to know Lee has a medicine cabinet full of first aid supplies."

"No," Bitsy said. "I don't wanta."

"I know," said Rusty. "You wanta go to the movies."

She shook her head. "I wanta go home."

Chapter Forty-two

Go home?" Rusty said. "No way."

"Wanta bet?" Using one hand to hold the top of her dress shut, Bitsy shoved at the ground with her other hand and managed to sit up.

"I'll drive you home," Slim said. "But you don't want your mom and dad to see you looking like this. Let's go in the house first, and. . . ."

"Huh-uh. I wanta go home. Right now."

Rusty looked pitiful. "Man, it's gonna be my ass."

"Should've thought of that," I said, "before you threw her down."

"It was an *accident*. Anyway, if you hadn't grabbed my shirt . . ."

"Oh, so now it's *my* fault."

With Slim holding her steady, Bitsy rose to her feet. "Let's go in the house," Slim said.

"I don't wanta." She tried to pull away, but Slim held on.

"You're *not* going home looking like this," Slim said, her voice firm. "We'll clean you up first and see if you've got any injuries. Then we'll do something about your dress. *Then* I'll take you home. Maybe."

I almost applauded.

Hobbling toward the front door in Slim's custody, Bitsy started to cry again.

Rusty and I stayed back. By the time we entered the front door, they were out of sight. Soon, we heard water running.

Rusty shook his head. "I'm really gonna get it," he muttered. "They'll ground me so long I'll be gray before they let me outa the house."

"You should've kept your hands off her," I said.

"She was trying to get away. She was gonna run home. It would've wrecked everything."

Slim came striding into the foyer.

"How is she?" I asked.

"*Really* upset. I mean, God." Slim shook her head. "At least she's not hurt."

"She's not?" Rusty asked. He seemed surprised and pleased.

"Not much. Mostly, she's grass-stained. She has a few little scrapes and scratches, but that's about it. I told her to wash up."

"How about her dress?" Rusty asked.

"Wrecked."

265

"Can't you fix it?"

"I could wash it," she told Rusty, and glanced at me in a way that brought back memories of her laundry room. "I might be able to mend it, too . . . sew some new buttons on. But the first time your mother takes a good look at it, she'll know it got wrecked. I mean, there's *fabric* missing where the buttons got torn off."

"In other words, I'm fucked."

Almost pleased, I said, "Yep."

"Not necessarily," said Slim. "There's one way out."

"Suicide?" Rusty asked.

"A little less drastic than that," Slim explained. "As a matter of fact, it's simple. All we've gotta do is win Bitsy over. You're off the hook if she doesn't tell on you."

"But what about the dress?"

"She can say she was fooling around . . . got into a game of touch footfall or something and had a little accident."

"Better make it *tackle* football," I said.

Slim grinned at me. "Yeah."

Rusty shook his head. "She'll never go along with it."

"It's your only chance," Slim said.

"What you've gotta do," I said, "is *really* kiss up to her."

"Barf."

Giving me a meaningful look, Slim said, "We've got to *all* be really nice to her."

"Never should've let her come with us in the first place," Rusty muttered.

Slim smirked at him.

"Hey, moron," I said, "it was the only way to get you out of the house."

"I could've snuck out."

"Sure. Maybe by around midnight. Which would've been a little late for catching the Vampire Show."

"Not gonna catch it anyway if we let Bitsy go home and rat on me."

"I shouldn't have pushed her," Slim muttered.

"That was Rusty."

"You know what I mean. We wouldn't be in this fix if I hadn't given her the third degree."

Rising out of his worries, Rusty flashed a smile at me. "What the hell *did* she do in your room?"

"Let's drop it," I said. "I don't know and I don't *wanta* know."

"Must've been pretty embarrassing."

Slim shook her head. In a low voice, she whispered to Rusty, "The kid's *in love* with him—*everything's* embarrassing."

I believe I snarled.

"Well, she is," Slim told me.

"I know."

"That's right," Rusty said.

At the sound of a door opening, we went silent and watched Bitsy step into the hallway. She was no longer crying. She seemed calm. Back straight, she limped toward us. She'd used a couple of safety pins to fasten the top of her dress together, but she hadn't done a very good job with them. Her front was open to one extent or another all the way down to her waist.

"How are you doing?" I asked her.

"Not so good."

"We're really sorry you got hurt."

"Yeah," Rusty said. "I'm sorry."

"You know what?" Slim asked her. "We're *glad* you're the one who did that stuff in our houses. I mean, we figured we had those weirdos from the vampire show creeping around, so it's a fantastic relief to find out it was only you."

"That's for sure," I said.

It wasn't a total lie. I was very glad we weren't being stalked by Stryker and his gang. But the notion of Bitsy creeping through my house—*while my mom was home*—gave me a bad case of the creeps. I knew that Rusty and I had sneaked into Slim's house that same day, but this seemed different. In fact, this seemed a trifle demented.

What if she sneaks into the house when I'm there?

I imagined her skulking through the hallways and rooms late at night, lurking in shadows, spying on me.

"I'm sorry I upset you," Slim told her.

"And I'm sorry you fell," Rusty said.

I just smiled at her and shrugged.

She smiled at me. A rather sad smile that used only one side of her mouth. "Anyway," she said, "I don't wanta go home, after all."

"Okay," Slim said.

Rusty looked as if he wanted to whoop for joy. He held it in, though, and simply sighed as if his death sentence had been commuted.

"All I ever wanted," Bitsy said, "was just to hang out with you guys. I didn't wanta wreck anything."

"That's real good," I said, trying to sound sincere.

"So can we all be friends?" she asked. "If I promise not to tell?"

"Sure!" Rusty blurted.

"And nobody tells on me, okay?"

"A deal," Slim said.

I nodded.

"What's to tell?" said Rusty.

Blushing, she looked away and muttered, "Nothing."

"Well," said Slim, "I'm glad that's all settled. Now we just have to decide what to do about Lee." She asked me, "What do you think?"

"I guess . . . since it was Bitsy who did the other stuff, maybe there really *isn't* anything to worry about."

Rusty gave his sister a look of exaggerated suspicion. "*You* didn't do something with Lee, did you?"

Bitsy narrowed her eyes. "No."

"Anyway," I said, "I guess we can either go on to the drive-in or wait here."

"There's no point in the drive-in anymore," Bitsy said.

We all looked at her.

"By the time we can get there . . ." She shrugged. "We'd just have to turn around and come back. Wouldn't even get to see a whole movie. Not if we have to be *here* by ten-thirty."

"We could at least watch part of one," I told her.

"Nah." A smile lifted her heavy lips. "Who wants to see a

couple of stupid movies, anyway? I wanta go see the Traveling Vampire Show."

Silence crashed down on us.

Slim, Rusty and I stared at each other.

Bitsy watched us, a funny smile on her face that made me suspect she knew exactly what she was doing.

Nobody else spoke up, so I did.

"We'd like to have you come with us," I said, "but we've only got four tickets."

She pointed at us, counting aloud. "One, two, three, four."

"The problem is, one of the tickets is for Lee."

"But she's not here."

"Thanks for the news flash," Rusty said.

Slim gave him a dirty look, then said, "They're Lee's tickets. She bought them, and she's intending to go."

"In fact," I added, "they might not let us in without her. We're all under age. Stryker only sold her the tickets on the condition that she'd come with us."

"How can she come with us if she isn't even here?" Bitsy asked.

"Well," I said, "we're hoping she'll be back in time."

"So *I* won't be able to go?"

"I didn't mean it that way. We'd *like* for you to come with us."

"Of course," Slim said. "But with only four tickets, I'm not sure we'll be able to manage it."

Lower lip bulging again, Bitsy said, "I guess I wanta go home now. If I can't go to the vampire show . . ."

"You can go!" Rusty blurted. "Jesus! Okay? No problem. We'll get another ticket, that's all."

"How are we supposed to do that?" I asked.

"For all we know," Slim said, "they might be sold out."

"Even if they aren't," I added, "they won't sell us one for a thirteen year old."

"I'm going home," Bitsy said.

"No!" Looking frantic, Rusty raised his open hands and flapped them at us. "Just hang on a minute. Nobody's going anywhere. I've got it all figured out. Okay?"

"Let's hear it," Slim said.

Calming down slightly, he patted the air in front of his shoulders and said, "We go now."

"Go where?" I asked.

"To Janks Field. We take three of the tickets. Slim drives. We leave Lee's ticket here so she can follow along later in her pickup. We leave her a note, too, so she'll know what's going on."

"That still leaves us a ticket short," Slim pointed out.

Rusty patted the air some more. "That's why we go now. We get there good and early, find us an adult and pay him to buy us one more ticket."

"What'll we use for money?" I asked.

"How much we need?" Bitsy asked.

"The tickets are normally ten bucks," Rusty said, "but we might have to pay more. Fifteen or twenty, maybe."

"I got more'n thirty," Bitsy said.

I remembered her white patent leather purse. She didn't have it now. When we first came into Lee's house, she must've left it in Slim's car.

Rusty frowned as if he couldn't figure out how his little sister had gotten her hands on that much money. But he played it smart this time and kept his mouth shut.

"Great!" he said. "We're in business." He glanced at Slim, then at me. "Okay?"

"Might work," Slim said.

"Worth a try," I said.

Narrowing her eyes, Bitsy looked at her brother. "What if we can't *get* another ticket?"

Rusty stared at her for a long time, then said, "That happens, you can have mine."

Chapter Forty-three

In the kitchen, I handed three of the tickets to Slim and left the fourth ticket on the table beside Lee's purse. Slim slipped them down a seat pocket of her cut-off jeans.

I found a pen and a pad of scratch paper by the phone. Back at the table, I wrote:

> Dear Lee,
>   Sorry we missed you. We took three of the tickets and went on ahead. We figured we had better get there early and beat the crowd, as the parking has been known to get wierd.
>   We took Slim's Pontiac. Please come as early as you can. We well be looking for you and save you a seat.
> Love,
>   Dwight

I showed the note to Slim. She read it to herself, then asked, "Who ever taught you how to spell?"

"What's wrong with my spelling?"

"Aside from it stinks?"

Rusty chuckled.

"Like *you're* some kinda whiz kid," I said to him.

"Let me see," Bitsy said, and plucked the note from Slim's hand. Her head bobbed up and down as she silently mouthed the words. About the time she came to the end, her brow furrowed.

"She's my sister-in-law," I explained.

Bitsy said, "I know that," but she looked relieved.

After she gave the note to me, I folded it and placed it beside the red ticket. "All set," I said.

271

"You don't want to correct the spelling?" Slim asked, a glint in her eyes.

"Not really."

"Lee's a teacher."

"I know that," I said, suddenly sounding like Rusty or Bitsy. Rusty let out a laugh. To Slim, he said, "Dwighty's hoping to get some private spelling lessons from her."

"Very funny," I said. "Are we going?"

"Let's go," Slim said.

In the living room, she picked up her bow and her quiver of arrows. Then we left the house. Hanging back, I shut the main door after I was out.

We crossed the lawn to Slim's car. When we got there, she put her bow and quiver of arrows into the trunk. Then we all climbed into the car. I sat in the back seat with Bitsy. Slim drove. Within about a minute, we were out on Route 3 with woods on both sides and no other cars in sight.

"What I think we'll do," she said, "is walk in."

"Huh?" Rusty said.

"Walk?" asked Bitsy.

"I'm not driving onto Janks Field," Slim said. "For one thing, I don't want the tires getting ruined. For another, we might be the only car there this early. We're too young to be going at *all*, so we sure don't want the whole crew watching us arrive."

"Good point," I said.

"Also, the place'll probably end up jammed with cars later on. We don't want to get stuck in the traffic."

"Hey," Rusty said, "maybe they'll have a riot like that other time." He sounded as if he hoped so and wouldn't mind participating.

"If there *is* a riot," Slim said, "we can just take off into the woods free and clear."

"Are we gonna have to walk through the woods?" Bitsy asked.

"Just if there's a riot," I explained.

"Or if we get chased by vampires," Rusty added.

"Quit it," Bitsy said.

"What we'll do," Slim said, "is park along the highway and walk in on the dirt road."

Bitsy moaned.

"You wanted to come," Rusty reminded her.

"I know that."

"You don't *have* to," I told her. "We've still got plenty of time. We could drop you off. . . ."

"I wanta come with."

"That's fine," Slim said. "The thing is, Bitsy, we might see some really bad stuff happen. *I* sure did. What they did to that dog . . . These are bad people."

"You're just trying to talk me out of it."

"No, I'm trying to warn you. You might end up wishing you'd stayed home."

"So how come *you're* going?" Asking that, she sounded a little snotty.

"Slim's the judge," Rusty said.

"Huh?"

"Dwight and I, we've got a bet going."

"What bet?" Bitsy asked.

"I say Valeria's a babe."

"Who's she?"

"The star of the show," I explained.

"Dwight says she'll be a loser, but I happen to know she'll be gorgeous. If I'm right, Dwight has to shave his head."

"*Slim* shaves my head," I reminded him.

"Oh, yeah, right. Anyways, Slim's the judge."

"That isn't why I'm going," Slim said. Turning her head to the left, she said, "There's the way in." She started to slow down. "We'll turn around . . . ," she muttered.

"Then why?" Bitsy asked.

"Huh?"

"How come *you* wanta go if it's gonna be so horrible?"

"Gotta watch out for my guys," she said. Slowing almost to a stop, she made a U-turn. "Anyway, my mom's away for the night and I didn't much want to stay by myself."

"Especially since she had a *prowler* today," Rusty added, and glanced back at his sister.

"I said I was sorry," Bitsy muttered.

"Here's the turn-off," Slim announced.

As she drove slowly past it, I glimpsed a couple of Traveling Vampire Show handbills and the makeshift cardboard sign on trees near the narrow dirt road. They were dim shapes in the darkness. If I hadn't already seen them a couple of times in daylight, I wouldn't have known what they were.

I thought, *Nobody'll be able to find the place*.

Then I realized it was a stupid thought. Everyone for miles around knew the location of Janks Field. Almost everyone *avoided* it whenever possible, but hardly anyone would have trouble getting there, even in the dark.

Slim eased her Pontiac off the road. We dipped down into a shallow ditch, then climbed out of it and rolled through some deep grass.

"What're you *doing?*" Rusty asked.

"Parking," Slim said.

The car shook as she steered it over the rough ground. Bushes squeaked against the sides. Fallen twigs crackled under the tires. But not for long.

Slim stopped the car behind some trees, killed its headlights and shut off the engine.

"Jeez," Rusty said.

"We don't want everybody seeing our car."

By "everybody," I'm sure Slim meant more than just people wishing to do us harm. She also meant any residents of Grandville who might drive by—either on their way to the show or going elsewhere. Because if anyone should see the huge old Pontiac, word would get around. Soon, everyone in town— including our parents—would know that Slim's car had been spotted out near the Janks Field turnoff the night of the Traveling Vampire Show.

The night of my dad's car accident.

The night Slim's mom had her overnight date on the river.

The night the parents of Rusty and Bitsy *thought* we'd taken their kids to a double-feature at the Moonlight Drive-in.

I suddenly had a bad thought.

"Rusty," I said.

He looked around at me.

"What time are you and Bitsy supposed to get home?"

"What time do *you* think?"

"Midnight?"

"Good guess."

"We can't be back by then," I said. "That's when the show *begins*."

"No sweat," Rusty said. "My folks're *never* awake by midnight. We'll just sneak in real quiet when we get home. They'll never be the wiser."

Maybe he was right. He had certainly gotten away, many times, with sneaking in and out of his house late at night.

"If we *do* get caught," he said, "I'll just say we had car trouble. And anyway, by then it'll be too late. We'll already've seen the show, right?" He chuckled. "*Let* 'em ground me. See who cares."

Chapter Forty-four

With the rest of us standing nearby, Slim opened the trunk of her car. Then she just stood there as if staring in.

"What're you waiting for?" Rusty asked.

Slim shook her head. "I'd better leave this stuff here," she said. "We might need to blend in with the crowd. Can't exactly do that if I'm armed like Robin Hood." Leaving her archery equipment inside the trunk, she shut the lid.

We started back toward the dirt road, staying in among the bushes and trees in case of traffic on Route 3.

"Nobody said we'd have to *walk*," Bitsy complained.

"You're the one that wanted to come," Rusty reminded her.

"But I got *sandals* on."

"So wait in the car."

"Nobody's going to wait in the car," Slim said.

275

"My feet are getting all scratched."

"Tough toenails," Rusty said, and chuckled.

"Ha ha. That's so funny I forgot to . . ."

"Let's hold up here a second," I said. We halted, and I pulled off one of my shoes. As I peeled the sock off, I said, "You can wear my socks, Bitsy."

"Really?" She sounded surprised and pleased.

"Sure." I handed her the sock I'd already removed. Still balancing on one leg, I put my sneaker back on. Then I shifted legs and took off the other shoe and sock. I gave the second sock to her.

"Thank you very much," she said.

As I put my shoe on again, Bitsy sat on the ground. She brought her knees up and spread them wide apart like a little kid. But she wasn't a little kid and she was wearing a dress.

There must've been a break in the clouds. Some moonlight made its way into the forest and she'd found a patch of it.

Almost as if she wanted me to watch.

I looked away and glimpsed Rusty staring down at her. He didn't say anything, just watched.

Being her brother, maybe he was used to seeing that sort of thing. I didn't have a sister, so I wouldn't know. But it seemed funny that he would stare like that.

It made me wonder about Rusty.

About Bitsy, too, for that matter. She had to know her brother was watching, but it didn't seem to faze her.

Bitsy was turning out to be more strange than I had ever imagined.

Slim, keeping watch as if afraid someone might sneak up on us, didn't seem to notice Bitsy's secret show—or audience.

After putting my socks on, Bitsy struggled into her sandals and stood up. She brushed off the seat of her dress. "Thanks," she said again.

"You're welcome."

"Ready?" Slim asked.

"Yeah," Bitsy said.

So we started off again, Slim in the lead, Rusty next. Instead of moving out behind her brother, Bitsy came over to my side and took my hand. "I wanta stay by you," she said.

"Sure."

She kept hold of my hand. Side by side, we made our way through the dark woods.

"The socks sure help," she said.

"Good."

"They're kinda sweaty, but I don't mind. I kinda like it."

"Ah," I said.

"Car!" Slim warned.

Off to the right and ahead of us through the trees, pale beams lit the night. A car was coming our way on Route 3. Slim stepped behind a tree trunk. Rusty crouched behind a bush. Pulling Bitsy by the hand, I gasped, "Come on," and rushed over to a waist-high boulder. We ducked behind it, Bitsy clutching my hand and gasping for breath.

Huddled together, we heard the car come closer. It sounded like a strong wind rushing through the trees. I felt one of Bitsy's breasts pushing against the side of my arm. It moved slightly, rubbing me, as if she wanted to make sure I noticed. I noticed, all right. And it made me wish I was somewhere else: hiding behind the tree with Slim, for instance.

Soon, but not nearly soon enough, the sound of the car faded like a sigh. We stood up. Slim waved when she saw us. Rusty shook his head. I tried to break contact with Bitsy. Though I got free of her breast, she kept her grip on my hand.

Slim and Rusty waited for us. When we were all together, Slim took the lead again. Rusty trudged after her. Bitsy squeezed my hand and looked up at me. We weren't in moonlight, so I couldn't see the look on her face. Just as well.

A couple of minutes later, we came to the dirt road.

Slim waited until we were all there. Then she said in a quiet voice, "Let's just stay on this and stick together. A lot easier than traipsing through the woods."

"What if a car comes?" Bitsy asked.

"We'll duck out of sight same as last time," Slim said.

Clustered together, we began walking up the dirt road toward Janks Field.

Soon, a car came along from behind us. We heard it and

saw the glow of its headlights in plenty of time to hide. It no sooner passed us than another was on the way. When both had gone, we returned to the dirt road.

"Early birds," Slim said.

"After the best seats," Rusty suggested.

"Or the best parking places," I said.

"*We've* got the best parking place," Slim said. "A good safe distance from the action."

"You still got the tickets?" Rusty asked her.

"Yep." She patted the seat of her cut-offs.

To Bitsy, he said, "You sure you got plenty of money?"

Nodding, she patted her purse. She had let go of me while we'd been waiting for the cars to pass. Now she was over to the side and slightly ahead of me. The white purse, hanging from her shoulder, seemed to be floating by her hip.

"You better have enough for a ticket," Rusty warned, "or the deal's off."

"I've got plenty."

We heard another car coming, so we ran for cover.

Our way was blocked by a fallen tree. All four of us scurried over its trunk and ducked behind it.

As we waited for the car to pass, I suddenly wondered why we were hiding and why we'd bothered to conceal Slim's Pontiac. If we hoped to buy a ticket for Bitsy, use our tickets to enter the grandstands, then sit among the other paying customers, we were sure to be seen and recognized. We would probably be *surrounded* by people from Grandville.

We started to rise, but then another car came along. It went by. As we began to climb over the trunk, another glow of headlights appeared so we dropped out of sight again.

"I'm not sure why we're hiding," I said.

Slim, crouched close to my left side, nudged me with her elbow and muttered, "So they don't see us, Mr. Brain."

"A few minutes, we'll be in the middle of them."

Was I the only one who'd thought of that?

Slim turned her face toward me. I couldn't see her expression, and she didn't speak.

"What'll we do?" asked Bitsy. She was crouched on my right.

"Should've brought disguises," Rusty whispered.

"It'll be all right," Slim said.

"I don't . . ." My voice stopped and I listened to the approaching engine. It had a powerful sound.

Hands on the rough, moist bark, I eased myself upward and peered toward the dirt road. A pickup truck was speeding along the dirt road, shaking and bouncing.

Its headlights ruined my night vision.

There seemed to be only one occupant, the driver. But I couldn't make out who it was—not even whether it was a man or woman.

As the pickup sped away, however, I was able to see its color in the glow of its tail lights.

Red.

A red pickup truck, the same as Lee's.

"Was that her?" Rusty asked.

We were all gazing over the top of the fallen trunk.

"I don't know," I said.

"Sure looked like her truck," Slim said.

"I bet it was her," Bitsy said.

"Did you see her?" I asked.

"No, but I bet it *was*."

"I hope so," I muttered. "Thing is, it's not like she's got the only red pickup in town."

"Did *any*one see the driver?" Slim asked.

"Nope."

"Huh-uh."

"I wish."

"Might've been her," Rusty said.

"She's *supposed* to come," I added.

"Well," said Slim, "we'll find out soon enough, I guess."

Chapter Forty-five

We walked for a couple of minutes on the dirt road, but then another car came so we hid again. This time, we crouched behind a clump of bushes about twenty feet from the roadside.

"We're *never* gonna get there," Rusty said.

"Maybe we'd better cut through the woods," Slim suggested.

"Have we *gotta?*" Bitsy asked.

"We'd better," Slim said. "If we keep hiding every time a car comes by . . ."

"We might as well walk up the road," I said. "Everybody's gonna see us when we get to the show, anyway."

Slim looked at me. She was silent for a few seconds, then said, "I don't know. Maybe you're right. But . . ."

Rusty gasped out, *"Holy shit!"*

The rest of us looked.

The car bouncing up the road and just about to pass our hiding place was a huge old Cadillac. Slammed by fear, I ducked. Bitsy was still staring at it, so I clamped a hand on her shoulder and jerked her down.

"What's . . . ?"

"Shhh."

Hunkered low, we waited for the Cadillac to pass.

It's probably not even the same one, I told myself. But I knew better. Around these parts, Cadillacs weren't nearly as common as pickup trucks. This *had* to be the one that had terrorized us after the drive-in.

For the past month, all the cops in the county had been looking for it.

Now, here it was.

The sounds of the Cadillac faded, but not with distance. Its engine noise decreased because someone had taken his foot off the gas pedal. Its tires no longer crunched along the dirt road because they had quit moving.

Cars stop for many reasons, but I *knew* why this one had stopped.

We'd been seen.

"Did they *see* us?" Rusty asked in a hoarse whisper.

Slim went "Shhh."

Rusty murmured, "Jesus."

"Who are . . . ?" Bitsy started to ask. I cupped an open hand across her mouth, catching the final word, dissolving it into warm breath. Though she didn't try to say more, I kept my hand on her mouth. She breathed into it.

I listened for the sound of a door opening.

What if they're already open?

Through the thick foliage in front of me, I could see nothing of the Cadillac exept the glow of its headlights.

I wanted to rise and peer over the top, but I didn't dare.

Then a man's thin voice sang out, *"Weee seee youuuu."*

I felt as if I had icy snakes in my bowels.

The same voice, but without the sing-song, asked, "Want a lift?"

I was afraid Slim might answer with a wisecrack, but she remained silent.

"What's the matter, kids? Cat got your tongues?"

A moment later, I felt *Bitsy's* tongue push gently against the palm of my hand.

She's licking me!

I jerked my hand away from her mouth.

"How about a ride to the Traveling Vampire Show?" the man asked.

I rubbed my wet hand on the leg of my jeans.

"Don't worry," the man said, "we won't hurt you." After a pause, he added, "Much."

His passenger giggled. That's when I remembered that they were supposed to be twins.

A matching pair of perverts.

The blast of a car horn made me jump.

"Be *seeeeing* you," the guy called out. The engine revved. The tires hissed and crunched on the dirt road.

Rising slightly, I saw that a pale station wagon now stood just behind where the Cadillac had been. It must've been the car that honked. As the Cadillac disappeared among the trees, the station wagon started forward. After it came a little sports car.

"This way," Slim said.

On hands and knees, she scurried away from the bush. We followed her into the trees. When the dirt road was a safe distance behind us, we got to our feet.

"It was *them*," Rusty said.

"Guess so," Slim said.

"Who?" Bitsy asked.

"Never mind," Rusty told her.

Bitsy turned to me for an answer.

The Cadillac twins were a well-kept secret. My dad and all the law enforcement agencies in the area knew about them, but hardly anyone else did. We'd been told to keep quiet. If the twins were long gone, there was no reason to panic everyone. If they *were* still around, the cops didn't want them to know they were being sought. "They find out we're after 'em," Dad had said, "they'll jackrabbit or go to ground."

So I said to Bitsy, "We can't tell you who they are."

"But they're very bad guys," Slim added.

"And they're going to the show," Rusty said.

"Still wanta go?" I asked him.

"You kidding? You think I'm gonna let a couple of pervs scare me off, you got another think comin'."

"You're not the one they're after," I said.

"Who is?" Bitsy asked.

"Slim."

Rusty groaned. "Tell her *everything*, why don't you?"

As if taking up the suggestion, Slim told Bitsy, "They tried to pull me into their car a few weeks ago."

"What for?"

Rusty said, "What do *you* think, dipshit?"

"Cut it out," Slim told him.

To Bitsy, he said, "You better not breathe a word of this to Mom or Dad."

"I won't."

"Sure you won't."

Turning toward me, Slim said, "I'm not so sure anymore."

"About going?"

"Yeah. It's bad enough, Stryker and his gang. But now *these* guys. It's getting a little *too* creepy."

Rusty went into his chicken impression, tucking his hands under his armpits, flapping his elbows up and down and going, *"Bwok-bwok-bwok-bwok!"*

"Up yours," Slim told him.

"Meow!"

"Shut up," I warned.

"I think maybe we'd better call it off," Slim said.

"No!"

"Yeah," I said. "I wanta see the Vampire Show as much as anyone, but it isn't worth getting killed over."

"Well, *I'm* going. You guys wanta chicken out, that's your problem. Fuck ya. And the horse y'rode in on." He jammed an open hand toward Slim. "Gimme one a those tickets."

"You don't want to go by yourself," Slim said.

"Oh, no? Y'wanta bet?"

"Hey, man," I said.

"Go to hell."

"Let's just all go back to the car and get out of here," Slim said. "We can go to the drive-in."

Rusty shook his head. "Not me. I'm going to the Traveling Vampire Show . . . with or without the rest of you chicken-shit pussies."

"You want to go, go." Slim jammed a ticket into his hand. "No skin off my butt."

"Thanks," Rusty muttered.

"It isn't worth it," I told him.

"I'm not scared."

"The hell you aren't."

Slim said to him, "You don't have to prove anything."

"I don't know what you're talking about."

"Yeah, you do," I said.

"Fraid not."

"Yeah, right."

He gave me the finger, then headed for the dirt road.

I muttered, "Damn it."

"You'd better go with him," Slim said.

"Huh?"

She called out, "Rusty, wait! Dwight's going with you."

"I am?"

Rusty stopped and turned around. "You coming?" he asked.

"Just a minute," Slim called. To me, she said, "We can't let him go by himself."

"Sure we can."

She shook her head. "Besides, what about Lee?"

Lee had temporarily slipped my mind.

"Whether that was Lee in the pickup or not," Slim said, "she'll probably turn up at the show sooner or later and she's expecting us to be there."

"She can hook up with Rusty," I said. It sounded feeble even to me.

"Suppose the Cadillac twins decide to go after *her?*"

Grimacing, I nodded. "Yeah," I muttered. "Maybe I'd *better* go. I don't want to, but . . ."

"Duty calls," Slim said. In the dim grayness of the forest, she seemed to smile at me. "Anyway," she added, "I *know* you want to see the Vampire Show."

"Don't you wanta see it?"

She shook her head. "Not hardly. Look, you go to the show and take care of Rusty. I don't think the Cadillac twins are likely to bother you guys if I'm not with you. They might not even recognize you. So just go on ahead. Find Lee. Enjoy the show. Bitsy and I'll wait for you in the car."

"I don't know," I muttered.

"Yes, you do."

"What if something happens to you and Bitsy?"

"We'll be fine. The car's well hidden. It'll be a hell of a lot safer for us than going to the Vampire Show, I know that much."

"Maybe you should drive on home."

She shook her head. "We'll wait."

"We'll wait," echoed Bitsy.

"Here's your ticket," Slim said. She held it out for me.

As I took it, she stepped in against me. She put an arm around my back, pressed her slender body against mine and kissed me. I felt the warmth of her belly, the soft push of her breasts, the gentle pressure of her lips. But only for a moment. Easing away from me, she whispered, "Be careful."

"You, too," I said.

"What about me?" Bitsy asked.

Slim stepped aside for her. Bitsy put both arms around me and tilted back her head for a kiss.

Slim gave a little nod.

So I hugged Bitsy.

She writhed against me, moaning. Her heavy, open lips mooshed against mine and squirmed like a pair of slugs.

When I eased her away, she whimpered.

"See you later," I said.

As I lifted a hand in farewell to Slim, Bitsy grabbed my other arm. "I'm coming with," she said.

"You'll be safer with Slim," I told her.

"But I wanta come with *you*. You *promised*! Everybody *promised*. If you're goin' to see the vampires, I getta go, too!"

"It's too dangerous now," Slim explained. "I'm not going, either."

"But *they* are! If they get t'go, I get t'go."

"You coming or not?" Rusty called to me.

"Hold your horses," I answered.

Slim patted Bitsy on the back and said, "Come along with me, Bits. We'll head back to the car."

"But I don't *wanta!*"

I jerked my arm out of her grip. She reached for me again, but I leaped out of range. So then she lurched toward me, reaching with both hands.

I caught hold of her wrists. In a voice that wasn't exactly gentle, I said, "Cut it out and go with Slim."

"But I wanta . . ."

"Shut the hell up and go with Slim!"

She gasped. Then she started to cry. When I let go of her wrists, she sort of sagged and stood there, sobbing.

"Sorry," I muttered.

As I ran to catch up with Rusty, Slim called out, "Nice going, Dwight."

I felt like bursting into tears, myself. But I called, "I'm sorry," and kept going.

Chapter Forty-six

Rusty and I trudged through the woods, staying away from the dirt road. With no path and very little light, it was slow going. And painful. We kept bumping into things, falling, getting scratched.

After a while, I muttered, "We should've gone with the girls."

"It's gonna be worth it, man."

"That's what you think."

"Just wait'll you lay your eyes on Valeria."

"Sure," I muttered. No matter how beautiful Valeria might be, she couldn't compare to Slim. I wanted *nothing* more than to be with Slim, but there I was—tromping through the woods with Rusty.

We were both out of breath, panting for air. The night was hot, the air heavy and moist. No wind at all seemed to penetrate the forest. Sweat poured down my body. My sodden shirt and jeans clinged to me. Without the socks I'd given to Bitsy, my feet slid around inside my sneakers and made squelching sounds.

Why am I *doing* this? I kept thinking.

Not so I could lay my eyes on Valeria, that was for sure. Not really so I could keep Rusty company, either—though that must've been part of it. The real reason was Lee.

No telling where she was or what had happened to her.

Maybe she was okay. If so, she would find the note we'd left in her kitchen and come to the Vampire Show. I needed to be there to meet her.

Maybe she had already arrived—if that had been Lee in the red pickup truck.

Or maybe she'd been taken there earlier. She'd given Stryker the check with her address on it. Would've been so easy for him to pay her a visit.

Then again, maybe her disappearance had nothing to do with the Traveling Vampire Show.

Maybe she wasn't even missing.

If nothing happened to her, I thought, she'll see the note and drive over. One way or another, Janks Field was where I stood my best chance of finding Lee.

At last, we saw a pale glow of lights through the trees ahead of us.

"That's gotta be it," Rusty said.

"Guess so."

The grandstands of Fargus's Folly were always brightly lighted at night to prevent the sort of mischief that often happened in the dark. But the grandstands weren't straight ahead of us. Also, their lights didn't move. Our way seemed to be illuminated, instead, by the headbeams of cars cruising Janks Field in search of places to park.

I thought about how smart it had been to park Slim's Pontiac off Route 3.

I wished I were there.

Slim and Bitsy had probably reached it already. If I were only with them . . . and if Bitsy weren't, so it could be just Slim and me sitting together in the front seat, waiting for Rusty. . . .

But Bitsy *is* there, I reminded myself. If I so much as *kissed* Slim, Bitsy would want me to kiss her, too.

Maybe I'm better off here.

Soon, Janks Field came into sight through the spaces between the trees. Cars and pickup trucks were moving about, headlights pushing through the darkness.

We crept closer and closer. With nothing more than a bramble between us and the field, we stretched out flat on the ground, side by side, our shoulders almost touching.

Off to our right, a stream of vehicles poured into Janks Field from the dirt road. They were met by black-shirted members of Stryker's crew who directed them toward the area of field in front of us. The place seemed to be filling up fast, but in an orderly way. Stryker's gang knew how to do their job.

I suddenly pictured them surrounding the one-eyed dog, poking it with spears.

They had no spears now—only flashlights. Watching them, though, I felt chills crawl up my spine.

Slim was smart not to come here, I thought.

Cars and trucks kept lining up, stopping, shutting off their headlights and engines. Doors opened. People climbed out. Doors banged shut. In couples and small groups, people walked away from their vehicles and headed for the brightly lighted bleachers. I could hear their voices, their laughter.

People I know, I thought.

I *had* to know plenty of them . . . any who'd come from Grandville, at least.

And they'll know us.

But I couldn't actually recognize anyone because of the darkness and the distance.

I nudged Rusty with my shoulder. His head turned. "See anyone we know?" I asked.

"Huh-uh."

"Me nei . . ." I gasped and flinched as someone flopped onto the ground beside me. The heat of her body seemed to wash over me. She was panting for breath.

"I'm back," she huffed.

I jerked my head toward her.

Bitsy's hair was glued down with sweat. Her face was shiny and dripping . . . and smiling. She nudged me with her shoulder.

"Shit, no," Rusty said. "What the hell is *she* doing here?"

Ignoring him, I twisted around and gazed behind me. No sign of Slim. "Where's Slim?" I asked.

"Goin' to the car."

"Why aren't you *with* her?"

"She said it's okay."

"*Slim* said you could come with us?" I asked.

"Yeah."

"She did not," Rusty said.

"Did so."

Fat chance, I thought. Keeping it to myself, I asked, "How'd you get away from her?"

Bitsy smiled. It gave me a creepy feeling. "I just said how I had to take a leak. That got her to let go of my hand, so then I ran away."

"Slim could've caught you easy," Rusty said.

"She did. And she ripped my dress and we fell down and I got hurt. So then she climbed offa me and said she was sorry."

That sounded like Slim, all right.

"And I was crying and saying how all I wanted was to go see the Vampire Show like everyone promised, but she said I shouldn't on account of I might get hurt and I said how I didn't care. So then she was gonna make me come with her anyhow. She pulled me off the ground and I tried to get away again but she wouldn't let go, so then I called her a name and she let go."

"Called her what?" I asked.

"Nothing," she muttered.

"What?"

Bitsy muttered, "A dirty whore."

"You called Slim *a whore?*"

Her voice a quiet whimper, she said, "Yeah."

Back in those days, you never heard the "c" word. I didn't, anyway. "Whore" was the worst thing anyone ever called a girl, and you rarely heard that. It's a commonplace word now, used in everyday speech, in comedy routines, all over the place. But not then. Back then, it was a dark, vile word. Calling a girl a "whore" was as lowdown as you could get.

I had a tight feeling in my throat—and an urge to punch Bitsy in the face.

"What'd you wanta call her *that* for?" I asked.

"Just to make her let go."

"She's always been your friend."

In a stronger voice, Bitsy said, "I wanted her to let *go* of me."

"That was really lousy," I told her.

Softly, she murmured, "I know. I'm sorry."

"Real neat play, fatso," Rusty said.

"So what happened after you called Slim that name?" I asked.

"She let go. She says 'You wanta go with Dwight so bad, go. And go to hell while you're at it.' So then she let me have my ticket. I told her thanks and she said 'Fuck you.' "

"Sure she did," Rusty muttered.

"She *did*."

I'd never heard the word come from Slim's mouth. I doubted she'd said it to Bitsy, but the worthless bitch had just called her a dirty whore so maybe Slim *had* used that language back at her.

"What happened then?" I asked. "After she called you that."

"Nothin'. I came looking for you."

"Where'd Slim go?"

"I don't know. Back to the car?"

I just stared at Bitsy. It was a good thing there wasn't enough light for her to see the look in my eyes. Turning to Rusty, I said, "I've gotta go and find Slim."

"Hey, no. Come on, man."

"You *can't*," Bitsy whined.

I looked at her. "Wanta bet?"

"You'll miss the show," Rusty said.

"Screw the show."

Bitsy went, *"Dwiiiight."*

I pushed myself up to my hands and knees. As I started to back away, Bitsy clutched my right arm with both hands.

"Let go," I said, keeping my voice low.

"Stay. Y'gotta stay."

"Bitsy, let go!"

"No!"

I wrenched my arm out of her grip, then whirled around on my hands and knees. Just as I was about to scurry off, a hand tugged at a seat pocket of my jeans and Bitsy said, "What about Lee?"

I stopped.

"You gotta find Lee, don't you?"

"Yeah," Rusty said. "You left her a note and everything. You can't just not show up."

Bitsy gave my pocket a couple of pulls. "Slim's just going back to the car, anyways. She doesn't need you."

Chapter Forty-seven

I looked around at Bitsy. She was on her knees, leaning toward me, left arm bracing her up while her right arm was extended toward my rear end. Behind her, a few cars were moving slowly toward their parking places. People were walking toward the bleachers. I saw a couple of the black-shirt gang waving flashlights.

Nobody seemed to be aware of us.

"Take your hand out of my pocket," I said.

She took it out. "Don't go," she whispered. "Please."

"Rusty, you're the one who's so hot to see the show. Why don't you and Bitsy go ahead? Keep an eye out for Lee. If you find her, stick with her. I've gotta make sure Slim's okay."

"Slim's fine," Bitsy insisted.

"I'll know that when I see her."

Rusty suddenly said, "I'm not gonna go to the vampire show with my *sister*. Screw that. I'm coming with you."

"No," Bitsy whined. "Never mind Slim. We gotta see the Vampire Show."

"Forget it," Rusty said.

Next thing I knew, all three of us were crawling through the forest *away* from Janks Field and the Traveling Vampire Show.

Fine, I thought. Now nobody gets to see it.

We never should've tried in the first place, I thought. The whole thing had been a rotten idea from the very start and we'd been in trouble of one kind or another all day long because of the stupid show.

I was *glad* we wouldn't be seeing it.

When we were a safe distance from Janks Field, we stood up. I led the way, moving carefully though the dark woods. Bitsy walked close behind me and Rusty followed her.

"Hold up a minute," Rusty said.

I stopped and turned around.

So did Bitsy.

Rusty said, "Here's good."

"Good for what?" I asked.

"This." He leaped forward, grabbed Bitsy by the front of her dress with one hand and smashed her in the stomach with the other. The sound was like punching a raw steak. Her breath whooshed out and she started to fold over. "Nuffa you!" he blurted, and slugged her again.

"Rusty!"

"Stay outa this."

Before I could make a move to help her, Rusty drove his fist into her belly again and again, very fast. Then he let go and staggered backward. Bitsy sank to her knees. Doubled over, she whined and sucked air. Her head was almost touching the ground.

"Jesus, Rusty," I muttered.

"She had it coming."

"God!"

"She asked for it. She's been askin' for it all day. Got no business messin' with us."

"You didn't have to do *that!*"

"Yeah, yeah." He stepped behind Bitsy, grabbed her hair and pulled. With a squeal, she struggled to her feet. She and

Rusty looked vague in the darkness, but I could see that Bitsy's dress was open, hanging off one shoulder. Her skin was a pale shade of gray, her nipple a black smudge. "Wanta take a swing at her?" Rusty asked me.

"Hell, no. Are you nuts?"

"Come on, man. She called Slim a dirty whore. You gonna let her get away with that?"

"I'm not gonna *hit* her."

"Chicken," he said.

"Leave her alone."

"Sure. Soon as she leaves *us* alone." He jerked her hair. She squeaked and went up on tiptoes. Mouth close to her ear, Rusty said, "You gonna leave?"

"Huh-uh."

"Wanta bet?"

"Rusty," I said.

"It's okay, pal. She's gonna go back to the car. *Aren't* you, Bitsy?"

"No."

"Yes you are."

"No I'm not."

"You're not coming with us."

"Am, too."

"You're gettin' one chance," Rusty said. Turning her so she faced the general direction of Route 3, he let go of her hair and shoved her. She stumbled a few steps, then fell to her hands and knees. "Now *go!*"

She stayed there for a while, her head drooping toward the ground. Then she pushed herself up and turned around.

"I don't see you *leaving*," Rusty said.

"Dwiiiiiight." Though she spoke my name, it sounded as if she were saying, *"Why are you letting this happen to me?"*

"You'd better go back and wait in the car," I said.

"But I wanta . . . come *with*."

"It isn't safe. That's why Slim changed her mind."

"*You're* going."

"We're guys. It's different."

"Now get your fat ass outa here," Rusty said, "or you're *really* gonna get it."

She slowly shook her head.

"That's it," Rusty muttered. He started toward her.

"Dwight!"

"Just go," I told her.

"No." She raised an arm and pointed straight at Rusty. "Better not," she said. "I'm gonna tell."

"Famous last words," Rusty said.

"Dwight!"

I just stood there and let it happen. It was her own fault. We'd told her to leave. And told her and told her. So I just stood there. It made me feel a little sick, just standing there and watching, but she had it coming. On top of everything else, she'd called Slim a dirty whore.

When Rusty was done, Bitsy lay sprawled on her back, wheezing and sobbing.

He stood over her. Gasping for air, he said, "Want more?"

She didn't answer. Probably couldn't. He turned around and staggered toward me. "Let's go, man."

Side by side, we headed for Janks Field. I looked back a couple of times. The first time, Bitsy was still flat on the ground. The next time, she was propped up on her elbows, watching us.

"Don't go 'n leave meeeeee," she whined.

Stopping, I called, "Go back to the car."

"I wanta come *with!*"

"No."

"But *Dwiiiiight!*"

I kept going, and hurried to catch up with Rusty.

"Dwiiiiight, don't leave me! Pleeeeese."

I called over my shoulder, "Shut up!" and sounded a lot like Rusty.

"Bitch," Rusty muttered.

I slugged him in the arm.

"OW!" He cringed away, clutching where I'd punched him. "What'd ya do *that* for?"

"Just felt like it," I said.

"Jeez."

"Bastard."

"Got rid of her, didn't I?"

"You didn't have to beat her up."

"Got the job done."

"You're gonna be in *so* much trouble. You and me both."

"Yeah, well, screw it. She asked for it and I gave it to her."

"There's no way she's gonna keep her mouth shut after *that*."

"Let her tell. It's what she's good at. But you know what? Nobody's gonna nail us for it tonight. By the time she blabs, we'll already've seen the Vampire Show . . . without her."

As we came to Janks Field, I noticed that it didn't seem as bright as before. I ducked behind a tree and peered around the trunk. In the few minutes we'd been away, so many cars and pickups had shown up that the field was almost packed. Soon, there would be no more space. The dirt road would end up jammed, maybe all the way out to Route 3. Just like the night of Fargus Durge's boxing spectacular.

"Come on," Rusty said and stepped out of the woods.

"Wait."

He didn't wait.

Nobody seemed to be nearby, so I went out after him and we rushed in among the parked vehicles. They were crowded close together. Staying low to avoid being spotted, we couldn't see where we were going. I simply followed Rusty. He led us through a dark, narrow labyrinth, gravel and bits of broken glass crunching under our shoes.

When we came upon a pickup truck, I wondered if it might be Lee's. It seemed to be a dark color, maybe red. But as I crept past the open passenger window of its cab, out came a reek of stale cigarettes.

Lee didn't smoke. The cab of her pickup always smelled as good as she did.

At the rear of the truck, a VW van blocked our way. We cut to the left and climbed over some bumpers before coming to another straightaway.

Crouched low between a couple of cars, Rusty looked back at me. "We're home free now," he said.

"Huh?"

"Bitsy'll *never* find us now. If she even tries."

"You think she'd *try?*"

"Wouldn't put nothin' past her, the dumb twat." He chuckled quietly, then moved on.

Every so often, we came upon pickup trucks. None seemed to be Lee's, though. Which didn't mean her truck wasn't there. So far, we hadn't even stumbled upon the red pickup that we *knew* had arrived. We saw nothing much except what was beside us and straight in front of us.

About halfway through the labyrinth, we came upon a big old black Cadillac.

Chapter Forty-eight

Parked close behind some sort of boxy delivery truck, the Cadillac took us by surprise. There it suddenly was, its front bumper close enough to touch.

Rusty must've noticed it an instant before I did. He gasped and dropped to his knees. At first, I didn't know what was wrong. I thought maybe someone had spotted us. Then I saw the hood ornament and felt as if my wind had been knocked out.

I hit the ground behind Rusty.

Twisting his head around, he whispered, "Is it *it?*"

"Uh-huh."

"You sure?"

"Pretty sure."

"Anyone in it?"

"I don't know."

Rusty moaned. "What if they're *in* it?"

"Got your knife?" Even as I asked, I shoved a hand down the front pocket of my jeans and wrapped it around Slim's folding knife.

Rusty reached back under the hanging tail of his shirt and pulled out Slim's sheath knife.

I opened my blade. My hands were shaking. "They're probably in the stands," I whispered.

"They better be."

I raised my head. The windshield had no glare. A pale glow from the grandstands lit up the rear window so I could see straight through the car.

If I'd found the twins staring back at me from the front seat, I probably would've dropped dead. Or at the very least filled my jeans. Instead, I let my breath out.

"It's okay," I whispered. "They're gone."

Rusty took a look for himself. Then he muttered, "Thank God."

We started forward again, moving through the narrow space between the side of the Cadillac and the station wagon beside it.

I suddenly got an idea. It sent a jolt of fear through me. Fear and excitement.

"Rusty, wait."

He stopped and looked around at me. "Huh?"

"Think it's really their car?" I whispered.

"Must be."

"Yeah. Look. I'm gonna check it out. Maybe we can find out who they are."

"But the show."

"Screw the show. Anyway, it's not gonna start for a while. Wait here." I switched the knife to my left hand. With my right, I reached up for the handle of the passenger door.

"Are you nuts?"

"Shhh. Keep an eye out. Yell if anyone comes."

The door wasn't locked. I opened it. No lights came on. Cigarette stink filled my nostrils. When I climbed into the car, stuff slid and crunched under my feet. There seemed to be a lot of junk on the floor in front of the seat. Magazines or maps, bags, food wrappers, maybe some small boxes. I couldn't see much in the darkness, but that was the impression I got.

I sat down and opened the glove compartment. It was full. I took out some cigarette packs, matches, maps, napkins, rubber gloves like my mom usually wore when she washed the dishes.

Rubber gloves.

I kept on searching, pausing to look at papers, hoping to find the car registration. There didn't seem to be anything of the sort, but I found an ice pick with a wooden handle.

"Jeez," I muttered.

"What?" Rusty asked through the door.

"An ice pick."

"Let's get outa here," Rusty said.

I put Slim's knife back into my pocket. Keeping the ice pick, I crawled out of the car. I eased its door shut and showed the pick to Rusty.

"Nasty," he said.

"Yeah."

"Gonna keep it?"

"I don't know."

"These've gotta be our guys."

"Oh, yeah."

"Find out who they are?"

I shook my head. "There's probably *something* with their names on it, but . . . too much crap in there. And it's too dark to see anything. Maybe if we took everything with us . . ."

"Forget it."

"Anyway, that'd take a gunny sack."

"Let's just get going," Rusty said.

"Wait."

"Now what?"

"We can make sure it stays here. The car, everything in it." I grinned. "Maybe *them*, too. The twins."

"Huh?"

Instead of trying to explain, I scurried over to the right front tire and rammed the ice pick into its side. The point punched easily through the rubber. I shoved the shaft in deep, then jerked it free. Air chased it out, hissing.

"Terrific," Rusty muttered.

At the front of the Cadillac, I checked for a license plate. There wasn't one. I opened the hood and propped it up. Leaning inside, I poked holes in all the hoses I could find. And I removed the radiator cap and gave it a toss into the darkness. Silently, I shut the hood.

I crouched by the left front tire, jabbed it with the ice pick, then hurried to the rear tire and gave it the same treatment.

No back plate, either.

I stabbed the right rear tire.

Looking up, I saw Rusty shake his head. "*Now* can we go see the show?" he asked.

"Yeah, I guess so." I rubbed the pick with my shirt tail to get my fingerprints off its handle, then tossed it under the Cadillac.

We moved on.

Rusty led the way, and I kept an eye out for Lee's pickup. We made good progress. Everything went okay for a while. But as we were sneaking alongside a Volkswagen, I glimpsed pale movement in its driver's seat. Couldn't see what it was, but I blurted, "*Watch out!*"

Not knowing what the problem was, Rusty stopped and twisted around to look back at me. The twisting swept his face past the open window.

"*No! Get . . . !*"

But he kept turning, luckily. His right upper arm, not his face, caught the dog's teeth. They clamped him through his shirt. He cried out in pain and lurched away.

The dog, hanging on, flew out of the car window. Might've been a white poodle. What they call a "toy." It looked like a toy, all right. Like a kid's stuffed doggie doll. But it growled like a real dog.

It swung by its jaws as Rusty twirled. "Get it off! Get it off!"

I tried to grab it, but it swung by too fast. And then it lost its hold, sailed off, and slammed against the shut window of the Chevy that was parked beside the VW. The dog yipped, bounced off the window and fell to the ground at Rusty's feet. He tried to kick it, but missed.

To get away from us, it scurried underneath the Chevy. About half a second later, it screamed.

If dogs can scream, that's what this one did—as if it had run into a nameless horror on the ground beneath the car.

One quick shriek, then silence.

Rusty and I stared at each other. His mouth was drooping open. He held Slim's knife in his right hand while his left arm was across his chest, hand clutching his wound.

We didn't say anything, just stared at each other.

No sounds at all came from under the Chevy.

Rusty suddenly whirled around and took off. I went after him. We cut to the right, climbed over bumpers and hurried through a narrow gap.

Rusty leaped over the side of an old gray pickup truck. I didn't, but I hung onto the side and gasped for air. Sprawled on his back in the bed of the truck, he held his chomped arm while he panted.

We were both too breathless to talk.

From where I stood, I could see that we'd made our way across most of Janks Field. There was only one more row of parked vehicles before the BEER—SNACKS—SOUVENIRS stand.

The shack was open, its door-sized flap raised and propped up at each end. It was brightly lighted inside. Julian Stryker in his shiny black shirt stood behind the counter, apparently selling tickets for the show. There must've been twenty people waiting in line. I recognized about half of them.

I saw no twins.

Lee wasn't in the line, either. But why should she be? She already had her ticket. Maybe she was already in the bleachers.

Or dead in the back of the hearse.

Where *is* the hearse? I suddenly wondered.

The Traveling Vampire Show's hearse, the black moving van and the bus were nowhere in sight. Maybe they'd been moved to the area on the far side of the bleachers.

Normally, I could look all the way through the stands and see whatever was over there. Normally, though, the stands were empty. Not tonight.

Tonight, the nearest bank of bleachers, about twenty-five or thirty feet high, was jammed with people. Through the spaces above and below the bench seats, I could see the backs of their legs. But I couldn't see much of the arena or the stands on the other side.

Down on the ground, the ticket line looked no shorter but had a few different people in it. Several customers were entering the stands. Others were heading for the ticket line from the direction of the dirt road where they'd probably left their cars.

"Hey," Rusty said.

I looked at him. He was still on his back, still clutching his arm, but now he had his knees up.

"What the hell's goin' on?" he asked.

"Stryker's selling tickets. . . ."

"The dog, man, the dog."

"It's a bad day for dogs," I said.

"What *happened* to it?"

"How should I know? How's your arm?"

"How the hell y'think it is?" He took his hand away. The sleeve of his shirt, dark with blood, was clinging to his upper arm.

"You're gonna need rabies shots," I said.

"Awww, man. Don't say that."

"And we'd better forget about trying to get into the Vampire Show."

"Huh?"

"You can't go in there. Not all bloody like that. The blood'll bring vampires like chum brings sharks. You said so yourself."

"Me?"

"This morning. To Slim."

"Yeah, well. . . . Screw that. I'm not gonna miss the show." He lowered his knees, sat up and took off his shirt. Then he looked at his arm. "Can't believe it," he muttered. "Fuckin' dogs."

I nodded, but he didn't see me. He was too busy studying the holes in his arm.

"What is it," he grumbled, "a fuckin' conspiracy?"

I shrugged. "Just coincidences, I guess."

"A fuckin' dog made your *dad* crash."

"Guess so."

"Not to mention the fuckin' one-eyed wonder."

When he said that, I pictured that dog getting speared to death by Stryker and his gang.

Where *is* his gang? I wondered.

Looking around, I spotted a couple of them near the entrance to the grandstands, taking tickets. I didn't see any others. Just those two, and Stryker in the shack.

Rusty used his wadded shirt to pat the bite wounds.

Just that morning, we'd tended to *Slim's* wounds on the roof of the shack after escaping from a different dog.

Strange.

And if some other dog hadn't caused Dad to crash his car, everything tonight would've happened differently. Much of it wouldn't have happened at all.

Including what went on with Slim and me.

Very strange, I thought.

"Y'wanta give me a hand?" Rusty asked.

I softly clapped.

"Har har."

So then I climbed over the side of the pickup truck and sat beside him. He thrust the bloody shirt at me. "Make me a bandage, okay?"

"With your shirt?"

"Why not? It's wrecked anyways."

"It's a day for wrecking shirts."

He frowned at me. "This has been a very weird fuckin' day."

"You're telling me."

I looked at his wounds. The poodle had left two small, curved rows of punctures near the back of his arm a few inches below his shoulder. Most of the bleeding was over, but they seemed to be leaking slightly. I tore a long strip off the back of Rusty's shirt, then wrapped it around his upper arm. With another strip, I tied it in place. "There you go," I said.

"Grassy-ass."

I looked toward the shack. Stryker still stood behind the counter, but the ticket line had dwindled down to three people. A few others were straggling in from the area of the dirt road.

"You sure you wanta go through with this?" I asked.

As if there were any doubt.

"You kidding me?" he said.

"How'll we get in?"

"We got our tickets, man. Why not walk in like anybody else?"

"We're under age."

"BFD," he said. I don't think anyone says BFD anymore. In those days, it stood for "big fucking deal."

Chapter Forty-nine

Rusty leaned over the tailgate of the pickup truck and stared at the ground. I knew why. He was thinking about the poodle, wondering what had gotten it and wondering if the same thing might make a try for him.

So was I.

"Whatever it is," I said, "I guess it's full."

"I don't know, man. That was an awful small dog."

"Wanta stay here and *listen* to the Vampire Show?"

He groaned, then leaped down. I jumped to the ground after him. Staying low, we rushed through the gap between a couple of cars. At the end of it, there were no more cars to conceal us. We stood up straight and walked toward the grandstands.

Over to the right, people were still in line to buy tickets. More were on the way. Stryker seemed busy behind the counter. I wanted to watch him the whole time to make sure he never looked at us, but I had to keep glancing at the ground.

In the glow of the stadium lights, the dirt looked pale gray. Broken glass glittered. Bumps and rocks cast dark shadows. Holes were blotches of blackness. I was looking for creatures. What I saw instead were cigarette butts, a mashed pack of Lucky Strikes, a flattened beer can, a dirty white sneaker . . .

Slim's sneaker?

It might've been one of those Rusty had thrown at the one-eyed dog. I was tempted to pick it up. But it looked as if it had been run over. No telling what else had happened to it—maybe a spider had crawled in. Maybe if I reached down for it something would spring at my hand. Besides, what good would *one* sneaker do Slim?

If Rusty saw the sneaker, he either didn't recognize it or didn't care. He kept on walking.

I caught up to him.

Just in front of us, a man and woman were about to encounter the ticket-takers. The man turned slightly and extended two tickets to a black-shirted member of Stryker's crew.

Rusty nudged me with his elbow, leaned toward me and whispered, "It's Hearn."

Sure enough, the man in front of us was Mr. Hearn, a history teacher from our high school. I didn't recognize the woman beside him, but figured she was probably his wife. Though we hadn't taken any classes from Mr. Hearn, we'd seen him around school and knew who he was. He probably knew who we were, too.

Everybody knew everybody.

He hadn't seen us yet, but . . .

Recognizing someone from our town came as no surprise to me. I'd expected it. It was inevitable. Before, however, it had been inevitable in some sort of distant, abstract way. Now, it was real.

Too real.

Even if plenty of spectators had come to the show from places like Clarksburg and Bixton—from all over the county—we were bound to be surrounded by people from Grandville who would recognize us and spread the news.

304

We're gonna get in so much trouble!

I stopped dead. Even as I reached for Rusty, he handed his ticket to one of Stryker's gang.

She was a slender, pale woman with straight black hair down to her shoulders. She wore a shiny black shirt and black leather pants. Her eyes narrowed slightly as she took Rusty's ticket. Her lips were bright red. She smirked and said to Rusty, "You're a big fella."

He nodded.

She slid a fingertip down his bare chest. He squirmed and grinned. "Not eighteen, though, I bet."

"Sure I am."

She turned to me. "And you." Still smirking, she shook her head. "I'm sorry, boys, but this event is for adults only."

Thank God, I thought.

Nodding, I was about to turn away.

"We have special permission from Mr. Stryker," Rusty said.

Away went her smirk. To the other ticket-taker, she said, "I'll be right back." Then she stepped past us. "Come with me, boys."

Rusty started to follow her. I put my hand on his shoulder. His bare skin was hot and moist. He scowled back at me and kept walking.

I tried to speak, but felt choked at first. Then I forced it out. "We don't have to see the show, ma'am. If it's a problem . . ."

Rusty gave me a murderous glance.

"If you've got Mr. Stryker's okay," the woman said, "it's fine with me. They're his rules."

Rusty's turn to smirk.

I gave *him* a murderous look. Didn't he know we were being taken to see Stryker? Had he forgotten what Slim had told us? Or didn't he care that this was the same guy who had rammed his spear up the butt of the one-eyed dog, picked it up with the spear and delivered it to the hearse?

I glanced toward the parking area.

If I made a run for it, would they come after me?

Probably not. Not with all these people around. The trouble was, Rusty might not come after me, either.

He *really* wanted to see the show.

So I stuck with him. The woman led us to the side door of the shack and rapped on it with her knuckles. A moment later, it was opened by Stryker. Light spilled out around him. He frowned as if annoyed by the interruption.

"Vivian?" he asked.

"I'm sorry to bother you, Mr. Stryker, but these boys claim they've got your permission to see the show." She stepped out of the way.

Stryker's eyes swept up and down Rusty. Looking somewhat disgusted, he shook his head. But when he saw me, his heavy black eyebrows slid upward and he smiled. "Ah, it's you."

I nodded. My heart was thudding. I wanted to whip around and run like hell, but I just stood there.

"Where are the others?" Stryker asked.

I just gaped at him and struggled to breathe.

"The lovely Lee Thompson and the spunky tomboy?"

I collapsed inside.

"They're on their way, sir," Rusty said. "We had to park pretty far off, so they sent us on ahead to save seats for 'em."

"I see," Stryker said. And the way he smiled . . .

He knows *everything*, I thought. Knows it's a lie, knows Lee isn't coming because he's already been to her house and knows exactly where she is.

Glaring into his eyes, I thought, *What have you done to Lee?*

Smiling into *my* eyes, he seemed to be thinking, *Wouldn't you like to know?*

He turned his smile on Vivian. "We'll make an exception to the age rule for my two friends here. See that they have excellent seats, will you?"

"Yes, sir," Vivian said.

"And stay with them until their friends arrive."

She nodded.

"Enjoy the show, boys." Stryker closed the door, shutting out the light.

"Come with me," Vivian said.

As we walked behind her, Rusty cast a smile at me. A very smug one, as if he had single-handedly made it possible for us to see the show.

In a way, he was right.

I wanted to slug him.

"You've really done it now," I muttered.

"Hey, man, we're gonna see it."

"Yeah, right."

"Valeria, here we come."

Didn't he realize we were now prisoners? Didn't he realize Stryker knew about Slim witnessing the death of the dog? She *must've* been seen, or why had Stryker thought to call her a spunky tomboy? And most of all, didn't Rusty catch on that Stryker had been to Lee's house? The bastard *knew* she wouldn't be showing up tonight.

What if he killed her?

An image filled my mind of Lee down on her elbows and knees, naked, Stryker driving a spear. . . .

No, I thought. She's fine. She *has* to be fine. Maybe she's his prisoner and we'll be able to rescue her. Maybe she's tied up on the bus, or . . .

"Oh, man," Rusty muttered.

We followed Vivian past the other ticket-taker and into the bright lights. With the noise, it was like entering a football stadium. A very small one. I walked beside Rusty, keeping my head down, hoping nobody would notice us.

I guess you'd call it the ostrich principle; if I can't see them, they can't see me.

Of course, I knew it was foolish. Even as we walked past the front of the bleachers, dozens of Grandville locals were certain to be watching us. Probably pointing us out to each other. *Hey, look, there's the Thompson boy. And Rusty Simmons, too. What're they doing here? Didn't anyone tell 'em this is "adults only" entertainment? You can bet your bottom dollar their FOLKS don't know about this.*

Within a day or two, Mom and Dad would be hearing about it from everyone in town.

I'd be grounded. Worse, I'd be humiliated. My parents had

always trusted me to follow their rules. I often *didn't* follow their rules, but I rarely got caught at it.

This time, I'd be caught big time. Everything would come out. Well, maybe not everything, but enough.

I heard my dad saying, *This is a real disappointment, Dwight.*

My mom was saying, *Of all things, to take advantage of your father's accident that way.*

Lee yelling, *"DWIGHT! RUSTY! UP HERE!"*

Lee's voice was real.

My head jerked up and turned. I searched the faces of the audience. Saw so many familiar ones. Neighbors, store clerks, teachers, friends of my parents . . .

"DWIGHT! HEY, DWIGHT! UP HERE!"

This time, I found the source of the voice.

There stood Lee, about halfway to the top of the bleachers, waving her arms overhead.

Chapter Fifty

Holy shit," Rusty said.

I couldn't believe it, myself. But the woman in the stands was Lee, all right. When she saw that we'd spotted her, she lowered one arm and waved with the other, beaming a smile down at us.

My eyes filled with tears, I was so glad to see her alive and free.

Rusty tapped Vivian on the shoulder. She looked back at us. "Our friends are already here," he announced.

Vivian frowned.

"Up there." Rusty pointed.

Vivian looked.

"The blonde in the blue shirt," Rusty said.

Nodding, Lee smiled and patted herself on the chest as if to say, *Yeah, it's me. I'm their adult.*

"That's your friend?" Vivian asked.

"Yeah," Rusty said.

"That's her," I threw in.

"I thought there was supposed to be a girl with her?"

"She's probably wandering," Rusty said. "She's my sister. A real pain in the butt."

The missing girl *wasn't* his sister, she was Slim. The switch was just part of his lie, but it annoyed me. Maybe because I didn't like to be reminded of Bitsy. Maybe because I wished Slim were with us. It was her choice to stay behind, I reminded myself. She never really wanted to see the vampire show, anyway.

But *I* wanted her to see it . . . wanted her sitting beside me. Slim on one side, Lee on the other.

"Okay, guys," Vivian said. "Go on ahead."

We both thanked Vivian. She stepped around us and headed away.

Apparently, I'd been wrong about us being prisoners.

I'd been wrong about a lot.

Rusty and I trotted up the nearest section of bleacher stairs. When we were level with Lee, I stepped into the row and waded toward her, audience knees on one side, heads and backs on the other. A few people nearby said, "Hi, Dwight," and "Hey, young man," and so on. I smiled, nodded, and greeted some of them by name.

Sitting two rows up was Dolly Desmond, the dispatcher. She didn't say hi, though. Just glared at me and Rusty.

We've had it for sure, I thought.

But it suddenly didn't bother me. Not very much, anyway. Trouble with Mom and Dad about coming to the Vampire Show didn't seem very significant anymore. Kid stuff. Not worth worrying about, now that I'd found out Lee was safe.

She had spread a folded blanket over about six feet of the bench to save space for us. She was sitting in the middle, her purse by her left hip. It was the brown leather purse we'd last seen in her kitchen.

The one Slim had searched.

I stepped past Lee, brushing against her knees, and sat on the blanket near her right side.

Rusty sat on her left.

She looked great. Her long, blond hair hung behind her in a ponytail. She had no makeup on, and looked about nineteen years old. She was wearing a blue chambray shirt, white shorts and white sneakers. The shirt didn't have any sleeves. Its top couple of buttons were open, and it was so short that it didn't quite reach the waist of her shorts. The shorts were white, small, and tight. Her white sneakers looked brand new, and she didn't have any socks on.

She watched the way I looked her over. "I'm glad to see you, too," she said, smiling. Then she turned her head. "And you, Rusty."

"Thanks, Mrs. Thompson."

"I've been looking for you guys. Thought you would've been here *before* me."

"We walked in from the highway," I explained.

"To avoid the parking tie-up?"

I nodded.

"No wonder I got here first," she said. Turning again to Rusty, she asked, "What happened to your arm?"

"Aaah, nothing. Some crappy little poodle took a bite outa me."

"A *dog* bit you?"

"Yeah. When we were coming through the parked cars."

"The same dog as this morning?"

"Nah. Different one."

"It's been a bad day for dogs," I remarked.

"I'll say," Lee said. "You'd better see a doctor about it, Rusty. You might need shots or something."

"*Rabies* shots," I added.

A disgusted look on his face, he said, "Yeah, I know."

"Are *you* all right?" I asked Lee.

"I'm fine." She spoke as if everything were perfectly ordinary. "Where's Slim?"

"Waiting in her car."

"What for?"

"Just . . . she didn't want to . . . where *were* you? We were over at your house and . . ."

Nodding, she said, "I got your note."

"We thought something had *happened* to you." I almost got through the sentence before my voice broke and tears again filled my eyes.

"Oh, God," Lee murmured. She leaned against me and put a hand on my back. "I was fine, honey. I just went out, that's all. I never expected you to show up so early."

Sounding amused, Rusty said, "Dwighty here, he had you kidnapped and murdered."

Not trusting myself to speak, I nodded.

"Your truck was still there," Rusty explained. "Same with your purse."

"I . . . thought Stryker got you."

"Jeez." She rubbed my back. "I'm so sorry. I just went down to the river, that's all. It's such a wonderful, windy night. I sat out on the end of the dock to enjoy the weather and have myself a little cocktail."

"My God," I said. I'd almost looked for her there. "But the screen door was locked."

"The back screen? Was it?" She frowned and shrugged. "I must've gone out the front." She was silent for a few seconds, then nodded. "Yeah, I *did* go out the front. Sat on the stoop for a few minutes before I got the idea to see what the river was doing."

"Man," Rusty said, and chuckled.

Lee rubbed my back some more. "I'm so sorry, honey. I had no idea. . . ."

"That's okay," I said. "We shouldn't have shown up so early." Why *had* we gone to her house so early? It took me a moment to remember. Then I explained, "We were worried about you. That's why we didn't wait till ten-thirty. I was afraid Stryker was gonna try something. . . ."

"Because I gave him that check?"

A few other reasons, too—but Bitsy, not Stryker, had turned

311

out to be the culprit behind most of them. I didn't want to get into all that with Lee.

"I guess it was mostly because of the check," I told her.

"I pay with checks all the time," she said.

"But Stryker's so creepy."

She smiled gently. "Oh, I don't know."

"He *is*."

"He's a pretty bad guy," Rusty affirmed.

"And he . . . he *likes* you."

"That's not so terrible. He probably wouldn't have sold us the tickets if he hadn't liked me."

"You know what I mean."

"Dwight thinks he's got the hots for you."

"He *does*," I said.

Looking mildly amused, Lee said, "Well, that may be so, but he never tried anything. I haven't even spoken to him since you and I were out here."

I stared at her.

"And he hasn't spoken to me. I did see him selling tickets on my way in, but he looked really busy so I didn't bother him. And he didn't bother me. I don't think he even *noticed* me. I figured he must've already let you guys in. . . . So *why* isn't Slim here?"

"It's her time of the month," Rusty proclaimed.

I couldn't believe my ears. I wanted to kill him.

"She got it all of a sudden on our way over."

"Rusty!" I gasped.

He leaned forward and smiled at me. "It's all right, pal. I'm sure Lee knows all about this sorta thing."

"Does Slim need . . . anything?" Lee asked. She seemed a little flustered, herself.

"You mean like a tampon?"

Lee nodded.

"Nah. She had some in her glove compartment. She walked off into the trees to put one on. Dwight and me, we waited in the car so as not to embarrass her."

If Slim ever heard about this, I wouldn't have to kill Rusty—she would beat me to it.

"So *where* is she now?"

"Back in the car, waiting for us."

Lee looked at me, frowning. Apparently, she wasn't completely buying Rusty's tale.

I shrugged.

She gave Rusty a perplexed look.

"You *can't* go to a vampire show when you've got your period," Rusty said, sounding exasperated by the need to explain something so obvious.

Lee looked at him as if he were nuts. She said, "Huh?"

"A *vampire* show? Your period? *Blood!* Get it?"

"You've gotta be kidding me," Lee said.

Rusty raised his right hand. "I kid you not."

"Jesus H. Christ," Lee muttered.

Rusty's eyes bulged. "It's not *your* time of the month, is it?"

She choked out a laugh. "As if I'm going to discuss that with *you*."

"Well, if it is . . ."

"LADIES AND GENTLEMEN, MAY I HAVE YOUR ATTENTION PLEASE?"

Chapter Fifty-one

Though the loud speakers hissed and crackled, I knew the voice. It belonged to Julian Stryker.

For the first time since entering the stadium, I turned my eyes to the arena. There stood Stryker on top of a canvas object that looked like some sort of large, rectangular tent. About ten feet high, maybe twenty feet long and wide, it took up most of the arena. The wind shook the canvas walls with a sound that reminded me of sailboats on the river.

It blew Stryker's long black hair and fluttered his shirt. His loose black shirt, half unbuttoned, gleamed in the stadium lights. His black leather pants looked as if they'd been oiled. He held a microphone in one hand, and turned slowly like the ringmaster of a circus. As he turned, the microphone in his right hand picked up the jangle of his spurs.

"WELCOME TO THE TRAVELING VAMPIRE SHOW!"

Some polite applause came from the audience.

"MY NAME IS JULIAN STRYKER. I AM THE OWNER OF THE SHOW AND YOUR MASTER OF CEREMONIES FOR TONIGHT'S EXTRAVAGANZA."

Lee nudged me, grinned, and said, *"Extravaganza!"*

"TONIGHT, YOU'LL FEAST YOUR EYES ON THE WORLD'S ONE AND ONLY KNOWN VAMPIRE IN CAPTIVITY . . . A DIRECT DESCENDENT OF THE GREAT COUNT DRACULA HIMSELF . . . THE GORGEOUS AND DEADLY *VALERIA!*"

More applause, along with some whispers and titters.

Stryker raised his arms for silence.

When the audience quieted down, he continued, "NOT LONG AGO, VALERIA ROAMED THE WILD REACHES OF THE TRANSYLVANIAN ALPS, FALLING UPON PEASANTS AT NIGHT, SINKING HER TEETH INTO THEIR THROATS AND DRAINING THE BLOOD FROM THEIR BODIES. AT MY RANCH IN ARIZONA, I KNEW NOTHING OF THESE STRANGE, UNGODLY MURDERS. NOT UNTIL THE NEWS ARRIVED THAT MY OWN UNCLE AND HIS FAMILY HAD BEEN VICIOUSLY SLAIN IN THEIR HOME NEAR BUDAPEST. LEARNING OF THIS, I UNDERTOOK AN EXPEDITION TO BRING THEIR SLAYER TO JUSTICE.

"FOR THREE LONG YEARS, MY TEAM AND I SEARCHED FOR THE VAMPIRE KNOWN AS VALERIA. GUIDED BY REPORTS OF EACH NEW ATROCITY, WE SLOWLY CLOSED IN ON HER. AT LAST, WE TRACKED VALERIA TO HER MOUNTAIN LAIR. WE ENTERED AFTER DAYLIGHT AND FOUND HER SLEEPING—AS IF DEAD—INSIDE HER COFFIN.

"THOUGH I HAD EVERY INTENTION OF PUTTING

VALERIA TO DEATH, I FOUND MYSELF OVER-
WHELMED BY HER BEAUTY AND WAS UNABLE TO
PERFORM THE DREADFUL TASK. STILL, SHE HAD TO
BE STOPPED. I COULD NOT ALLOW HER TO CON-
TINUE HER RUTHLESS CAMPAIGN OF MURDER. AT
LAST, WITH THE AID OF A WISE MAN WELL VERSED
IN THE ARTS OF MESMERISM, I GAINED CONTROL
OVER VALERIA'S MIND AND THUS ENSLAVED HER
TO MY WILL.

"AND SO I REMOVED HER FROM HER NATIVE
TRANSYLVANIA AND BROUGHT HER TO MY OWN
COUNTRY ... OUR COUNTRY, YOURS AND MINE,
AMERICA."

Good patriots, most of the people in the bleachers cheered
and applauded.

When the noise subsided, Stryker continued his speech.
"UNFORTUNATELY, DUE TO HER BLOOD-THIRSTY
NATURE, VALERIA IS NOT A WELCOME GUEST IN
OUR LAND. LIKE THE WANDERING JEW, SHE MUST
FOREVER CONTINUE HER TRAVELS, NEVER STOP-
PING LONG ENOUGH TO REST, NEVER FINDING A
HOME. AND SO WE ARE HERE TONIGHT, PAUSING
BRIEFLY ON OUR JOURNEY TO PROVIDE YOU GOOD
FOLKS WITH A CHANCE TO VIEW AN ACTUAL VAM-
PIRE ... VIEW HER *AND MORE!*"

While he paused, I heard whispers hissing through the audience.

Then he said, "LADIES AND GENTLEMEN, I'LL MAKE
YOU WAIT NO LONGER. HERE SHE IS! THE WORLD'S
ONLY LIVING VAMPIRE IN CAPTIVITY! THE LOVELY!
THE LETHAL! THE MOUTH-WATERING TEMPTRESS
OF TRANSYLVANIA! *VALERIA!*"

He flung his arms high and the audience erupted. As we
clapped and cheered, several members of his black-shirted
crew hurried into the arena. For the first time, I noticed that
ropes were hanging down the canvas walls ... three on my
side of the enclosure and three (I assumed) on the opposite
side.

Each of the ropes was picked up by a member of Stryker's crew. I spotted Vivian in the arena with the center rope from our side. She and the others walked backward, pulling. The ropes came off the ground, lifted away from the canvas, and stretched taut to the place where they were secured on top of the enclosure.

Stryker swung his arms down. It was a signal.

Vivian and the others tugged their ropes.

"VALERIA!" Stryker cried out.

All around him, crackling and whapping, the sheets of canvas fell to the ground.

Stryker was standing atop a steel cage. Its roof and every side were made of thick bars like a jail. It was raised a couple of feet off the ground on cinder blocks. It seemed to have a floor of some kind—maybe wood over more bars. Whatever the floor was, it seemed to be covered by a foot-thick layer of dirt.

Near the center of the floor lay a simple, wooden casket. Its lid was shut.

I took my eyes away from the coffin for a moment and looked around. Every spectator seemed to be staring at it.

For a while, the only sound came from the wind blowing through the trees around Janks Field.

Hands on hips, Stryker gazed down through the bars.

"VALERIA!" he shouted. *"ARISE!"*

The coffin lid flew off as if kicked. I flinched. So did people all around me. Most of the audience seemed to gasp. A few people let out startled squeals. The coffin lid flipped over a couple of times and hit the dirt floor. Dust drifted up and blew away.

Valeria sat up very slowly as if in a trance.

At first, I could only see her in profile. Then, very slowly, she turned her head away. She seemed to be studying the audience in the bleachers across from ours. While she did that, I studied the thick, black hair flowing down her back.

Slowly, her head turned to the front, then to *our* side.

All around me, people moaned and whispered.

Rusty was one of those who moaned.

To say that Valeria was gorgeous would be like calling Mount Rushmore a nice piece of sculpture. Rusty won our wager by a landslide. I would get my head shaved by Slim.

Valeria's head turned toward the front again.

She sat motionless. The audience was dead silent.

"Valeria, arise," Stryker commanded in a low, firm voice from the top of the cage.

She glided upward, rising to her feet with the elegance of a ballerina. Standing upright inside her casket, she must've been well over six feet tall. She spread her cape wide open like the wings of a bat and slowly began to turn.

When she turned toward us, I saw the outfit she was wearing beneath her cape: a top that looked like a bright red leather bra, a very short skirt of matching red leather, and red leather boots. The coffin blocked my view of the boots except for their very tops, which came up nearly to her knees.

All around me, people were murmuring. I heard Rusty say, "Holy shit."

I might've said it, myself. I don't know what I said, if anything. I only know that I gazed at Valeria, stunned.

Gazed at her amazing, beautiful face.

Gazed at her deep cleavage.

Gazed at the magnificent globes of her leather-encased breasts.

Gazed at her flat belly and the swell of her hips and her smooth, solid-looking thighs.

Then I saw her in profile. Then I saw only her back: the wide-spread cape and her thick, raven hair.

Completing her full turn, she lowered the cape and wrapped it around herself. As she walked toward the foot of her casket, I heard the jangle of spurs and glanced up at Stryker. He stood motionless on top of the cage, staring down at her.

She stepped out of the casket. The spurs were on her scarlet boots. She halted and stood motionless, staring straight ahead.

Stryker raised the microphone to his mouth. "LADIES AND GENTLEMEN, VALERIA HAS BEEN ENCLOSED IN HER COFFIN SINCE OUR LAST PERFORMANCE SEVERAL

NIGHTS AGO." He paused for a few moments, then said, "AND SHE IS HUNGRY."

Murmurs swept through the audience.

Lee glanced at me and grinned.

"SHE IS HUNGRY FOR BLOOD."

Laughter, cheers and applause.

Stryker raised his arms, signalling for silence.

When the audience settled down, he announced, "THE TRAVELING VAMPIRE SHOW IS *MORE* THAN A PERFORMANCE BROUGHT HERE FOR YOUR EDIFICATION AND ENTERTAINMENT, LADIES AND GENTLEMEN. IT IS ALSO OUR METHOD OF SUSTAINING VALERIA'S EXISTENCE.

"BEFORE BEING TAKEN INTO CAPTIVITY, SHE ROAMED THE NIGHT AND SUPPED AT RANDOM, DRAINING HER PREY OF THEIR BLOOD—TAKING THEIR LIVES. SHE NO LONGER KILLS. NOW, IN THE COURSE OF EACH PERFORMANCE, SHE GAINS HER NOURISHMENT NOT FROM ONE SOURCE BUT FROM SEVERAL . . . *MEMBERS OF THE AUDIENCE!*"

The people in the stands went wild with cheers, applause, whoops and whistles.

When the noise subsided, Stryker continued. "WE MAKE A CONTEST OUT OF IT, LADIES AND GENTLEMEN. A CONTEST OF STRENGTH, COURAGE AND ENDURANCE. AUDIENCE MEMBERS MAY VOLUNTEER TO ENTER THE CAGE OF VALERIA. ONE AT A TIME, OF COURSE. AND ONE AT A TIME, SHE WILL DRINK THEIR BLOOD . . . OR PERHAPS NOT. THOUGH SHE POSSESSES UNCOMMON STRENGTH AND AGILITY, HER CHALLENGERS FROM THE AUDIENCE ARE SOMETIMES ABLE TO RESIST HER.

"RESIST HER FOR A PERIOD OF FIVE MINUTES . . . PREVENT HER FROM DRINKING SO MUCH AS A SINGLE DROP OF YOUR BLOOD DURING A BOUT OF FIVE BRIEF MINUTES . . . AND YOU WILL WIN THE SUM OF FIVE HUNDRED DOLLARS. THAT'S FIVE HUNDRED

DOLLARS CASH MONEY, LADIES AND GENTLEMEN—
HALF A THOUSAND DOLLARS."

Someone in the grandstands on the other side of the arena
called out, "You mean we gotta *fight* her?"

"ONLY IF YOU VOLUNTEER, SIR. BUT THAT'S EX-
ACTLY WHAT I MEAN. VALERIA IS VERY HUNGRY.
SHE'LL WANT THE BLOOD OF ANYONE WHO STEPS
INTO THE CAGE WITH HER—SHE'LL WANT IT *BADLY*.
WHOEVER TAKES HER ON WILL HAVE A DESPERATE
FIGHT ON HIS HANDS. OR ON *HER* HANDS. WOMEN
ARE WELCOME . . . EVEN ENCOURAGED . . . TO CHAL-
LENGE VALERIA." He chuckled in a way that sounded very
phony, then said into his microphone, "FIVE HUNDRED
BUCKS WILL BUY A LOT OF GROCERIES, WON'T IT,
LADIES?"

Another audience member, a woman this time, yelled,
"Ain't enough groceries to *die* for!"

"VALERIA'S CHALLENGERS RARELY DIE, MA'AM.
SHE KNOWS WHEN TO STOP. HAVING YOUR BLOOD
SUCKED BY VALERIA IS NO MORE DANGEROUS
THAN DONATING A PINT TO THE RED CROSS . . . BUT
MUCH MORE PLEASURABLE."

Laughter and murmurs came from the crowd. A man
shouted, "All *right!*" Another man yelled, "Sounds good to
me!" Someone else, "I'm in!"

"BEFORE I ASK FOR VOLUNTEERS," Julian continued,
"I MUST WARN YOU THAT THOSE WHO CHALLENGE
VALERIA DO RUN A RISK OF INJURY. OVER THE
YEARS, A FEW HAVE EVEN SUCCOMBED TO THEIR
INJURIES."

Lee leaned toward me and I felt her upper arm against mine
as she said in a quiet voice, "They died."

I nodded.

"SHE IS VERY POWERFUL. THOUGH I'VE TAMED
HER TO SOME EXTENT, SHE *IS* A VAMPIRE AND EX-
TREMELY DANGEROUS. I MUST ASK EVERY CHAL-
LENGER TO SIGN A WAVER BEFORE STEPPING INTO
THE CAGE . . . RELEASING US OF LIABILITY FOR

WHATEVER MISFORTUNES MAY OCCUR IN THE COURSE OF THE STRUGGLE."

He looked down through the bars at Valeria. She still stood motionless just past the end of her coffin, staring straight forward.

"VALERIA, ARE YOU HUNGRY?"

She flung off her cape, threw her arms wide open as if to embrace the night, and *roared*.

"AUDIENCE, DO WE HAVE A VOLUNTEER?"

Chapter Fifty-two

We did.

Scattered throughout both grandstands, maybe twelve or fifteen people stood up. Those of them who were timid or polite raised one hand like a school kid, while others waved both arms overhead. A couple of them even shouted and whistled. Though I didn't get a good look at everyone who volunteered—including some who had their backs to me—they all seemed to be men.

They had friends in the audience who cheered and yelled.

Stryker, from his perch atop the cage, pointed toward someone on our side of the stands and said, "YOU, SIR!"

The man punched both fists at the sky as if he'd already won. He was nobody I recognized. As the audience cheered, he sidestepped through a crowded row, reached the cleared area of stairs, and hurried down to the arena.

He wore a plaid shirt, blue jeans and work boots.

The shirt and jeans fit him snugly. He looked handsome and rugged. His haircut was a flat-top, brushed straight up so it looked like a bristly triangle. I figured he was probably some sort of construction worker.

When he got to the ground, however, he shoved both fists at the air again and shouted, *"Semper Fi!"*

A United States Marine!

Back in those days, with fathers who had fought in World War Two and Korea, we all knew about places like Guadalcanal, Tarawa, Iwo Jima and the Chosin Reservoir. To most of us, every Marine was a hero. We held them in awe. Some of us still do.

Realizing that the volunteer was a leatherneck, I think I muttered, "Wow."

The audience went crazy, cheering and whistling.

He took off his shirt. He had a dark tan and the sort of muscles that made guys like me want to keep our shirts on forever.

I looked over at Lee. She was leaning forward slightly, staring down at the volunteer. She must've caught the motion of my head, because she turned to me and smiled. "This should be good," she said.

"A Marine," I said.

Leaning way forward, Rusty said, "Anybody know this guy?"

"Not me," I said.

Lee shook her head.

"Good thing I'm not a homo," Rusty said. "I'd fall in love."

Lee swatted his leg, but not very hard.

Down in the arena, Vivian walked up to the Marine with a clipboard. She took his shirt, spoke to him, and handed him the clipboard. He signed, then gave it back to her.

As she led him toward the cage, Stryker leaped to the ground. The microphone cord came down after him like long black rope. When he landed on the ground, his spurs jangled. They jangled some more as he stepped up to the volunteer.

Stryker said into the mike, "AND YOUR NAME IS?"

"WALLACE, SIR."

Vivian skidded the fingernails of one hand down his spine. He squirmed a little and smiled.

People in the audience laughed.

"CHANCE WALLACE," the man said.

"CHANCE, IS IT? WELL, DO YOU THINK YOU STAND A *CHANCE* AGAINST VALERIA?"

"YES, SIR!"

Vivian patted his rear end through the tight seat of his jeans. "GOOD LUCK TO YOU."

"THANK YOU, SIR."

Stryker stepped away from him and swung open the door of the cage.

Valeria continued to stand motionless just past the foot of her coffin, her back to the door, the cape wrapped around her body.

"LADIES AND GENTLEMEN . . . WE WILL LEAVE THIS DOOR WIDE OPEN SO THAT THE VIC . . . THE *VOLUNTEER* . . . WILL BE ABLE TO MAKE A QUICK ES-CAPE IF THE NEED SHOULD ARISE." He nodded at Chance. "ARE YOU READY?" he asked.

"MAY I ASK A QUESTION, SIR?" Chance asked into the mike.

"FIRE AWAY."

"WHAT ARE THE RULES, SIR?"

"YOU DON'T HAVE A WEAPON, DO YOU?"

"NO, SIR."

"THEN FEEL FREE TO DO WHATEVER YOU DEEM NECESSARY IN ORDER TO PREVENT VALERIA FROM SUCKING YOUR BLOOD. LAST FIVE MINUTES IN THE CAGE WITH HER AND YOU WIN FIVE HUNDRED DOL-LARS. ARE YOU READY?"

"YES, *SIR!*"

Stryker gestured for Chance to enter the cage.

Chance climbed a couple of wooden stairs and stepped through the doorway.

Stryker removed a timepiece from a pocket of his leather pants. From where I sat, it looked similar to the stopwatch that always dangled around the neck of my high school track coach. Also like my track coach, he wore a silver whistle around his neck. He glanced at the stopwatch, then spoke into his microphone. "LADIES AND GENTLEMEN, LET THE CONTEST BEGIN!"

Chance moved forward, eyes on Valeria. He walked slowly, hunkered low but keeping his head up, his arms open and his knees bent like a wrestler approaching his opponent.

Valeria still stood motionless, her back to him.

With one foot, Chance shoved the coffin out of his way. Another couple of strides took him within reach of Valeria. He halted.

The audience watched in utter silence. All I could really hear were the sounds of the wind.

I don't know why, but it struck me just then that somewhere in the audience were the two degenerates who had tried to take Slim—the Cadillac twins. They might be sitting directly behind me . . . or in the stands on the other side of the arena . . . or anywhere.

Peering across the arena, I started to look for them.

And missed Valeria's first move. As gasps exploded from the audience, I jerked my eyes back to the cage.

Already, Chance was draped from head to waist by the black shroud of Valeria's cape. While he struggled to get rid of it, she twirled away and raised both her arms in triumph, her spurs ringing out with each stride. She looked glorious, her raven hair blowing, her skin golden under the stadium lights, her red leather outfit gleaming.

Chance flung the cape aside. The wind caught it, carried it across the cage and pinned it to the bars.

Facing Valeria, he smiled. Then he shook his head and said something, but I couldn't hear what.

They started circling each other.

Chance might've been happy just to circle her for whatever was left of the five minutes. Plenty of us in the audience might've gone along with it, too. If Lee's reaction meant anything, the handsome and shirtless Marine was a real treat for the gals to watch. And every guy in the audience could've sat there all night watching Valeria. She would've been fine to watch if she were simply standing still. In motion, though, she was spectacular. The way the muscles moved under the smooth skin of her thighs and calves, the way we kept getting different views of her leather-harnessed breasts, and how they wobbled and shook.

She was a wonder to behold.

But Chance would be winning five hundred dollars in the next couple of minutes unless she did more than circle and prance and look gorgeous.

She had to know it, too.

We all knew it.

What's she waiting for? I wondered.

Maybe she's afraid of him. Who wouldn't be? A Marine, for godsake.

She attacked.

Went straight at him, roaring, leaping, reaching out with both hands.

People in the audience gasped. Others yelped with fright.

Must've been Judo.

Suddenly, Chance twirled and bent, took Valeria down across his hip and threw her. I glimpsed her red boots high in the air. An instant later, her back slammed the dirt. Dust rose around her.

She lay sprawled on her back, apparently stunned.

Chance stared down at her for a few seconds as if not quite sure what to do next. If she'd been an enemy soldier, he probably would've finished her off. But she was a beautiful woman. And he didn't *need* to finish her off; all he had to do was remain unbitten for a while longer.

The audience, sensing Valeria's defeat (and maybe fearing that her loss might put an end to the entire performance), started cheering her on.

"Get him, Val!"

"Come on, honey, you can do it!"

"Time's a-wastin', darlin'! Nail this gyrene's hide!"

She rolled onto her side. Instead of rising, however, she curled up as if she had a stomach ache.

We clapped and stomped our feet and chanted, "*UP! UP! UP!*"

Chance, assuming the victory was his, began to stride around Valeria, waving at the audience, smiling and nodding.

And got too close to her.

With a sweep of one leg, she kicked his right foot forward. Chance's leg flew high. He yelped with surprise and waved his arms. It looked as if he would slam down on his back. In the moment before he hit the ground, however, he turned his body. He shouted, "YAH!" and slapped the ground and landed on his side.

Unhurt, he rolled to get away from Valeria. But not fast enough. She hurled herself onto his back, hooked an arm across his throat, and darted her face down against the side of his neck.

He let out a yelp of surprise and pain.

Then he just lay underneath her, not resisting. Valeria no longer seemed to be struggling, either. She was sprawled on top of him, hands on his shoulders, her body squirming as if Chance were her lover, not her victim.

I couldn't see what was happening with her mouth, but I was pretty sure what must be going on.

Stryker entered the cage, trailing the microphone cord. "AND THE WINNER IS . . . *VALERIA!*"

The audience erupted with clapping, cheers, shouts and whistles.

Valeria stayed on top of Chance's back, face still down against his neck.

Stryker frowned at her. "VALERIA! QUIT!"

She didn't quit.

She went on with Chance as if they were all alone in the world.

"*VALERIA!*"

She ignored him.

Stryker stepped over to her, raised his right leg and raked the rowl of his big silver spur across her bare back just above the waist of her skirt.

Her head darted up and swung around. Glaring over her shoulder at Stryker, she roared. Blood flew from her mouth.

As I gaped at her, shocked, she turned her head the other way to let those in the other bleachers get a good look.

Silence.

Nobody spoke or laughed or clapped . . . or moved. The wind blew, hissing through the forest and lifting the long black hair from Valeria's shoulders.

Into the microphone, Stryker said, "IT'S OVER, MY DARLING. YOU'VE WON."

Chapter Fifty-three

After Valeria climbed off the Marine, several members of Stryker's black-shirted crew came into the arena wheeling a gurney. While they hurried toward the cage, Chance rolled onto his back and managed to stand up.

Applause rippled through the crowd even before Stryker's voice boomed out, "LET'S HEAR IT FOR A REAL CONTENDER!"

The applause grew to a roar.

Chance raised his hand in a game but embarrassed wave, sort of like a cowboy who has just gotten tossed off the back of a Brahma bull. Staggering out of the cage, he waved off the gurney in spite of the fact that he appeared to be bitten on the right side of his neck. He had blood all over his shoulder and running down his back and chest. He must've not considered it very serious, though. Not serious enough to merit a visit to an emergency room—or wherever the gurney crew had planned to take him.

As he hobbled back toward the bleachers, Vivian came along with his shirt. She didn't give it to him, though. Instead, she took hold of one arm and spoke to him. He nodded, then walked off with her.

Maybe to get himself bandaged.

Stryker proclaimed, "CHANCE WALLACE, LADIES AND GENTLEMEN!"

More wild applause. Chance waved again, then walked out of sight with Vivian.

"CHANCE'S TIME IN THE CAGE WITH VALERIA . . ." Stryker glanced at his stopwatch. "THREE MINUTES, FORTY-EIGHT SECONDS! A FINE DISPLAY OF COURAGE!"

Valeria, standing near Stryker in the cage, was using a wet towel to wipe the blood off her face and neck and chest.

"THAT WAS ONLY THE BEGINNING, LADIES AND GENTLEMEN! CHANCE'S BLOOD DID LITTLE MORE THAN WHET THE APPETITE OF THE GLORIOUS . . . AND VERY THIRSTY . . . VALERIA!"

She dropped the towel to the ground. One of the helpers hurried in to retrieve it.

"WHO WOULD LIKE TO GO NEXT?"

Leaning forward, Rusty looked past Lee and said to me, "Was that bitchin', or what?"

"Pretty cool," I said, and suddenly wished Slim could've been here to watch it with us. She would've gotten a kick out of seeing this woman wipe out a Marine. Also, I would've liked to have her sitting beside me. Lee on one side, Slim on the other.

I supposed she was probably sitting in her Pontiac, listening to the radio.

Or maybe listening to Bitsy. I could just see the poor thing sitting in the front seat with Slim, crying her eyes out, sobbing her tale of getting pounded by her brother. . . .

Why didn't I stop him?

Slim would be shocked and outraged by what we'd done. And sympathetic toward Bitsy in spite of the names the girl had called her.

"YOU! YOU THERE. YES, YOU."

Stryker's tinny, amplified voice startled me, tore me out of my daydreams and planted me in the present.

I saw a man climbing down the bleachers across the arena from us. He was a skinny guy, bald on top, and wearing glasses. He couldn't have been more than forty years old, but he dressed like a codger in a white polo shirt, plaid Bermuda shorts, knee socks and loafers. He sort of laughed and waved at the crowd as he made his way down to the arena.

"Here's a sure winner," Lee said.

Rusty and I laughed.

Down in the arena, he kept his shirt on and signed Vivian's clipboard. Then she led him up the stairs and through the doorway of the cage.

Stryker asked his name. The gawky man leaned close to the microphone in Stryker's hand and said, "I'M CHESTER."

"Go, Chester!" yelled someone in the audience.

Grinning, he nodded and waved.

"READY TO TAKE ON VALERIA?" Stryker asked.

"OH, WELL, SURE." He shrugged. "CAN'T SEE WHY NOT."

"THAT FIVE HUNDRED DOLLAR PRIZE MUST LOOK AWFULLY GOOD TO YOU."

"IT AIN'T HAY," said Chester.

Rusty leaned forward. "This guy's a goner."

"WOULD YOU LIKE TO LEAVE YOUR GLASSES WITH OUR BEAUTIFUL ASSISTANT?"

Chester shook his head. Into the mike, he said, "I'LL KEEP 'EM ON, THANKS." Stryker started to pull the mike away, but Chester grabbed it and pulled it close to his mouth. "YOUR GAL HERE, THIS VALERIA, SHE'S A FINE LOOKING WOMAN. A GUY'D HAVE TO BE NUTS TO GO IN THAT CAGE WITH HIS GLASSES OFF."

With that comment, he won the audience. The grandstands erupted with laughter and cheers.

I looked at Valeria. She had her eyes on Chester, and didn't crack a smile.

Stryker was chuckling, though. He patted Chester on the back and said, "BEST OF LUCK, MY FRIEND."

Chester bobbed his head, grinning.

"ANY QUESTIONS?"

"NOPE. JUST LET ME AT HER."

Stryker walked out of the cage and trotted down the stairs, his spurs jangling. At the bottom, he hauled out his stopwatch.

"LADIES AND GENTLEMEN," he announced, "LET THE CONTEST BEGIN!"

Valeria planted her hands on her hips and stared at Chester.

He stood there, arms hanging by his sides, and studied her. He didn't even try to be sneaky about it, just ogled her, his head moving slowly up and down. After doing that for a while, he wiped the back of a hand across his mouth.

Nervous-sounding laughter ruffled through the crowd.

Chester looked around, grinning at his audience. Then he leered at Valeria, raised both hands to chest level, and flexed his fingers as if honking her breasts.

That bought him wild laughter and cheers . . . along with a chorus of *boos*.

Smirking, Valeria walked toward him. She moved slowly, her back arched, arms by her sides, as if offering to let him squeeze more than just air.

He pointed a finger at himself and mouthed, "Me?"

She nodded.

He reached out, actually clutched the red leather cups and squeezed them. He squeezed them a couple of more times, turning his head and mugging for the audience.

"I bet he's a ringer," Lee said.

"Huh?" I asked.

"Someone they planted in the audience. He can't be for real."

Rusty leaned forward. "I bet you're right. She isn't gonna let some *stranger* grab her . . . her you-know-what's."

Lee chuckled and shook her head.

Down in the cage, Chester had stopped making faces. He'd stopped pretending to honk Valeria's breasts. Now he was stroking their bare tops while she stood there motionless, letting him.

Lucky Chester.

Then one of her hands glided forward and she rubbed the front of his Bermuda shorts.

His mouth fell open and his back arched.

Everyone in the grandstands probably couldn't see where Valeria had put her hand—the angle was only right for some of us—but half the crowd went *"EWWWWWWWWW"* and so many shrill whistles ripped through the air that my ears cringed.

Chester stood as if frozen.

I heard Rusty murmur, "Man, oh man."

Lee grinned at him and patted his knee.

My mouth was dry, but I managed to say, "This guy *has* to be a ringer."

"Oh, yeah," Lee said.

I wondered how much time he had left. At least a couple of minutes must've gone by so far. If he really was a ringer, maybe the plan was to let him win.

Valeria pulled down the zipper of his shorts.

"Oh, great," Lee grumbled. "You guys shouldn't be . . ."

Valeria reached into Chester's open fly.

". . . seeing this."

The reaction of the audience was a wild mixture of joy, consternation and excitement. Through all the hoots and whistles and applause, I heard shouts of, *"No!"* and *"Go for it!"* and *"All right!"* and *"Someone put a stop to this!"* and several suggestions that were extremely foul and vulgar.

Instead of doing what most of us probably expected, however, Valeria turned her hand upward and clutched Chester's pants: not only the upper areas of the zipper, but apparently the waistband of his Bermudas and also his belt buckle. Then she hoisted him off his feet.

He squealed, flapped his arms and kicked.

With just her one arm, Valeria rammed him all the way up. Luckily (or due to plenty of rehearsals), his head missed the bars. It passed through a space between two of them and poked out the top of the cage. The bars stopped him at the shoulders.

Letting go of him, Valeria twirled out of the way.

Chester yelped and started to fall. Then suddenly he grabbed the bars. He pulled himself up until his head was again jutting out the top of the cage.

"Help!" he yelled.

Far as I could tell, nobody in the audience seemed very upset by his plight. A good many of us must've already suspected he was a ringer. And some of the audience, especially women, probably figured he was getting his just deserts.

There was nervous laughter—and cheering—when Valeria reached out with both hands and jerked his Bermudas down. For underwear, he wore baggy white boxer shorts decorated with red polka-dots.

This guy was *definitely* a ringer. His antics had been nothing but a stage performance.

I felt a strange mixture of relief and disappointment.

Is it ALL fake?

Most likely, I thought.

Then Valeria jerked the boxers down to Chester's ankles. From the waist down, he was naked.

She pulled the Bermudas and boxers down over his shoes and tossed them across the cage. Now Chester was dangling there in nothing but his polo shirt, knee socks and loafers. He had a skinny, pale butt. He also, much to the shock and delight and amusement and dismay of the spectators, had a boner.

It didn't matter where you were sitting; the way he kicked and twisted, everyone in the bleachers got to see both sides of Chester.

I was suddenly very aware of why they tried to keep kids away from the show.

And I was suddenly embarrassed to be watching this with Lee sitting beside me. And glad that Slim had decided against coming.

Chester's groin area was just about level with Valeria's face. She stepped up to him and opened her mouth.

Some people screamed. Including Chester. Others cried out *"NO!"* and *"Oh, my God!"* and a few suggestions such as *"Bite it off!"*

I figured the five minutes must be running out. Valeria had better do something fast or Chester would win the five hundred bucks.

She slowly leaned closer, her mouth wide open as if ready to take him in. . . .

He squealed *"No!"* and kicked out, driving his right shoe into Valeria's midsection. She grunted and stumbled backward, bending over, hugging her belly. As she fell to the dirt, Chester let go of the bars and dropped.

Huffing for breath, he stared down at her. He was standing at her feet. Her legs were parted, her knees up. Chester seemed to be staring up her short leather skirt.

He swung around and looked toward the open door of the cage.

Thinking about it.

Wondering how much time he had left?

Or maybe no longer caring about the time or about the five hundred dollars or about anything other than what was sprawled on the ground behind him.

Pulling the polo shirt over his head, he whirled around. He flung the shirt away. Naked down to his knee socks, he dived for Valeria, arms extended, hands all set to grab her breasts. He would've landed between her knees in perfect position for thrusting into her body, but one of her feet shot up.

In an instant of silence, I heard the jingle of a spur.

Then Chester squealed. Braced up by Valeria's right leg, he was thrown over her body. He flipped over in midair and landed on his back across her open casket.

He'd been split open from navel to sternum.

"Holy shit," Rusty muttered.

Lee blinked, shook her head and said, "Maybe he's *not* a ringer" as Valeria, down in the cage, buried her face in Chester's bloody abdomen.

Chapter Fifty-four

The black-shirted crew hustled into the cage and lifted Chester onto the gurney. As they rolled him away, Valeria took a wet towel from one of the helpers and started to wipe the blood off her body. Stryker spoke into the microphone. "LET'S

HEAR IT FOR CHESTER, LADIES AND GENTLEMEN! A REAL SCRAPPER!

Down beside him in the cage, Valeria raised her right leg and propped her boot on an edge of the coffin.

Bending down, she used the towel to wipe the blood off her spur. As she did that, I stared at the red mark across her back . . . the wound inflicted by Stryker's spur.

Hers was just a scratch.

She'd really opened up Chester.

"AND HOW ABOUT THAT PHYSIQUE!" Stryker went on. "IF ANY OF YOU LADIES ARE INTERESTED, I'M SURE YOU'LL HAVE NO TROUBLE FINDING CHESTER LATER AT THE LOCAL EMERGENCY ROOM."

Here and there, people were making their way down the bleachers. Mostly women. Several towed men along behind them.

Apparently, they'd had enough.

Ignoring the exodus, Stryker studied his stopwatch. "CHESTER LASTED A GRAND TOTAL OF FOUR MINUTES AND FORTY-THREE SECONDS. CAME UP ONLY SEVENTEEN SECONDS SHORT, LADIES AND GENTLEMEN."

Vivian hurried over to Stryker and leaned in close to his side. As she started speaking into his ear, he lowered the microphone. Whatever she was telling him, we couldn't hear it.

"Maybe we should be going, too," Lee said.

Rusty blurted, "No! We can't!"

"This is worse than I thought it'd be. You boys shouldn't be seeing this sort of thing. *I* shouldn't either."

"*Please*, Mrs. Thompson."

She shook her head. "I don't know what I was thinking, bringing you boys to a show like . . ."

"It's not so bad," Rusty said.

"That man was naked."

"So? It was just a *guy*. I mean, maybe *you* didn't like to see that, but it wasn't any big deal for me and Dwight. It ain't pretty, but we see that sorta stuff in gym class all the time. Right, Dwight?"

I just shrugged.

"You don't see guys get ripped open," Lee said.

"It's just a show, Mrs. Thompson. You said so yourself. I'll bet Chester didn't even get a scratch on him. It was probably all a big fake-out. They can do that sorta stuff, magicians and people like that. It's easy."

Lee frowned and shook her head, but I noticed she was still sitting down. In my opinion, she felt that she *ought* to take us away from the evil show, but she didn't much want to miss the rest of it, herself.

I finally opened my mouth. "Why don't we just stick around for one more bout and see what happens?"

Lee frowned and sighed. "I suppose we can stay for *one* more." Glancing from Rusty to me, she said, "But you guys have to promise you'll never breathe a word about any of this to your parents." To me, she added, "Or your brothers. If they find out I dragged you guys to something like . . ."

"I'll never tell," Rusty said.

"I sure won't," I said. "I promise."

"Okay. Well, I guess we can stay a little while longer."

Rusty grinned and clapped. "You're the best, Mrs. Thompson."

"Yeah, sure."

Just about then, Vivian got finished whispering to Stryker. As she hurried out of the cage, he raised the microphone to his mouth. "I'VE JUST BEEN ASSURED THAT CHESTER WILL NEED A FEW STITCHES, BUT HE'LL BE FINE. LET'S HEAR IT AGAIN FOR HIM!"

Some applause came from the crowd, but not much.

"PERHAPS HE DESERVED WORSE THAN HE GOT."

With that comment, Stryker won over a good portion of the remaining spectators. They laughed and cheered.

"BUT THE SCRAWNY LITTLE BASTARD CAME WITHIN A MERE SEVENTEEN SECONDS OF WALKING HOME WITH FIVE HUNDRED DOLLARS CASH MONEY IN HIS POCKET! HE LASTED *THAT* LONG, FOLKS. IF HE CAN STICK IT OUT—NO PUN INTENDED. . . ."

Laughter, groans, applause.

"IF CHESTER CAN *LAST* THAT LONG, WHY NOT YOU? OUTLAST HIM BY A MEAGER SEVENTEEN SECONDS AND YOU'LL WIN THE BIG PRIZE. NOW, HOW ABOUT IT, FOLKS? DO WE HAVE A VOLUNTEER?"

"I'll take her!" shouted someone behind me.

I recognized the voice.

As shouts and cheers erupted from the crowd, I twisted around and saw Scotty Douglas near the top of the bleachers. Though standing up, he wasn't going anywhere yet. He stood there smirking, flanked by five or six of his hoodlum friends including a couple of tough-looking gals. Not letting the hot night get in the way of fashion, they *all* wore black leather jackets. I didn't know any of the others, but I had no trouble recognizing Scotty.

Even though I hadn't seen him in a long time (he'd dropped out of high school after his junior year and moved to Clement), the sight of him gave me a sickish feeling in my stomach. It was pretty much the same feeling I'd gotten a couple of years earlier when he and his two buddies, Tim and Smack, went after Slim and Rusty and me when we were at Janks Field for archery practice.

He looked about the same as always: greasy hair piled high on his head, long sideburns, black leather jacket, white T-shirt and blue jeans. He wore a familiar sneer on his face. A cigarette dangled from a corner from his lips.

"YOU!" Stryker announced. "YOU UP THERE IN THE LEATHER JACKET!"

Scotty nodded, winked toward Stryker, then turned to his friends. He spoke to them for a few seconds—probably cracking wise about how he would decimate Valeria. After that, he stripped off his leather jacket and handed it to one of the gals. Then he started to work his way across the row.

He'd gained a scar on his left cheek since the last time I'd seen him. Also, he looked as if he'd gained about twenty pounds of muscle.

Rusty said, "Jesus H. Christ, is that who I think it is?"

"It's him, all right," I said.

"The Douglas kid?" Lee asked.

335

"Yeah."

"I knew his big brother. A real . . . jerk."

"Must run in the family," I said.

I watched Scotty make his way down the bleachers and enter the arena. He didn't seem to have a limp anymore, but I bet he still had a scar from Slim's arrow.

He was wearing motorcycle boots, the same as always.

Cigarette hanging off his lower lip, he took the clipboard from Valeria and signed it. Then he tossed his butt into the dirt, climbed the stairs and entered the cage.

"NAME'S SCOT DOUGLAS," he said into Stryker's microphone. "I'M HERE TO COLLECT MY FIVE HUNDRED BUCKS."

The grandstands went wild with shouts and hoots and whistles. The worst of the noise came from behind us. Looking over my shoulder, I saw what I expected: Scotty's friends were on their feet, a couple of them waving and shrieking while three were busy giving out ear-splitting whistles with the help of fingers buried in their mouths.

"THINK YOU CAN BEAT CHESTER'S RECORD?" Stryker asked.

"DAMN RIGHT, SPORT."

"WELL, GOOD LUCK TO YOU." Spurs jingling, Stryker walked out of the cage and trotted down the stairs to the ground. He raised his stopwatch. "LADIES AND GENTLEMEN, LET THE CONTEST BEGIN!"

For a while, Scotty and Valeria stood a few feet apart, looking each other over . . . Scotty smirking, Valeria glaring back at him with narrow eyes. Then they started circling like a couple of wrestlers.

The crowd went silent.

Scotty peeled off his T-shirt. Holding it in one hand, he swung it like a towel, sweeping it past Valeria's face, snapping it at her bare midriff.

Way off beyond the other bleachers, the sky flashed as if a monstrous light bulb had burst to life inside a thunderhead, shuddered and quickly died.

Scotty whipped his T-shirt at Valeria's face. She tore it from his hands and the wind tossed it across the cage.

Thunder grumbled through the night.

Here it comes, I thought. All day long, the sky had been grim with clouds, the air heavy and moist and hot. *Now* the storm would come . . . in time to spoil the show.

It isn't here yet, I told myself.

Besides, Lee's going to drag us out of here as soon as Valeria finishes with Scotty.

Maybe.

While I'd been busy worrying about the storm, Scotty had been busy pulling his thick leather belt out of the loops in his jeans. Now he was swinging it instead of the T-shirt, snapping it at Valeria as she circled him.

She didn't seem to be in any hurry to rush him. Nor did she seem very concerned by the belt. Though she dodged and feinted fairly often, she didn't make any great efforts to avoid its lash. Every so often, the leather smacked against her skin with a sound like a face being slapped. Each time that happened, she flinched but just kept circling Scotty.

Why didn't she close in and put a stop to it?

I started to wince myself each time the belt struck her.

Turning to Lee, I said, "Why doesn't she . . . ?" But even as the words started to come out, I noticed that Lee seemed entranced by the spectacle. Her eyes had a glazed look and her mouth hung open.

Though I hadn't finished my question, she blinked and turned her head. "Huh? What was that?"

"I was just . . . why is she letting him *do* that? He's hurting her."

Lee shook her head, muttered, "Don't know," and returned her attention to the cage.

Rusty leaned forward and said to me, "Bet she *likes* it. Some gals *like* to get knocked around, you know? Turns 'em on."

I nodded. "Yeah, that's probably it."

We both stopped talking.

Eyes on the show again, I flinched as the tip of Scotty's belt cracked against Valeria's belly. That one must've *really* hurt, because she cried out and twisted away.

As Scotty rushed after her, swinging his belt, she backed away from him. A couple more strides, and a wall of the cage would stop her retreat.

Suddenly, she reached behind her back, undid whatever fasteners were there, and swept off the bright red leather top of her costume. The sight of her naked breasts tore my breath away. All through the audience, people gasped. I could feel myself growing hard. A moan came from Rusty's direction, but I didn't look over at him. Couldn't look anywhere except at Valeria.

Clad only in her short red skirt and boots, she whipped the bra-like garment through the air in front of her. The quick motion swung her breasts.

In midair, the red leather of Valeria's top met the black leather of Scotty's belt. They tangled.

Valeria's arm leaped back and the belt flew from Scotty's hand.

The crowd roared with delight.

Most of the crowd, that is. The bunch behind us—Scotty's friends—hissed and booed. Someone from back there shouted, "Get her, Scot!" Another shouted, "Ream her!"

Down in the cage, Valeria flung away the tangled leather of Scotty's belt and the top of her costume. They landed inside her open casket. Scotty watched them drop out of sight with a look on his face as if his favorite hat had just been blown over the edge of a cliff.

Beyond the other bleachers, a jagged dagger of lightning ripped through the night.

Scotty made a dash for the casket.

He wanted that belt.

Valeria raced to intercept him, her large breasts leaping and swinging.

Thunder grumbled.

She dived, wrapped her arms around Scotty's waist as he ran, and tore him to the ground. They rolled through the dirt. Then Scotty was on his back. Valeria, straddling him, grabbed his shoulder with one hand and his head with the other. She shoved his head sideways, then plunged her face against the side of his neck.

He thrashed and writhed underneath her.

Stryker's voice boomed from the speakers, "AND THE WINNER IS . . . VALERIA!"

She stayed on Scotty, not done with him yet.

Stryker ran into the cage. "THAT'S ENOUGH, VALERIA! STOP IT."

She didn't stop.

"NEED ANOTHER TASTE OF THE SPUR?"

She clung to Scotty for a few seconds more, then raised her head and rolled off him. She flopped on her back, gasping for air. Her lips and cheeks and chin—even the tip of her nose— were crimson with Scotty's blood. The rest of her body gleamed with sweat.

As the crew rushed into the cage, Stryker announced, "SCOT'S TIME WITH VALERIA, THREE MINUTES AND TWENTY SECONDS."

He hadn't lasted nearly as long as the frail Chester, but the audience showed lots of appreciation. Maybe because he'd gotten Valeria to remove her top.

The crew lifted Scotty onto a gurney and hurried away with him.

There was a lot of blood on the dirt floor where he'd been sprawled.

The audience cheered Valeria as she rose to her feet. Her body gleaming with blood and sweat, she thrust both arms toward the sky in triumph and pranced around in a circle as if doing some sort of victory dance. The way she looked— beautiful and shiny, hair blowing in the hot wind, breasts bouncing and swinging—drove the audience to a frenzy. All around us, people stood up.

My view was blocked, so I stood up, too. As did Lee and Rusty.

Apparently enjoying her ovation, Valeria danced around even more wildly.

As she leaped and twirled, lightning in the shape of an upside-down tree turned the sky brilliant. Every detail of Valeria trembled in stark relief—the wild look on her face, the curves of her muscles and ribcage, the jutting tips of her breasts. . . .

I felt hard and achy. Without underwear on, I was pushing tight against the inside of my jeans. I started to worry about having another accident so I sat down. This not only relieved the pressure, but it took Valeria out of sight.

Thunder roared, shaking the night.

Lee sat down beside me. "You okay?" she asked.

I nodded.

"We'd probably better get going," she said.

"I guess so."

"Before something *else* happens."

"Guess so," I said.

She patted my leg, then turned her head the other way. Toward Rusty.

But he wasn't there.

Chapter Fifty-five

All I could figure was that Rusty must've had an accident, himself, and hurried away to prevent Lee or anyone else from noticing it.

"Come on," Lee said. She started to stand up.

"No, wait."

"What?"

"Why don't we wait here for him? He probably just went . . ."

Lee shook her head. "He knows we're about to leave. Maybe he just went on ahead."

We were both wrong.

In front of us, the spectators sat down and we saw Rusty halfway down the bleacher stairs, waving both hands overhead. Shirtless and bandaged, he almost looked as if he'd *already* been in the cage with Valeria. Racing toward the bottom, he shouted, *"Me! Me! I'm next! I call it! My turn!"*

The audience cheered him.

Lightning ripped through the sky.

"Oh, my God," Lee muttered.

I couldn't believe my eyes—oh, yes I could. Though stunned, I wasn't very surprised. Of *course* Rusty wanted to get into the cage with Valeria. He probably saw this as the opportunity of a lifetime.

And maybe he was right.

The thunder came . . . a long, rumbling noise. I could feel its vibrations in my chest like the drums of a parade band.

The storm was coming closer.

But wasn't here yet.

Valeria stood in the cage, breathing hard, slowly rubbing her body with the towel. She hadn't put her top back on. It was probably still inside the casket.

"Rusty!" I shouted. The crowd was clapping and yelling, so maybe he couldn't hear me. *"Don't!"* I called out.

"Come on," Lee said. She stood, sidestepped past the empty space left by Rusty, and started to make her way through the seated spectators.

I stayed close to her.

"Excuse me," Lee said to the people we had to disturb.

We were facing forward. The knees of those behind us jammed the backs of our legs. Our thighs rubbed the backs of people the next row down. I'd lost my boner by then, or it would've poked some heads.

"Excuse me," Lee said. "Excuse me. Excuse me."

A few people stood up to let us by. Others didn't budge and we had to shove past their legs.

"Excuse me. Excuse me."

"Sit down!"

"Down in front!"

"Y'make a better door than window!"

As we struggled across the row, I watched Rusty scribble on Vivian's clipboard. She took his arm and led him up the steps to the cage. As they entered the cage, another tree of lightning cracked across the night.

Lee and I broke through the end of the row.

Thunder crashed.

But still no rain.

If the rain starts, I thought, will they stop the fight?

Probably not.

I followed Lee as she raced down the stairs toward the arena.

"I SEE WE HAVE AN EAGER YOUNG VOLUNTEER," Stryker said, his amplified voice loud and crackling.

"I'M RUSTY," Rusty said into the microphone.

The audience cheered.

Rusty turned all the way around, grinning like a dope and waving at the crowd.

Someone called out, *"Go get her, Rusty!"*

Another, *"Nail her!"*

"Give them titties a squeeze for me!"

And worse.

Suddenly, near the bottom of the bleachers, our way was blocked by half a dozen black-shirted members of Stryker's crew.

"READY TO TAKE ON VALERIA?" Stryker asked.

"Excuse me," Lee said, and tried to keep going.

"YOU BET," Rusty said.

The man directly in front of Lee shook his head and spread out his arms.

"Let us through," Lee said.

"You'll just have to wait your turn, miss."

"Down in front!"

"Hey, sit down!"

"That kid can't fight Valeria," Lee said.

"Sure, he can."

"He's underage."

The man smirked. "Big deal."

"Outa the way, for cry-sake!"

"I'm his mother and I forbid . . ."

"BEST OF LUCK, RUSTY!"

"His mother, my ass."

"THANK YOU, MR. STRYKER."

A thin, tough-looking woman beside the guy said, "We don't want any trouble here."

"Then don't let Rusty fight!"

"Move yer asses!"

"Down in front!"

The woman shook her head. "Why don't you both return to your seats and enjoy the show?"

"LADIES AND GENTLEMEN, LET THE CONTEST BEGIN!"

Another harsh flash of lightning.

"You can't *do* this!" Lee shouted.

"Hell we can't. Sit down or we'll have you removed from the premises."

The crowd roared.

So did the thunder.

The fight had started. We didn't stand much chance of stopping it, now. I wanted to watch. And so did a dozen or so people whose views we were blocking.

Apparently, so did Lee. "Okay, okay," she said.

Though there were empty spaces down low, Lee raced halfway up the stairs before moving toward the center, squeezing past half a dozen spectators and taking a seat. If she couldn't stop the fight, at least she wanted a good vantage point for watching it. Breathless, I sat beside her.

The black-shirted crew watched us for a few more seconds, then spread out and seemed to vanish.

From the look of things in the cage, we hadn't missed much. Rusty and Valeria were both hunched over, arms out, circling each other slowly.

Which seemed to be the standard way to begin such contests.

I felt scared for Rusty. But I also envied him. There he was, face to face with Valeria, probably one of the most beautiful women to ever walk the earth—three or four feet away from that amazing face and those incredible, naked breasts.

It seemed like madness.

Glorious madness.

This must've been like a dream come true for Rusty.

He was sure to pay dearly for it, but it might be worth the payment.

Valeria seemed in no hurry to attack. Neither did Rusty—not with the kind of view he had. But I knew him. What he really wanted, now, was to reach out and feel those breasts.

He *had* to get his hands on them.

Even in front of an audience brimming with people who knew him and his parents?

You bet, I thought. He won't let a little thing like that stop him.

I could just see him grin and hear him say, *Hey, man, by the time someone tells on me, it'll be over. What're my folks gonna do, ground me? They can't make it not've happened, know what I mean?* And he would be showing me his hands as if they were trophies.

He went for her.

Rushed forward, ducking and reaching out with both hands. I thought he was going for her breasts, but then he dived and grabbed the sides of her leather skirt. His weight tore the skirt from her hips.

As Rusty fell, Valeria stumbled backward until the skirt tripped her. She landed on her back. The impact jolted her entire body, bounced her head off the dirt floor and jarred her breasts.

The audience exploded with delight.

The night exploded with lightning.

On his knees, Rusty snatched Valeria's skirt off her boots. The spurs seemed to give him trouble for a moment. Then the skirt pulled free and he flung it out of reach.

Thunder pounded through the air.

Valeria was now naked except for the crimson boots that reached almost to her knees.

She just lay there, sprawled out and limp, staring at the sky . . . either knocked into a stupor by the blow to her head or faking it.

I figured she *had* to be faking. Vampire or not, she'd outmatched much tougher men than Rusty tonight.

"Get away from her!" I shouted.

He probably couldn't hear me through the tumult of the crowd.

Lee joined my shouts. In unison, we yelled, *"Get away from her, Rusty!"*

If Valeria really *was* stunned or unconscious, Rusty actually stood a chance of winning the contest. Five hundred bucks was a ton of money for a guy who forever spent his allowance the day he got it. But he needed to keep his distance. . . .

Instead of getting away from her, he scooted forward on his knees, sliding his hands up her bare legs.

The audience cheered him on.

"Rusty!" I yelled. *"No!"*

But the lure must've been irresistable. I knew him well. He claimed he'd never seen a naked woman in real life, much less touched one. And he'd never *seen* a woman as beautiful as Valeria.

These were probably the most fabulous moments of his entire life.

"Is he nuts?" Lee asked.

As his hands traveled up Valeria's thighs, the crowd roared with delight and advice.

Lee yelled, *"Rusty, watch out! She's playing 'possum! Get away from her!"*

Rusty spread Valeria's legs apart. Either that, or she spread them herself. I missed who did it. I just suddenly realized her thighs were wider apart than a moment earlier.

"It's a trick!" Lee shouted. *"Get away from her! Run!"*

On his knees between her legs, Rusty leaned forward and put a hand on each of her breasts. He rubbed them slowly as if she'd asked him to spread suntan oil on them. They wobbled around under the motions of his hands. When he squeezed them, they seemed springy.

Valeria just lay there, not reacting.

Maybe she *isn't* faking, I thought.

If she's hurt, shouldn't Stryker put a stop to this? Was he

planning to just let Rusty spend the rest of the five minutes feeling her up? •

Rusty hunkered down and put his mouth on Valeria's right breast. He seemed to be kissing or sucking its nipple. Then his head was moving all around. I didn't know what he was doing at first, then realized he was *licking* her breast.

A dagger of lightning stabbed down from the sky, roaring, and struck the top of one of the light poles. It was just behind the other bleachers. The bank of stadium lights exploded . . . along with the top of the pole.

All the lights surrounding the grandstands suddenly died.

Chapter Fifty-six

We were plunged into darkness . . . except for a fluttering yellow-orange glow of firelight. It came from the blazing top of the pole that the lightning had struck.

Suddenly, warm rain was pouring down.

The blazing pole loomed over the bleachers like a giant torch, dimmed by the rain but still on fire.

All around us, people began leaping to their feet.

They wanted *out*.

As they shoved and bumped us in their rush to escape, Lee and I stood up. We climbed onto our seats and looked down. On both sides of the arena, people were fleeing through the downpour. Some were falling. Others were fighting. But I didn't care what was happening to them.

I turned my eyes toward the cage in the center of the arena.

By then, the fiery light post had nearly been extinguished. Through the heavy rain, I could barely make out the shapes of Rusty and Valeria.

Then came another blast of lightning.

It turned the rain into slanting silver streaks and filled the cage with a shuddering white glare. I glimpsed Rusty on top of Valeria, jeans down around his ankles, his white rump shoving, flexing.

Darkness.

Someone bumped me from behind. I don't know whether it was deliberate or one of those careless collisions of the kind that happens when people are in a hurry. Either way, the result was the same. I yelped and teetered.

Lee grabbed me. She couldn't stop me, though. We both fell forward, grappling with each other, colliding with a few people below us, knocking them off their feet before we crashed down on the slick, wet bleachers. We rolled and fell between two rows.

I struck a board. Then Lee mashed me against it.

She seemed very heavy for such a slender woman. I couldn't budge. She lay on top of me, gasping for breath. Her cheek was warm and wet against the left side of my face while the right side got pelted by rain. Under my back, I felt the vibrations of all the shoes and boots and sandals and bare feet pounding their way down the bleachers.

Nobody stopped to help us.

For that matter, with the darkness and downpour and the way we were down in a low place between the rows, maybe no one even *saw* us.

The bleachers trembled and shook.

Out behind the stands, car doors thumped. Engines began to sputter and cough and race. Headlights came on, casting a pale glow into the rain-filled air above Janks Field. Horns honked. People shouted. More doors slammed. More engines revved.

I suddenly remembered the Cadillac twins and what I'd done to their car.

I'd intended to strand them, but I hadn't planned on *us* being trapped in the grandstands when it happened.

Brilliant move, Thompson.

Directly above us, lightning fluttered across the sky and thunder crashed. Lee flinched.

Which surprised me. She seemed too strong for that. But

all her weight was on top of me, so there was no mistake about it: she jerked like a startled little girl. Suddenly feeling protective of her, I raised my arms and wrapped them around her back.

"You okay?" I asked.

She nodded, her cheek sliding against my face. "How about you?" she asked.

"Guess I'm okay."

"Am I crushing you?"

"Nah."

"Maybe we'd better stay here for a few minutes. Give the crowd a chance to clear out."

I almost told her that I wanted to get up and check on Rusty . . . but then I remembered my last glimpse of him in the lightning flash. It made me feel a little sick.

Valeria obviously wasn't a vampire, after all. Just a beautiful woman with a very strange and dangerous job. And she hadn't been playing 'possum, after all. She'd been stunned or out cold.

You don't *do* things to someone in that condition.

You just don't.

Not even if she's gorgeous and naked and pretends to be a vampire.

I knew Rusty was always horny, always making crude remarks, always talking (when Slim wasn't around) about how much he'd like to "do it" to this or that girl. Or "jump her bones" or "give her a taste of the one-eyed monster" or so on. Maybe it shouldn't have been a shock to catch him doing that to Valeria.

But it was.

How did he even know *how?*

The way he'd been going at her, I couldn't help thinking that maybe he'd had some previous experience.

No. He would've bragged about it.

Unless the girl was . . .

From somewhere behind the bleachers came a scream.

Looking back toward Janks Field, all I could see was a pale

glow given off by headlights. I was too high in the stands for a view of the ground or even the vehicles.

"Glad we're not mixed up in that," Lee said.

"Yeah."

"How you doing?"

"Fine."

"You're not squished yet?"

"Nah. I'm okay."

"You make a pretty good mattress."

"Thanks."

"Maybe a little lumpy here and there." She squirmed as if looking for a more comfortable position.

All of a sudden, I was acutely aware of being flat on my back with *Lee* on top of me.

Through her soaked, clinging shirt, my hands felt her back—and no bra straps. Her breasts were mashed against my chest. The way her belly touched mine, I could feel each breath she took. Her groin was tight against my crotch. Though we were thigh to thigh, her legs were slightly apart and squeezing mine together as if to hold herself in place.

I started to get a boner.

Squirming, I pushed at Lee. "We'd better get up."

"I'll try."

She reached up to the bench with her right hand, pulled at it, shoved at my shoulder with her other hand, unclenched her thighs and managed to sit up on me, straddling my hips, her legs dangling off the sides.

If anything, this position was worse for me. Didn't she realize what she was sitting on?

Didn't she care?

Maybe she *liked* it.

Lightning flashed.

Lee flinched again.

For just a moment, through the slanting streaks of silver rain, I saw her sitting upright on top of me with her head turned toward the arena. Her soaked hair was flat against her head. Her face, shiny as oil, streamed with water. So did her bare arms. Her drenched shirt was half unbuttoned. It adhered to her body and took on the shapes of her breasts. Her stiff nipples pushed out the clinging fabric.

I saw all this in the starkness of the lightning, a glare that probably lasted no more than a second but seemed to go on much longer. And just before the darkness returned, I saw Lee's jaw drop open.

"Oh, my God!" she gasped.

"What?"

"He's down! She's on him!"

My insides cringed. I tried to sit up but I couldn't—not the way Lee was sitting on me.

She began to climb off. Trapped between the bleacher seats, her legs dangling, it was a struggle. Finally, she freed herself.

The moment she was off me, I lurched upright and looked for Rusty. Whatever cars remained on Janks Field, their headlights weren't pointing in our direction. All we had in the arena was darkness and pouring rain. I could hardly see the cage, but there seemed to be pale shapes inside it. They might've been naked bodies squirming in a tangle, but I couldn't be sure.

Lee dropped onto the bench in front of me, twisted around, reached out and squeezed my arm. *Let's get down!*

She helped me climb out from between the bleacher planks. Then, side by side, we hopped carefully but as fast as we dared down the slick boards like a couple of hikers leaping from rock to rock in an effort to cross a stream.

No one was in our way.

The stands on both sides of the arena looked empty. It seemed that everyone except us had already fled. By the sounds of engines and car horns and shouts, many of them were still in Janks Field, fighting the traffic jam.

What're the Cadillac twins up to?

I hardly got a chance to start worrying about them, however, before several dark shapes hurried into the cage with a gurney.

Then several more came running toward Lee and me.

We almost reached the bottom of the bleachers before they stopped us.

The man blocking our way said, "Show's over, folks. Time to go home."

"We're not going anywhere," Lee said. "Not without my son."

"Your son, right." Though I couldn't make out the details of his face, he was obviously the same man who had stopped us the last time. "Go on, get outa here."

"You can't make us," I blurted. I was angry and scared. I needed to get past these people and stop the others from taking away Rusty. "This is public property. And anyway, my dad's the chief of police. So you'd better just get out of our way."

"Sure, kid."

"Please," Lee said to him. "We only want to . . ."

I broke to the side, my feet somehow not flying out from under me, and leaped. One of the gang tried for me. I shouldered him or her out of the way, but the impact knocked me crooked. I managed to plant one foot on the bottom row of the bleachers and spring off. In midair, I saw several dark figures moving inside the cage . . . rolling the gurney. A pale body was sprawled on the gurney. Someone else stood nearby, hands on hips.

Balance gone, I landed on the ground with a splash, stumbled and started to fall.

I was caught by strong hands. They clamped me just below my armpits and hoisted me upright. After I was standing, they didn't let go.

"What seems to be the problem here?"

It was the voice of Julian Stryker.

"My friend," I blurted. "They're taking away my friend." In case he didn't know who I meant, I said, "Rusty. The one who . . ."

"I know who he is," Stryker said. "He's been hurt. They're taking him to an ambulance."

The sky suddenly trembled with lightning.

Stryker's mane of black hair was plastered to his head, his stark white face dripping and shiny, his lips crimson. So much like a beautiful woman, but rugged and craggy like a man.

351

His silk shirt was clinging like ebony skin to his powerful shoulders and chest.

In the last moment of brilliant light, I saw past Stryker's side—the gurney gliding by, weighted down by Rusty.

Rusty, naked except for his white socks. Chubby, pale, shiny.

His arm was no longer bandaged.

Where his arm had been nipped by the poodle, he now had a mouth-sized patch of gory pulp.

The blood'll bring vampires like chum brings sharks.

Thunder rumbled.

Darkness clamped down and Rusty was gone.

Chapter Fifty-seven

Let go of me!" I shouted into Stryker's face.

"Just settle down."

"They're taking him away!"

"Nothing to worry about."

"Where're they *going?*"

Stryker ignored my question. He called out, "Bring the woman here."

Over my shoulder, I looked for Rusty. No sign of him or the gurney or those who'd been bearing him away.

But I saw Lee being led toward us, members of Stryker's gang clutching both her arms. Though she struggled to pull free, they hung on. I realized that the rain was no longer falling so hard. It still poured down, but with less force than before. I could see better. . . .

Lee's chambray shirt, sleeveless and hardly long enough to reach her waist, was no longer buttoned. Down its middle was a strip of skin the same dusky shade as her bare legs. Her white shorts looked like snow on a cloudy midnight.

Stryker released my sides. Before I could make a move, however, he grabbed my upper right arm. "Just take it easy," he said. "Everything's fine."

"Like hell," I said.

"Let her go," Stryker told his people.

They released Lee's arms. Facing Stryker, she said, "Now *you* let go of Dwight."

Stryker's teeth showed. They were as white as Lee's shorts.

"Giving me orders?" he asked. But his hand dropped away from my arm.

I almost took off to go after Rusty, but changed my mind. With half a dozen of Stryker's gang spread out close behind us, I wouldn't have gotten far.

"We want Rusty back," Lee said.

"I'm afraid he was seriously injured in the competition, but we'll see that he gets proper attention."

"We'll take care of him," Lee said.

"He's already being looked after."

"*We'll* look after him."

"Where *is* he?" I demanded.

Stryker's head turned toward me. By the way the white showed, he was obviously smiling. "Wouldn't you like to know?" he said.

"Yes!"

He chuckled.

Lee took hold of my hand. "Come on, Dwight."

"We can't leave without Rusty!"

"Come on." Her voice was firm.

I had an urge to jerk my hand from her grip and refuse to leave, but then I realized she probably had a plan. Lee wasn't a quitter.

Maybe she figured we should leave peacefully, then double back and spy on the gang.

Or maybe the plan was to hurry into town and come back with the police. My dad was in the hospital, but Grandville still had a police department of sorts. If necessary, they could bring reinforcements from the county sheriff and even the state troopers. We could come back in force and rescue Rusty.

353

"Let them go," Stryker ordered.

His gang spread out.

As we walked away from them, I looked over at the parking area. The structure of the bleachers blocked some of my view. So did the BEER—SNACKS—SOUVENIRS shack. But I could see plenty of Janks Field, anyway.

Just about the only people still wandering around over there appeared to be members of Stryker's crew. Equipped with flashlights, they were busy directing traffic. From the look of things, they'd been doing a good job. Though a few cars and pickups sat motionless as if abandoned, the field was mostly empty. A line of vehicles inched toward the mouth of the dirt road.

Not an ambulance among them.

No sign of Rusty, either.

"What're we gonna do?" I asked.

"I'm not sure," Lee said.

"We can't just leave Rusty."

"I know."

"I don't think they're sending him to a hospital. Or the others, either. I haven't even seen an ambulance."

"Ambulances couldn't get out of here, anyway," Lee pointed out.

When we rounded the end of the bleachers, I had a clear view of Janks Field. I spotted Lee's pickup truck, the disabled Cadillac and a couple of other cars. And then I heard the jangle of spurs behind us.

Something seemed to crumple inside me. "Uh-oh," I muttered.

"Lee! Dwight!"

We stopped and turned around.

"What is it that you want?" Stryker asked, sounding almost as if he'd forgotten. But you could tell by his voice that he was playing with us.

"Rusty," Lee said. "We just want Rusty."

"How badly?"

In a solemn voice, Lee asked, "What've you got in mind?"

"You give me what I want, I give you what *you* want."

"And what is it that *you* want?" Lee asked.

"You and Valeria. Five minutes."

"What?"

"In the cage."

"You want me to *fight* her?"

"That's the idea."

"Why? The show's over. Everybody's gone."

"Not everybody." Stryker placed a hand on his own chest. "I love a good contest of strength and will. Frankly, I feel cheated. The show usually goes on for a couple of hours, at least." He shrugged elaborately. "It was especially disappointing that our only challengers were men. I *love* to see an attractive woman take on Valeria. Warms the cockles of my heart."

Lightning flashed again. All I noticed was Stryker's dripping, grinning face.

When the darkness returned, he said, "Take her on. I *know* you'll give us a great show."

I pulled at Lee's hand. "Let's get out of here."

She stayed put. "What if I don't win?" she asked.

"If you don't win, my dear, Valeria will suck your blood."

Scared that Lee seemed to be considering it, I pulled harder at her hand. "Come on!" She didn't budge.

Thunder grumbled through the night. It came from a distance. Rain continued to fall, but I realized the worst of the storm had moved on.

"What about Rusty?" she asked.

"What about him?"

"Do we get him even if I lose?"

"Certainly."

"No!" I blurted. I wanted Rusty back, but not if it meant Lee getting ripped up by Valeria. *"Are you crazy?"*

Lee turned her head toward me. "I'm the reason Rusty came here tonight. I bought the tickets, remember?"

"I know, but . . ."

"And I'm not leaving without him. Not if I can help it."

"Then we have a deal?" Stryker asked.

"We have a deal," said Lee.

Richard Laymon

"You can't fight her!"

She gave my shoulder a gentle squeeze and said, "It'll be all right."

"Leeeee!"

"Don't worry, honey. Please."

Stryker stepped away and spoke to some of his crew. Three of them went hurrying off through the rain. Two others came over to me.

While Stryker stayed in the arena with Lee, I was led up the empty bleachers. My two guards were Vivian and a muscular man with a crewcut. They chose seats in the middle, about halfway up, and positioned themselves on both sides of me.

From there, we would have the best view possible of the activities inside the cage.

Vivian patted my leg. "This is gonna be good," she said.

I didn't respond.

"So who's the lucky gal? Not your mom, is she?"

I shook my head.

"Didn't think so. She looks way too young. What is she, your big sister?"

I had no reason to tell this woman the truth, so I said, "Yeah, my sister."

"Good lookin' gal," said the guy on my right.

Go to hell, I thought. But I didn't say it. I'm not that stupid.

"Your mom know you're here?" Vivian asked.

I shook my head again.

"Bet your folks think you're home in bed, don't they?"

"Maybe."

"Glad you came?"

I frowned at her. "Not very."

"Bet your friend Rusty had himself a good time. For a while there, anyway . . . till Valeria put the bite on him."

Her attempt at humor angered me. I opened my mouth. Mostly, I intended to tell her to shut up. But different words came out. "Is she real?" I heard myself ask.

"Real? Sure she's real."

"I mean, a vampire."

Vivian let out a harsh laugh. "What do *you* think, kid?"

"Is she?"

"Nah. She's the tooth fairy."

The guy laughed. "Good one," he said.

Off ahead of me, behind the other stand of bleachers, three sets of headlights lit the night. I couldn't see the vehicles behind them, but figured they must be the Traveling Vampire Show's hearse, bus and truck.

The beams of the headlights reached through the stands. In their pale glow, I saw Stryker and Lee standing together on the ground, and Valeria alone in her cage.

She no longer wore her boots. Totally naked, she was leaning back against the bars, arms and legs spread out, stretching and writhing as if she relished the flexing of her muscles and the feel of the rain on her bare skin.

When the light beams shifted, I looked away from Valeria.

One pair of headlights continued to aim at the arena, but the other two sets slid away through the rainy night.

In the jittery glare of a lightning flash, I caught a glimpse of the vehicles. The hearse remained in place behind the opposite bleachers. Moving slowly to the right was the large black truck. Moving to the left was the black bus.

Where're they going? I wondered.

Is Rusty in one of them?

We had no guarantee that Stryker would keep his part of the bargain.

What if they're taking Rusty away?

Through the sounds of their engines and the hiss and patter of the falling rain came a soft rumble of thunder.

The truck and bus rounded the ends of the bleachers, then turned. They weren't leaving, after all.

They drove straight toward each other until the bright beams of their headlights filled the cage. Then they stopped. I heard brakes squeak.

Now, headlights reached through the night from three directions. All of them met in the cage.

Stryker climbed the steps and entered.

Lee walked in after him.

Valeria let go of the bars. Still stretching and writhing in a languid way that seemed almost catlike, she glided toward the middle of the cage. Her sleek black hair was flat against her scalp and clinging to the sides of her face and neck. In the glare of the six headlights, her skin looked like alabaster gleaming and dripping with baby oil.

Stryker raised a hand and signalled her to stop.

She halted.

Like a boxing referee, Stryker spoke to both contestants. I couldn't hear a word he said.

For our benefit, he held up an open hand—the unstretched fingers apparently representing five minutes. Then he hurried backward from between the two women and brought his arm down fast.

As Lee and Valeria started to circle each other, Stryker left the cage. Outside it, he shut the door and did something to its latch.

I gasped, "Hey! He shut the *door!*"

"No sweat, kid," said the man on my right.

"Don't worry about it," Vivian told me. She patted my thigh. "Door or no door, your gal won't be getting out of there alive."

Chapter Fifty-eight

Down in the cage, Lee and Valeria kept circling each other, staying apart but bent over, their arms wide open, their heads up.

Though both women were about the same size and I couldn't make out their faces very well, they were easy to tell apart. Lee's blond hair swung and flipped behind her head in a soaked, stringy ponytail. Valeria's straight black hair was plastered down against the back of her skull. Lee wore her sleeveless chambray shirt, white shorts and blue sneakers; Valeria was stark naked. Every so often, I glimpsed the smooth, inner slopes of Lee's breasts through the gap of her open shirt; except when her back was to me, Valeria's breasts were in full view, bouncing and swaying with the motions of her body.

Suddenly, Valeria growled and swept an open hand at Lee's face as if to claw her cheek open.

Lurching back, Lee grabbed the hand. She seemed to fall away, stretching Valeria's arm. Valeria staggered toward her, then stumbled sideways, breasts leaping. Lee let go. Valeria twirled away and her back slammed against a wall of the cage. The impact shook her. She stayed against the bars as if she needed them to hold her up.

Instead of rushing in to take advantage of the situation, Lee retreated to the other side of the cage.

"Get her!" I shouted. *"Knock her out!"*

Hearing me, she looked over her shoulder. She probably couldn't see me, though, because of all the headlights and how I was sitting in the darkness.

It only took a few seconds for Valeria to recover. Then she came for Lee.

Prancing sideways with her back to the bars, Lee put the casket between herself and Valeria.

Valeria chased her around the casket. It was like some sort of lame comedy skit . . . goofballs circling a dining room table. Except both the goofballs were beautiful women and one was completely naked and I hated to think of what would happen if she caught Lee.

I got the impression that Valeria was enjoying the chase. But she couldn't let it go on forever. In whatever remained of the five minutes, she needed to catch Lee and sink in her teeth.

Suddenly, she bowed at the waist, grabbed the casket with both hands and swung it off the ground. On its way up, it overturned. Out fell a red leather skirt and top, red boots with spurs attached, and a black leather belt. Holding it high, she marched straight toward Lee.

Oh, God, she was something to behold!

Though I knew that she planned to smash Lee with the

casket, I suddenly noticed a stiffness in my jeans. No telling how long I'd had it. I felt guilty and ashamed, but it didn't go away.

"Look out!" I yelled at Lee.

She needed no warning, though; she could see what was coming. She backed away until she was stopped by a wall of the cage.

Then she ducked and charged. Apparently, she meant to go in under the casket and crash her head into Valeria's belly. But she wasn't quite fast enough.

Valeria slammed the casket down on Lee's back. I heard the whomp of its impact, heard a grunt from Lee. An instant later, she was face down on the mud floor of the cage, sprawled flat.

Valeria tossed the casket out of the way. Then she leaned over Lee, grabbed her by the pony tail and the seat of her shorts, picked her up and hoisted her overhead.

Lee's arms and legs drooped. Her shirt hung open. I could see her breasts.

I didn't want to look at them, but I couldn't help myself. My eyes were latched to them. I grew harder. I felt as if I were betraying her. Betraying Slim, too. But I couldn't look away. I'd been wanting to see them for so long, and here they were, pale and shiny, glorious . . . and suddenly lurching on her chest as Valeria ran with her across the cage.

Oh, my God!

Valeria planned to ram her into the wall of bars.

"NO!" I cried out. *"LEE! WATCH OUT!"*

I don't know if she heard me, but both her arms suddenly darted up and she grabbed a bar above her face and came to an abrupt stop.

Unprepared for it, Valeria almost tore Lee loose, but not quite. Though Lee cried out in pain, she clung to the ceiling bar. Valeria lost her hold on Lee's pony tail and shorts and stumbled on, waving her arms, trying not to fall.

Suspended by her arms, Lee twisted and swung.

As Valeria came back for her, she chinned herself up and kicked a foot toward the ceiling of the cage. If only she could hook a foot through the bars, she might be able to pull herself all the way up . . . maybe out of Valeria's reach.

But one leg was still hanging down. Valeria grabbed it with both hands.

I yelled, *"NO!"*

On both sides of me, my guards clapped and cheered.

Valeria tugged at Lee's leg until the other one came down beside it. At that point, it would've been simple to pluck Lee down from the ceiling bar. She didn't do it, though. Instead, she pulled off both of Lee's sneakers and tossed them aside. Then she smiled over her shoulder—at me?

After the smile, she stepped behind Lee and peeled her white shorts down and off. First her shorts, then her panties.

Lee dangled from the bar, facing me, her open shirt barely reaching past her ribcage, her body naked from there down. She looked as if she were being stretched by her own weight. Her arms almost seemed longer than usual. Her belly looked taut. I saw a golden tuft of hair between her legs.

Her legs began to spread apart. Then a hand appeared between them. Valeria's hand. Stroking her.

Lee's jaw was clenched. She had a strange, tight look on her face. A tightness that trembled. She was wet and shiny all over, so there was no way of knowing if she had tears running down her face.

But I knew she was crying.

When I see a girl cry, something happens to me.

Especially if it's a girl I love. Like Slim or Lee.

Shouting, *"Leave her alone!"* I leaped up and drove the point of my elbow into the face of the big man on my right. He grunted and grabbed his nose. Vivian grabbed my other hand, but I didn't let her stop me. Pulled by my weight, she rose off the bench. I tried to fling her and we both tumbled down the bleachers.

When we came to a stop on top of a wet board near the bottom, Vivian was sprawled under me. She raised her head. I slugged her in the nose. Her nose crunched. The back of her head struck the wood with a sound like knuckles on a door.

I scurried off her.

The big guy was coming for me, leaping down the slippery face of the bleachers.

I jumped off the bottom row and ran for the cage.

I still had to get through Stryker.

But he wasn't even looking at me. He stood with both hands on the cage door.

Racing toward him, I looked into the cage. Lee no longer hung from the ceiling bar. She had Valeria backed up against the rear of the cage. Head down, she was slamming punches into Valeria's belly.

Yes!

Maybe she didn't need my help, after all, but it was too late to back out.

"Open the door!" I shouted as I ran toward Stryker.

I hardly thought he would do it.

But he stepped backward swinging it open, grinning at me through a space between its bars. "The more the merrier," he said.

I rushed into the cage.

He swung its door shut. *Clang!*

Valeria was still on the bars. Lee kept landing punches to her belly. They were strong punches. Her fists sounded like mallets smacking wet meat. Each blow shook Valeria and made her breasts lurch. With each blow, she grunted.

"Good going, Lee!" I called out.

"Very good going," Valeria said, smiling at me. She spoke with a fluid, languid drawl. "For a girl," she added. Though Lee was still pounding her, she wasn't reacting. Just calmly talking to me. "Do you suppose you can do better, Mister Thompson?"

Okay, so she knew my last name. I wasn't going to let that bother me. Much. It bothered me a lot more that Valeria didn't seem the least bit fazed by the punches.

"Lee's doing just fine," I said.

"Is she?" Valeria grabbed the front edges of Lee's shirt, swung her around and slammed her against the bars. Lee's whole body jerked with the impact. She started to sag.

A hand to Lee's throat, Valeria pinned her to the bars. With her other hand, she dragged the shirt off Lee's right shoulder, baring her upper arm and breast.

Then she stepped back, keeping Lee pinned to the bars. "Lee *is* doing just fine, isn't she?"

"Let go of her!"

"Oh, I don't suppose so." Reaching out, she slipped a hand beneath Lee's right breast. "Lovely, isn't it?" She squeezed it, but Lee didn't react.

Out cold?

Maybe that's good, I thought.

"How do you suppose it tastes, Mister Thompson?"

"Leave her alone."

Valeria licked her lips, then spread her mouth open wide.

"NO!" I yelled.

As I plowed into her, she stumbled away and let go of Lee. In the corner of my eye, I glimpsed Lee sliding to the floor.

Arms clamped around Valeria, forehead pressed between her breasts, I chugged with my feet and drove her across the cage. I had a vague notion of slamming her against the far wall and going at her with my fists the same as Lee had done.

But Lee's punches hadn't hurt Valeria, so why should mine?

Anyway, we didn't make it to the far wall. Valeria fell flat on her back and I landed on top of her.

Aren't the five minutes up yet? I wondered.

Maybe they've stopped counting.

"TIME?" I shouted.

Valeria, beneath me, said, "This is not a game anymore."

She was under me, breathing hard. I felt the quick rise and fall of her chest against the side of my face. It was wet and hot and I heard her quick heartbeat.

She's no vampire!

Of course not, I thought. No such thing.

Just a woman.

Just.

I pushed myself up. Sitting on her pelvis, I pinned her wrists to the muddy ground by her sides.

She smiled up at me. "Now what?" she asked.

I had no idea.

I looked to Lee for an answer, but she was sprawled on the ground, apparently unconscious.

"Give up?" I asked.

"I don't believe so." Smiling, she writhed. I watched the rain bounce off her shiny breasts. Her nipples were dark and rigid. "I know what you would *like* to do."

I shook my head.

"Go ahead. I'll let you. I let your friend Rusty do it, and he's not *nearly* as cute as you."

"You *let* him?"

"Did you honestly believe he'd over*powered* me?" She chuckled softly. "I hardly think so. Nothing happens to me unless I *allow* it. And I hereby allow *you*, Dwight Thompson."

I shook my head.

A smile spread over her face. "I know you *want* to. I know you *lust* for me."

"If you say so."

"Now's your chance," she said. "You have me at your mercy, Mr. Thompson."

"Yeah, well. . . ."

"I'm all yours."

"Forget it. All I wanta do is get outa here. Come on, okay? It's been five minutes." I looked over my shoulder and saw Stryker outside the cage door, staring in. My two guards were standing beside him. "Come on!" I yelled. "The five minutes are up! Let us have Rusty back and we'll . . ."

Smiling, Stryker shook his head.

"You don't want to die a virgin, do you?" Valeria asked.

I suddenly didn't feel too good.

"Die?"

"This may be your one and only chance to avoid such a miserable fate."

I just sort of stared at her.

"Kiss me," she said.

I shook my head. "We just wanta get out of here. With Rusty."

"Kiss my breasts."

I shook my head.

"Fuck me."

"No thanks."

"Last call. You're about to die, either way. You might as well die happy."

"You're really beautiful and everything," I said, "but I don't even like you. I wouldn't *do it* to you if you were the last woman on . . ."

She roared in my face and flung me off her body. As I rolled across the floor of the cage, she sprang to her feet. She swept down, grabbed my shirt and ripped it open. Then she picked me up by it.

She raced across the cage, holding me out in front of her, and rammed me into the bars. My ears rang. Barely conscious, I felt her rip the shirt off my shoulders and down my arms.

She rubbed her wet, slippery breasts against my chest. Writhing against me, she kissed me on the mouth. "See what you'll be missing?" she asked. Then she clutched my right shoulder and my head. She shoved my head sideways, stretched her mouth open wide and went for my neck.

Shrieking, I pushed at her.

I knew it wouldn't do any good, but I shoved at her breasts with both hands and a weird little part of my mind thought how nice they felt.

I knew that the next thing I felt would be her teeth sinking into my neck.

Instead, I felt Valeria yielding to my push.

She's just letting me think. . . .

Then I saw the thin wooden shaft protruding from her right eye. Sort of like a pencil. . . .

Someone stabbed her with . . .

As she stumbled backward, I saw how long the shaft was. I saw the feathers near its end. Then came a heavy *thunk*, a second arrow hitting her. This one popped through the nipple of her right breast and blood squirted. The arrow went in deep, skewering her breast, holding it rigid while she staggered backward.

Still on her feet, backing away from me, she got it with a third arrow. This one caught her high on the left side of the chest, just over the heart. Her left breast jumped. Unsteady now, she raised her arms for balance. Only a couple of inches of the last arrow showed. She looked as if she had a strange, feathered broach pinned to the skin of her chest.

Waving her arms, she fell. She landed with a splash and lay spread-eagled on her back in the mud.

Chapter Fifty-nine

I stared at Valeria. She twitched and shuddered. Blood poured out of her wounds, but was quickly washed away by the rain. When she stopped moving, I looked toward the cage door.

Nobody there.

Stryker and the others must've run when the arrows flew. Probably to their bus. It was stopped about twenty-five feet away, its engine running, its headbeams bright in my eyes.

The cage door was shut.

Lee, conscious now, was braced up on her elbows. Except for her shirt, she was naked. Her shirt was mostly off. It covered her left shoulder, and that was about all. Face scrunched, she scowled through the rain at Valeria's body.

"You okay?" I called to her.

She looked at me, frowning. "What happened?"

"I guess Slim happened."

"Jeez."

I hurried over to the sodden rag of Lee's shorts and snatched them out of the mud. They were white in front, filthy in back. I turned them over and the rain sluiced off some of the dirt.

When I got back to Lee with them, she was on her feet and leaning back against the bars. I handed the shorts to her. "Thanks," she said. She shook them open. As she raised a leg to put them on, I turned away and tried to spot Slim.

I figured she must've shot her arrows from somewhere under the bleachers where I'd been sitting earlier. Because of the headlights on me, though, I couldn't see very well into the darkness. If Slim was crouched beneath the bleachers, I sure couldn't see her.

I could see through them, though. To the back of the BEER-SNACKS-SOUVENIRS shack, to the area that had earlier been crowded with parked cars and trucks. There, all the headlights and taillights were gone. The field was dark except for the thin, moving beams of six or eight flashlights.

Stryker's crew.

Apparently unaware of what had just happened in the cage, they seemed to be checking on the abandoned vehicles and other things they found interesting in Janks Field.

"Damn," Lee said.

I looked at her. She was bending over, shoving the shorts down her legs.

"What's wrong?"

"Can't get 'em on."

"Huh?"

"Too tight." With a kick of her right foot, she sent the shorts flying. Then she ran toward the other side of the cage. She slid to a stop, bent down and plucked Valeria's red leather skirt out of the mud. Stepping into it, she said to me, "Try the door."

I hurried over to it. There was no handle. I grabbed the bars and shoved. The door rattled in its steel frame and stayed shut.

On the other side was a hasp and a padlock.

Groaning, I turned my head. "We're locked in!"

Lee came running over. The red leather skirt was so short it hardly covered her groin. She'd straightened her shirt, but only fastened one button, down near her belly.

"Let's see," she said.

I stepped out of her way. Lee studied the situation, then reached through the bars, grabbed the lock and jerked at it.

"Oh, boy," she muttered.

"What'll we do?"

"I don't . . ."

"Hey!" Slim's voice. It seemed to come from the area of the bleachers.

Lee and I both started to turn.

"Don't look." She sounded a little strange, her voice tight like someone talking through pain. "They're in the bus. Probably watching you. Fiddle with the door or something."

We turned again to the cage door.

"Locked in?" Slim asked.

"Looks that way," I said.

"It's a combination padlock," Lee explained.

Slim didn't say anything.

"You still there?" I asked.

"Yeah."

"Maybe you'd better go get help," Lee called.

"Nice outfit, Lee."

"Thanks."

"Red becomes you."

"You'd better get going," Lee said. "Try to get the police out here. . . ."

"Not a good idea. I need to keep you covered."

"Are you okay?" I asked.

"Okay enough. Took care of Valeria, anyway."

"You sure did. That was great shooting. But what's wrong?"

"I'm a little beat up, that's all."

At first, I thought she meant her earlier injuries . . . those from the dog and falling down.

"I got worked over a little," she said.

"What?"

"Bitsy. She jumped me from behind."

"Bitsy?"

"Yeah. Clobbered me with something. Then she beat the crap out of me. Turned out my lights."

Through my rage, I felt confusion. "When did she do it?"

"A few minutes after we left you guys. Guess she wanted to 'go with.' "

"That creepy little . . . !"

"She adores you, pal."

"Yeah," I muttered, suddenly glad that Bitsy had gotten herself pounded by Rusty. If I'd known what she'd done to Slim, things would've gone a lot worse for her.

"Seen her around?" Slim asked.

"Yeah. She said you got mad and told her to *F* off."

"Real nice."

"Anyway, we sorta ditched her in the woods. Haven't seen her since."

"So where's Rusty?" Slim asked.

"We don't know. They took him away after Valeria bit him."

"She *bit* him?"

"After he *made* it with her."

"Huh? Rusty *made* it with Valeria?"

"Yeah."

"You mean sex?"

"Yeah. Right in the cage here. In front of everyone."

"Holy jeez."

"Then she tore into him. Next thing you know, they were taking him away on a gurney. We don't know where he is now."

"Maybe in their bus or something," Lee said.

"They were gonna give him back to us," I explained, "if Lee went five minutes with Valeria. That's how we ended up like this."

"Looked like she was about to take a piece out of your neck."

"Thanks for saving it," I said.

"Hey, it's my favorite neck."

I blushed.

"You still have the knife?" Slim asked.

The knife?

I slapped the front right pocket of my blue jeans and felt a solid bulge. Slim's folding knife?

I couldn't believe it.

I'd forgotten I had it.

"Take it out," Slim said.

I shoved my hand into the tight, wet pocket of my jeans. No wonder Lee hadn't been able to get her shorts back on.

Something about wet cloth . . . But I managed to shove my hand in deeply enough to grab the knife.

I pulled it out.

"Now come over to my side of the cage. Make it fast."

I wanted to ask why, but didn't bother. Whatever her reasons, they were probably good. As I've mentioned before, Slim had more brains than me and Rusty put together.

So I whirled away from the door and rushed across the muddy floor. Through the bars on the other side, I saw a vague shape squirming on the ground in front of the bleachers. It had to be Slim belly-crawling toward the cage.

Suddenly, an engine revved.

Slim scrambled up. Rushing the final few feet to the cage, she entered the headbeams. Her short blond hair was matted and curly with rain. Her black silk shirt, torn in several places, was clinging to her body. She had her bow in one hand and her quiver of arrows in the other.

It felt great to see her.

But she had a gash above one eyebrow and her face was swollen.

I felt like killing Bitsy.

A moment before slamming against the cage, Slim shoved her bow and quiver of arrows through the bars. "Trade," she gasped.

"Huh?"

The bus was on its way. Though I didn't look at it, I heard it going through its gears, picking up speed like a school bus after dropping off a load of kids.

"Take my stuff! Gimme the knife! Quick!"

I did as she asked.

"Protect yourselves," she said. Then she put her face between two of the bars. "Kiss me."

Valeria's words exactly. This time they came from Slim and the sound of them hurt my heart.

I dropped to my knees and kissed her on the mouth, forgetting about her puffy, split lips. She winced. I started to pull away, but her hand caught the back of my head. We continued to kiss. I felt the warmth of her lips, the heat of her breath. I tasted her blood.

The brakes of the bus groaned.

Though I didn't look, the sound told me that the bus was stopping somewhere near the front of the cage.

Slim pulled back. "I love you, Dwight. Don't let yourself get hurt, or I'll have to kill you."

"Oh God, Slim." I had a catch in my throat.

"See you."

"What're you gonna do?"

She tugged open the blade of the knife. "Tell you after I've done it."

I heard the familiar hiss of a bus door opening.

"Run!" Lee yelled.

In a low crouch, Slim rushed for the bleachers.

A big man sprinted in from the side at an angle to intercept her. He was my guard, the guy I'd elbowed in the nose.

As he chased Slim, I heard the bus engine roar. I glanced toward the sound and glimpsed the bus racing backward as if to put a safe distance between itself and the pursuit.

Just in front of the bleachers, Slim flopped to her belly and squirmed forward.

"Leave her alone!" I yelled.

The man didn't even so much as glance at me.

He was about to leave his feet for a dive at Slim when I let an arrow fly. I was no expert archer like Slim, just a normal American kid of my times . . . a kid who'd done plenty fooling around with all things lethal: knives, firearms, blowguns, home-made spears, explosives, swords, bows and arrows.

My arrow went in just under the man's armpit and sank into his ribcage. He hit the mud skidding.

Slim scurried under the bleachers and vanished.

Bleachers I'd thought were empty.

From somewhere near the top, however, came applause. It sounded like one or two people clapping their hands.

Chapter Sixty

My skin went all crawly with goosebumps. I couldn't see who was up there, but I knew anyway.

As I peered toward the top of the bleachers, the beam of a flashlight reached up through the darkness, swept this way and that, and found two men at the very top of the stands—found them for an instant, then lost them as they lowered themselves behind the structure.

"Look out, Slim!" I yelled, getting to my feet. "The Cadillac twins! They're coming after you!"

She didn't answer.

The beam of the flashlight lowered and whipped back and forth through the lower rows of the bleachers. Shadows jerked and leaped. I looked for Slim, didn't see her, then turned my head to find out who was holding the flashlight.

Its beam came from a cluster of three or four people standing just outside the door of the bus. The bus had stopped about twenty feet back from the cage. Not very far, but the people were in darkness and I had headlights shining in my eyes so I couldn't tell who they were. Stryker was probably one of them, though. And Vivian.

I turned in their direction, readied an arrow and drew the bowstring back to my chin.

"Shut off the flashlight or I'll shoot!" I yelled.

The light went dead.

"Thanks," I said. A dumb thing to say, but it came out before I had a chance to think. "Now come over here and let us out."

"Why would I do that?"

Before I had a chance to think about it—much, anyway—

372

I released the arrow. It vanished into the darkness. Then came a quiet *thump*.

"Ah!" a woman cried out. A dark figure broke away from the group, hunching over and twisting away, then dropping to its knees. *"You fucking bastard!"* yelled the same voice. It didn't sound like Vivian, but I'd noticed earlier that Stryker had several women in his crew.

I reached down to the quiver clamped between my knees and pulled out another arrow. Before I could shoot it, though, my targets had disappeared inside the bus. They'd left the wounded one on the ground, writhing and whimpering.

"That's two down," Lee said. "Three, counting Valeria. Not bad."

"Except they've got us trapped and surrounded."

She shrugged one shoulder. "Big deal."

I laughed and so did she. As she came toward me, I slipped the arrow back into the quiver.

When she hugged me, the quiver fell over. But I didn't care. My shirt had been ripped off by Valeria, so Lee's chambray shirt was the only thing between me and her skin.

"You're doing really well," she said into my ear.

"Thanks."

"I always knew you were a good guy, but you're even better than I thought."

"Well . . . I'm trying."

Her arms tightened around me. The way she was standing, I figured she could see the bus over my shoulder. And I could see the headlights of the truck over hers. If anything started to happen in either direction, we would know it.

"The thing is to stay brave," she said.

"I'll try."

"Me, too."

I let out a sad little laugh. "And we don't have to worry about Slim."

"Huh?"

"Staying brave. That's the least of her problems."

"I just hope she's careful," Lee said.

"Yeah, me too." Then I started to cry.

Lee stroked the back of my head. "It'll be all right," she whispered. "She'll be fine."

"I don't know," I blubbered. "If anything happens to her . . ."

"It's okay, honey. It's okay."

I kept crying, Lee holding me and stroking my head.

"You know what?" she asked. "It's like you said when Valeria got shot. 'Slim'll happen to *them*.'"

I sort of laughed and sobbed at the same time. Then I mumbled, "God, I hope so."

Lee stepped back slightly, moved her face in front of mine and looked me in the eyes. To me, she looked blurry. As I blinked, she wiped the tears and raindrops off my face with her fingers. All that touched me were her fingertips and breasts. It would've been very sweet and exciting if I hadn't felt so scared.

After a while, she asked, "Feeling any better?"

I nodded. "A little."

She eased forward and kissed me gently on the mouth. Then she stepped back and put her hands on my shoulders. "We'd better get ready for the attack."

"What attack?"

A smile flashed across her face. "The one that's sure to come."

"Oh, that. What'll we do?"

"First . . ." She stepped away from me, bent down and picked up the quiver. After counting the arrows, she muttered, "Eight. Plus three is eleven."

"Three?"

"Put it on." She gave me the quiver.

While she held the bow. I swung the quiver onto my back so its strap rested on my left shoulder and ran diagonally down my chest like a bandolier. Then she handed the bow back to me. "Keep us covered, okay?"

Nodding, I slipped an arrow out of the quiver and nocked it on the bowstring. Then I followed Lee toward Valeria's body.

She crouched beside it.

374

I said, "Oh, my God," as she reached for the feathered shaft that protruded from Valeria's eye socket. "Hey, no. Come on."

"Sorry," Lee said. "But we might need these."

She started to pull at the arrow. I turned away fast.

And took the opportunity to check our situation. The truck was still in position, engine rumbling quietly, headbeams reaching into the cage. The hearse remained motionless behind the other bleachers, shining its headlights at us. And the bus was where they'd stopped it after dropping off the guy who chased Slim.

The wounded gal was gone. She'd either gotten away on her own or someone had helped her.

On the other side of the bleachers into which Slim had vanished, the parking area was dark. No headlights, no taillights, no brakelights. Except for the abandoned vehicles such as Lee's pickup truck and the twins' Cadillac, all the vehicles were gone.

Stryker's gang no longer directed traffic or roamed the field. They were over here, now, sneaking through the darkness. I couldn't see them very well—not with so many headlights aimed into the cage, not with the darkness and falling rain.

They wore black clothes and they'd switched off their flashlights. They looked like human shadows. I almost couldn't see them at all. They were easier to see when I didn't look straight at them.

They were all around us, crouching and skulking under the bleachers on both sides, kneeling in the darkness near the bus and truck.

"Here," Lee said.

I turned. She held an arrow. The first few inches of it were dripping blood. I glanced at Valeria's eye socket and almost gagged.

"Catch." Lee tossed the arrow to me.

I snagged it out of the air.

"They're all around us," I said.

"I noticed."

She reached for the arrow that had gone through Valeria's nipple, so I turned away again.

I held out the bloody arrow that she'd just handed me, hoping the rain would wash it clean. Its shaft was so thin that not many raindrops landed on it. Each time one hit, I saw a tiny explosion of pink.

"This one's really stuck," Lee said.

"Maybe just leave it?"

"Huh-uh." Lee stood up, planted a bare foot on Valeria's ribcage—directly between the breasts—bent down and grabbed the arrow with her right hand. She started to tug at it. I turned away again.

Off in the distance, someone raced past the front of the truck, sprinting through its headbeams. I couldn't tell whether it was a man or woman, but it held a long, thin shaft in one hand.

A spear?

My skin prickled.

"Oh, jeez," I murmured.

"You'd better give me a hand here," Lee said.

I didn't want to. More than that, though, I didn't want to disappoint her. I guess I would've done *anything* she asked. So I handed the bow and arrow to her, then put a foot on Valeria's chest, just as she had done. Only three or four inches of the arrow protruded—enough room for just one hand.

I wiped my right hand on my jeans (which were also wet), then grabbed the arrow around its feathers, being careful to stay away from what remained of Valeria's nipple. Squeezing the shaft, I gave it a hard pull. A quick slip and my hand flew off it.

"Damn," Lee said. "Give it another try, okay? If we end up one arrow short . . ."

"I'll get it," I said.

And I meant it. I wasn't going to let Lee think I was weak or chicken. "Get me a rag," I said. Not waiting for it, I cupped Valeria's breast with my left hand, my thumb hooked around the arrow. Her breast felt slippery and cool. I pushed, mashing it, sliding it down the shaft until there was room on the arrow for both my hands to fit.

Lee muttered, "Oh jeez." Then she gave me my shirt.

Released, Valeria's breast swelled upward, climbing the arrow.

Though my shirt was wet, it took some of the slipperiness off my hands. I used it to dry the protruding shaft. Keeping the shirt around my hands, I once again compressed Valeria's breast to make space for two hands on the arrow. Then I clutched the shaft with both hands, put most of my weight on her chest, and pulled with every ounce of my strength. The shirt, I think, gave me the extra friction that was needed.

I felt a force under my shoe as if Valeria were trying to sit up, but my weight kept her down.

The arrowhead, embedded in God-knows-what, suddenly let go. I glimpsed her breast stretching upward, pulled into the shape of a tall cone. Then the arrow leaped out like Excaliber, flinging blood. I held it high in both hands as I stumbled backward.

I slammed into Lee. She grunted, but stayed up. So did I.

"You okay?" she asked.

"Guess so."

"Good work."

"You too," I said, knowing that she must've thrown herself in my way on purpose to stop me from falling.

We stood there, back to back. The quiver was in the way, but I could feel Lee's rear end against mine.

Under the bleachers in front of me, a shape flitted across the headlights of the hearse. It was hunched low and carrying a spear.

"What's going on?" I asked.

"They've got us pretty much surrounded," Lee said. "But they're staying back. So far."

"What're they waiting for?"

"No idea. Maybe they're just afraid of catching an arrow."

"I'll get the last one," I said, feeling very powerful and brave now that I had retrieved the breast arrow.

"Better leave it," Lee said.

"Huh?"

"Just in case."

I thought about that for a moment. "Because it's the one in her heart?"

"She's probably *not* a vampire, but . . . I don't know, everything's so crazy. I don't know what to make out of all this, but . . . I'd hate to be locked in this cage if she suddenly comes to life."

"You and me both," I said.

"I know she won't, but . . . I don't want to stake my life on it."

"That arrow's probably broken anyway," I said. "It went all the way through her and she fell on it."

"Might've just buried itself in the dirt. But let's leave it. For now, anyway."

"Okay."

"If we start to run out . . ."

. . . *if we last that long*, I thought.

". . . I'll try to get it out of her later."

Chapter Sixty-one

"I'll make you a deal!" Stryker shouted.

Lee whirled, drawing back the bowstring.

I saw a dark shape hunkered by the front door of the bus.

"That him?" Lee asked.

"Not sure."

Lee called out, *"What sort of deal?"*

"We'll let you and the kids live if . . ."

Her arrow flew, hissing through the rain.

"Fuck!" Stryker yelled.

The arrow must've come close, but it missed him. Lee shook her head, then turned and handed the bow to me. "You'd better do the shooting."

As I got ready with the arrow I'd plucked from Valeria,

Stryker shouted, *"Don't do that again or I'll have you writhing on lances, screaming your lungs out."*

Lee yelled, *"Chuck you, Farley!"*

"Just listen to my offer! Do you want to die in that cage? Do you want the kids to die?"

Kids? He meant me, of course, but who else? Rusty and Slim? Bitsy?

Though I took aim at the shape that was probably Stryker, I didn't release the arrow. At this distance, I'd be lucky to hit him. So I lowered the bow.

"You said you'd let Rusty go if I went up against Valeria," Lee shouted. *"So where is he?"*

"You weren't supposed to KILL her."

"Fortunes of war, buddy."

"Here's the new offer."

"You didn't keep the OLD offer. Screw you."

"Would you like a demonstration?"

I didn't like the sound of that.

Suddenly, Stryker blew his whistle. It shrilled through the night like the sound of an angry track coach.

For a few seconds, nothing happened.

Then spears were flying out of the darkness toward our cage. Lee threw me to the ground and shielded me with her body. I heard a clamor as if something had struck a bar and bounced off. Then came the wet thunking sounds of spears punching into the mud.

Lee climbed off me. Raising my head, I saw six or seven spears sticking out of the ground. They formed a rough circle around us.

We got to our feet. I still held the bow, but it didn't seem like much of a weapon after the storm of spears. And I'd lost the arrow.

"Next time I blow the whistle," Stryker yelled, *"they won't miss. Interested in hearing my offer?"*

"What is it?" Lee asked.

"You killed our sole attraction."

"Not me," Lee said.

"You, your friends, it's all the same. Valeria's dead. We're

out of business unless we replace her. I want YOU to be her replacement. Agree to surrender and come with us as our vampire, and I'll let the kids go home."

"Why me?" Lee asked.

"You're perfect. You're brave and strong . . . and luscious."

"I'm not a vampire."

"No problem. All you need to do is travel with our show and take on all comers in the cage."

"For how long?" Lee asked.

"You can't!" I blurted at her.

"For as long as I say."

"And you'll let everyone else go?"

"Certainly. I would HAVE to, wouldn't I? If I don't release them, you won't keep your side of the bargain."

"You're right about that."

"How about it?"

"Give me a few minutes to think it over."

"Of course."

We turned away from Stryker and faced each other. "You can't do it," I said.

"What other choices do we have?"

"Fight."

"They'll kill us easily."

"Maybe, maybe not. At least maybe we can take some of them with us."

"I don't want you to get killed, Dwight. Or *me*, for that matter. Not to mention Slim and Rusty. For all we know, maybe they've even got Bitsy. We might *all* die if I don't take his offer."

"You *can't!*"

"I've got to."

"What about Danny?" I asked.

At the mention of my brother's name, her chin started shaking. In a voice that trembled, she said, "Tell him that I love him. This . . . this is something I had to do. Tell him I'll always love him. And I'll come back to him if I can."

I started bawling again. This time, I didn't feel embarrassed about it. I was in too much anguish for embarrassment.

"I have to do this, honey. It's the right thing to do. You know it and I know it."

"No!"

"Let me have the bow," she said, her voice gentle and sad. Though I blurted, *"NO!"* I didn't resist when she pulled it from my hand. Nor when she removed the quiver from my back. "I thought we were gonna *fight,*" I protested.

"I'm sorry," she said.

She carried the bow and the quiver of arrows to the side of the cage, reached through a space in the bars, and let them fall to the ground.

Turning toward Stryker, she raised her arms in surrender and called, *"It's a deal!"*

"Very good. You won't be sorry."

He stood up, stepped in front of the bus and made some gestures with his hands. All around us, black-garbed men and women came out of the darkness. Some appeared from behind the bus and truck. Others climbed out from under bleachers. I didn't count, but got the impression there must've been fourteen or fifteen of them. About half of them carried spears.

They all walked toward our cage.

A few paces from the bars, they stopped. One of them bent down and picked up the bow and quiver. All of them gazed at the body of Valeria. Some were scowling. Many shook their heads and looked dismayed. Others appeared to be weeping.

Stryker stepped up to the cage door.

Looking around at his crew, he said in a loud voice, "This has been a terrible night." Heads nodded in agreement. "I know how much Valeria meant to all of you . . . and to me. She was a very special lady. Very special. We'll all miss her terribly." He took a deep breath and sighed. "However, the show must go on. To that end, let me introduce the woman who will take over Valeria's role . . . our *new* vampire, Lee Thompson."

Murmurs and quiet applause came from the crew.

Stryker stepped forward, bent over slightly in front of the door and turned the dial of the combination lock. A few seconds later, he removed the lock and swung the door open.

Lee moved toward it, but Stryker entered. Taking her by the shoulders, he guided her backward toward the middle of the cage. "You're already in part of the outfit," he said. "Let's see how you look in the rest of it."

The crew applauded again, this time with some eagerness.

Standing rigid in the middle of the cage like a proud soldier, Lee removed her sleeveless chambray shirt. She stood there in the rain, naked except for the very short skirt of red leather.

Stryker picked up Valeria's red, bralike top.

Lee stood motionless while he slipped the straps up her arms, cupped her breasts inside its stiff leather, and stepped behind her to fasten its back.

Vivian entered the cage, carrying the black cape.

Stryker took the cape and swept it over Lee's shoulders.

As he backed away from her, she spread the cape wide open, swept it high like bat wings and called out, *"I AM LENORA THE VAMPIRE!"*

Stryker's black-shirted gang of thugs went crazy, cheering and clapping and shouting.

I thought to myself, *Holy shit. What's this?*

With all eyes fixed on Lee and with so much noisy appreciation coming from the crew of The Traveling Vampire Show, nobody seemed to notice the hearse.

Including me.

Not until it came roaring through the rainy night, headlights off. At the last moment, half a dozen of Stryker's people turned and yelled and tried to jump out of the way.

They didn't make it.

The hearse, probably doing sixty, roared between the side of the cage and the bleachers (the stands under which Slim had disappeared), ramming through everyone there. They bounced off the grill and hood and roof. They did cartwheels through the rain. A few spears, along with Slim's bow and quiver of arrows, leaped from hands and flew off into the night.

Stryker gaped at the mayhem.

I whirled around, crouched and snatched an arrow out of

the mud—the arrow I'd struggled so hard to pluck from Valeria's breast.

I'd dropped it when Lee threw me to the ground during the storm of spears.

Leaping up, I spun around and drove its razor-sharp point into the side of Stryker's neck so hard it popped out the other side.

His eyes bugged out.

I grabbed Lee's arm. *"Let's go!"* I yelled. I jerked her arm.

She looked at me, a frenzy in her eyes, then flung off the vampire cape and let out something that sounded the way I always imagined one of those "rebel yells" from the Civil War must've been like . . . an ear-splitting cry full of rage and wild joy.

On our way toward the cage door, we each jerked a spear out of the mud.

We were just outside the cage when the hearse skidded to a stop near the rear of the bus.

We ran for it.

It started backing toward us.

I had a pretty good idea who must be behind the wheel.

A few spears flew past us, but missed.

Somebody leaped out of the bus door and confronted us with a machete. Before he could swing it, Lee shoved her spear into his mouth and I plunged mine into his stomach.

Leaving the spears in him, we sprinted for the hearse.

It slid to a halt. I was first to reach its passenger door. I grabbed the handle and jerked it open.

"In!" I yelled at Lee. *"Jump in!"*

She dived in and I scurried in after her.

Slim turned her head. "I'm back," she said.

She stepped on the gas. The hearse lurched forward, its passenger door slamming shut without any help from me.

I figured we should finish the escape, but Slim had different plans. She made a high-speed pass along the other side of the cage. This time, she didn't have quite the same element of surprise working for her. She only managed to mow down one of Stryker's people.

"Can we go now?" I asked.

"Sure."

With that, Slim steered around the end of the bleachers, put on the headlights and sped across Janks Field. The hearse shuddered and shook over the rough muddy ground. We bounced and swayed.

I saw the crippled Cadillac sitting abandoned. And Lee's pickup truck. And two or three other cars that had been left behind.

"Want me to drop you off at your pickup?" Slim asked.

"No thanks," Lee said. "Just get us out of here."

"You sure? I'd be glad to."

"I lost my keys."

"We'll go back to my car," Slim said, and sped toward the dirt road that would return us to Route 3.

Chapter Sixty-two

On the narrow and curvy dirt road, Slim slowed down a lot. She kept glancing at the side mirrors.

"I don't think they'll come after us," Lee said.

"I don't know," Slim said.

"Can't hurt to keep an eye out," I added. I didn't mean it as any sort of pun, but the words forced a picture of Valeria's eye socket into my mind. And then I pictured the arrow embedded in her nipple.

"They've got so many dead," Lee said.

"We decimated their sorry butts," Slim said.

"You did a great job," Lee told her.

"Saved our lives," I added.

I half expected a quip, but Slim only nodded. In the glow of the dashboard lights, her face looked grim.

"What happened, anyway?" I asked her.

"Huh?"

"After you went off under the bleachers."

"Just sort of snuck around."

"Did you see the Cadillac twins?" I asked. "They were up at the top. Looked like they were on their way down to get you. I yelled to warn you."

"Yeah, thanks. I took care of them."

"Huh?"

"You know, the knife. I was sort of waiting for them when they climbed down the back of the stands. Did away with them."

"You *did away* with them?"

"Yeah. Sent them south. Deep south."

"Jeez," Lee said.

I said, "Holy shit."

"As Mike Hammer says, 'It was easy.' "

"So you *killed* them?" I asked, hardly believing it.

"Yeah. Some others, too. I sort of snuck up on anybody I found and cut their throats. A couple of them saw me coming, but I think they figured I was with the Show because of the black shirt."

"The morons," I said.

"I was trying to find Rusty," she said.

"Any luck?" Lee asked.

I think we both knew what the answer would be.

"No. I don't know where they took him. I searched the truck. It's where they keep the cage and stuff when they're on the road, I guess. Nobody was in it, though. Just the driver. He was in the cab. I took care of him before I searched the back. Then I didn't get a chance to search the bus or the back of the hearse. Just about the time I got to the hearse, I looked over at the cage and saw they were moving in on you guys. So all I did was kill the driver and come to the rescue."

"Mighty good job of it," Lee said.

"Thanks. I just wish . . ." She shook her head. "I wanted to find *Rusty*." As she said that about Rusty, her voice cracked. "I don't want to leave him *behind*."

I put my hand on Slim's thigh. The leg of her cut-off jeans

was warm and damp. "Wanta go back?" I asked her.

"I don't know. I think maybe." She must've taken her foot off the gas pedal; the engine quieted and we slowed down. "What about you?" she asked.

I *hated* the idea of going back to Janks Field. We'd been lucky to get out of there alive, and the chances of finding Rusty alive were slim.

"Yeah," I said. "Let's go back and find him."

"What the hell," Lee said. "In for a penny . . ."

" 'And gentlemen in England now a-bed,' " quoted Slim, " 'shall think themselves accursed they were not here, and hold their manhoods cheap. . . .' "

"You bet," Lee said.

Slim stopped the hearse. She shifted to reverse, started speeding backward, then twisted toward me in her seat to look back over her shoulder. "Damn!" She slammed on the brakes.

I looked over my shoulder. The window behind the front seat was shrouded with a curtain.

Slim glanced at the side mirrors. "I can't drive backward without a rearview mirror."

"Guess you'll have to turn around," I said.

"Too narrow."

"Maybe go on to the highway," Lee suggested. "Easy enough to turn. . . ."

From behind us came a *thud* as if someone riding in back— in the coffin area—had stomped on the floor or dropped something.

Slim looked over her shoulder at the glass just behind our heads. *"Rusty!"* she called.

Lee was already throwing her door open.

As Lee leaped out, Slim shut off the engine and plucked the key from the ignition. Then she flung her door open.

I scurried out Lee's side.

Lee was first to reach the rear of the hearse. She was trying to open its door, but not having any luck. "I think it's locked," she said.

"I've got the keys," Slim said. She picked one and tried to put it into the lock hole. Her hand was shaking so badly that she couldn't get it in for a while. When she finally poked its tip into the slot, it wouldn't go in any farther. Wrong key. So she pulled it out and tried another. Again, she had trouble because she was trembling so badly. Then it went in.

She turned the key and worked the door handle. The door unlatched. She stepped back, pulling it toward herself, swinging it wide open.

The night, until then fresh and sweet with the aromas of a rain-soaked forest, suddenly went foul. The stench made me hold my breath. Lee clapped a hand across her mouth. Slim stepped around the open door, her lips pressed shut and her chest out. It was the way she sometimes looked out on the river just before she plunged below the surface.

I *wished* we were out on the river. Or anywhere else, just so we were miles away from here.

Inside the hearse a light had come on. It must've been triggered by the opening door.

We all gazed in.

The volunteers who'd gone up against Valeria in the cage were there: Chance Wallace, the handsome Marine; geeky Chester; our old enemy Scotty Douglas the hoodlum; and our chubby, sweet, stupid best friend, Rusty.

They were all naked.

They were all in pieces, piled up next to the casket within easy reach of . . . its occupant.

Inside the casket, propped up with his head against the curtains of the window we'd been trying to look through, sat an obese, legless, hairless man. I *guess* it was a man. He looked like a bloated sack of slippery white skin. Except the skin was mostly scarlet with blood.

His bulgy eyes looked like a pair of bloodshot golf balls.

Clutched in both hands, upside-down just under his chin, was Rusty's head. Snuffling and grunting, he shoved his maw into the raw gore of the neck stump. He ripped out a large gob, then raised his head, bumping it against the window, and seemed to smile at us . . . with a dripping load of Rusty slopping out of his mouth.

Chapter Sixty-three

All things considered, I think we handled ourselves very well up to the point at which we looked into the back of the hearse.

What we saw in there . . . it knocked out whatever remained of our brains and guts.

I have vague memories of noises coming from us. Things like *"Whoa!"* and *"Yahhh!"* and *"Eeee!"* as we backed away from the rear of the hearse. And someone—Slim, I think—slammed the door shut. And then we were running down the middle of the dirt road as if we had the boogey-man after us.

We ran and ran and ran. Finally we came to Route 3 and Slim led the way to her Pontiac. We all piled into the front seat. The three of us sat side by side, me in the middle, all of us huffing and whimpering while Slim tried to get her key into the ignition.

At last, the engine roared and we were off.

We sped down Route 3 toward town.

At Lee's house, we turned on all the lights. Then we took turns taking showers. After our showers, we got into clean dry clothes that Lee had gathered for us. I wore my brother's stuff. Lee and Slim wore Lee's. We got together in the living room. Lee let us drink beer. She even made popcorn. We were so freaked out that we hardly talked . . . not for a while, anyway. By the time we'd each polished off a couple of beers, though, we had calmed down.

The talking began. And decisions were made.

In the early morning hours before dawn, we went out to Lee's garage to start getting ready. We made a couple of stakes by sawing off a broom handle and whittling a point on one end of each shaft. We gathered a hammer and a hatchet. We also equipped ourselves with the tin of gasoline that Danny kept around for his power mower. And a box of wooden matches and a cigarette lighter.

We loaded all this into Slim's Pontiac.

After sunrise, we climbed in and Slim started the car. But Lee said, "Just a minute. I just thought of something."

She climbed out of the car and hurried back into her house. A couple of minutes later, she came back with my brother's Winchester .30-caliber lever-action repeater. As she climbed in with it, she said, "In case we have human trouble, too."

"Always thinking," Slim said.

Then she drove us up Route 3 until we came to the turnoff. She made the turn and drove slowly up the dirt road toward the place where we'd left the hearse and its awful cargo.

It was a lovely summer morning. Sometime before dawn, the rain had stopped. You could still smell it, though. There is nothing like the scent of a forest after a heavy rainfall.

The sky was cloudless. Birds were twittering all around us, bugs buzzed and sunlight slanted down through the treetops like transparent rods of gold.

It was one of those mornings that makes you feel great.

At least if you're not on an errand like ours.

After a while, Lee said, "Where is it?"

"I don't know," Slim said, and kept on driving.

I think we all expected to find the hearse around every bend, but the dirt road ahead of us remained empty.

"Somebody must've moved it," Lee said.

Then we came out the other end of the dirt road. Ahead of us was Janks Field, all rutted and muddy, puddles and bits of broken glass flashing sunlight.

Lee's red pickup was still there. So was the Cadillac I had disabled. So was a VW bug. I supposed it had probably belonged to one of the other volunteers—Chester, most likely. Scotty had been with a bunch of his hoodlum friends; they must've gone off without him after the lightning struck. As for Chance the Marine, who knows?

On our way over to the bleachers, I noticed several fresh holes in the dirt. They weren't filled in. Just holes. I didn't know who or what had made them, or why, but I suddenly remembered the poodle that had nipped Rusty's arm and how it had squealed underneath one of the cars.

Slim drove us all around the bleachers and between them. There was no sign of the black bus or the black truck or the black hearse or the black-shirted crew of the Traveling Vampire Show.

The cage was gone, too.

" 'Folded their tents like the Arabs,' " said Slim, " 'and silently slipped away.' "

It seemed they had left nothing behind except Slim's bow, her arrows, and the special quiver she'd won at the Fourth of July archery contest.

When she spotted them, she cried out, *"Ah-ha!"* and stopped the car. Lee jumped out and retrieved them.

A few minutes later, Lee jumped out again. This time, she ran through the mud with spare keys in her hand and climbed into her red pickup truck.

We followed close behind her all the way back to town.

Chapter Sixty-four

There was a big investigation, of course, but the Traveling Vampire Show was never seen or heard of again. Neither were the bodies of the volunteers or Stryker or Valeria or any of the workers we'd killed.

Or Bitsy.

Yeah, Bitsy vanished that night, too. I don't know, she simply never turned up again. Searchers, including me and Slim and Lee, scoured the woods for her. Parts of Janks Field were even dug up. Four bodies were found, but not Bitsy (no one else from that night, either, strangely enough). To this day, Bitsy is a big mystery. I keep hoping she's alive and happy somewhere, that she chose that night to run away from home, that she didn't end up getting grabbed by remnants of the Vampire Show or by some other form of degenerate . . . or whatever it was that got the poodle. If anything bad happened to her, it would've been partly my fault.

I won't get into the whole mess about Mr. and Mrs. Simmons, the parents of Rusty and Bitsy. Let's just say it was grim.

Rusty had won the wager about Valeria's beauty, no doubt about that. We didn't have to go through with the pay off, but we did. As sort of a tribute to Rusty, Slim shaved my head. We never told anyone why. Only Lee. We pretty much told her everything.

My father recovered nicely from the injuries he'd sustained in the car accident.

The next year, Lee and my brother Danny had a baby girl.

Slim started calling herself Fran, short for Frances, and we began going steady and everything was just about as great as it could possibly be . . . except for Rusty being dead and Bitsy being gone and Lee and Fran and me never being able to completely get away from memories of what we saw that night in the back of the hearse.

I guess maybe it was the "real" vampire, and maybe Valeria had been some sort of bait. . . .

I don't want to think about it.

Anyway, that's my story.

I just want to say, if you ever get word that a Traveling Vampire Show is coming to your town, stay away from it. For God's sake.

AMONG THE
MISSING RICHARD LAYMON

At 2:32 in the morning a Jaguar roars along a lonely road high in the California mountains. Behind the wheel sits a beautiful woman wearing only a skimpy nightgown. She's left her husband behind. She's after a different kind of man—someone as wild. daring, and passionate as herself. The man she wants is waiting patiently for her . . . with wild plans of his own. When the woman stops to pick him up, he suggests they go to the Bend, where the river widens and there's a soft, sandy beach. With the stars overhead and moonlight on the water, it's an ideal place for love. But there will be no love tonight. In the morning a naked body will be found at the Bend—a body missing more than its clothes. And the man will be waiting for someone else.

___4788-8 $5.99 US/$6.99 CAN

Dorchester Publishing Co., Inc.
P.O. Box 6640
Wayne, PA 19087-8640

ONE RAINY NIGHT

RICHARD LAYMON

"If you've missed Laymon, you've missed a treat."
—Stephen King

The strange black rain falls like a shroud on the small town of Bixby. It comes down in torrents, warm and unnatural. And as it falls, the town changes. One by one, the inhabitants fall prey to its horrifying effect. One by one, they become filled with hate and rage . . . and the need to kill. Formerly friendly neighbors turn to crazed maniacs. A stranger at a gas station shoves a nozzle down a customer's throat and pulls the trigger. A soaking-wet line of movie-goers smashes its way into a theater to slaughter the people inside. A loving wife attacks her husband, still beating his head against the floor long after he's dead. As the rain falls, blood flows in the gutters—and terror runs through the streets.

"No one writes like Laymon, and you're going to have a good time with anything he writes."
—Dean Koontz

___4690-3 $5.99 US/$6.99 CAN

Dorchester Publishing Co., Inc.
P.O. Box 6640
Wayne, PA 19087-8640

Please add $1.75 for shipping and handling for the first book and $.50 for each book thereafter. NY, NYC, and PA residents, please add appropriate sales tax. No cash, stamps, or C.O.D.s. All orders shipped within 6 weeks via postal service book rate. Canadian orders require $2.00 extra postage and must be paid in U.S. dollars through a U.S. banking facility.

Name_____

Address_____

City_____ State_____ Zip_____

I have enclosed $_____ in payment for the checked book(s).

Payment <u>must</u> accompany all orders. ❑ Please send a free catalog.

BITE RICHARD LAYMON

"No one writes like Laymon, and you're going to have a good time with anything he writes."
—**Dean Koontz**

It's almost midnight. Cat's on the bed, facedown and naked. She's Sam's former girlfriend, the only woman he's ever loved. Sam's in the closet, with a hammer in one hand and a wooden stake in the other. Together they wait as the clock ticks down because . . . the vampire is coming. When Cat first appears at Sam's door he can't believe his eyes. He hasn't seen her in ten years, but he's never forgotten her. Not for a second. But before this night is through, Sam will enter a nightmare of blood and fear that he'll never be able to forget—no matter how hard he tries.

"Laymon is one of the best writers in the genre today."
—*Cemetery Dance*

Sips of Blood

MARY ANN MITCHELL

The Marquis de Sade. The very name conjures images of decadence, torture, and dark desires. But even the worst rumors of his evil deeds are mere shades of the truth, for the world doesn't know what the Marquis became—they don't suspect he is one of the undead. And that he lives among us still. His tastes remain the same, only more pronounced. And his desire for blood has become a hunger. Let Mary Ann Mitchell take you into the Marquis's dark world of bondage and sadism, a world where pain and pleasure become one, where domination can lead to damnation. And where enslavement can be forever.

___4555-9 $5.50 US/$6.50 CAN

Dorchester Publishing Co., Inc.
P.O. Box 6640
Wayne, PA 19087-8640

Please add $1.75 for shipping and handling for the first book and $.50 for each book thereafter. NY, NYC, and PA residents, please add appropriate sales tax. No cash, stamps, or C.O.D.s. All orders shipped within 6 weeks via postal service book rate. Canadian orders require $2.00 extra postage and must be paid in U.S. dollars through a U.S. banking facility.

Name_____
Address_____
City_____ State_____ Zip_____
I have enclosed $_____ in payment for the checked book(s).
Payment <u>must</u> accompany all orders. ❑ Please send a free catalog.
CHECK OUT OUR WEBSITE! www.dorchesterpub.com

Quenched

MARY ANN MITCHELL

An evil stalks the clubs and seedy hotels of San Francisco's shadowy underworld. It preys on the unfortunate, the outcasts, the misfits. It is an evil born of the eternal bloodlust of one of the undead, the infamous nobleman known to the ages as . . . the Marquis de Sade. He and his unholy offspring feed upon those who won't be missed, giving full vent to their dark desires and a thirst for blood that can never be sated. Yet while the Marquis amuses himself with the lives of his victims, with their pain and their torture, other vampires—of Sade's own creation—are struggling to adapt to their new lives of eternal night. And as the Marquis will soon learn, hatred and vengeance can be eternal as well—and can lead to terrors even the undead can barely imagine.

___4717-9 $5.50 US/$6.50 CAN